PRAISE FOR KJEL

'A masterclass in plotting, atmosphere an[d] shocking twists' *The Times* Crime Club

'A chilling novel about betrayal' *Sunday Times*

'More than gripping' European Literature Network

'The perfect example of why Nordic Noir has become such a popular genre' *Reader's Digest*

'Utterly convincing' *Publishers Weekly*

'If you have never sampled Dahl, now is the time to try' *Daily Mail*

'Dramatic, fast-paced and character-focused' *Crime Review*

'Skilful blend of police procedural and psychological insight' Crime Fiction Lover

'Fiercely powerful and convincing' LoveReading

'Crisp and current' My Chestnut Reading Tree

'Vividly described' Jen Med's Book Reviews

'Elaborately plotted, well constructed and gratifying' Claire Thinking

'Killer ending' Liz Loves Books

'Burning with tension and haunting in its lingering prose' Book Drunk

'Intelligently crafted and infused with a truly unique personality' Crime by the Book

'A shocking conclusion that left me reeling' Novel Gossip

'Before you realise it you have raced through half the book' The Last Word Book Review

'Flawlessly plotted, with a beautifully nuanced translation' Raven Crime Reads

'A darkly entertaining thriller that kept me guessing to the end' Never Imitate

'Chilling and compulsive reading' Life of a Nerdish Mum

'Some of the chapters had me gripping my seat, shocked' Ronnie Turner

'Unbelievable amount of talent and beautiful prose' Mumbling about…

'Dahl masterfully leads his readers on a journey of misdirection' The Quiet Knitter

'A slow-burning and subtle story' Bibliophile Book Club

ABOUT THE AUTHOR

One of the fathers of the Nordic Noir genre, Kjell Ola Dahl was born in 1958 in Gjøvik. He made his debut in 1993, and has since published eleven novels, the most prominent of which is a series of police procedurals cum psychological thrillers featuring investigators Gunnarstranda and Frølich. In 2000 he won the Riverton Prize for *The Last Fix* and he won both the prestigious Brage and Riverton Prizes for *The Courier* in 2015. His work has been published in fourteen countries, and he lives in Oslo.

Follow Kjell Ola on Twitter *@ko_dahl*.

ABOUT THE TRANSLATOR

Don Bartlett completed an MA in Literary Translation at the University of East Anglia in 2000 and has since worked with a wide variety of Danish and Norwegian authors, including Jo Nesbø and Karl Ove Knausgård. For Orenda he has translated several titles in Gunnar Staalesen's Varg Veum series: *We Shall Inherit the Wind*, *Wolves in the Dark* and the Petrona award-winning *Where Roses Never Die*. He also translated *Faithless*, the previous book in Kjell Ola Dahl's Oslo Detectives Series for Orenda. He lives with his family in a village in Norfolk.

THE ICE SWIMMER

KJELL OLA DAHL

Translated by Don Bartlett

ORENDA
BOOKS

Orenda Books
16 Carson Road
West Dulwich
London SE21 8HU
www.orendabooks.co.uk

First published in Norwegian as *Isbaderen* by Gyldendal, Norway, 2011
First published in the United Kingdom by Orenda Books, 2018
Copyright © Kjell Ola Dahl 2011
English language translation copyright © Don Bartlett 2017

A catalogue record for this book is available from the British Library.

ISBN 978-1-912374-07-6
eISBN 978-1-912374-08-3

Typeset in Garamond by MacGuru Ltd
Printed and bound in Denmark by Nørhaven

This publication of this translation has been made possible through
the financial support of NORLA, Norwegian Literature Abroad

For sales and distribution, please contact: *info@orendabooks.co.uk*

Oslo. Thursday, 10th December

1

Nina threads her way through the stream of people pouring up the steps at Egertorget Metro Station. She continues along Karl Johans gate, where the heating cables under the flagstones keep the pavement free of snow. She speeds up. The traffic lights change to red, but Nina doesn't stop. She glances over her shoulder and sets off at a run. The exhaust fumes spreading across the open tarmac reflect the lights of the morning rush-hour cars and creep up their bodywork. In shop windows plastic Christmas pixies in woollen jumpers and coarse fabric trousers stand and laugh. Others wear frozen smiles and wave stiff arms. Nina races past, a shadow on the glass.

Nina runs down the steps of Jernbanetorget Metro Station.

A train roars in and screeches to a halt. The doors open. Passengers disgorge onto the platform.

Nina hesitates. Waits. Looks around. The doors close. At the last second she makes a lunge. A man does the same into the carriage behind.

The train sets off. The temperature inside is warmer, but Nina is frozen. The carriage jerks and lurches around the bends. Passengers cling to the poles that connect the floor to the ceiling. Nina sits facing backwards. Her eyes flit across the other people, all squeezed close together, some staring at the ceiling, some with their noses in a book or a newspaper. Nina continues to search. And makes eye contact with her pursuer.

He is sitting right at the other end and raises his hand in a wave.

Nina jumps up. She works her way forwards. The train is packed and she hides behind backs as she moves towards the door. The train stops at Grønland.

The doors open.

Nina waits and gets off just as the doors close.

The train pulls away.

Nina is left standing on the platform. She doesn't move, as though afraid to look, afraid to know the result of her sudden manoeuvre. Finally she turns. She sees her pursuer standing a few metres away.

They stare into each other's eyes for several long, mute seconds. Nina is on the point of saying something. The words are drowned by the noise of another train braking and coming to a halt alongside the platform. The man can read her fear.

The doors open, passengers spew out and a few get on.

The two of them are motionless. Only Nina's eyes roam.

The doors close.

Nina flings herself in.

In some miraculous way the pursuer manages to follow suit before the doors are closed.

The train moves off. Nina advances through the carriage, pushing people aside. She is at the front now. Soon she won't be able to go any further. Slowly she turns and meets her pursuer's eyes. She is standing like this when the train arrives in the next station. The doors open. Nina waits. The doors are about to close.

Nina makes a lunge at the last instant.

Nina walks slowly, glancing to each side.

As the train picks up speed, she looks around. Sees only passengers, no sign of her pursuer. The crowd on the platform is thinning.

Then she sees him. She has walked past him. The man starts walking. Towards her.

Nina backs away, down the platform. They are alone now. Nina is forced against the wall. But there is a gap in the wall.

She spins round and jumps down onto the tracks. She runs into the tunnel. Soon she has merged into the blackness.

2

The lowest strip of sky formed a purplish line above the horizon: a red incision in a frieze of grey hues. Steam rose off the water in the harbour. Twenty-four degrees below zero outside. In a few days the harbour would freeze over.

Lena Stigersand braked for the traffic lights in Kontraskjæret. The mere thought of minus twenty-four made her shiver.

'Is that what you keep in here?' Emil Yttergjerde asked. He was bent over in the passenger seat, rummaging through the glove compartment for a CD. He held up an unopened packet of o.b. tampons.

'You won't find it in there,' she said. 'It's probably in another cover. I can't keep them tidy when I'm driving.'

'Another cover? We're talking Tom Waits here,' Emil said. 'You don't treat Tom Waits like that.' He continued to search through the glove compartment. The lights changed to green and Lena pushed the gearstick into first.

'What's this?' Emil asked as she changed back down, turned and crossed the tram tracks.

Lena was startled. 'Put it back,' she said quickly. 'It's a pepper spray.'

'It's dangerous, you know,' Emil said.

'That's why you should put it back!'

Lena steered towards the City Hall Quay, where a patrol car and a yellow ambulance were parked.

Lena stopped and pulled the handbrake. Took the spray out of Emil's hand. 'Where's the lid?'

'It wasn't on.'

'Give me the lid.'

'I'm telling you the truth. It wasn't on.'

Lena threw down the spray, opened the door and got out. Her body hit the cold; it was like a solid wall. The snow creaked with every step as she made her way towards the two uniformed officers who were putting up barriers and securing cordons. Two other figures were operating a yellow crane on the edge of the quay.

She stepped over the cordon, walked past the stone building on the pier and went to the edge. The engine of the winch purred. A man in a diving suit stood on a life raft attaching a strap under the arms of a lifeless man floating in the icy water.

One of the paramedics tapped Lena on the shoulder. 'I've been given to understand you're in charge here.'

She nodded.

'He's dead and has been for quite a while. There's nothing we can do, so we're off.'

She nodded again. 'OK.'

The ambulance started up and drove away.

The winch raised the body from the water. The stiff corpse banged against the quayside and the crane driver cursed.

A tram glided away from the Vestbane stop and was soon lost behind the pointed roofs of the stalls in the Christmas market, which looked like a festively illuminated village in front of the City Hall.

The crane driver cursed again. The dead man rose higher and rotated in the air. The lapels of his jacket hung like heavy pennants. Water dripped and immediately froze into icicles on his clothes. The crane driver shouted for someone to grab the body. Hands stretched into the air, be-gloved and be-mittened. They couldn't reach. The body was too high.

'Down, down, down,' Lena whispered to the driver.

The body was lowered to the ground. Emil Yttergjerde grabbed the strap and turned the body onto its back. The water on the dead man's face froze to ice as they watched. A glassy face belonging to a young man with short, fair hair. Lena knelt down and examined the man's hands. No wedding ring, but an expensive watch on his left wrist: a Tissot Chronograph model that was still ticking. It was nine o'clock.

The sound of a choir singing far away could be heard, coming in waves through the grey light. Lena turned to look. Behind the fences, between the Christmas-market stalls, she caught a glimpse of a group of nuns singing a hymn for the first arrivals. Dressed in black. Like crows.

A knot of spectators had assembled behind the police cordon. Lightning flashed.

'Suit and smart shoes in minus twenty-five,' Emil mumbled, and added, as if to explain: 'Heading home after a Christmas dinner, rat-arsed, and then he went to the harbour edge for a piss.'

Lena knelt down, searched the wet pockets and found a bunch of keys. In the inside pocket of the jacket, a wallet.

She opened the stiff leather. Had to take off her gloves. Blew on her fingers and studied the bank card: the owner's name was Svei-nung Adeler. The date of birth showed he was thirty-one years old. The wallet also contained a prescription for cortisone cream and a wad of notes, which as yet hadn't frozen into a block. She counted two thousand, two hundred kroner.

The dead man was tall, slim and well proportioned. *Two years younger than me*, Lena reflected. *This is a guy who, yesterday, could have been sitting on the same bus as me or sweating profusely in the same gym, on a bike.*

Just unutterably sad, she thought, with a shiver. The nuns had finally stopped singing. It had become lighter, a December grey. The Nesodden ferry clanked to a halt a hundred metres away. A flock of black, winter-clad passengers hurried out and dispersed towards Vika-terrassen and the National Theatre.

The only people interested in the scene where she stood were the clutch of reporters behind the cordon.

✻

By the time the mortuary vehicle started up and took the deceased man to the Pathology Institute, two SOC officers had secured the pier. Lena and Emil strolled back to the car.

Reaching the cordon where the press were waiting, Lena took a deep breath and told them: 'We don't know any more than what you've seen. A man, ethnically Norwegian. An accident we presume occurred at some time during the night. We'll establish the facts and send a press report when we know more.'

She hurried past the group.

A hand grabbed her arm.

Lena turned.

The man holding onto her was around forty with long, brown, wavy hair, a becoming unshaven face, and grey eyes that sought hers above a smile that revealed a little gap between his front teeth.

'A photo?' He flourished a camera. His eyes twinkled and she smiled back.

'No, thank you,' she said, opening the car door. She got in.

'Here!'

She took the business card he handed her and pulled the door to.

Emil was behind the wheel. The press reporters were moving away. She watched the figure walking alone across the square, knotting his scarf and pulling a cap over his head. She read his card: *Steffen Gjerstad, journalist.*

'I know that guy a bit,' Emil said. 'That is to say, my girl does. Monica. She's on the reception desk at *Dagens Næringsliv*. He works there.'

'Nice bum,' Lena said.

'Lena,' Emil grinned, and shook his head, smiling. He started the car and crunched it into first.

3

Axel Rise was a tall, lean guy with long hair, which he kept combing back with two fingers as he tried to secure it behind his ears. The hair had to be a relic of twenty years before, when Axel was a motorbike cop, rode a big BMW and dazzled women with his hippy ways. Now he maintained the style with a short leather jacket. But his hair had thinned and greyed over the years.

'It's just incredible,' Rise said in his Bergen dialect. 'One of the Metro drivers sees someone running down the tracks in the tunnel. He sounds the alarm. The ops room in Tøyen brings all the traffic to a halt and sends staff in to check. They trawl through without finding a single living soul – they claim. Then the trains resume service. The Grorud train's standing at the Grønland stop. It only manages two hundred metres. Guess what happens. This woman's behind one of the pillars between the tracks. And she throws herself in front.'

Gunnarstranda's biro died. He looked up. Straight at Rise. Rise appeared to be waiting for some comment. Gunnarstranda tried the biro again. No luck. 'Have you got something to write with?' he asked.

Rise took a silver Ballograf from the breast pocket of his biker jacket.

'The woman was cut to pieces. You could've put all of her into an IKEA bag,' Rise said. 'If it hadn't been such a messy business. Twenty minutes of high-pressure hosing in winter temperatures is hell for everyone.'

Gunnarstranda wasn't interested in Rise's Metro job. But his chuntering was making him lose concentration. He had half filled in the football pools coupon. But where was he in his system?

Emil Yttergjerde came through the door and sat down beside Gunnarstranda.

'Quite a start to the day,' Rise said.

'What's he blathering on about?' Yttergjerde whispered in Gunnarstranda's ear.

Gunnarstranda gave up on the pools. He pushed the Ballograf pen back and collected his coupons together.

'What was that, Rise?'

'A woman threw herself in front of a train,' Axel Rise said. 'It's tragic, of course, and we know suicide victims are resourceful. But how was it possible? The Metro people claim they checked the tunnel but didn't find her. Standing in front of the train, I could see there were lots of places to hide. Niches in the wall with locked gates in front. But they can be opened.'

'I feel ill every time I hear about a suicide,' Yttergjerde said.

'I just can't understand how it's even possible,' Rise intoned again.

'The staff searching the tunnel must know it pays to search properly. Traffic's held up for much longer after a suicide.'

'I'm sure they do,' Gunnarstranda said drily. He didn't like hearing complaints about other people's work. It reminded him of gossip. The cackle around the village pump.

'Was she young?' Yttergjerde asked.

Rise shrugged. 'No teeth, a syringe and the whole kit and caboodle in her pocket – junkie. Plata type. If only she knew the trouble she's caused. Why didn't she kill herself in Plata? Couldn't she have done it with a shot of heroin?'

'Junkie?' Yttergjerde said. 'Anyone we know?'

Rise shrugged again. 'Her name's Nina Stenshagen.'

Yttergjerde shook his head.

'How is it possible?' Rise rumbled on again. 'To search a tunnel with torches and the lights on and not find…?'

Gunnarstranda, who had decided to do the pools somewhere else, wasn't listening any more. The door closed with a bang behind him.

4

Lena found a gap between two 1.5 metre-high piles of cleared snow in Vogts gate. This was Lena's speciality, parking in tight spots. She signalled and drove past the car in front, ignored the queue braking behind her, reversed straight into the gap, twisted the wheel hard over and pulled the handbrake. The car slid into position as though the car and the gap were made for each other. Lena got out and checked her handiwork before strolling off to the entrance of the apartment block. The bells on the wall showed that Sveinung Adeler lived on the second floor. Could the dead man have a partner? It didn't seem to be the case. There was just one name on the bell tab.

Lena pressed and waited as she sorted the keys on the ring she had found in his pocket.

Not a sound from the intercom by the bells. No buzz of the lock.

She pressed the button twice more, then opened the door with a key. She found the name S. Adeler on one of the post boxes attached to the wall. Inserted the correct key in the lock and opened the box. Advertising. No letters. She locked the post box and went up the stairs.

There was only his name on the door. Presumably he had lived alone. She fumbled with the security lock. She had to turn it three times before the door to the flat opened.

She stood in the hall and breathed in the atmosphere. The flat was utterly silent apart from a low buzz from a fridge. Lena sniffed and smelt a faint scent of green soap.

To the left a sliding door was open. It led to a bedroom. A white double bed dominated the room. It was made and tidy. On the wall there was a poster of Rihanna wearing a full white bodysuit. She might just as well have allowed herself to be photographed nude. Lena continued into the living room. One wall was almost completely covered with the spines of DVDs. A large flatscreen filled another wall. Surround sound. She looked at the film titles. A lot of action movies. She recognised a few: *Pulp Fiction*, *Fargo*, films with Jason Bourne. Also: Hong Kong films and American B films with Travolta and Cage. On the lowest shelf there were a couple of films with the Playboy bunny logo. This was obviously a single man's room. On the table there were two empty bottles of Mexican beer – Corona. No ashtrays.

In a corner there was a kitchenette. A sheet of paper on the worktop. A neatly written note: '*Need more washing powder and Jif*'.

The note was signed. 'Pamina'. Probably a home help. This Pamina might have just been in to clean. There were no pans of leftovers on the stove.

Lena opened the fridge. The remaining four bottles of a six-pack were on the top shelf. Otherwise there were two tomatoes, a Fjordland ready meal, a carton of apple juice and an unopened packet of two chicken filets. This fridge belonged to someone who lived alone.

She went back to the hall. Opened a cupboard. Piles of trainers and ski sticks. Sveinung Adeler liked to stay fit.

The mirror cabinet in the bathroom was overflowing. An electric toothbrush and a shaver between bottles of fancy after-shave and deodorants: Dolce & Gabbana, Armani, Hugo Boss, Tommy Hilfiger. There were almost more bottles than Lena had at home.

She turned to the laundry basket. It was stuffed full: jeans, training kit, underwear.

This flat didn't tell her much. No calendar, not even a desk. No computer. Why not? Had he had a laptop with him last night? In which case it would lie in the mud at the bottom of Oslo harbour until archaeologists scoured through it at some point in the future.

Lena needed some personal information. She had to contact the relatives. She went through the bedroom again. No desk, no files, nothing.

She left the flat. Sealed the door with police tape. Went downstairs and onto the street. The cold gnawed at her nose.

Vanity and winter weather did not go together, Lena thought, as she stalked off in her long, thick puffa jacket, tying the cord of her fur hat under her chin. She felt like a penguin and probably looked like one too, but it didn't matter. When the cold bit, health came before beauty. The people on the uncleared pavement were a study of hats, long coats and solid winter boots – also the man a few metres ahead of her. Reefer jacket and knitted beanie. Mittens.

This man was holding the mittens on either side of his face and peering in through the window of her car.

She coughed loudly.

The man straightened up. She recognised him beneath the hat – just about. It was the journalist, Steffen Gjerstad.

Gjerstad smiled when he saw her. 'We meet again.'

'We do indeed,' she said, taking off one mitten and pulling the car key from her pocket.

'I recognised Sveinung dangling from the crane,' Gjerstad said. 'I've interviewed the guy a few times. I suppose you've searched his flat?'

'We have to inform the relatives,' Lena said.

His icy breath formed hoar frost on the tips of the hair sticking out from under his hat. 'He was a Vestlander. Came from Jølster, I believe. Quite a broad accent and mentioned the place once. So I'm sure his mother and father live there – Jølster.'

Lena involuntarily ran her bare hand through her hair and tucked the tips under her scarf. 'And you've interviewed the guy? In what connection, may I ask?'

Steffen Gjerstad grinned. 'We can swap information,' he said with a conspiratorial wink. 'Was it an accident?'

'Looks like it.'

'But you don't know for certain?'

She liked the look of Steffen Gjerstad and smiled from behind her scarf. 'It would be wrong to state anything until we've properly investigated what happened when he fell in. Do you know what his job was?'

Gjerstad put his mittens under one arm then took a pinch of snus from a box he'd produced from his jacket pocket and shoved it into his mouth. 'Civil service,' he said, with a bulging lip. 'Finance department.' He dusted the snus from his hands.

It struck Lena that taking snus was not the greatest seduction technique in the world. Then she said to herself: *Seduction? Control your imagination.*

Steffen continued: 'I haven't got anything in print. The interviews, two of them – it was research – were for articles we were working on. By "we" I mean the newspaper.'

'But you knew Adeler?'

'No. I knew who he was, if I can put it like that. He met estate agents and financiers. The paper where I work focuses on the economy and markets, and those circles aren't big.' Gjerstad thought for a few moments. 'Sveinung Adeler was something of a parvenu.' He grinned. 'Wanted to be interviewed at the Beach Club and places like that. He was a namedropper – "the other day I met such and such a celeb". Always wore the latest fashion and held his nose in the air – that type. But he was alright, macho, trained hard, pretty high standard, told everyone LOUDLY AND CLEARLY that he skied the Birkebeiner and the Vasa and that race down in Italy…' Gjerstad snapped his fingers searching for the right name. 'Marcialonga.' He ruminated. 'Not exactly my style.'

Lena unlocked the car. She had done the Birkebeiner three years in a row. 'Nice to meet you, Gjerstad.'

'Steffen.' He winked.

She had to smile again and repeated: 'Steffen.'

'And you?' he asked.

'What about me?'

'What's your name?'

'Lena.'

He waited with a furtive smile at the corners of his mouth.

'Stigersand,' she added.

'And do you have a phone number by any chance?'

He didn't waste any time, she thought, but she liked that. She liked the subtext. She ratcheted the atmosphere up a notch and asked: 'What do you want with my phone number?'

They looked into each other's eyes, both smiling. He said: 'In case something should occur to me, as they say in TV crime programmes.'

She nodded, tongue-tied.

He took a biro from an inside pocket. With his mittens under his arm he jotted down the number she gave him on the back of his hand. Both his hands were covered with notes in biro. There was something boyish about the sight and Lena felt a stab of tenderness in her chest. *Enough is enough*, she thought, and got into her car.

She drove off without looking back. Stopped at the lights outside Soria Maria. Her phone beeped. Message: *Forgot to say have a nice day, Steffen.*

He lifted her mood. She had to give him that.

5

Gunnarstranda had just sat down when the door opened.

Rindal watched him from the doorway without saying a word.

'My wife used to look at me like that,' Gunnarstranda said, slamming the desk drawer, 'if she'd cocked up the Christmas dinner or forgotten to go to the Vinmonopol on a Saturday.'

Rindal didn't smile. He came straight in and closed the door behind him. 'Would you mind contacting the Metro ops room in Tøyen?'

'Regarding what?'

'We've just received a phone call,' Rindal said. 'From their security department.'

Gunnarstranda angled his head, intrigued.

'The incident today. There's more to it than we assumed.'

'We?' Gunnarstranda mused, although he said nothing. He waited for Rindal to continue.

'The traffic controllers had been warned there were people in the tunnel. They stopped the traffic. They switched off the electricity and sent in security officers to inspect. It was all called off as a false alarm. No one was seen. The trains and trams get the green light. Traffic starts up again. Next thing they know, a woman throws herself under a train. It's happened before. People contemplating suicide are cunning. They hide. I've walked the stretch between Grønland and Tøyen myself several times. I'm sure you have, too. There are bomb shelters and corridors down there. The woman in question found a hiding place and jumped out when the first train came. But now the Metro's security people have rung me to say that they'd registered an alarm going off at an emergency exit inside. It happened after the collision and none of the staff went out through that exit.'

'What about Axel Rise?'

'What about him?'

'I thought he was handling this case.'

Rindal took a deep breath. 'There's something I think you should know about Axel Rise,' he said in a low voice.

Gunnarstranda stood up and put on the coat hanging over the back of his chair.

'Rise and his partner had a son two years ago. This boy has a syndrome – brain damage and some mucus stuff. He needs round-the-clock nursing, a respiratory aid and regular oxygen infusions. The boy lives at home, but there are night nurses and alarms, and if he starts thrashing about in bed he's straight to hospital, and apparently he does that quite often.'

Gunnarstranda sank back down on his chair. 'The poor man,' he mumbled.

'It doesn't end there,' Rindal said. 'A sick child is one thing, but it takes its toll on your relationship if you have no private life and have your home invaded by a variety of nurses day after day, month after month. It's even worse trying to keep your career going, especially as a police officer. He applied for a job here to get some mental space. But he goes to Bergen every weekend and once or twice a week. When he isn't working or on duty he's plagued by a bad conscience. What I'm trying to say is that I'm not sure he's the right man to draw conclusions in a case such as this.'

'I see. But it doesn't seem such a good idea to work in Oslo when you've got a wife and child who need you twenty-four hours a day in Bergen.'

'Strictly speaking, that's none of our business,' Rindal said. 'But having a child who needs you twenty-four hours a day must affect your mind. The man needs some space.'

Gunnarstranda sat looking at Rindal, silent.

'I'd just like you to know how the land lies,' Rindal said. 'I'm asking you and the others to be considerate towards Rise; that's why I'd like you to do this extra job. Check out the alarm and reassure the traffic controllers. They're upset and want clarity.'

✳

Gunnarstranda hadn't been to the Metro's new operational switchboard before. But he remembered the old one very well. There had been flashing analogue bulbs, a control panel mounted on cardboard, all connected to chunky switches and grey telephones that reminded you of the 1960s.

The new switchboard was separated from the world by a large, glass sliding door. The room was impressive. One long wall was a gigantic computer screen on which the train network was lit up with colour codes for various stations, and for turning loops, train markings, track changes and the movements of the trains from station to station. It was reminiscent of pictures from the Pentagon, Gunnarstranda thought, as he turned from the broad screen and walked towards the employees controlling the surveillance cameras. On the wall were monitors showing pictures projected by fifteen of the several hundred operative cameras. They showed stretches of rail, tunnel openings, ticket machines, platforms and a train pulling into a station that Gunnarstranda recognised as Majorstua.

Gunnarstranda was on nodding terms with most of the staff in the ops room. These were people who had worked at Oslo Metro for years – who had started as conductors, barrier guards or train drivers when the network was still called Oslo Sporveier. These operators knew the network inside out.

He nodded to one, knew exactly who he was, but couldn't put a name to him.

Two minutes later the operator had rewound the Grønland tape to 06:30. The picture was in colour with a high resolution.

'What are we looking for?' the operator asked.

'A woman dressed in a red track suit.'

The picture showed people standing still, people walking to and fro.

'She was a junkie from the Plata area,' Gunnarstranda added, 'but you might not be able to see that.'

Nothing. They had the road going down to Grønland Station on the screen, they had what was known informally as the junkie staircase, then the corridors, the halls, the platforms, but no red track suit. The minutes ticked by on the CCTV.

'My mistake,' the operator said. 'The driver who rang the alarm thought she was on her way south from Tøyen.'

They watched new footage. 'Tøyen has lots of platforms.'

People walked to and fro, got off and on the train.

But they didn't see anyone in a red track suit.

'Perhaps she came by train,' Gunnarstranda said.

'We have the same picture that the train drivers have on their screen before the doors close,' the operator said.

'If there's a sighting of someone on the track at 06:30, we're looking for a train that dropped her off just before,' Gunnarstranda said.

The pictures came up. The whole length of the train. Passengers getting out. Doors closing. Train setting off. Another train arriving. Doors opening. Passengers getting out.

There. A passenger jumping out just as the doors closed.

'That's her.'

The person moved out of the picture.

'The tunnel,' Gunnarstranda said.

They watched the same red figure back down the platform, turn and jump onto the track. She was swallowed up by the darkness of the tunnel.

Both Gunnarstranda and the operator stared intently at the screen.

'There,' said Gunnarstranda with a smile. 'There were two of them.'

Pictures don't lie. On the screen it was clear. Someone wearing a short jacket and a hood over his head hurrying after Nina Stenshagen, scrambling over the plastic barrier at the end of the platform, running down the steps and disappearing into the tunnel.

'That man knows what happened,' Gunnarstranda said. 'It must have been him who went through the emergency exit after the incident.'

'That doesn't help us much,' the operator said darkly. 'It means our security officers missed both of them when they were inspecting the tunnel. That's impossible.'

'The lights were on when they were searching the tunnel, were they?'

The operator nodded. 'But there are no cameras in the tunnel.'

Gunnarstranda sat deep in thought. This case was beginning to stimulate his interest. The man in the picture followed Nina Stenshagen into the tunnel. Why? What was he doing when she threw herself in front of the train? Why did he keep hidden? Why did he leave the tunnel only after the collision?

'Can you see if you can get the face of the guy in the hoodie?'

The operator rewound the tape.

He shook his head. 'Looks like we've only got his back.'

'He must have got on the train at some point,' Gunnarstranda said.

'There are lots of stations to choose from,' the operator said.

Gunnarstranda stood up. 'Would you mind working on it a bit more and contacting me if you find anything?'

6

In the break Lena found a table with the day's tabloids on it. Empty and half-empty cups were scattered across the surface. On top of the papers was a plastic box of cinnamon snaps. Beside it a poinsettia. She pressed a fingertip into the soil. Dry. She grabbed a half-full tea cup and emptied the contents into the pot, then lifted the box of biscuits and took the top newspaper. Nothing about the drowning in the harbour by the City Hall. What about the online papers?

Lena got up and went into her office. Took her laptop from the bag hanging over the chair.

VG-nett and *Dagbladet.no* had pictures of the ambulance and staff in the hi-vis jackets. *Aftenposten* had found an old archive photo of Lena. She never liked seeing herself in photos. In this one her hair was awful. The articles said nothing except that a man had been found dead in the sea.

She couldn't resist the temptation. On the Birkebeiner website she looked for the name of Sveinung Adeler. His results popped up. Adeler had been a fit man. 2.57.06. That was phenomenal. Skiing from Rena to Lillehammer in less than three hours. Her own PB was 3.48.24. On that occasion she had been so tired over the last ten kilometres that pure willpower was all that had held her upright. Stopping would have meant she would have been teased by all her male colleagues for eternity and beyond – by Emil Yttergjerde in particular.

She decided to google the journalist Steffen Gjerstad. There were a number of hits. He clearly did a lot of social networking. She was invited to click onto Twitter, Facebook and LinkedIn. Instead she looked for pictures on Google. She flicked through them. A pretty good-looking guy. His own man. In two of the photos he was with a group of young women. They were laughing. He obviously liked being the only man. In one photo he was looking up at the photographer with a tentative expression. She liked that. That, and his smile.

She clicked on the *Dagens Næringsliv* website and searched his name. The titles of a series of articles he had written rolled out. Finance and feature articles. One about sailing boats, one about modern dress codes for men and one about trends and mechanical Swiss clocks. Not exactly her sphere of interest.

What kind of guy was Steffen in private? Did he like Tom Waits, for example? Did he have posters of erotic female singers on his bedroom wall?

She bookmarked all Steffen Gjerstad's newspaper articles and closed her laptop.

The phone rang. It was Ragnhild, who worked in the Sogn and Fjordane Police District. Lena and Ragnhild had gone to police college together. They chatted for a bit then Ragnhild came to the point. Sveinung Adeler's relatives in Jølster had been informed of his death by the parish priest. Ragnhild offered to visit his parents.

Lena agreed. 'Ask if they have his cleaner's phone number. I'd also like to know who he mixed with in Oslo,' she said. 'If his parents could give us a hand there, it would be good. Ask if he had a girl-friend or if there were any exes. Ask when they last spoke to their son and if they knew what plans he might've had for Wednesday evening. Oh, and Ragnhild?'

'Yes.'

'Could you ask them for a photo? As recent as possible.'

She stared into the distance. Again she was thinking about Steffen Gjerstad. At that moment the phone rang.

Two minds – one idea. It was Steffen Gjerstad. She grabbed her phone. It thumped in her hand like a little heart. Should she answer it? She liked him well enough. But things were going too fast, and they shouldn't.

Emil Yttergjerde came in, strode towards the plate of cinnamon snaps. 'Lena, your phone's ringing.'

She nodded and put it back in her bag. 'Let it.'

7

'It was my understanding I'd be working in the missing persons section,' Axel Rise said.

Section Head Rindal said nothing. He leaned back in his arm-chair and observed Rise from under lowered eyelids.

'I applied for Frølich's job,' Rise explained. 'Frølich was responsi-ble for missing persons.'

'Frank Frølich's suspended from duty,' Rindal said. 'His case is still pending. And we're reorganising this section until further notice.'

'But the job description—'

'That's irrelevant,' Rindal interrupted. 'This is my responsibility. I assign staff to reports of missing persons.'

Rise appeared put out.

Rindal drew a deep breath. 'You did a good job on the Metro this morning, but apparently there was a hiccup regarding the emergency exits.'

'OK, I'll sort it out.'

'Gunnarstranda's there.'

Rise's face tautened.

'I couldn't find you,' Rindal said, taking a strip of chewing gum from the packet on the desk.

'You've got a tough situation at home and you travel,' Rindal said. 'But some jobs need an officer round the clock.'

When Rindal went to carry on, Rise flicked his hair behind his ears and interrupted him:

'The reason I applied to work here was to have more responsibility. I need to grow. You know that. It makes no sense to commute between Bergen and Oslo only to get bits and bobs.'

Rindal leaned back in his chair and reflected. At length he took a piece of paper. 'I've got something here, sent to us from the security service, PST.' He added: 'A garbled letter to a female MP at Storting. Probably nothing. But check it out. Apparently a woman wrote the letter. The parliamentary administrators at Storting regard this letter as threatening.'

Rindal pushed the sheet across the table to Rise, who sat studying it disapprovingly.

Rindal fixed him with his eyes.

Axel Rise took the sheet and left.

'Rise,' Rindal said.

He turned by the door.

'I'd like you to get to know Gunnarstranda.'

'Why?'

Rindal looked down. 'We can discuss that later.' He swivelled round on his chair and concentrated on the computer screen.

Rise stared at him for a few seconds and then left.

8

On the way to Rindal's office Gunnarstranda met Lena Stigersand.

'Can you do me a favour?' he asked.

Lena tilted her head, curious.

'Ring me in eight minutes.'

Linda looked at her watch. 'From now?'

Gunnarstranda nodded and carried on walking. He didn't want to let this case go. There were a number of unanswered questions regarding the Metro suicide.

✳

Rindal listened in silence as Gunnarstranda reported back on what he had seen in the Metro ops centre.

When Gunnarstranda had finished he said: 'There are two possibilities. Either the mysterious second man has something to do with the incident or he hasn't.'

Gunnarstranda resisted the temptation to comment.

'So there are two people hiding from the search teams,' Rindal summarised, 'and as the searchers don't find anyone, the electricity is switched back on, the lights are extinguished and the trains start to run, then this woman throws herself in front of one. Everything is stopped again and there's a full alert. The passengers are evacuated, are they?'

Gunnarstranda nodded. 'They had to climb down onto the track and were guided back to Grønland Station.'

'When?' Rindal asked.

'The collision occurred at 07:19.' Gunnarstranda took out his notes. 'This is the timeline: A train driver sees someone running on the track from Tøyen to Grønland Station and reports it. The electricity is switched off almost immediately. The time is 06:37. The search team starts walking from Tøyen down to Grønland at 06:43. It takes them just over twenty minutes. It takes that long because they have to search bomb shelters and corridors and so on down there.

They shine torches through gates and check for anyone hiding. They don't see anyone. The tunnel is about eight hundred metres long. When they reach the end, at 07:03, the conclusion is that either the train driver was mistaken or the person had run back out. So they send two men back, one on each track, for safety's sake. These two move faster and it takes them ten minutes. They report the all-clear at 07:17. The electricity is switched on. The Grorud train starts up and hits the woman at 07:19.'

'And the alarm shows the emergency exit being used?'

'At 07:22. At that time all the train doors were closed and the train driver was in conversation with the ops room. He was reporting what had happened. The evacuation of the passengers doesn't start until half an hour later.'

Rindal and Gunnarstranda looked at each other.

'There was a person in the tunnel who saw her commit suicide,' Rindal said, his brow furrowed with doubt.

Gunnarstranda corrected Rindal's conclusion. 'There was one person in the tunnel, one person who knows what happened.'

Rindal raised both palms in defence. 'Control your imagination. This was a suicide. Case closed.'

'She was a hardened junkie. Why didn't she OD if she wanted to die?'

Rindal closed both eyes. 'I'm not listening to what you're saying.'

Gunnarstranda's phone rang. He looked at the display and stood up. 'Sorry,' he said. 'I have to take this one.' Gunnarstranda left the room with the phone to his ear. 'Just a moment,' he said, and turned to Rindal. He lowered the phone. 'Two people, Rindal. Both hiding. How is it possible that the security officers didn't see them? This is a tricky situation for Oslo Metro, but also for the police. I intend to follow this line of enquiry.'

After he closed the door behind him he thanked Lena and rang off.

9

When Lena called Gunnarstranda she was queueing outside Mikels Kebab Shop in Grønlandsleiret. She asked to have hers wrapped. The low sun cast long shadows and made the cold air seem even colder as she trudged up the path to Police HQ. On her way in she met Axel Rise on his way out. She nodded to him.

'Stigersand?'

She stopped.

'You've got the case with the guy they fished out of the harbour, haven't you? Sveinung Adeler?'

Axel Rise stood winding a long scarf around his neck. When he had finished he looked at her as if expecting a report.

'Looks like an accident. He was probably pissed after a Christmas dinner and slipped on his way home,' she said to fill the silence. 'May know a bit more after I've spoken to the pathologists.'

Rise observed her without speaking, the same hangdog eyes.

The icy air was nipping at her ears, she was hungry and wanted to go in and eat. She made as if to move on.

'I've received a tip-off,' Axel Rise added quickly. 'About the Christmas dinner last night. Sveinung Adeler was having dinner with a Storting MP.'

'And who was that?'

'Aud Helen Vestgård.'

Lena waited for him to continue, to give her more context. It didn't come. Talking with this guy was like coaxing old wax out of a narrow candlestick holder with a broad-bladed knife, she reflected. Somehow it wouldn't come out.

'Where did you get that from?'

Rise gave her a sly wink, turned and walked down the hill.

Confused, Lena stood watching him disappear for four long seconds before following him at a jog. 'You must have more than a name.'

Rise stopped. 'What more do you need?'

Lena racked her brains for a sensible answer. 'Anything. The woman has to be eliminated from enquiries.'

'Of course she has,' Rise said. 'Ask her,' he grinned. 'That's not hard.' Axel revealed a set of broad, even teeth as he smiled. 'Are you worried about talking to Vestgård? If you need help I'm at your service.'

Lena felt her irritation rise. 'You and I are colleagues; we pass on what we know to each other. We don't sit on secrets or buy and sell info.'

Axel Rise angled his head as though unaware of what she meant: 'What are you talking about? We work in teams, yes. I just passed on a tip-off to you and I'm offering you help.'

'You can start by saying who gave you the tip-off.'

Rise went quiet and the silence persisted. He didn't want to say any more, that much was obvious. Lena spun on her heel and walked off. She tore open the door and marched in without looking back. She was already blaming herself. She hadn't needed to lose her temper at Rise. His tip-off was useful. Sveinung Adeler worked in the Finance Department. Having dinner with a politician would be quite normal. But Rise had in some way suggested that they were *alone*. Aud Helena Vestgård was an attractive, married female politician. She occasionally appeared on TV. She took stands on controversial topics and could do the banter on popular satirical TV programmes. If she was having dinner with a younger civil servant, would that make matters more complicated?

Lena dismissed the idea. She would have to talk to Aud Helen Vestgård whatever.

10

The mirror had the same shape and size as a piece of A4 paper. The frame was narrow, but delicately wrought. The surface of the mirror had cracked at the edges. *Old*, thought Gunnarstranda. *The edges of the mirror have aged, in the same pattern that cobblestones do.* Looking at the mirror, he barely recognised himself. Cheeks puffed out, nose like a potato. In other words, the mirror was useless. Nevertheless he considered buying it. He knew Tove would love a mirror like this. It would be the perfect gift for someone who was interested in antiques. But the decision still hadn't matured enough in him. Even if the mirror was a treasure, he couldn't bring himself to do it. He put it back, avoided eye contact with the sales assistant and left the second-hand shop.

It had become dark outside. The only reason he had come this way had been that he was looking for the bus the Salvation Army used to help severe cases of drug addiction. He needed to know more about the dead woman, Nina Stenshagen. The challenge was to find someone who knew something and was also reliable. People like this were thin on the ground in Nina's milieu.

He headed towards Jernbanetorget and caught sight of the bus as it turned into Dronningens gate. The bus was old, from the 1980s, and the diesel exhaust it spewed out as thick and black as the smoke from burnt tyres. Gunnarstranda flagged it down. It pulled in to the kerb and stopped. The front door opened and Gunnarstranda jumped in.

There was hardly anyone on board. Only three or four jaded-looking addicts sitting at the back and eating their packed lunches.

The bus drove on as he leaned against a pole and showed his ID card to the guy behind the wheel: a man in his forties with long grey hair in a ponytail and wearing the Salvation Army uniform.

'Nina Stenshagen,' Gunnarstranda said.

'What about her?'

'She's dead.'

'OD?'

Gunnarstranda shook his head. 'She fell under a train in the tunnel between Tøyen and Grønland this morning. I'm trying to establish the circumstances.'

'Well, you won't find them here.'

'Did you know her?'

'You don't know people like Nina, but I was aware who she was. I've dealt with her a few times.'

Gunnarstranda held on tight as the lights changed to green and the bus accelerated. 'Did she have any enemies?'

'Nina? Hardly. It was hard enough for her to survive, poor thing. No enemies – unless she'd pinched someone's shot for the following day.'

Gunnarstranda glanced over to the back of the bus. One of the passengers was passing round a carton of chocolate milk.

'Is that likely?'

'Is what likely?'

'Was Nina the type to pinch stuff?'

The man behind the wheel smiled at Gunnarstranda as though the answer was obvious.

'Do you know the names of anyone she hung around with?'

'She had a boyfriend. She has had for a long time. Stig. That's another tragic story. Once, Nina went on methadone. Five or six years ago. She tried to go straight. Stig's never been on methadone. The inevitable happened. Just a mo and I'll ask.' He turned and shouted down the bus. 'Any of you know where Stig is – Nina's fella?'

No one answered. But one of them got up and stumbled to the front.

'Nothing else?' Gunnarstranda asked the driver. 'She had a boyfriend, tried to go straight and otherwise, what? How did she end up on drugs? Where did she come from? Did she speak dialect for example?'

'Nina was an Oslo girl.'

'Past? Job?'

The driver shrugged. He stopped at the lights. 'No idea.'

'I know,' said the guy who had joined them from the back. A skinny man with a very wrinkled face. He leaned against the back of a seat and rolled a cigarette with trembling hands.

Gunnarstranda watched him stick the roll-up between his lips and the pouch into his trouser pocket. Red Mix. He had smoked that brand – once.

'Nina worked at Oslo Metro,' said the guy, the cigarette bouncing up and down between his lips. 'When her hands were steady she drove on the Østensjøbane for many years. Shift work, right. Then they have problems sleeping, and then they start on pills, then they start mixing them, and then they don't get prescriptions any more, and then they have to buy them on the street. In the end they join us.' He grinned and revealed a row of dark stumps in his lower jaw. 'That's how crazy it can get.'

The driver opened the door for him. The man jumped down and out. 'Keep an eye on your kids,' he shouted up to Gunnarstranda and the driver, and was gone.

11

It was too cold for the highway maintenance department to salt. Light snow mixed with previous falls and frozen salt brine made the carriageway on Drammensveien smooth and treacherous. Lena drove carefully and stayed in the right-hand lane the whole way out of Oslo. Grey and brown snow lay on the verge. She turned off at Lysaker. The further she drove towards Bærum, the cleaner and whiter the snow.

The street lamps along the road dotted with large detached houses cast a deep-yellow light over the countryside. Lena parked by the edge of a pile of snow.

The house where Aud Helen Vestgård lived towered like a castle in the winter darkness a few metres behind a wire netting fence. All the windows shone with light, but there were no occupants in sight.

Lena's timing was calculated. The most important TV news programmes were over and there was still at least an hour before the debates started. So she wouldn't be disturbing, she assumed.

Two figures came walking up the hill. Two young women, it turned out. One had long blonde curls that bounced on her shoulders as she walked. The other had wound a large scarf around her head and shoulders. Both disappeared into the gates of the Vestgårds' house. The daughters of the house, Lena concluded – or the daughter of the house and a friend. Lena watched them enter through the front door. When it closed behind them she got out of the car.

Not a sound could be heard when she pressed the bell. A few long seconds passed, then the broad door was opened by a man in his mid-forties. Lena recognised his face. It was Frikk Råholt, Aud Helen Vestgård's husband and a state secretary in some ministry or other. She had seen him many times before – on TV. Nevertheless she was taken aback by how small in stature he was. His face was square and attractive; his hair combed back, greying at the temples. He inclined his head in an enquiring smile.

Lena showed him her ID. 'Lena Stigersand, Oslo Police District. I'd like to speak to Aud Helen Vestgård, if I may.'

Frikk Råholt was clearly curious, but his manners prevailed over his curiosity. He held the door open and moved aside. 'Come in.'

He closed the door behind her. 'Please wait here. I'll call you.' He left.

The hall was large and welcoming. Wide sliding wardrobe doors on one wall. Big, black tiles on the floor.

A song on the radio came from the depths of the house: Dean Martin. *Let it snow, let it snow, let it snow.*

Dean Martin was faded out and a voice took over.

Lena felt a sneaking sense that she had made a bad decision steal down her body. She looked at her watch. It was several minutes since Råholt had let her in. What were they doing?

Another Christmas song: 'I Saw Mommy Kissing Santa Claus'.

Lena plumped down on a stool beside the front door. If Aud Helen Vestgård had been out with Sveinung Adeler last night she would of course have informed the police. After all, the name of the drowned man had been made public many hours ago. And if there was one thing MPs did it was to follow the news on the TV, radio and internet.

Lena turned her head and almost jumped out of her skin.

Aud Helen Vestgård was standing in the doorway watching her.

Lena shot up like a schoolgirl caught sleeping in class.

'Stigersand, wasn't it?' Aud Helen Vestgård stretched out a hand.

The owner of the hand was in good shape for a woman over forty. She obviously spent a lot of time keeping fit. And she had quite a different style from her husband. Vestgård wore jeans and a bright-red top – clothes that emphasised her figure and made her seem youthfully casual.

'As you can perhaps imagine, I'm quite curious to know more,' Vestgård said in her pleasant speaking voice. 'Have you found anything yet?'

Lena had no idea what she was talking about and had to admit it with a tentative smile.

Vestgård regarded Lena with surprise, but explained: 'Parliament reported a letter I'd received to the police. It was confused, but there was no misunderstanding its intent. It was a death threat. Am I to understand that is *not* why you're here?'

Lena concentrated hard and chose her words with care: 'I'm afraid I know nothing about that case. I'm investigating the circumstances surrounding the death of Sveinung Adeler.'

Aud Helen Vestgård turned her head in a friendly yet inquisitive way: 'Oh, yes?'

Lena hesitated, but again chose her words with care: 'I understood you knew him.'

'I don't.' Aud Helen Vestgård stuck both hands in her pockets. Her jeans were so tight there was only room for her fingertips. 'Excuse me for asking, but where did you get the idea I know this man?'

This meeting was taking a very different turn from what Lena had expected. She was feeling warm in her thick clothes and unzipped her jacket. 'Your name has been mentioned and so we're obliged to check. We're trying to clarify the circumstances regarding Adeler's death and what might've happened—'

She didn't get a chance to finish her sentence.

'Could you bring me up to speed here? Who is this Adeler and what has happened?'

Lena let her words sink in. The questions made the MP look exceptionally bad. An official in the Finance Department had been found floating in the harbour that morning. The young man's death was on everyone's tongue and she, a Member of, the Norwegian Parliament, didn't know what had happened?

'A drowning incident,' Lena said with a poker face. 'Last night or early this morning. Tragic story. Sveinung Adeler died when he fell into the water by the City Hall Quay. But no witnesses have come forward and before we draw any conclusions we have to detail what exactly happened. He was dressed as if he had been out dining last night, and we've received a tip-off suggesting he was at a Christmas dinner where you were also present, but you're saying that isn't the case?'

'Yes. Your tip-off is incorrect.'

Lena waited. But nothing was forthcoming. 'Where were you last night?'

Vestgård put on a weak smile, almost of acknowledgement. 'At home.' She added: 'Here with my husband and child.'

Lena made to leave.

'You know, I suppose, I regard this as strange,' said Vestgård, still with her fingertips in the tops of her pockets. 'The security service reported the death threat to the police. If I hadn't been concerned before, I was petrified then – this is just a bit over the top, isn't it, someone wishing you dead? PST is taking this case seriously.'

Lena nodded. She understood.

'Then the police come and ask me about this instead.' The woman fixed Lena's eyes with her gaze.

'I can only apologise,' Lena said sympathetically. 'On the other hand, it's a positive that I've got a little further in my case.'

Lena took off her gloves and gripped the door handle behind her. 'Thank you for taking the time to talk to me.'

Vestgård said nothing.

'Have a nice evening,' Lena said, stumbling out.

✳

Lena walked briskly down the drive and out of the gate. She fumbled as she inserted the key in the car lock. Her little Micra was as out of place here as she was.

Immediately the thought had been articulated she lifted her head and inhaled the fresh, cold air. Then she noticed another little car a few hundred metres down the road. It was a black Fiat 500.

Lena thought the model the height of cool – it was chic and rounded and loyally designed like the original classic of many years before. This one even had a hood – a cabriolet. She would have loved to buy one herself – if only she could have afforded a new car. In the meantime she would have to make do with dreaming.

When Lena was small her father had kept an original Fiat 500 in the garage. This veteran car had been his great hobby, and every winter he spruced it up in preparation for the summer. He had loved the car and he had loved fiddling around with it. The car had also been an adventure for her. Small and compact, it had been like riding a dodgem on the road. And whenever Lena saw a picture of a Fiat 500 she thought about the pillow she'd had when she was a child. A white pillow with a black stain. She smiled at the memory. It hadn't been her fault. She had forgotten she was dirty. Her father had dabbed oil on her nose when he was lying on his back, working under the car, and she had bent down to tell him dinner was ready.

She opened the Micra door and was on the point of getting in. Then she noticed someone sitting inside the Fiat beneath the street lamp further down.

Lena got in. Started the engine and put the heating on full. The person in the Fiat must have been frozen. The car must have been there for a while because there was frost on the inside of the glass. Why hadn't they started the engine and the heating?

She cast a final glance at the house. From a window on the first floor Vestgård and her husband were watching her. She considered what Vestgård had told her about the threat. *Nothing on this earth is straightforward*, Lena thought. *But in the end I am a cop.* She opened her bag and took out a pen and something to write on. Made a note of the car's registration number.

Lena was in her own world all the way down to Drammensveien. She drove home in a dream. Planning what she was going to do – maybe go skiing. Yes, that was definitely what she was going to do.

She fumbled blindly for a CD in the pile and shoved it in. Soon Tom Waits was singing 'Rain Dogs' accompanied by a hurdy-gurdy.

She was completely immersed until she arrived home at the block of flats in Tvetenveien and drove down into the garage complex. Then she glanced into the mirror. A car drove slowly past on the road behind her. A modern version of a Fiat 500 in black – with a hood.

Was that possible? She stopped. Two identical cars? It seemed almost too improbable. She sat watching the garage door roll down behind her, immersed in thought.

Seeing two Fiat 500s in the space of twenty minutes – well, maybe. But if both were black and cabriolets?

Could that be chance?

She dismissed the idea and parked.

12

The snow on the illuminated piste was packed hard. The intense cold would presumably keep most skiers indoors. So there would probably be ice on the tracks, which would make for heavy going. She wouldn't need to apply much grip wax. More like glide wax. She fetched her skis from the tall cupboard in the hall and leaned them against the worktop, underside up. Ran her hand along the blades. What wax did she use last time? Purple? Or blue? May as well remove it. She looked for the wax iron and plugged it in. Ran the hot iron back and forth so that the paper absorbed the rest of the old wax. The last bits she removed with a knife. Then she rubbed in a good layer of wax. Melted the glide wax with the hot iron. Fetched the box of waxes from the cupboard under the worktop. Checked the thermometer outside the window. Minus eighteen. So it might be less than minus twenty on the piste. Light-blue VR30 should do the trick. She put two light layers under the binding and spent time distributing the wax with a cork. *There we are. Perfect.* If Lena was going to complete the Birkebeiner she would need to get a few kilometres in her legs every week. To progress. Gradually increase distance and speed. She changed into woollen underwear and ski pants. She allowed herself an extra woollen jumper under her jacket and ran down the stairs to the car.

✳

She drove to Ellingsrud and did her usual circuit to Mariholtet and back. The piste was compacted and icy, as expected. And the grip was good. The snow underneath sucked. Even on some gentle descents she had to dig in to maintain her speed. On the other hand, she could easily ski up the steepest sections without slipping once. The cold gnawed at her toes and chin; her frozen breath condensed into hoar frost in her hair. But she warmed up as she skied. The powerful lamps along the piste cast a strong light on the snow, and the total darknesss created a scenic backdrop for the run. The only sounds to be heard were the dry clicks as she used her sticks and the low whoosh of her skis on the snow. At times it was so quiet she could hear the crackle of the floodlights. There was no one else on the piste this evening. Most people considered twenty below too cold to train. Lena mentally thanked the piste manager for being such a sport as to keep the lights on. In these conditions it would have been possible to put in a shift in the darkness too, but the light made the experience memorable.

After a shower she stood in front of the mirror, rubbing herself down. The area under her eyes was dark. *I look exhausted. I'm getting on for thirty-four and look drained.* She straightened up and took a step back. Scrutinised her naked body, turned around 360 degrees and stretched: taut stomach, muscular upper arms.

But her breasts were too pendulous.

She put down her towel and lifted them. Then she felt it, with her forefinger – a hardness, near the nipple.

For a fraction of a second she met her own fearful eyes in the mirror. Held her left breast in both hands once more.

Felt again. She had been right the first time. A lump.

She repeated the movement with her right breast. All soft, no hardness.

At once Lena was as hot as she had been after skiing. The steam and the silence in the bathroom were suffocating. She opened the door to the hall, walked naked into the sitting room, stood staring into the air. Images flickered through her brain:

There were images of her beloved father who, in the space of a few weeks, experienced all the side-effects of a cytotoxin: the enormous weight loss, one bout of pneumonia after another, before losing mobility in his legs, getting infections in his blood, having problems with his teeth, then losing his hair – until there were only a few strands left, which he defiantly combed back. Her father had been turned into a shadow of his former self, a caricature, trapped in the claws of death, which squeezed and pressed and tormented the lean figure, shrank him from inside and brought him closer to the end with every day that he had to suffer.

Lena was soon as cold as she had been hot.

Was it possible? That you could touch a breast and have your whole life turned on its head?

No, she told herself, *I'm strong!* She focused on her reflection in the window. A supple body, fit and muscular.

Yes, she was strong, but what about in a few months' time? What about when her body was weakened by radiotherapy and cancer and no longer had any immune protection?

She slumped onto a chair and talked herself round: *Take it easy. This might be an innocuous cyst or a glass splinter you trod on when you were four, an object that has become trapped and moved around your body and turned up somewhere completely different.* Now she was sure.

That was the explanation. It was exactly what had happened before, when she was sixteen and had a lump on her arm. After a couple of weeks she had been able to coax out a tiny, harmless grain of sand.

Suddenly the idea of illness was absurd. She was healthy. There was no lump. There couldn't be. It had to be something else.

Warily, she stroked her left breast. Felt nothing. Encouraged, she squeezed harder. Then she felt it again; it was small, tiny. A slight hardness. She looked up, glimpsed her eyes in the window reflection and caught herself in the lie.

She got to her feet, hot all over. Dressed on autopilot. She went down to the cellar and fetched the cardboard box with the Christmas decorations. Back in the sitting room, she sat taking out Christmas pixies and candleholders while her thoughts were elsewhere. *I am sitting here holding an ageing female pixie.* Lena studied its wrinkled face and thought: *My God, what am I doing?*

She put the figure back in the box and went to the kitchen. Opened the fridge. On the lowest shelf were eight quarter-bottles of champagne and prosecco. All Lena's good friends knew she liked fizzy wine, which she kept in small bottles. They were the presents they gave her after trips abroad. Lena searched through the selection until she found a prosecco. She read the label – Villa Sando Fresco – opened it and filled a stem glass. Took the packet of spelt biscuits from the cupboard. Cheese. She wanted some cheese. Chèvre. The cheese in the bell had seen its best days. But with honey and nuts this was the greatest luxury on earth. Three thin spelt crackers, each with a bit of goat's cheese, every bite with a hazelnut glazed with honey.

She put everything on a dish. Carried it into the sitting room. Zapped through the channels. Serious male faces talking. Another channel: a reality show with blondes and plummeting cleavage.

But Lena wanted something to laugh at. She got up and went into her bedroom where she had a shelf of DVDs. Her eyes found *The Piano*. She loved that film. The relationship between the mute Ada and tattooed George – desire and forbidden love. But *The Piano* was not the sort of film to make you laugh. Lena put it back and instead flicked through for *Notting Hill*.

Soon she was back in front of the TV, watching Hugh Grant play the good-looking bookshop owner while the princess in the fairy story was browsing the books. Lena couldn't concentrate. But she noticed her glass was empty. She went to the kitchen. No more prosecco in her selection on the lowest shelf of the fridge. The bottles clinked as she took out a Henkell Trocken. Sat down in front of the screen again. Rewound the film to where Hugh Grant pretended to be a journalist and introduced himself as a rep for the magazine *Horse and Hound*. But the scene wasn't funny any more.

She went to prod her breast again, but forced herself to refrain.

Lena put her feet on the table and a blanket over herself and stared at the ceiling. When she woke up, the film was over. She was cold under the blanket.

Lena got up with difficulty, shuffled into the bedroom and slipped under the duvet.

1

Rikard Svenaas opened the window on counter two.

Svenaas always walked around with his teeth bared in a lop-sided grin, as though someone had cut off his lips with a sharp knife. Gunnarstranda jumped every time he caught sight of the man even though he had witnessed the same sight for close on twenty years.

'Can't you cover your teeth for once, man? Seeing you like that makes me nervous.'

'I've been like this my whole life, Gunnarstranda. You and my wife can found Naggers Anonymous, but it won't help. This is what I do when I'm concentrating. What are you doing here, anyway?'

'I want to see what Nina Stenshagen had in her pockets when she was run over in the tunnel.'

Gunnarstranda stood waiting by the window as Svenaas disappeared inside. 'Can't have been much,' he called to the broad back. 'It was handed in yesterday morning.'

Svenaas returned with a small plastic bag labelled 'Nina Stenshagen'.

The bag contained two syringes packed in cellophane, a mobile phone, a shrunken pouch of Petterøes roll-up tobacco, nail-clippers, a disposable lighter with the Rema 1000 logo and a few coins.

'The phone,' Gunnarstranda said. 'Can you ring Telenor and crack the PIN?'

Svenaas grabbed the phone and studied it with his teeth bared in an even broader grin. 'Not necessary. It's switched on. But the battery's weak.' He passed the phone to Gunnarstranda, who put on his spectacles.

It was a Nokia, quite similar to his own. He tapped on the menu

until he found Nina's phone list. Flicked down until he found the
name Stig. He took a biro from his pocket, noted the number and
was about to pass the phone back to Svenaas, then hesitated. 'You're
quite a dab hand at these things. Can you see who she called yesterday – just before she was killed?'

'We can see the last number she called.' Svenaas fumbled with
the phone. 'Here you are.' He read out the number. Gunnarstranda
compared it with his piece of paper. It was the same number: Stig
Eriksen.

'When did she ring this number?'

'Tuesday evening.'

Gunnarstranda frowned. 'Are the date and time correct on the
phone?'

Svenaas checked, and nodded.

'If she rang someone with this phone on Wednesday or Thursday
morning, it would be registered, wouldn't it?'

Svenaas nodded again. 'Doesn't look as if Nina Stenshagen has
used this phone since Tuesday evening.'

Gunnarstranda pushed the bag back over the counter. 'Would
you be so kind as to copy the phone numbers in the list – before the
battery dies?'

Svenaas grunted an answer and disappeared inside again.

Gunnarstranda tapped Stig Eriksen's number onto his phone. It
was still early, but Stig lived on the street. People living outdoors in
below-zero temperatures don't tend to sleep in. The phone rang in
his ear. Gunnarstranda was on the point of giving up when at last
there was a crackle at the other end. He heard the din of traffic as Stig
fumbled with the phone.

'Yes?'

'Stig Eriksen?'

'Who's that?'

'Gunnarstranda, Oslo Police. I'm ringing about Nina Stenshagen.
Nina…'

He hesitated. Stig had rung off.

Gunnarstranda looked at his phone for a few seconds. He called again – same number. It rang three times in his ear, then Stig's phone was switched off.

Gunnarstranda gazed into the air thoughtfully.

Svenaas peered out from behind a shelving system. 'What did he say?'

'He didn't want to talk to me.'

'Surprised?'

Gunnarstranda didn't answer.

Svenaas waved the phone. 'This might take a while.'

When Gunnarstranda was back in the department, he stood in front of the window thinking about Nina Stenshagen. A homeless woman who dies at the age of forty-four. If it was true that as she had worked as a train driver on the Metro she would have known the tunnels under Oslo city centre like the back of her hand. She would have known where the bomb shelters and the emergency exits were.

He looked out of the window. It was early, but still dark outside. In the streets down in Grønland there were long lines of car lights, white and red. Stig Eriksen was out there somewhere, freezing. Well, OK, thought Gunnarstranda. Stig didn't fancy a conversation with the police.

Was it Stig who had followed Nina into the tunnel? And if it was, why had he done so?

Gunnarstranda turned away from the window and looked straight at Emil Yttergjerde.

'Have you seen anything of Axel Rise?' Gunnarstranda asked.

Emil shook his head. 'I saw him yesterday afternoon, when he was on his way to check out a death threat on an MP.'

Gunnarstranda went into the corridor.

Rindal was in the doorway of his office waving a bit of paper. 'Are you free?'

2

In Rindal's office the department head closed the door and passed Gunnarstranda the piece of paper.

It was a copy. The original was written on a perforated sheet of lined paper from a pad. It was a quite a clumsy letter, addressed to Aud Helen Vestgård, Storting: Vestgård had better wise up. She should know that as a woman she had a historic duty to oppose men's repression of women. If she continued as she was doing, subjecting herself to society's male values, it would be to her cost.

The letter was signed with a name and address.

'The parliamentary admin chief sent the letter to PST in Nydalen,' Rindal said, 'and they sent it on to us. They've concluded that the letter was written by a confused person, so the case does not concern national security or the counter-terrorist forces.'

Gunnarstranda raised both eyebrows. 'Terrorism?' He read aloud from the letter:

'"…it would be to her cost".' He looked at Rindal enquiringly: 'What bright spark thinks that line is a terrorist threat?'

Rindal ignored the question. He said: 'PST doesn't want to take on the case. On the other hand, the parliamentary security takes the view that an MP has been threatened and wants an investigation into what might lie behind it. I agree with PST. The woman who sent this letter is probably out of it. But parliament has raised the issue and wants an answer. Can you check this matter out ASAP?'

Rindal sat down again and concentrated on the computer screen. Gunnarstranda stayed on his feet.

'Close the door on your way out,' Rindal said.

Gunnarstranda didn't budge.

Rindal swivelled round on his chair and looked at him. 'Yes?'

'I thought you'd asked Mr Bergen to do this.'

'His name's Rise,' Rindal replied curtly. 'We like to call each other by name at this station, Gunnarstranda. It's best for everyone. You wouldn't like to be called "Baldy", would you.'

Gunnarstranda sighed. 'Could I have an update?' he asked.

'On what?' Rindal jutted out his chin.

'On what Rise's job is and on why I'm doing all the legwork for another person. Is Rise not happy with doing this?'

Rindal grimaced. 'Rise's a competent officer,' he said, and then added: 'I know he is.' He raised a hand as Gunnarstranda made to say something. 'You don't need to object. I know he's competent because he's worked under me before. You'll discover the same as I did. You'll be working together, you see.'

Gunnarstranda eyed Rindal closely without saying a word.

Rindal shrugged and swivelled the chair back to his desk to concentrate on a pen lying on some papers.

'Yup,' Rindal said to the pen. 'As I told you, the guy's having a hard time. Things happen to people who have it tough. Well, Rise hasn't taken this threatening letter very seriously. That's a matter between Rise and me, and of course I'll take it up with him. But you and he have to work together from now on. Which will apply to the Metro incident if it turns out there's any more to it.' Rindal swivelled back and eyed Gunnarstranda: 'You don't have to look so bloody miserable. You outrank Rise and I expect you to ensure your co-operation proceeds without any problems. But until I've informed Rise about the situation there's still someone who wants an answer to what's behind the letter threatening Vestgård. She regards it as extremely unpleasant. Vestgård talks about this to colleagues in parliament. The people sitting and chatting about this over lunch are the same people who decide your salary and mine, and future overtime packages. So I'm sure you can see the need for something to happen. I expect a report clarifying this matter before twelve o'clock, *capisce*?'

Gunnarstranda was at a loss for words. Rindal realised and beamed at him in triumph, his famous Gene Hackman smile.

Gunnarstranda turned and let himself out. *Capisce*? Was Rindal doing an evening course in Italian, or what? he wondered.

3

Lena waited impatiently until it was two minutes past eight. She locked the office door, then took out her phone and called.

The voice that answered was gentle and warm, but still Lena was unable to relax. She explained the reason for her call, how the lump close to the nipple felt and said it was sensitive when she pressed it. It was difficult to estimate the size. She had never noticed it before, but had to concede she didn't check her breasts regularly.

The gentle voice talked about mammograms and tissue samples, and asked whether there was any discharge from her nipple.

Lena shuddered.

At the same time someone was trying her door. How annoying. Anyone pulling the handle would wonder why she had locked it. Whoever it was knocked.

Lena raised her voice. 'Just a minute!'

She walked towards the door with the phone to her ear. No, not as far as she knew.

The voice continued: If the nipple did have discharge she wanted Lena to take note of the colour and whether there was any blood in it.

Lena turned her back to the door. 'I've read quite a bit about this online,' she said, slightly frustrated. 'But I'd like an appointment as soon as possible.'

'By far the majority of lumps are benign,' the voice said.

'I work for the police,' Lena said, 'and I have a meeting in a second. When do you think…?'

'Monday,' the voice said. 'Twelve-thirty.'

'I'll be there,' Lena said, and rang off. She turned to the door, unlocked and opened up. The person who had been knocking had gone.

Lena walked down the corridor and almost collided with Rindal.

'My office,' he said, and marched off ahead of her.

*

Once inside the closed door, they stood looking at each other.

'Can you give me an update on the Sveinung Adeler case?'

Lena cursed internally. She had the reports on her laptop at home. 'I'm afraid they're on my home computer…'

'Just give me an update,' Rindal said softly.

Lena explained that she was trying to assess what had happened before Adeler fell in the water. There were no CCTV cameras on the pier by the City Hall Quay. No witnesses had come forward. Just one transaction on his bank card that Wednesday: a withdrawal of three thousand kroner. They had found a little over two thousand in his wallet. Nothing unusual about spending eight hundred, particularly in December, just before Christmas. There was every reason to suspect that he had fallen in accidentally.

'Why should this *not* be an accident?'

'The pathology report isn't clear. Formally, we don't know what he died of. Also, his flies weren't open,' Lena said. 'If he was drunk and went to the harbour edge to urinate, his flies would've been open. The belt and the top button of his trousers were untouched as well.'

'Perhaps he didn't have time. He was dressed up and coming back from a Christmas dinner pissed, wasn't he?'

'As I said, we don't know anything about his alcohol level. Accordingly, I think it's too early to shelve this case.' All while cursing her own goodie-goodie syndrome. Good girl, doing her homework. Thorough examination. What was the point of believing that Adeler's death was anything but an accident? Absolutely no point at all. Except that Lena knew Rindal would have preferred to have Emil Yttergjerde doing this job. Several people in the department thought that Lena had benefited from positive discrimination; she was the pussy vote and in some gentlemen's eyes not as good as the other officers, i.e. those police employees with a dick between their legs. And now Lena had a strong instinct that Rindal intended to get even for his defeat over her nomination.

But Rindal just stood there, watching her, silent, waiting.

It struck Lena that she should have made a note of the doctor's appointment before she forgot. She looked at her watch and was about to go when Rindal spoke up.

'Excellent,' he said distantly, and coughed. 'So far, so good. But of all things – of all the possible decisions to take – you chose to go to the home of an elected MP and ask her to account for her movements? Isn't that a bit much?'

Who had Rindal been talking to, Lena wondered, but instantly corrected her line of thought. Who had been talking to Rindal?

'On the contrary,' she said. 'I got a tip-off that Adeler was with this Storting woman the evening before he drowned. My view was that Vestgård might be able to give us useful information about Adeler's actions before his death. That's why I went to Vestgård's private address. Yes, I was aware that she was a VIP and for that reason I decided to approach her discreetly. I intentionally visited her after working hours and drove there in my own car and in plain clothes. I just wanted to eliminate her from the case.' Lena continued in a firmer tone: 'Vestgård, however, blathered on about death threats. That put me in a difficult spot. If we at HQ knew Vestgård had received death threats when I drove there, I should've been told about them, so why wasn't I?'

Rindal was deaf in that ear. He said: 'You should've informed me about the Vestgård tip-off *before* you left and invaded her home.'

'I didn't invade anyone's home. This was pure routine stuff. Surely I don't have to consult a superior officer for clearance before I eliminate a witness from our enquiries?'

'The witness this time was an MP. In this case, that is precisely what you should've done.'

Lena relaxed. Rindal might not have been on the defensive, but he certainly didn't seem quite as worked-up any more. He was thinking now. She backed towards the door.

Rindal coughed.

She stopped.

'Sooner or later this harbour incident is going to be shunted down our list of priorities,' Rindal said.

She nodded.

'The sooner, the better,' he went on. 'We have a lot to do.'

Lena didn't reply.

'Off you go then,' Rindal said brusquely.

Lena let herself out. In the corridor she stopped and thought: *What actually* is *going on in there?*

4

The voice on the intercom belonged to a woman. The door buzzed as soon as Gunnarstranda said he was from the police.

Naturally the woman had to live on the top floor of a block with no lift. She stood waiting in the doorway as he panted his way up the last flight of stairs: a fair-haired woman in her late twenties, dressed in baggy jogging pants and a large, hand-knitted jumper.

The flat was as hot as an oven. A strong smell of fried eggs and morning filled the air. A low, familiar, homely voice sang from the mini stereo. Gunnarstranda hung his winter coat over his arm and spotted the CD over on one speaker: Norah Jones. The young woman's taste in music immediately predisposed him in her favour.

He asked if she had any ID.

'I've got a bank card with a photo on. If you want my passport I'll have to start a search.'

'The bank card's fine.'

She picked up her shoulder bag and rummaged nervously through it.

Gunnarstranda asked: 'What comes to mind when I mention the name Aud Helen Vestgård?'

The woman shrugged. Her fair hair was held up with slides. She continued to hunt for her bank card.

Gunnarstranda took in the room. On the sitting-room table was a jumble of worn textbooks, loose paper and an open exercise book. Beside them was a plate of unfinished bread and eggs. She had been interrupted in the middle of her breakfast. She hadn't had time to throw on anything more than a jumper and jogging trousers. She was a student and worked from home. He felt a sudden wave of solicitude for the young woman. And a hungry rumble in his stomach.

At last, she handed him the card. He studied it. The picture on the card was of her. Judging by the signature in the threatening letter, it had been written by this woman. He passed the card back.

'Do you know who Vestgård is?' he asked.

'I know she's a politician, yes, but I'm not interested in politics.'

He nodded towards the books. 'What are you doing?'

'Studying for an exam.'

He took one of the books. The title was in English and the cover was illustrated with a picture of the human body with only the muscles showing. An anatomy textbook.

'Medicine?'

'Kinesiology – sort of medicine, yes. Alternative though.' She still seemed taken aback and uncomfortable. Three pairs of panties and some red tights were drying on the radiator below the window. She quickly grabbed the clothes and stood with the bundle in her hand, not quite knowing what to do with it. 'Sorry,' she said.

'You don't need to tidy up for me,' he said. 'Kinesiology – so you're learning about energy pathways in the body and that sort of thing?'

She smiled at his attempt to meet her halfway. 'Something like that. But a bit more.'

'My partner's into all that alternative stuff,' he said.

She nodded and switched off the stereo.

'Homeopathy and healing and so on.'

She nodded again.

Gunnarstranda lifted an exercise book from the table. It was her notes. He examined her handwriting – it was clearly different from the writing in the letter. Her notes were extremely tidy. The 'A's and 'R's were formed almost like printed letters – consistent – and quite different from how they were written in the letter. 'Your notes?' he asked.

Another nod.

'I'd like you to look at this.' He dug into his pocket and passed her the copy of the letter.

She tucked her underwear under her arm and held the letter with both hands as she read. She rolled her eyes when she saw the contents.

She gasped: 'Signed using my name?'

'Can you explain that to me?'

She shook her head. 'I've never seen this before.'

He flicked through her notes. Noticing that she finished the letter G with a fish hook that went below the line. In the letter it looked more like a loop.

'Aud Helen Vestgård received this letter at Storting,' he said. 'As the contents might be construed as a threat we have to find out if there's any substance to it. The signature points to you and now you're telling me you never wrote it. The question is whether I should believe you or not. What's your opinion of Aud Helen Vestgård?'

'I don't have one. She doesn't interest me. I don't have the time to read newspapers. Haven't had for several weeks. I don't understand any of this.' She regarded him with her clear blue eyes – wide open.

'Do you think someone might've done this as a prank?' Gunnarstranda asked. 'Someone trying to get you into trouble, to disrupt your studies?'

The young woman considered the question, then shook her head. 'I simply have no idea.'

'A boyfriend you've just finished with or maybe your current boyfriend's ex?'

She shook her head again. 'I'm engaged; we have been for quite a while.'

'Someone who might've been jealous of you?'

Again she shrugged. 'How could they be?'

'You're a student, maybe a clever one. Do you know of anyone who would be capable of such mischief, maybe because they're nursing a grudge against you?'

'Nope.'

'Anyone who's annoyed by your personality?'

She reflected. At length she shook her head. 'No one I can think of.'

'Someone's written a threatening letter in your name. Why yours?'

'I'm sorry. I don't have the slightest idea.'

'What's odd about this letter is that it's signed,' Gunnarstranda said. 'No genuine threatening letter would be signed. They're always anonymous. I think someone's trying to get you into trouble.' Gunnarstranda interlaced his fingers behind his back. 'I hope this won't upset your studies. However, someone has shown with this letter that they wish to cause you some grief. Should it occur to you who this might be, just get in touch.' He passed her his card. 'Shall we leave it like that?'

She nodded.

Gunnarstranda went to the door. He motioned to the table. 'Good luck with your swotting and the exam.'

5

A crow flapped its wings and hopped across the snow. The sight reminded Lena of a hunchback – the bellringer in *Notre Dame de Paris*. She had hardly articulated the thought before another crow appeared. Then wings flapped behind one of the tree trunks. There were lots of them. Grey crows and black crows with strong, black beaks. One of them was staring at her. The eye looked like a button. One of the others had something red in its beak. Fibres, Lena thought, and saw the body the very next second. It was lying at the foot of the tree. The remains of flesh and a ragged furry coat. A squirrel? The crows pecked and tore at a little indeterminate animal, perhaps a kitten.

The traffic lights in Grønlandsleiret changed to green, and when she crossed the street and approached the tree the crows took fright and hopped off. She looked away and spotted a figure in a short leather jacket and motorbike boots walking towards her. Lena hurried towards him.

'Rise!'

'Yes?'

Lena got straight to the point: 'I need to ask you about something. The tip-off about Sveinung Adler dining with Vestgård on Wednesday night – it's important you tell me where you got it.'

Axel Rise held her eyes for a long time without speaking. 'How come?'

'I got a bollocking for questioning her at home.'

Rise let out a whistle. The information seemed to have cheered him up. 'I was given it by a journalist,' he said.

'Who?'

'He works for *Dagens Næringsliv*. Steffen Gjerstad.'

Now it was her turn to be lost for words.

'We talked about you, and he said he'd been trying to ring you, but you didn't pick up.'

I'm a conceited fool, Lena thought as she trudged on, up the hill to Police HQ.

When Steffen Gjerstad rang the previous day she hadn't answered because she had assumed he was after her. But he had only wanted to give her a tip-off in the Adler case. Everything she did went wrong.

Lena took the lift up and walked to her office. There, she took out the business card Gjerstad had given her.

Her fingers trembled as she tapped in the number.

The phone rang once before he picked up. 'Lena here,' she said. And hastened to add, 'Stigersand.'

'Hi, Lena, I've been waiting for you to ring.'

'You tipped off a colleague of mine, Axel Rise, that Sveinung Adler was out for dinner on Wednesday evening,' she said.

'Yes,' Steffen replied, in the same contented tone.

'There are a few inconsistencies,' Lena said. 'Where did you find out the two of them were together?'

'That's precisely what I want to talk to you about,' he said. 'Shall we discuss this over a meal tonight? My treat.'

So he didn't want to answer her question. He wanted to use this opportunity to get to know her better.

'What do you reckon?' he asked in the same slick way.

Is it such a big deal? she thought at first. *Would it really be that bad?* she thought next. But she had to give an answer. Yes or no, she wondered. Heads or tails.

'Let's go for a beer,' Lena said. 'I'll pay for my own.'

After she hung up, the phone rang again at once. It was a secretary from the Pathology Institute.

6

Gunnarstranda was given a yellow hi-vis jacket and a blue helmet with a head torch by Torleif Mork, a man with a white beard and eyes that twinkled under his helmet.

'When the train comes we stand back against the tunnel wall and look up at the driver,' Mork said, then added: 'If we're lucky, he sees us and slows down and then the suction isn't so bad.'

They strolled down the platform for trains leaving from Tøyen to the city centre. Mork rang the ops room. Soon the lights came on in the tunnel.

They climbed stiffly down the metal ladder onto the gravel beside the track. Mork pointed to the yellow electric rail about thirty centimetres above the ground. 'That's got enough power to supply all our trains with speeds of fifty to sixty kph at any one time, so please don't touch it.'

There was silence in the tunnel. They walked on a flagstone path that reverberated with a hollow echo with every step they took. Mork explained that the flagstones also functioned as lids for the cable trunking alongside the tracks. Their monotonous footsteps were short-lived. What came next started as metal scraping against metal, but grew in volume. Gunnarstranda regretted not bringing ear defenders with him. This had to be worse than being in a church tower when the bells rang, he thought, pressing back against the wall. The train that came rushing around the bend seemed incredibly big. Carriage after carriage thundered past. Gunnarstranda saw Mork moving his lips, but could hear nothing over the din of the train and screeching metal.

'What was that you said?' Gunnarstranda yelled when the last carriage was finally gone.

'I said we'll soon be below sea level,' Mork grinned.

They walked on and passed a niche carved into the wall. The opening was closed off with an iron gate secured with a solid padlock. They continued onwards, shining their torches into all the cavities as they passed.

'No one can hide in these niches unless they destroy the padlock first,' Mork said. 'All the padlocks are intact and every niche was inspected with a torch.'

A few seconds later they had to squeeze back against the wall again. They had reached the middle of the bend now. The train leaned towards them and Gunnarstranda imagined he felt metal against the tip of his nose. This train went faster and was longer than the last. He counted six carriages.

They walked on. The tunnel was changing character. This part was concrete and the ceiling was supported by immense pillars.

'There,' said Mork, pointing. 'That's where she was standing until she threw herself forwards. It's a fairly standard method, by the way.'

They looked at the pillars between the railway tracks. Another train raced in, from the opposite direction. It was so fast you couldn't distinguish the faces of the passengers behind the windows. Gunnarstranda shuddered as he thought about the woman being chopped to pieces.

There was silence again.

'Let's go on,' Gunnarstranda said.

The tunnel widened. A staircase ascended to a side tunnel, which rose steeply.

Gunnarstranda found it liberating not to have to stand back as the next train thundered past.

They went up the stairs and on through a narrow, gently rising tunnel until they reached a double door with a panic handle in the middle.

'Same type of door as in the cinema,' Mork said. 'You just have to push to get out. This is an emergency exit of course.'

'And it was this alarm that went off?'

'Yes. The person leaving the tunnel after the incident came out here.' Mork pointed upwards. 'The sensor. The alarm's triggered when the door opens.'

Mork rang the ops room. 'When the alarm goes off, it's just me, Torleif Mork,' he said, and hung up.

They opened the door and walked into Åkerbergveien, directly behind Police HQ.

Gunnarstranda turned and ambled back. One thing he was able to confirm: in this side tunnel leading to the emergency exit there was nowhere to hide.

Where could the two of them have hidden?

They walked back to the railway tracks. Apparently there was a lull in the train traffic. The silence was total.

'Are there any other emergency exits?' Gunnarstranda asked.

Mork raised an arm and pointed. 'There,' he said.

Gunnarstranda turned. It was like an image from a horror film. A broad, dusty, pitch-black staircase leading to an even darker grotto. Gunnarstranda felt his stomach constrict at the sight. It was possible to hide *here*.

Here there was a gap in the electric rail, which made it possible to cross the tracks. Gunnarstranda went over first.

'There should be a light here somewhere,' Mork said as they went up the stairs. 'Hm…'

The staircase led into a long corridor. The beams from their head torches cut diagonal lines across the wall and revealed an old graffiti tag.

They came to a double metal door, which was open.

'This is an old bomb shelter,' Mork said. His voice echoed through the large room. 'You know, the Metro was built in the 1960s and there was a very different climate then than now. Politically, I mean.'

Gunnarstranda shone his head torch across the walls. There were some doors that opened into narrow corridors and rooms. An immense ventilation pipe rose into a shaft to the right. 'What's the ventilation for?'

'It belongs to a multi-storey car park above us, I think.'

'Someone could've hidden in here,' Gunnarstranda stated with conviction.

They went on. The floor was wet.

They pushed open some double doors with the panic handle. Behind them was another long, dark grotto.

'Once these doors have closed you can't get back without special keys,' Mork said. He took a breeze block from beside the grotto wall and placed it in the doorway to stop the door closing. They went on. And came to another double door. Gunnarstranda pushed it open. The sunlight blinded them. They were in Grønlandsleiret.

'Are these emergency exits covered by CCTV?' he asked.

Mork shook his head.

They walked back. The doors locked behind them. The transition from light to darkness was stupefying. Gunnarstranda stood still to allow his eyes to get used to the darkness again.

Mork bent down to put the breeze block back. The beam from his head torch swept across the concrete floor.

'Wait,' Gunnarstranda said. 'Don't move.'

'What is it?'

Gunnarstranda removed his helmet and pointed the beam of light at the floor just inside the door. 'That's blood,' he stated. 'That is, without any doubt, blood.'

The two men stood still, silent. Their torches shone on a pool of blood the size of a drain cover, smeared at the edges. 'Someone has been bleeding here,' Gunnarstranda said at length. 'A lot. Someone has been lying here bleeding and was later dragged backwards into the bomb shelter.'

Mork raised his head and let the torch sweep around them. 'What shall we do now?' His voice was dry, metallic.

A train rumbled past in the tunnel.

'We have to do some looking,' Gunnarstranda said when he could hear himself think.

'Look for what?'

'The hiding place.'

It took them five minutes. In one of the side rooms of the old bomb shelter there was a broad ventilation pipe running from the floor to the ceiling with a ninety-degree angle in it. Where the pipe ended there was an equally broad pipe running horizontally. From wall to wall. A ladder lay in front of this pipe. Why was it there? Gunnarstranda went down on his knees and shone his torch under the pipe. There, the opening between the floor and the pipe was narrow, but not too narrow. Under and behind the pipe there was just enough room to hide someone.

'Here,' Gunnarstranda said, shining his torch on the concrete floor. The line of blood was unmistakeable.

'It shouldn't be possible to hide here.'

'If there's no light in here, it's possible,' Gunnarstranda said.

'Who was lying there bleeding?' Mork asked.

'It was either the man who ran through the emergency exit or it was the woman who threw herself in front of the train.'

'But if someone was bleeding our people must have heard them! If you're in pain you make a noise.'

Gunnarstranda refrained from commenting.

'What do you think?'

'I'd like to keep that to myself for the time being,' Gunnarstranda said quietly. 'In fact, I think I've seen enough now,' he said, and pointed. 'Shall we go?'

Mork nodded.

Gunnarstranda felt something brush against his face. He grabbed it.

'What's that?' Mork asked, almost bumping into him.

'A cable,' Gunnarstranda said, showing him the lead that hung from the neon tube on the ceiling. 'Someone has deliberately shorted the light in here.'

7

'Sveinung Adler was absolutely sober,' Schwenke said, leafing through the thin pile of papers in his hands. He straightened his glasses. 'Zero alcohol level. He could've driven a car.'

The pathologist turned and opened the door to the lab. The smell of formalin and butchery rushed towards them. Schwenke led the way to the corpse.

'When did he die?' Lena asked.

'Hard to say. We don't know when he ate or when he fell into the sea. The food was well digested. *Lutefisk*, pork and potatoes. Incidentally it was the third stomach I've opened up this week that didn't have mushy peas with the *lutefisk*. Do you think we're witnessing a trend?'

No one could tell when Schwenke was joking or serious. Lena looked away and thought to herself: Adeler had been sober. Would a man with no alcohol in his body fall from a harbour into the water?

'What do you think the cause of death was?' Lena asked. She tried not to look at the body on the zinc trolley with the stomach sewn up.

'He drowned. There's no question about that,' Schwenke said. 'But there's another little thing I asked you to come and see, as you're trying to clarify the circumstances.'

'Oh, yes?'

Schwenke bent down and picked up a carrier bag. From this he took a damp white shirt. 'He was wearing this. Look,' Schwenke said, showing her the collar, which was ragged and torn. 'Three tears.'

'When could that have happened?'

'I'll show you something else,' the pathologist said, walking around the table.

Schwenke lifted the dead man's head. Carefully he twisted it to the side. He pointed with his fingertips. There were clear wounds in the neck behind the ear, just under the hairline at the back of the head. 'Cuts,' Schwenke said. 'Grazes and cuts where the shirt is torn as well.'

Lena didn't know what to make of this. She asked him straight out: 'What do you think it means?'

'The first question is whether the wounds were inflicted before or after he fell into the sea. When I first saw the injuries I assumed he must've received them when he fell from the harbour. We don't know how he came to fall, of course – whether he fell forwards or slipped backwards or hit something on the way down. But then I examined the shirt and found the tears. Then I examined the jacket. But it doesn't have any tears. So the question is how he could hit himself on the way down and tear the shirt but not the jacket? He was wearing both items of clothing when he was found. This made me re-read the SOC officer's report.'

'And?' Lena said, still as bewildered as before.

Schwenke grimaced, as though he found it difficult to say what he had to say. 'As the shirt is damaged, but not the jacket, the cuts may have been caused by an object that came between jacket and shirt. At first I thought the tears in the shirt and the injuries sustained were caused by some kind of tool – a boathook or another hook of some kind that someone had attached to his clothes.'

Lena tried to imagine it: Sveinung Adeler splashing in the water and someone hooking him by his shirt collar.

'To fish him out of the water?' she asked.

'Or to force him down,' Schwenke said.

They exchanged glances. Lena didn't follow this line of thought. 'I just can't imagine him falling from a boat,' she said.

'I don't think he fell from a boat, either. I'd like you to see this,'

Schwenke said, and showed her the SOC officer's report. 'I searched for a boathook. But I found this.'

Lena read: '"Two hundred and fifty-four centimetre spruce lath, three-quarters, four".' She looked up. 'What's that?'

'A plank two and a half metres long,' Schwenke said drily. 'Three-quarters of an inch thick and four inches wide. The piece of wood was on City Hall Quay 1. That's the pier closest to the fortress. The SOC officers think that's where he fell. And they noted that the lath was there.'

Lena had to articulate the emerging conclusion. 'So you think someone tried to force the man under the water with the plank and it was responsible for the tears in his shirt and injuries to his neck?'

Schwenke didn't answer. As always when confronted with weighty conclusions, he ruminated.

'I'm going to put in my report that he drowned. However, the tears in his shirt and the injuries to his neck were most probably inflicted after he fell into the water and before his heart stopped beating. That's all. If I were you I'd ask the lab to examine the lath with great care and compare it with the shirt. There may be shirt fibres lodged in the wood, assuming my theory is correct. If this turns out to be the case, you have proof that there was someone on the quay while the man drowned. The temperature of the water would have meant he lost consciousness within a minute. In these circumstances someone was forcing him down so hard that his shirt tore. As to the intention of this person? I wouldn't like to comment, but someone was definitely there. Someone was holding the lath.'

Lena closed her eyes and opened them. She looked straight at the white body.

In a flash she saw herself lying on a similar zinc trolley. A body, a carcass this cynical pathologist cut up with relish. A kidney for the highest bidder – or what about the liver? Used but in good condition, thirty-three years old, well treated by the owner, not much abuse beyond quarter-bottles of champagne and a couple of paracetamols for high temperatures; some discount available in view of the strong radiation…

'Someone was holding the lath,' Schwenke repeated.

'I hear what you say,' Lena said. 'It's all up to the lab now, then.'

8

There was a pixie on the bar. Woollen tunic, corduroy breeches, red stockings and clogs on his feet. It had no beard – so it wasn't a model of the man who lived at the North Pole, but a Norwegian farm pixie. He had his left arm raised and was opening his mouth, which was hinged like an Ivo Caprino puppet. He had his head twisted to the left and was saying '*ho ho ho*' as his hinged mouth opened and shut. The staring eyes gave the pixie a wild and, to Lena's mind, slightly frightening expression.

The barwoman pushed a glass of beer towards her. The pixie lowered his arm and almost knocked over the glass. Lena pushed the glass back and out of danger. But the barwoman slid the glass in her direction again.

'It isn't mine. I didn't order one.'

'It's on me,' shouted a voice from the right.

She turned round slowly. Steffen Gjerstad had taken off his winter coat and was posing in a tight suit jacket and neat faded jeans – Hugo Boss, she thought, or Dolce & Gabbana. Slim, long-legged and self-confident, he was propping up the bar. He had folded his hands and was watching her. Was she nervous? Maybe a bit. But also wary. They exchanged glances. Lena felt something in her stomach and looked down.

Steffen was an attractive man. Her body had acknowledged it. And Lena was terrified that her reaction would show. So she didn't dare look up straightaway, but took the glass, lifted it in a toast, her eyes still cast down, and drank.

It was a dark ale, which tasted slightly bitter, though not bad at all. Anyway, as she was swallowing it, she felt that this was something she should keep away from.

No, she told herself. *Don't think illness. Not now.*

Steffen Gjerstad said something, but his words were drowned out by the music.

She raised her head. 'What did you say?' she shouted and went closer.

'Why did it take you so long to ring?'

She shrugged her shoulders a second time.

He didn't change his stance, leaning sideways against the bar. It was her turn to say something.

'Why should I ring you? You aren't even a crime correspondent.'

He laughed out loud. 'You googled me!'

She smiled back instinctively. Relaxed, she leaned back against the bar and scanned the room. Though her concentration wandered. She needed serenity, harmony. She would have preferred to go home, run the bath and calm herself down.

A table by the window became free. He reacted before she did, nodded towards the table and said: 'Are you up for it?'

They sat down facing each other. 'The tip-off you gave Axel Rise doesn't hold water,' she said, 'but I was stupid enough to follow it up.'

'How so?'

'Aud Helen Vestgård. I asked her if she'd been with Adeler on Wednesday evening. But she didn't understand what I was talking about.'

'She's lying.'

The response came with surprising speed and confidence.

'Before you tell me why I should believe you and not her, I should inform you that I've already been reprimanded for inappropriate behaviour.'

He whistled.

'Admit it,' she said. 'You don't have a clue what Adeler was doing on Wednesday evening, least of all who he was with.'

Steffen, who had been sitting forwards with his chin resting in his hands, straightened up and regarded her pensively in silence.

'Why did you tip off Axel Rise and not me?'

'You didn't want to talk to me, did you,' Steffen said. 'I rang you. You didn't pick up and you didn't ring back either.'

Lena looked down again.

'I know Rise from when he used to work in Bergen,' he continued. 'We met yesterday. He's new in the job, isn't he. I asked him how he was doing and your name came up. I said I'd bumped into you at the harbour and I'd tried to ring you because I'd been tipped off about what Adeler was doing on the Wednesday evening.'

She felt a fool. 'I didn't mean to grill you,' she said. 'I was just a bit put out when Vestgård denied it.'

'Naturally,' Steffen said, warming to the topic. 'It doesn't make sense for Vestgård to deny knowing Adeler. The two of them know each other very well. She was almost a mentor to him. That's widely known. Adeler was a fully paid-up member of the party; she was an MP.'

Lena raised both hands in defence: 'Fine. Your source says Adeler was out with Vestgård on the Wednesday. Where?'

Steffen grinned. 'In Grefsen. The Flamingo Bar & Restaurant – an anonymous hangout. The local eatery up there. Why did they choose to meet and dine there of all places? My guess is,' he waggled his forefinger, 'so as not to attract attention.'

'Are you dropping a hint?' Lena asked sceptically. 'Were they having an affair?'

Steffen twirled the glass between his fingers. It was empty. He got up. 'Another?'

'Red wine,' she said quickly.

Just one glass, she told herself. She could allow herself to sit there for as long as Steffen was coughing up relevant information. She observed him ordering. He clearly knew the barmaid – an attractive, Asiatic-looking woman with a fringe. She laughed at something he said as she was filling his glass. He knew a couple of the regulars too, exchanged a few words with a man in a brown cord jacket on the way back to the table.

'House wine,' Steffen said, placing the glass in front of her.

They sat looking at each other. She liked the way he looked at her. She raised her glass and sipped the wine. 'Level with me,' she said.

'Hm?'

'What's your agenda in all this?'

'I've been waiting for you to ask,' he said, shifting on his seat. 'The newpaper's preparing a big series of articles on raw materials – their production and the stock exchange.'

He interlaced his fingers and mused – as though he were considering how to choose his words, then he said: 'Interested?'

'As long as it's relevant.'

'Let's see then.'

'I've vowed I'll stop after this glass.'

The response derailed him for a moment. He smiled absent-mindedly and then renewed his concentration. 'Well, the fact is that one of the world's most important raw materials today is phosphate. It's needed to make things grow. Phosphate is an important ingredient in fertilisers. The world needs phosphate for food and it's mined from phosphorus ore. But the problem is there's almost no ore left in the world. Quite frightening actually. When the world's phosphate resources have been used up there won't be enough food to feed the Earth's current population. We're talking a potential ecological crisis here, the like of which the world has never seen. Never ever. Already we can see the first signs. Obviously the less phosphate there is, the higher the prices of fertiliser. Today the prices have risen so high that many farmers in poor countries can barely afford to buy it. And these price increases have just started.' Steffen sipped from his glass.

Lena asked: 'But is this relevant to…?'

'I'm coming to that,' Steffen grinned. 'I'm trying to be pedagogical. Don't be so impatient, Lena. To sum up, phosphates are one of the most valuable raw materials in the world. There's a lot of money to be earned here. Do you understand? Who invests in this market?

Many people. And among them the *Norwegian Oil Fund* – the *Government Pension Fund Global*. Take it easy, I'm getting to Adeler. The Norwegian Oil Fund behaves like any other capitalist. They buy and sell shares and bonds; they short sell shares and gamble with derivatives. The Oil Fund's like a standard investor except in one area: the Oil Fund's a capitalist who is *INCREDIBLY* rich! I doubt if there's been such a rich investor in this or the previous century. He's so fat and well nourished he can hardly walk. He's like Theodor Kittelsen's troll in Karl Johans gate. But he doesn't scatter moss and trees when he walks. He scatters money and gold. He's so fat and enormous he barely dares sit down for fear he'll never be able to get up again. But ask any Norwegian in the street if they know what the Oil Fund does – no one has a clue. This is where Norway's free press comes in. We – that is, I – educate the public with active, critical investigative journalism. What we know is that it plays a *crucial* role in international business where the Oil Fund invests its money – simply because the fund is so big! Other investors listen to what the Oil Fund does. If they move their money, other investors follow suit. If the Oil Fund makes an investment, others fight to follow suit. In other words, the Norwegian Oil Fund has considerable *power* because it's the world's biggest and most important bellwether in the finance market. Its size means that its investments affect share prices. They also give companies credibility, of course. Whatever the Oil Fund does is of significance. As soon as it invests in a company, this company becomes an interesting investment for other investors.'

'Very interesting,' Lena said, trying hard not to sound bored. 'But Sveinung Adler was a low-ranking official with only one interest in life: to train hard enough to beat his pals in the Birkebeiner.'

Steffen blinked again and flashed his charm-attack smile. 'I'm afraid you're somewhat mistaken. It's exactly at this point that Adeler becomes interesting. Or his job does. Adeler worked with the Oil Fund. He did research for the Oil Fund's Ethics Council, which reports back on businesses they invest in. Adeler worked in the secretariat. He was the person who researched facts about companies. After he had investigated a company he submitted a report, which he delivered to the Ethics Council, who in turn used it as a document in a thorough discussion. Afterwards the Ethics Council would draw its conclusions and pass on its recommendations to Norges Bank – who control the Oil Fund.'

Steffen straightened his back as if weighing up the pros and cons. At length he seemed to have decided. 'OK,' he whispered in a low, intense voice. 'Can I rely on you for the utmost discretion?'

She nodded and leaned forwards as well. Barely twenty centimetres separated their heads.

'The world's last great deposits of phosphate rock are found in Western Sahara. Several producers operate there. One of the companies is MacFarrell. The Oil Fund has invested in MacFarrell and they make a lot of money. Do you know the history of Western Sahara? No? Let me give you the edited highlights: The country was a Spanish colony until the 1970s. Since then, the neighbouring country, Morocco, has laid claim to a great swathe of it. So we're talking *occupation*. Well, the dilemma for the Oil Fund is that this conflicts with the Norwegian policy towards investing in companies that do business in occupied territories. That is why the Ethics Council is investigating companies that have dealings in Western Sahara. Some companies are regarded as kosher, others aren't. We at the newspaper ask why. What are the interests that dictate policy here? To find the answers we've started to dig.'

Lena nodded and smiled weakly into her glass. She was having a nice time and could feel her head buzzing.

'The Oil Fund's Ethics Council has a secretariat,' Steffen continued. 'Which is where Sveinung Adeler works. He did research into the Oil Fund's investments. In the early hours of yesterday he fell into the harbour after a Christmas dinner.'

Lena anticipated what was about to come. She closed both eyes and said: 'Don't mention the name Aud Helen Vestgård.'

'I asked for discretion and you promised to keep stumm.'

The moment was still magical. She was still sitting with her eyes closed. 'OK.'

'The newspaper – that is, me – I get a tip-off that Adeler was having Christmas dinner with a party member. That doesn't have to mean anything; not even the fact that the party member is an attractive, married woman has to mean anything. Her being a prominent member of the parliamentary finance committee doesn't have to mean anything, either.

'But then the news of Adeler's death was on the net for several hours. The man's identity is made public. Sveinung Adeler drowned, dressed in a suit and smart shoes, at twenty-five degrees below zero. The police need information to determine what he was doing before he drowned. Has anyone come forward?'

Lena shook her head.

'Right. Who was Adeler having dinner with? Who hasn't come forward?' Steffen grasped Lena's hand.

She looked down at the two hands, raised her head and looked him in the eye. She had a tingle in her stomach. Despite the tingling, Lena didn't want things to go too fast.

Slowly she extricated her hand and said: 'If what you say is true, why does Vestgård deny that she knew Adeler – to me, to the police?'

Steffen leaned forwards, excited. 'Exactly! There's something fishy about the whole case. Why does Vestgård whisper in your superior officer's ear and you're reprimanded for interviewing her?'

Lena straightened up. 'Neither of us has a clue whether she did that. If she had done, it'd be the most natural explanation in existence. Firstly, Vestgård was put on the spot when I rolled up at her house. She thought I was there because of the death threat. Instead she was confronted with a suspicious death. Bad press could ruin Vestgård's career.'

Steffen grasped her hand again. 'Suspicious death?'

For a few seconds she looked down at the hand that was covering hers, before, once again, slowly extricating it. And once again they exchanged looks.

The signals between them now were like salvoes. No point pretending. Her mouth was dry and it wasn't the odd butterfly fluttering around in her stomach, it was a swarm, and an unknown species.

'My mistake. I meant the drowning incident.'

She was aware they were both looking at their hands.

Then they glanced up – at the same moment.

At once she lowered her gaze.

Steffen said: 'You can believe what you like, but I'm convinced there's something fishy about the rendezvous in the restaurant. The journalist in me has caught the scent. I know there's a big case waiting for me out there.'

Lena smiled. Steffen Gjerstad had a fascinating personality. The impression of a leggy model had first given way to a sharp analyst, then the analyst had given way to a little boy with Lego bricks, ready to shout '*broom, broom*', as soon as he had a toy car in his hands.

Her glass was empty. And her mind was in a whirl. On the one hand she needed time for herself; on the other she was tempted a little now to drink and laugh without a care in the world. The problem was that pub and flirting sessions like this generally had one outcome. She didn't want the outcome to be a mistake. Not now. Not today. She chose therefore to listen to the solemn voice in her head. She rose to her feet.

He looked up at her. 'Are you going?'

She nodded.

'Me too.'

The door wouldn't close properly after them. They almost collided when they both went to shut it. They were standing close to each other, and it was cold outside. Neither of them said anything, Lena turned and set off.

They walked side by side, silent. They were crossing Akersgata when she saw the bus coming. 'That's my bus,' she shouted. 'It's half an hour to the next one. Bye!'

She broke into a run.

The bus stopped at the shelter fifty metres ahead. The door opened. As she got on she turned.

Steffen was behind her. He had also got on. He was gasping for breath. They exchanged looks and both had to laugh.

They sat down beside each other on a double seat by the rear door. Neither said a word.

In the end she couldn't bear the silence any more and asked: 'Where do you live?'

'Hegdehaugsveien 31.'

'Then you're on the wrong bus. This one goes to Helsfyr.'

He didn't answer.

Lena stared into the black night and saw only the reflection of Steffen's face. They exchanged glances again.

She took a deep breath and turned her face to him. Neither of them spoke. When he swallowed, she rested her head on his shoulder and closed her eyes.

9

The drone of a floor-washing machine approached in the corridor. It was the signal that told him it was beginning to get late. Gunnarstranda got up. He looked down at what he had written. A variety of scenarios that boiled down to the same questions: Who had been bleeding in front of the door with the panic handle? Nina Stenshagen or her pursuer? Why?

Of the various scenarios, Gunnarstranda had most faith in the one based on the following roles: She ran first. He sprinted after her. Presumably she was fleeing from him. She knew about the bomb shelter with the emergency exits in the tunnel. She was counting on giving her pursuer the slip down there. Either because the pursuer didn't dare run after her in the tunnel or, if he did, because she could hide and escape from him through an emergency exit. However, he did go after her and caught her before she managed to get out. There was a struggle. He injured her. Perhaps he killed her. At any rate he injured her enough to cause haemorrhaging. When the light was switched on and the traffic stopped he tore down a cable and shorted the light circuit in the bomb shelter. The crime scene was in total darkness. He hid with her. When the electricity came back on, he pushed her in front of the first passing train.

Well, this theory *might* hold water. But if this was how it happened the question was why did he push her in front of the train?

Had he only hurt her and therefore wanted the train to finish the job off? Or was she already dead? Was he trying to disguise a murder as suicide? But once more: why? It was so much bother. If he killed her by the emergency exit, he could have left her there and made his escape through the door. There must have been something that made him decide to throw her in front of the train instead.

What would have happened if he had left her lying by the door? She would have been found by the search teams. If she had lived she could have told them who had injured her. If she had died the alarm would have been raised instantly and the murderer didn't know if the CCTV cameras had caught him. That might *possibly* be one explanation.

Gunnarstranda rubbed his eyes. The telephone on the desk rang. He stood for a few seconds, looking at it. Heaved a big sigh. Went back and lifted the receiver.

'Gunnarstranda?' The voice belonged to Iqbal in the undercover team.

'Yes.'

'Stig Eriksen. You asked where he was. Right now he's sitting on the footbridge between Oslo Station and Hotel Plaza, begging.'

Gunnarstranda thanked him and put down the receiver. He shrugged on his jacket.

The drone of the floor-washer was getting louder. But it wasn't a cleaner who appeared in the doorway. It was Axel Rise.

'Heard you looked at the CCTV cameras and went through the tunnel,' Rise said.

Gunnarstranda nodded.

'I'd like a copy of your report,' Rise said.

Gunnarstranda angled his head.

'Rindal's told me you're in charge of this investigation and we should liaise, but to do the latter I'll have to see what you've done so far.'

'It hasn't struck you that I might need to do the same?'

Rise passed him a pile of papers. 'Here.'

Gunnarstranda didn't move a muscle. 'I understand you spoke to the Metro's security service after the incident?' he said.

Rise nodded. 'They said they'd examined the tunnel, but they couldn't have done. She was there all the time, inside.'

'Did you walk along the track?' Gunnarstranda asked.

'Why would I?'

'Well, for example, to find out how the security staff could go in and not see there was actually someone there.'

Rise blinked. 'As I said, I'd like to read your report and see the CCTV pictures,' he intoned.

Gunnarstranda walked past Rise into the corridor. From there, he turned and pointed to his desk. It was covered with loose sheets and documents. 'It's all there. Since you're here anyway, you can tidy up. I'd appreciate that.' He took three steps. Then he spun on his heel with a raised finger and said, 'One thing…'

'Yes?'

'You might find the report, and the CD. But what you're looking for, you will never find.'

'How can you know that?'

'I'm talking from experience.' Gunnarstranda smiled. 'Tomorrow morning we can synchronise our watches, as they say in crime fiction. I think this case has much more to it than meets the eye – more than a suicide.' He swivelled round and continued down the corridor.

'Tomorrow's Saturday,' Rise shouted after him.

Gunnarstranda stopped and turned.

'Rindal said he'd told you. I go home to Bergen every weekend.' Rise raised his hand and looked at his watch. 'The plane goes in three hours.'

Gunnarstranda nodded amiably. 'Have a good weekend.'

✷

Gunnarstranda had a suspicion this liaison was not going to be of the intense variety. But it didn't matter much. He didn't really get on with Rise. Besides, he liked working on his own.

His car was parked in one of the police bays in Åkerbergveien. The air was damp. *It's going to turn to snow*, he thought, and got in. The engine was cold and he shivered, despite the hat on his head and the gloves on his hands, while he drove the few metres to Tøyenbekken. He wondered about driving into the multi-storey car park, but decided against it. Instead he parked at the Statoil petrol station. He got out, crossed the street at the lights and hurried towards the taxi rank outside the bus terminal. When he was level with the taxis in the queue he went inside. Here, in the terminal building, he headed towards the stream of passengers hurrying in the direction of the departures hall.

He left the immense hall, took the travellator up to Galleriet then continued to the exit that led to the hotel and the footbridge over to Oslo Station.

The icy wind hit him as soon as he came out. The first snowflakes were dancing in the air. He didn't envy anyone sitting still and begging in this weather. He passed Café Fiasco. Some frozen smokers sat huddled with rugs over their shoulders as they sucked in nicotine under the patio heaters. He immediately spotted the Buddha-like figure on the footbridge. A steady flow of people hurried back and forth.

Stig Eriksen was sitting on a flattened cardboard box. He had his hands buried in his jacket pockets. His long hair was held in place by a woollen hat. In front of him lay a piece of paper that was prevented from blowing away by a cup with a few coins in it. On the paper he had written that he was freezing cold and needed a warm meal. Under the bridge cars raced in both directions across four lanes.

Gunnarstranda stopped. 'Stig?'

Slowly the beggar raised his head. His face was pitted and his eyes were listless.

'I'd like a word with you. I'm investigating Nina's death – Nina Stenshagen.'

'Piss off,' Stig said. 'You're blocking the sun and I'm losing customers.'

Gunnarstranda grinned. He took a bank note from his pocket, two hundred kroner. He put the note in the cup.

Stig scowled at the note and snatched it in a flash.

'My name's Gunnarstranda and I only want to talk to you, nothing else. We know Nina took the Metro to Tøyen at about half past six yesterday morning. After it continued on its way she jumped down onto the track and ran into the tunnel. Had she done that kind of thing before?'

Gunnarstranda noticed that the garment under Stig's coat was a hoodie. The man who jumped down onto the track half a minute after Nina had worn a hoodie. In fact, it could have been Stig who ran into the tunnel. But Stig wasn't saying anything.

'Where were you yesterday morning?' Gunnarstranda asked.

Stig smiled. It was a toothless grin.

He did something behind his back. A moment later he was holding two crutches and hauling himself up.

It was an impressive manoeuvre. Stig Eriksen had, it turned out, only one leg. His left leg had been amputated; his trouser leg was knotted under the knee. Now he was resting on his crutches and eyeing Gunnarstranda, who realised this man could not be the perpetrator he was after.

Stig bent down and grabbed the cardboard seat and paper. He rolled them up and put them in his back pocket. 'You won't want to know where I hang out,' Stig said. 'But it's a long time since I've seen Nina. We used to be together, but that was several years ago.'

Beneath them the traffic stopped for a few brief seconds as a blue tram glided slowly east.

'And you're wondering what Nina was doing on the Metro?' Stig said in a croaky voice. 'Do you know what *I'm* wondering? I'm wondering why Nina's become so bloody popular now that she's dead.' With which he turned his back on Gunnarstranda and hobbled away.

'Stig,' Gunnarstranda shouted after him.

Stig stopped, rested on the crutches and glowered at him.

'I think Nina was murdered,' Gunnarstranda said.

Stig fixed him with a stare – a long one. 'You think so?' he said at length.

'We know someone followed her into the tunnel. I believe this man inflicted terrible injuries on her and afterwards pushed her in front of a moving train. I want that person punished.'

Stig watched him thoughtfully without speaking.

Gunnarstranda was at a loss as to how to interpret his looks, but felt his attitude was thawing.

'You can help me by getting the perpetrator punished,' he said, then went over and put his police card in Stig's top pocket. 'My number,' Gunnarstranda said. 'Ring me if you change your mind.'

Stig turned his back on him again and hobbled off.

10

It wasn't how she had planned the evening.

Lena was lying on her side and holding her head in one hand. Steffen was lying on his stomach. He seemed to be asleep. She stroked his mane of hair, long and thick. She continued the movement down his back, over his buttocks and down his thigh. He didn't stir; he was asleep. She lifted his hand, which was completely limp. The notes and one-word reminders on the back of his hand were a hotchpotch of blue letters and numbers. She laced her fingers through his and thought: *It wasn't seventh heaven, nor sixth or even fifth. Let's say it was fourth. I've never been in fourth heaven when I've been with a man for the first time. What about next time when we know each other better?*

She lowered his hand. Took the remote from the floor and switched on the stereo. Sade's velvet voice filled the air. 'By Your Side'.

This moment can go on and on, Lena reflected, and glanced across at Steffen, who was stirring now.

'Hi,' he smiled drowsily.

'I thought you were asleep,' she whispered and snuggled up to him. They lay entangled and silent for a long time as Sade's music caressed them.

When she opened her eyes he was on his side and looking at her. 'What's up?'

His eyes twinkled. 'How old are you?'

'I'm over thirty, if that's what you're asking.'

It was his turn to support his head on his hands. A tall, slim man's body on the bed. She let her eyes bask in the sight and she liked it.

'I'm closer to thirty than forty,' she said. 'And you?'

'A bit closer to forty than forty-five.'

She closed her eyes and felt his lips brush hers.

'When I fall for a woman it's like a tree hitting the ground,' he whispered. 'Branches crack, soil and gravel fly and, after the crash, there's a long, long silence.'

She opened her eyes. 'A big tree, in other words?'

He gazed at her without speaking. She felt the atmosphere change and wished she had bitten her tongue. She gulped. Was he annoyed?

She cleared her throat. 'Sorry.'

He raised his eyes and ran his fingers over the pile of books on her bedside table. 'Which of these are you reading?'

'All of them,' she said, relieved to talk about something else.

'All of them at once?'

'I read one at a time. But generally I start a new book before I've finished the last. I've always done that.'

'But do you get anything out of a book, reading like that?' he asked with a wry smile on his lips, as though he didn't believe her.

'It's my way of reading,' she said, and sat up. She put on the wrist-watch she had taken off a few hours before. Got up from bed.

'When a woman puts her watch on her wrist, the bedsheet will go chilly,' he said. 'Japanese haiku,' he added with a teasing smile.

＊

In the bathroom she closed her eyes and could feel her body was heavy and sluggish, but she was fine. She was just a little stiff. She opened her eyes and saw herself in the mirror. In the end she stared at her left breast.

No.

She turned on the water for a shower and let it run as she waited. When the jet was warm enough she stepped into the cabinet and enjoyed the hot massage of her shoulders, back and stomach. She leaned back and let the hot water wash over her face for ages. Then she shampooed her hair. Soaped her body.

In the distance she heard a phone ring.

Involuntarily she opened the shower door a fraction.

It had to be Steffen's phone. She could hear him talking. Heard him pacing up and down the sitting room. She hoped he was still naked, then the two nosy neighbours opposite would have something to talk about.

She finished the shower, found some clean underwear in the cupboard by the door.

The sitting room had gone quiet.

Then she heard him fiddling with his shoes in the hall.

She poked her head out.

Steffen was in the hall, fully dressed.

'Did your wife ring?' she asked, surprised.

Steffen didn't find the joke funny. His face was very serious. 'Got a call. It was a source. I have to be off. That's my job, be prepared. Let's keep in touch.'

Before Lena could react, his lips brushed hers. A second later he was gone.

11

The snow had become heavier. Street lamps and windows shone – yellow and inviting, like on Christmas cards. A taxi with poor tyres and spinning wheels dragged itself slowly and crookedly up the hill in Åkebergveien. Gunnarstranda kept his distance in case the taxi should come to a halt and start sliding back down. The lights changed to red and Gunnarstranda prepared to wait. He couldn't bear the thought of having to get out and push the car in front. Snowflakes, downy and light, fell onto the windscreen, where they lay without melting. He put out a hand for a CD and pushed it into the player. Coltrane's sax in the speakers, accompanied on the piano by – who was it? Bill Evans? Maybe. No. Too slow and blue. It had to be the quartet with McCoy Tyner on the ivories.

The lights went green, and strangely enough the taxi with the poor winter tyres managed to cross at the first attempt. It went towards Galgeberg and was gone. Gunnarstrand bore left to Kjølberggata.

The phone rang.

He put it to his ear.

'Stig here. Stig Eriksen.'

Gunnarstranda pulled into the nearest bus lay-by and stopped. He turned down the volume of the CD player.

'We've just been talking.'

'Yes.'

'I've remembered something.'

'Fire away, Stig.'

'Not on the phone.'

'You do want to talk to me then. What about?' Gunnarstranda could hear that his tone was unnecessarily dismissive, but it was late, he was looking forward to getting home, lighting the fire, putting his feet up and collapsing with Miles Davis in the speakers and a glass of whisky or Calvados in his mitt.

Stig coughed hesitantly. 'I was lying.'

'Oh, yes?' Gunnarstranda said.

'It's right that Nina was killed. I know what happened, why she was killed, that's why I have to talk to you.'

'Oh, yes?' Gunnarstranda repeated, turned off the CD player, and said: 'I gave you two hundred spondoolies and you slung your hook by way of thanks. Now I have to go looking for you in this shit weather. Don't waste any more of my time, Stig. You have to give me something right now, on the phone, something that'll make me think it'd be worth my while looking for you.'

He looked in his mirror. A bus was coming. He drove forwards a few metres to give it some room.

Stig still wasn't talking.

'What's it going to be?'

'I'll give you something,' Stig whispered. 'Nina saw what happened to the fella who was fished out of the water by the City Hall Quay yesterday. Nina told me how he was killed. Nina watched as they threw the man in.'

They, Gunnarstranda thought, but said nothing. Singular or plural, the situation had been turned on its head. Now it was important to find Stig Eriksen before he did another disappearing act.

'That was why Nina was killed afterwards!' Stig said.

'Where are you?' Gunnarstranda asked.

Stig chuckled. 'Thought that'd put a rocket up you,' he laughed.

'Are you stringing me along?'

'No,' Stig said quickly.

'Who threw the guy off the quay?'

The bus indicated, the driver hooted angrily as he drove past.

'Not on the phone,' Stig said.

Gunnarstranda glanced at his watch and deferred Miles and the drink for two hours. He said: 'Where will I find you?'

12

The whole of the brick wall behind the Statoil petrol station was now obscured by cars sneaking in to park for free. Gunnarstranda told himself this would be a lightning visit and parked behind a car with snow on the roof. To the east, new glass buildings towered over half-finished constructions. There was a lot going on in Bjørvika.

Gunnarstranda grabbed a torch from the glove compartment. Got out.

He dug his chin deep into his scarf and headed for the building site.

He stopped by a temporary wire fence. Several signs warned that access was forbidden. He was going the right way. The snow lashed his face. He pulled his coat tighter around him and walked into the wind. Continued alongside the fence until he found the hole in the wire netting.

A trail in the snow led to the unfinished building. The ends of the wire pointed in all directions. He wriggled through the hole and stared into the darkness. Straight ahead was the base of a huge crane. The yellow machine rose towards the sky and disappeared in the blackness and the driving snow. Beside the crane he could make out the outline of a compressor.

The unfinished building gaped at him with its dark, rectangular orifices. He followed the trail in the snow to the nearest opening.

No Stig.

Gunnarstranda took a deep breath and regretted allowing himself to be duped.

It was as black as night. Now he was standing in an enclosed area that smelt of cellar and refuse. At any rate, he was sheltered from the wind. He brushed the snow from his coat, switched on his torch and realised he was in some kind of stairwell. A bare concrete staircase led up to the higher floors.

There was a crunch of cement particles under his shoes as he began to walk. He shone the torch over the walls. The yellow beam swept across sprayed artwork. There was a black plastic bag on the landing. It was full of bits of cable and debris.

He heard footsteps.

'Stig?' he called.

No answer.

Someone was up there. No doubt about that.

He pointed the torch upwards. It went out.

Leaving him in the pitch black.

Gunnarstranda shook the torch. It wouldn't come back on. He banged it against the wall. There was a flash of light and then it went dark again.

He needed light. He turned the screw cap at the end of the torch, slid out the batteries and put them back in. Tightened the cap.

Then he heard the footsteps again. Closer now. Very close.

'Hello?'

He held his breath and listened. Now there was only the sound of the town outside.

No footsteps.

Was this Stig's latest trick? If so, what bright idea had he come up with this time?

Gunnarstranda tried the torch again. It worked.

Lit up his surroundings. He couldn't see anyone. But he had heard footsteps. Where?

He walked slowly up the staircase with the torch in front of him.

Second floor. Here some light from the town came in through an opening in the concrete wall. But he couldn't see anyone. Had he really heard footsteps? Or had he been imagining it?

He stood in front of a forest of steel pipes. Deep inside, behind the beams, a little flame flickered. It had to be from a candle.

He shouted: 'Stig!'

The building was as quiet and still as before.

He walked slowly towards the light. Groping his way forwards. The ends of reinforcement bars poked out from the concrete. The air was dead and stale, the smell a mixture of damp concrete, urine and vomit.

He made it to an open door in the wall.

Inside, the meagre candlelight revealed a den that must have belonged to a homeless person.

Frightened that the torch would go out with any sudden movement, he held it absolutely still.

The candle was in an empty wine bottle and well burned down. On the floor there was a creased sleeping bag, the remains of a pizza and the packaging of what might have been hamburgers or kebabs.

No Stig.

He shone his torch slowly over the abject inventory. Smashed glass, a half-full bottle of Coke…

He cleared his throat and shouted again: 'Stig!'

No answer.

He switched off the torch. Took out his mobile. Called Stig's number.

A phone rang. The ringtone was a metallic version of 'Jingle Bells'. Gunnarstranda followed the sound.

With the phone in one hand and the torch in the other, he followed the tune. Passed through a corridor of bare concrete.

The sound suddenly died.

Gunnarstranda stopped and listened.

All he could hear was the rumble from the town in the distance. His mouth was dry. He pointed the yellow beam behind him. No one.

He shone his torch in front of him. He was close to the end wall. Noise from the town carried through a hole in the wall, the opening for a window.

The torch beam formed a yellow circle. It wandered along the wall, down to the floor, passed something. Stopped and slowly went back.

An oblong bundle lay under the gaping hole in the wall.

Gunnarstranda feared the worst and proceeded with care.

The bundle was a body.

The body had only one leg and lay in a contorted position. His foot pointed to the sky while he lay face down on the concrete. Gunnarstranda crouched down.

The back of Stig's head was a mass of coagulated blood.

He turned the dead man onto his back. The hole in his forehead was as round as a one-krone coin.

Gunnarstranda switched off the torch and crouched without moving. He held his breath and listened, but could hear nothing except the sound of traffic drifting through the window.

The footsteps he had heard were the footsteps of an armed murderer. And all he had to defend himself with was a semi-defective torch.

But he couldn't stay here.

With a dry mouth and a pounding heart he went through Stig's pockets. No phone. He had to find it. Took out his own and called Stig's number.

'Jingle Bells'.

Gunnarstranda stood up. Orientated himself. Took two steps. Then the sound died.

Gunnarstranda crouched down.

He sat still, but nothing happened. Only the sound of footsteps resonated now, as clearly as church bells on a Sunday morning.

With infinite lentitude, his eyes became accustomed to the dark. He made out the shape of an opening in the wall.

He concentrated and saw a shadow moving towards the opening.

Gunnarstranda got up. The shadow slipped through. Gunnarstranda went after it, through the door opening. The wind blew harder here. He came to a sudden stop.

The wind came from below. He shook his torch and tried to switch it on. It lit up.

He was standing on the edge of a sheer drop. A square hole in the floor.

He gasped as his hands groped for something to hold on to. They found nothing, but he regained his balance.

A vibration made him step back two paces without his knowing why. A crash made him start. A concrete block had landed where he had just been standing. It smashed into pieces and sprayed his face with bits of cement and gravel.

The shock made him drop his torch. He squatted down and scrabbled around for it, but the torch rolled towards the edge and vanished down the shaft.

He went down on all fours and blinked the cement dust from his eyes.

Then he stood up and fumbled for something to grab on to. His hand found the wall.

Slowly he groped his way through the darkness to the staircase. The man was somewhere above him, he would have to use the staircase to get out.

He heard footsteps again.

At that moment he received a violent push and fell. He broke his fall with his hands and grazed both palms. Someone jumped over him and ran down the stairs.

Gunnarstranda struggled to his feet and stumbled after him. But then he fell again. Hitting himself on the head. Once more he struggled up.

At last he made it to the bottom.

No one around. Only snow, a crane, a compressor and a gaping hole in the fence.

Gunnarstranda leaned against the bare wall, breathless. Once again he took out his phone, rang Stig's number and put the phone to his ear. This time there was an answer. He could hear the traffic and the sound of footsteps.

'Who are you?' Gunnarstranda asked and listened.

He heard the footsteps come to a halt. A long silence followed. Gunnarstranda was about to repeat the question when the sound ended.

He lowered his phone. End of conversation.

1

A bright ray from the low winter sun struck the glass of water, was refracted and hit him in the eyes. The alarm clock never stopped beeping. Gunnarstranda raised an arm, groped and managed to turn it off. It was a few minutes past nine in the morning. He had slept for three hours. Swinging his legs to the floor, he took the glass and downed the water in one.

Tove had gone to work. An empty plate lay on the worktop beside a packet of muesli.

The room smelt of burnt coffee. Tove had left the machine on. There was still half a litre in the jug. He poured himself a cup. It was strong. He diluted it with milk from the fridge. Looking at the contents of the fridge he couldn't decide if he was hungry or not. All he knew was he was tired.

He went to the bathroom and considered whether to have a shower or not. What he most wanted was to go back to bed.

He looked at his watch again. Almost twenty minutes had passed and all he had achieved in the day so far was to pour a cup of coffee.

He went to the telephone and called the Pathology Institute. He asked if they had received a request for an autopsy of Nina Stenshagen. They hadn't. He asked to be put through to Schwenke.

'It's Saturday.'

'So?'

'I'm not sure he'll be there.'

'Try,' Gunnarstranda said, irritated.

The phone rang for a long time. Gunnarstranda was thinking of hanging up. He didn't have time.

'Schwenke.'

'Gunnarstranda here. Nina Stenshagen. She was hit by a train on Thursday morning. Could you fix up an autopsy?'

Schwenke wanted to know why he should.

'I want to know if she was shot before she was hit,' Gunnarstranda said. 'And yes, I have reasonable grounds to suspect that she was.'

He rang off.

Gunnarstranda squinted into the low sun outside the window. He felt lousy. The previous day, which he had thought would culminate in a quiet evening at home, had turned into a long night at a murder scene. And on top of that he had found himself the victim of a murder attempt! He deserved more than three hours' sleep.

He trudged back to the bedroom and crawled under the duvet.

As soon as he closed his eyes he felt wide awake. Opened his eyes and looked through the window at the blue sky. It was no good. He wasn't going to be able to sleep.

He got up and sipped at the coffee he had poured himself. That, at least, was a start.

2

Lena started Saturday morning by switching off her phone. She had a lot to do and needed an hour away from the tyranny of total accessibility. Then she wrote a to-do list. She had to buy mutton ribs, smoked and salted; she had to buy icing sugar and almonds for the marzipan; Kong Haakon chocolate. Three boxes at least. And Christmas presents.

She sat chewing her pen. Her mind drifted to the man in the harbour. He wasn't coming home for Christmas. But there were relatives still waiting. She had to tell them which day the body would be released. She mustn't forget.

Lena had two to-do lists. One for work. One for Christmas.

Thank God I'm such a control freak, she reflected, *that I start my Christmas shopping in January*. On every holiday trip or mooch through an exotic shop in town this random thought would strike her. A candle with cinnamon fragrance? Would that be suitable as a gift for Ingeborg? Or a jar of Italian chestnut honey? Or that beautiful top? *But I'm not enough of a control freak,* Lena mused. *There are still two names on the list without a present. And I still haven't bought anything for Mum.*

What should she buy for her mother? She hadn't a clue. She chewed her pen, unable to come up with a single idea. She got to her feet and went over to her laptop, which was on. A little search online – the list of Christmas radio stations was long. She chose xmasmelody.com. Chris Reah's breathy voice immediately began to sing 'Driving Home for Christmas'. Back to the list. Still a blank. Lena went to the kitchen and put the kettle on. *Perhaps* that *could be a present for Mum? A kettle? A cafetière?* She took the tea-light holders on the table and scraped out the remaining wax. Eleven burnt-out metal cups. She ought to go to IKEA and buy five or six bags of cheap tea-lights. She had almost run out in the cupboard. *That's all I'm really good at,* she thought. *Drinking tea and burning tea-lights.* But first things first: Oslo city centre and Christmas presents.

✳

Lena caught the bus to the centre and set off on a peregrination lasting several hours, first through Arkaden Mall, then Oslo City shopping centre. But as she had no clear idea what she was after and she hadn't planned who she was buying for, her wanderings ended in Platekompaniet and her buying a DVD for herself: the classic *Pride and Prejudice* from 1995 with Colin Firth starring as Mr Darcy.

She stood weighing the DVD in her hand. Actually she would have liked to receive this film herself, but knew she wouldn't be able to wait until Christmas and so decided it would be a pre-Christmas present. She was already wildly excited about spending the weekend on the sofa and following the emotional struggle of a decent romantic drama. She was looking forward to despairing with Lizzie, looking forward to crying with Jane.

Her attention was caught by a display model in a window, wearing stockings, a suspender belt, transparent knickers, a bra and a very intricate Santa Lucia wreath on her head. With Christmas tree candles. The cables for the candles were taped to the stomach and the thighs of the model. Lena took a deep breath. Tomorrow it was Santa Lucia Day, 13th December. Children singing: '*Black the night descends…*' She turned and looked outside. It was already getting dark. The Vinmonopol would be closing soon.

Lena took the escalator down, laid in for a minor siege and wrapped every bottle in Christmas paper so that they wouldn't clink. Suddenly she felt hungry.

Should she go straight home or have a bite in town first?

Lena considered the options and had a brainwave.

She could have a bite to eat at the famous Flamingo Bar & Restaurant. She checked her shoulder bag. The photo of Sveinung Adler was there.

A little later, as the tram whizzed up Grefsenveien, Lena was sitting by a window, looking at the detached houses with welcoming yellow windows beneath snow-covered roofs with grey wisps of smoke swirling upwards into the sky.

Lena got off the tram and trudged towards the restaurant with the carrier bags in her hand.

The place was closed. Typical.

Lena, who was starving now, didn't give up. She banged on one of the windows facing the street.

The door was opened by a young man in jeans and a yellow jumper with a chic cap on his head.

'I might not look like it,' Lena said, 'but I work for the police.'

She put down her carrier bag and fished her ID card from her shoulder bag.

*

The room was empty, but still smelt of the previous day's Christmas meals. A small girl of three or four was crawling on the floor between the tables. She grabbed Lena's trouser leg and wanted to play.

The man apologised and lifted the girl up.

'Wednesday evening,' Lena said, abandoning all hope of a quick bite to eat. She took out a photo of Sveinung Adeler. 'Can you tell me if this man was here then?'

The man took the photo and studied it. 'It's possible. I think I've seen the guy, and if he was here on Wednesday that might be right, but I can't remember exactly. Only the face. It seems to ring a bell.'

'Were you working here on Wednesday night?'

'Every night. All of us are here – my brother and sister, my father and my mother.'

'Do you have a full house on Wednesdays?'

'Not usually. But this is peak period. From the beginning of November it's a full house, so to speak, every night, right through to the twenty-third.' He splayed his hands. 'Christmas dinners, *lutefisk*, you know what it's like. The most popular places in the centre are already fully booked in October and many people turn to us when Christmas approaches, but we have lots of regular customers too, in the Christmas rush.'

'Who was serving here, apart from you?'

The man put the child down on the floor, took the photo with him and went into the kitchen. Judging by the noise, it was busy.

Lena's stomach rumbled. When she got home she was going to run wild, make cheese toasties with lashings of butter and mustard and ham. At least four. No champers. She would drink beer. Lager, Mexican, the kind Adeler had in his fridge. Her stomach rumbled again. She stood up in the hope it would stop. Looked at the little girl with golden skin and gorgeous black locks. The girl smiled secretively and grabbed her leg.

Lena capitulated. 'What's your name?' she asked.

The girl shook her head, bursting with laughter and embarrassment. She ran to the kitchen door after her daddy.

They almost collided in the doorway. The father was followed by a woman in her fifties with a sharp, weather-bitten face.

Now the woman was holding the photograph. 'I remember him,' she said with a whisky voice. 'Has he done something?'

Lena shook her head. 'What I'd like to know is who he was with.'

'There were three of them,' the woman said, pointing to a table by the window. 'I remember them because one was a VIP. The good-looking one, the one in parliament. Aud Helen Vestgård. That was a bit special. We do have celebs here now and then, but not every day, and I thought that was nice, you know. I like her, and I was pleased it was me serving her, you know. There were three of them. Him, Vestgård and one more.'

'Man or woman?'

'Man.'

'So this third person wasn't a VIP?'

'No. Never seen the man before. But it was a bit of an unusual order. The man in the photo wanted *lutefisk*, beer and aquavit, while Vestgård wanted mutton ribs and red wine, of all things; and the third person was a veggie and drank water. So that was a bit different, but fine.'

'What did the third person look like?'

'Bit over fifty, I'd say. Good-looking, brown eyes, a little beard around his mouth and chin – not on his cheeks though; short hair, dark, grey streaks. He was wearing a suit. Very elegant. Gold watch and a ring with jewels in on his finger. The type that takes a lot of care about his appearance, if you ask me. Both of the men wore suits, and Vestgård had a woollen dress on, rather chic actually, sort of earthy colour, although I can't imagine she knitted it herself.'

'You're very observant,' Lena said.

'As I said, he was a good-looking guy,' the woman replied with a smile.

'I assume they booked the table in advance?'

'They must've done. We don't go in for preferential treatment here.'

The little girl had crawled under the table where Lena was sitting. She pulled her trouser leg and wanted some attention again.

The guy with the cap went to the kitchen door, reached inside and brought out a wad of booking sheets. 'Let me see now, Wednesday.' He flicked through. 'Vestgård, eight-thirty pm.'

Lena got up and went over to him. 'So, she booked the table?'

'Looks like it.'

'I'd like a copy of the booking sheet,' Lena said.

'I can scan the page and email it to you.'

Lena nodded and searched for a police card in her back pocket. She passed it to him. 'Email address and phone number. How long were they here?' she asked.

The woman sat thinking. 'They split the bill,' she said at last, 'Vestgård and the older man. No. She paid for two, cash. The other man – him,' she said, pointing to the photo of Adeler, 'paid for himself, cash. Off the top of my head, it would've been around eleven, maybe a bit before. The kitchen closes at half past ten and the restaurant begins to thin out then.'

'Is there a credit-card receipt with the time on?' Lena asked.

The woman shook her head. 'No. They paid cash. But they asked me to ring for a taxi, I do remember that.'

'They left here together?'

'That was my impression. I only rang for one taxi.'

Lena straightened up on her chair. 'Do you remember the number of the taxi?'

'Are you out of your mind? The taxi was one of a hundred that evening. At least.'

Lena thanked her and made ready to leave.

The little girl whispered something to her father as Lena wound her scarf around her neck.

'You do that,' the father said.

The little girl blushed.

Lena crouched down. 'What is it?' she asked.

The little girl gave her a flower. It was a crinkled plastic flower.

Lena took it. 'Thank you very much.' Lena was moved and happy. She stretched out her arms to give her a hug. But the girl ran off into the kitchen.

Her father winked at Lena. 'My daughter wanted to give you a present, but she's so shy.'

✳

Lena stuffed the flower into her pocket. While waiting for the tram to take her back down to town, she called the Pathology Institute. She got a pathologist on the line and told him Sveinung Adeler had ingested *lutefisk*, beer and aquavit on Wednesday evening between seven-thirty and eleven. Would that make it easier to define the moment of death?

The pathologist she was talking to was unsure. She was passed over to Schwenke.

'What is it now?' Schwenke barked with irritation. 'It's Saturday. Why do the police keep phoning me?'

Lena apologised and promised him a Christmas present if he could answer her question on the hoof.

When Schwenke hesitated she repeated her question about Adeler's last meal and when he ate it.

Schwenke didn't waste any time, he said: 'From the way the food was digested my conclusion is that Adeler drowned somewhere between five and six o'clock on Thursday morning.'

Lena thanked him and hung up.

The blue tram glided in, stopped and opened its doors. Lena got on. Schwenke was right, of course.

Saturday was a free day and she had several hours of a tussle for love ahead of her.

She found a free seat. Alone, she reflected. A whole weekend on her own.

She took out the crinkled plastic flower she had been given by the little girl. Twirled it between her fingers. Again she was moved, felt a lump in her throat and was reminded of the lump in her breast. When you are weighed down by negative thoughts it is good to feel acknowledged. She took a deep breath and closed her eyes. *This is a sign. I am vulnerable. I have to use my freedom properly, use it on myself, meditate, train.*

Monday, 14th December

1

'I'm sorry,' Lena said. 'But I didn't get your message until last night.'

Gunnarstranda didn't answer.

'My phone was off and at home while I was out preparing for Christmas. I have a mother who has certain requirements regarding Christmas celebrations.'

She didn't need to apologise, but she did anyway.

A kind soul had baked too many saffron buns at the weekend and decided to share the surplus with the gang of officers. A red woven basket with the glistening Kringle cakes was placed between two half-full cups of coffee that had stopped steaming. Lena watched Gunnarstranda take one of the buns and break it into two. When he saw the yellow contents inside, he put the two pieces back.

'You can't do that,' she said.

'We were talking about what you were going to do,' Gunnarstranda said, but took note of her objections. He grasped the two halves and threw them in the wastepaper basket.

Lena lifted one of the cups and swirled the cold liquid round. The coffee grounds stained the sides.

The conclusion was indisputable. One or more unknown persons had been with Adeler at the moment he fell in the water. It was as clear as crystal now that the lab had done its share of the work. The plank that was floating in the water beside the corpse bore fibres that came from Adeler's shirt. Someone had been standing on the quay and pressing the plank down onto the neck of the man splashing in the water. To give him a hand, push him down or to pull the body in. Whatever this person was doing they hadn't come forward. Six luminous letters flashed in Lena's head: M-U-R-D-E-R.

'*Tempus fugit*,' Gunnarstranda said. 'I'm just as keen as you to find out what occurred on the quay that morning. We have a witness – Stig Eriksen. On Friday night he was shot dead by someone with an automatic weapon ten minutes after he admitted he knew what happened to Adeler and Nina Stenshagen.'

Lean nodded. The case was assuming new dimensions. But she felt a need to analyse the information thoroughly, spend a bit of time separating the wheat from the chaff.

'Aud Helen Vestgård's lying,' Gunnarstranda said.

'Thanks. I know.'

'Vestgård booked the table,' Gunnarstranda said, drumming his fingers on the copy of the Flamingo booking sheet. 'You have a witness. Furthermore, you have proof of Vestgård lying about her contact with Adeler. A new scenario has materialised. Both you and I need to know what Adeler did after the meal on Wednesday night. The unknown third man probably knows what Adeler was doing that night. It might've been him who pushed Adeler off the quay in the early hours and held the poor man under the water with the plank.'

Lena agreed.

'The two of them – the unknown guy and Sveinung Adeler – may have said goodbye to Vestgård, who then went home in the taxi. What about if the two of them went on the town and got into an argument?'

Lena shook her head. 'Adeler had *no* alcohol in his blood when he drowned.'

They sat brooding in silence.

It was broken by Gunnarstranda: 'You *know* there were three people around the table at the Flamingo. Adeler's dead. Only Vestgård can tell us who that third person was.'

'I think I'll have to take this up with Rindal,' Lena said. Gunnarstranda was right, but Rindal had made it very clear that he wanted a say in anything to do with Vestgård's involvement in this case.

'The clothing fibres on the piece of wood from the quay explain everything,' Gunnarstranda said. 'Someone was forcing Adeler under water to drown him. That's *premeditated* murder. Nina Stenshagen saw what was going on and fled. The perpetrator ran after her. If the drowning had been a normal accident or misadventure there would've been no point running after Nina and killing her.'

Lena took her phone and called Rindal for a third time. And still got the voicemail. She put it down.

They exchanged looks.

'We can both talk to Vestgård if you don't want to do it alone,' Gunnarstranda said.

'Why doesn't he pick up?' she said in a low voice.

'Stig Eriksen rang me wanting to tell me who killed them. But I was too late. First he shot Stig. When I turned up he tried to kill me too. It was only a freak of fate that prevented a concrete block landing on my nut.'

'What?! And you're telling me that now?'

'Bang!' Gunnarstranda said, smacking his palm down on the table. 'Bits of concrete flying everywhere!'

'Hang on a mo,' Lena said, getting up. She couldn't sit still any longer.

Gunnarstranda went quiet.

Lena realised that if she wanted to talk to the Storting politician once more she needed an angle that would rule out any possible repercussions.

Then she had an idea. 'I need your help,' she said, 'but afterwards I'm talking to Vestgård on my own.'

2

Lena decided she wouldn't go in for any pre-arranged tactical strategies. She wanted this over and done with. She would walk into the lion's den – unannounced. Although parliament was in recess she reckoned people would be at work anyway.

The first surprise she encountered was in the reception area. Today the entrance to Norway's National Assembly was guarded by one Ståle Sender.

Lena hadn't spoken to Sender since she finished with him in a text when he went on a summer holiday with his wife. Lena saw no reason to talk now either. She nodded curtly to him and said she believed Vestgård was expecting her. Ståle, for his part, took the time and trouble to accompany Lena in.

'What's new?' he asked.

'Nothing special,' Lena said. 'We're a bit short-handed, have a lot of overtime, the usual.'

'I mean, with you,' Ståle said.

Lena hesitated. 'Not much, until I start listening to my heart.'

Ståle kept quiet. Fortunately. They were there now. She read the name Aud Helen Vestgård on the door and knocked.

Ståle waited as well.

'Thank you, Ståle,' Lena said.

'What about a meal before Christmas?' Ståle chipped in quickly.

Why didn't Vestgård's door open? She glanced at Ståle. 'What? Like, just you and me?'

He nodded.

She didn't answer. There weren't the words.

'My treat,' Ståle said. 'The Theatercafé, Gamle Raadhus, Annen Etage, you choose. One of the perks of this job is that you're on informal terms with the right people.' Ståle smiled, flexing his muscles. 'What do you say to an evening together? *Toi et moi?*'

'Soon be Christmas,' Lena said coolly. 'Spend your money on something sensible. Buy your wife something nice.'

Then the door opened.

On this occasion Aud Helen Vestgård was sporting a dark suit with a narrow stripe, which looked good on her.

'You again?' Vestgård said, with an annoyed frown.

Lena got into her stride. 'I'm here about the threatening letter you received.'

'Oh, yes?'

Lena pointed. 'Perhaps we could take this in your office?'

Vestgård glanced at her watch. 'I have an important meeting, I don't know.'

'It won't take long,' Lena said.

'Well,' Vestgård said, holding the door open.

The office was immense. A tall ceiling. The acoustics. Her heels click-clacking like on a stage floor. The echo of the door closing. The window looked out over Wessels plass and Halvorsens Conditori.

As if to emphasise how unwelcome this visit was, Vestgård stood in the middle of the floor. She snatched another glance at her watch.

'The threatening letter was a false alarm. Someone wrote the letter to embarrass the sender. Apparently she's a student, not very interested in politics and not at all interested in you – no record, not politically active. Our people lean towards the view that the perp wanted to target her. Your name has no relevance at all to the case.'

'That's reassuring to hear,' Vestgård replied curtly. 'Thank you very much.'

She headed for the door again, but waited for Lena to exit first.

It's now or never, Lena thought, and went for it: 'Aud Helen Vestgård, you lied to the police. We have witnesses who say you were at the Flamingo Bar & Restaurant in Grefsen on Wednesday evening with Sveinung Adeler.'

Vestgård took a step forwards.

'I would advise you to take a minute now to clear this matter up. If you don't, I'll have to apply for a legal order to carry out an official interview later,' Lena said.

Vestgård stepped back, as if the response had shocked her. 'What is this impertinence? You have no authority here. You're in Storting, Norway's National Assembly. If you don't behave, I'll have you thrown out!'

'I can leave here now if you insist,' Lena said softly. 'But the circumstances will not change. The fact is that you lied while making a statement to the police. I'm offering you a chance to change your statement now. What you say to me will be recorded and inaccuracies will be amended. You are completely within your rights to change the statement you made earlier. On the other hand…' Lena left the alternative hanging in the air.

Vestgård stepped closer to her. 'Are you theatening me?'

Lena took a pace back.

'Do you think I have something to hide? What could it be? Or is this your modus operandi – whispering into the ears of media types so that they can help you to hang respectable members of the public out to dry every time reality is not as you think it is?'

Lena knew she was near her goal now and she had only to resist the pressure. 'Not at all,' she said as calmly as she could. 'You're not listening. I'm offering you the chance to change your statement.'

Aud Helen Vestgård's eyes were still flashing. But she was obviously considering what Lena had said. In the end she lowered her shoulders and went to the desk, where she shuffled some papers as she continued to reflect on her situation.

'Sveinung,' she said at length. 'Sveinung and I had a Christmas dinner together. Let me stress the following so that there are no inaccuracies in your damned reports. Sveinung and I were *not* having an affair. This was a *professional* relationship that became a *friendship*. I was, one might say, a kind of mentor to Sveinung. He hadn't been a member of the party for very long. We met during the election campaign. I was at a stand out there,' she pointed towards the window. 'Sveinung stopped by and started a discussion about drilling for oil outside Lofoten.' Vestgård smiled weakly at the memory. 'It was raining, dreadful weather, but we had a heated debate; he had strong opinions. Sveinung was good at marshalling his arguments. Well, anyway, Sveinung, it transpired, was a member of the party and we met in that context soon afterwards. And became friends. We simply liked each other. On Wednesday we ate together at this restaurant in Grefsen because it was the only place where it was possible to get a table. And he wanted *lutefisk*, you see.' Vestgård shrugged. 'The Christmas dinner was the reason for going there. All the usual restaurants in the centre were fully booked. If he'd wanted sushi or tapas or something Lebanese – even Thai for that matter – we could've found somewhere in the centre.'

Lena had to ask: 'Why did you deny that you knew him the last time we spoke?'

Vestgård turned away from Lena and stared pensively out of the window. 'That was foolish of me, of course. But you caught me on the hop. I was expecting the police's clarification of the death threat. When you marched in talking about Sveinung – well, I didn't want any media speculation. It would've been unrelenting. After all, Sveinung was fifteen years younger than me.'

'According to our witnesses there were three of you eating in Grefsen. Who was the third person?'

A silence grew between them. Aud Helen Vestgård fixed Lena with a hard stare.

The seconds ticked by.

Lena could almost hear the cogs in her brain whirring round.

'Your witness is mistaken,' Vestgård said at length. Her voice trembled. 'There were *not* three of us. Only two. Sveinung and I. The restaurant was packed and your witness probably thought someone from another table was with us. But that was not the case. It was a typically boisterous Norwegian *lutefisk* evening. People were toasting one another from table to table, and we joined in. But it was only the two of us. That was precisely why I didn't want to talk about this meeting, because my eating alone with Sveinung was likely to be misinterpreted.'

'That's your last word?' Lena asked.

'Of course,' Vestgård riposted.

Lena weighed her words carefully before saying, 'We're trying to work out Adeler's last movements before he died. Where did you go after you finished the meal?'

'I went home. I have no idea what he got up to.'

'Could he have gone with this unknown third person?'

'Are you hard of hearing? There was no third person!'

It was clear to Lena that Vestgård wasn't going to back down on this, so instead she asked: 'How did you get home?'

'I took a taxi. I suppose Sveinung did the same.'

'According to the employees in the restaurant only one taxi was ordered.'

'Sveinung was a modern man and capable of looking after himself.'

'Did you see him getting into a taxi?'

'No, but I assume he did. He was in a good mood. When the taxi came he let me take it. He said he would get another. He was a grown man of over thirty and I had no compunction about leaving him on his own. I doubt it was any later than eleven.'

'Did he say where he was going after midnight – back home or to see someone?'

'No. I assumed he was going home.'

'Why did you assume that?'

Vestgård lost her cool again. 'Because it was the middle of the week? I have no idea. Listen: I left the restaurant before eleven. I've got the receipt from the taxi driver, which I can show you. My husband and two daughters were still up and can confirm when I got home.'

Before Lena had a chance to protest Vestgård had grabbed the phone on the desk and tapped in a number: 'Vestgård for Frikk Råholt.' There was a pause. 'Frikk, it's me. I've got the policewoman here again. Yes, I've told her I was out with Sveinung on Wednesday night. Now she wants to know when I got home. Can you tell her?'

Vestgård passed the receiver to Lena. 'Ask Frikk, my husband.'

Lena was uncomfortable with this situation, but she obeyed. 'Lena Stigersand here—'

She got no further as Frikk Råholt interrupted her. 'I have received assurances from your superior officers that all communications with my wife or anyone else in our family will be discreet and through secure channels. Taking a statement from Aud Helen in Parliament itself could hardly be called discreet. I will therefore take this up with your superior officer, which I am sure you understand. As a matter of form, may I ask you to note the following: My wife arrived home in a taxi at eleven-thirty on Wednesday, the ninth of December. If you insist on a signature confirming this statement, please fax a document to the Department of Justice – after first conferring with your superior officer.'

The conversation was at an end and the dialling tone buzzed in Lena's ear. She watched Aud Helen Vestgård take the receiver from her and return it to its place.

3

Apart from Lena there was another patient waiting – a blonde in her mid-twenties. The woman was reading a fat book and didn't react when Lena came in and sat down. Lena stole furtive glances. Perfect figure, tight jeans going down to high black boots with heels.

On a low table there was a pile of old weeklies and the odd health magazine with a glossy cover. On the walls hung posters about the damage caused by smoking and excessive drinking.

Lena leaned forwards and took a weekly from the pile on the table. The woman looked up from her book. They nodded briefly and politely to each other.

Lena flipped through the gossip rag, which was several months old. There were pictures of a film première with beautiful young women posing on a red carpet. Their dresses were commented on and rated by an 'expert' using numbers on a dice. Lena was relieved she didn't have her attire assessed by the expert. Moreover, she regretted not having brought something to read with her.

She sneaked another peek at the woman. She was curious to see what she was reading. It certainly was a thick book. A novel. What kind of novel would a woman with an hourglass figure and a solarium tan read? Probably a doctor novel, Lena mused; at any rate nothing with any shelf-life – like Jane Austen.

The blonde with the book raised her head and gazed at her.

Lena immersed herself once again in Norwegian TV celebs' problem-free love affairs. Looking at the photos made her feel uncomfortable. She put down the magazine, stretched her legs and leaned back in the chair.

The woman put a bookmark in the novel and closed it.

The title was *Moby Dick*.

Lena had to laugh at her own prejudice.

At last the door opened. A plump woman in a green doctor's uniform stood there. She nodded to the blonde and eyed Lena. 'Stigersand?'

Lena stood up and walked in.

✳

An hour later she got into her car. She sat looking through the windscreen, pensive and disorientated. For the first time she had gone to a doctor's surgery concerned about the outcome. She couldn't take it in. She didn't want to think about it. Nevertheless she opened her shoulder bag. In it was the envelope she had been given when she left. She weighed the envelope in her hand. Made a decision. Tore it open and took out the sheet. Read the first sentences: '*Make sure you are not on your own when you ring for the test result. It might be good to have someone to talk to.*'

The gravity of the words was too much for her. She sat for some seconds with her eyes closed. But then she couldn't stay still. She got out of the car and locked it. She had to move.

She mooched around with no clear destination and ultimately found herself in Steen & Strøm, wandering through the heated store in her padded winter clothes, feeling like an astronaut waggling from side to side in an alien world. She went into the perfume section. How come women who worked in perfume departments always looked the same? How could they be so attractive and fashionable in all towns, in all countries? When Lena had been a little girl she had come here and ogled the beautiful women wearing pink aprons and smelling of perfumes and powders. She had dreamt about being one of them, being like them – a sweetly scented beauty in a perfumery surrounded by creams and make-up and chic lingerie.

What was it that had just happened?

She'd had an insight.

I'm mortal.

I am thirty-three years old and actually hadn't absorbed this fact until now. I have wasted thirty-three years on trivial nonsense. I despised my mother and missed my father, cried over a stupid love affair at school. I became a cop. Why did I become a cop? Because it was difficult. Because you had to have good grades and pass entrance exams. Because Kenneth, my ridiculous teenage love, wanted to become a cop. He never did though. He wasn't able to fulfil the entrance requirements. I was. But what's the point of all this? Why work shifts and endless overtime? Why push your body, deprive it of sleep, why wear yourself out doing what you think is right when you receive only ingratitude and severe reprimands in return? Why did I apply for a job as a detective? Little Lena, the class creep.

She moved slowly up the escalator. On the step in front of her was an unusually beautiful Asiatic woman accompanying an overweight man of a similar age. Lena followed them. The two of them looked at ladies' underwear. The dusky beauty put some transparent panties and a provocative corset over her arm and showed them to her beefy lover, who nodded encouragement. Lena walked past them and took the escalator back down. She wasn't someone who had no cares in the world. She was mortal.

There was no question of her going to work today. She walked almost blindly to her car. Got in and drove. She thought of her mother, thought of her dead father and was startled when a car hooted.

She had gone through the crossing on red! *Pull yourself together, Lena!*

She snapped out of her thoughts and concentrated on driving. Then she held her hand to her breast. Why did she do that? She felt a stab of pain.

She pulled in and stopped. Released her safety belt. It helped, the pain went. On the other side of the road a multi-storey block of flats towered above her. On the third floor lived someone with a passion for Christmas. The balcony was festooned with red, green and yellow lights. Above all this a message flashed to the world, like an advertising slogan in red and white: *Happy Christmas*.

Lena indicated and pulled onto the carriageway. She wanted to go home, away from everything and into her dreams, put a match to tea-lights and burn incense. She still had three episodes left of *Pride and Prejudice*. Lizzie still hadn't been to Blenheim with her aunt and uncle. Mr Darcy hadn't ridden in on his white charger yet and Lydia hadn't eloped with Wickham.

4

Going through the door to the noisy Asylet pub was like going back years in time. The wall- and floorboards looked as if they had been cut with a chainsaw. Winter logs were piled up against the wall. The big fireplace was roaring, and Frank Frølich was sitting at one of the long tables in the room with the bar.

Frølich was good friends with the barmaid, who had sat down next to him with a coffee. She stood up as soon as Gunnarstranda appeared.

'Stay where you are,' he said.

'I won't if you want something to drink,' she grinned. 'Besides I've poured out my heart enough for this evening.'

'What do you want?' he asked Frølich, who was leaning back against the wall. He had placed a large fur cap and two big fur mittens beside him on the table.

'A pils and a Gammel Dansk.'

'Same for me,' Gunnarstranda said to the barmaid. 'How's it going?' he asked Frølich.

'So-so,' Frølich said. 'I've had two offers of work. One as Father

Christmas and one as a security guard at Oslo Station. It's a toss-up which one to take.'

'No point trying to tickle my funny bone,' Gunnarstranda said. 'I never laugh.'

The barmaid came over with the beer and shots of bitters. The two men raised their dram glasses and drained them in one.

'Another,' Frølich said.

'Don't they come in smaller glasses?' Gunnarstranda enquired gently.

The barmaid shook her head.

'OK, another.'

'Soon be Christmas and I'm living on my savings,' Frølich went on. 'I've decided to make my own Christmas presents. And to save electricity by staying in bed longer in the morning. That's going well with the sleep deficit I've accumulated over years of night shifts. Now I'm horizontal for up to ten hours a night. Soon I'll be able to go to the doctor and have my new illness ratified: narcolepsy. Then I'll go to social security, apply for early retirement, buy a yacht on the never-never and travel around the world. I'm like the lion in that zoo in Kabul. I've got enough food, enough leisure time, I've got everything.'

'Just no lion friends,' Gunnarstranda said.

'How's the newbie?' Frølich asked.

'Axel Rise works in Oslo, but lives in Bergen and has a tragic personal life.'

Frølich drank instead of making a comment.

'Did you know that Bergen calls itself the town between the seven mountains?' Gunnarstranda said. 'But they can't agree on which seven they are. There are more than seven, you see. Maybe fourteen or even more. Isn't it a bit strange to reduce the number to seven when you're trying to put your town on the map?'

'*Skål*,' Frølich said.

'I've got a riddle for you,' Gunnarstranda said, putting down his glass.

'Come on then.'

'OK, this is what happened. At eight o'clock on Thursday morning we receive a message about a guy floating in the water off the City Hall Quay. Lena goes down, and what looks like a drowning accident isn't.'

'He was pushed in?'

'Someone not only pushed him in, but found a piece of wood and forced the poor devil under – at minus twenty-five. Anyway, Lena discovered that this guy, Sveinung Adeler, died from drowning at about six o'clock in the morning. The same morning Nina Stenshagen ends up under the wheels of a Grorud train and dies. She's one of the junkies at Plata. By then it was half past seven.'

'Suicide?'

'She ran into the tunnel, chased by some guy. Three minutes after Nina falls under the train an unknown person leaves the tunnel through an emergency exit a few metres away.'

'So it's not necessarily suicide. What does the train driver say?'

'She's still in shock at the moment and didn't see anything. She just heard a bang, according to my partner Rise, who took her statement.

'This Nina turned out to be the girlfriend of another junkie – Stig Eriksen. I talked to him the day after. He wouldn't say anything, but rang me half an hour later. This time he told me – on the phone, that is – that Nina was killed because she saw who threw the guy off the quay and drowned him.'

Gunnarstranda took a deep breath and drank some beer.

'Haul Stig Eriksen in. Put him in a cell until he goes cold turkey and then he'll tell you everything you want to know,' Frølich said.

'The problem is that Stig Eriksen's dead,' Gunnarstranda said bluntly. 'Shot with an automatic weapon a few minutes before I was going to do what you suggested.'

Frølich whistled.

'Just like in American films,' Gunnarstranda continued. 'Entry wound in the forehead, blood and gore everywhere.'

Gunnarstranda realised that the barmaid had brought another round of Gammel Dansk. Frølich's glass was already empty.

Gunnarstranda sipped from the glass and swallowed the bitters down with some beer. 'Now, the thing is I have Nina Stenshagen's mobile phone. And it wasn't used – neither on the Wednesday nor on the Thursday morning. The last time it had been used was on Tuesday evening – when Nina and Stig talked on the phone.

'So a man's drowned in the harbour on Thursday morning. Nina sees what happens. She's frightened and runs from the crime scene with the perpetrator hard on her heels. In her happier years she worked at the Metro, so decides to lose her pursuer by running into the tunnel. I think she was caught and killed. The riddle I'm trying to solve is this: How could Stig know Nina was killed because she saw someone kill Adeler *when they hadn't spoken?*'

'You've always said simple is best,' Frølich said.

Gunnarstranda nodded.

'The simple solution is that Stig was bluffing. He knew nothing.'

'Of course I've considered that possibility,' Gunnarstranda said. 'But my gut instinct is that Stig knew. Don't forget, at first he refused to talk to me. Then he rang and wanted me to go back. Stig could've lured me with anything to make me go back. He could've claimed he knew who ran after Nina into the tunnel or said he knew what was really happening. I would still have turned round and run straight to him. Instead he talked about the *motive* for the murder of Nina – he talked about the man who drowned in the harbour. I hadn't mentioned Adeler or the drowning. So Stig was telling the truth. I know it in my bones. Nina saw what happened on the harbour. And I want the mystery solved. You're a smart guy, Frølich, and you read crime novels. Help me. How could Stig have known what Nina saw that morning?'

'That's obvious,' Frølich said with a smile. 'Stig was also there and saw what happened!'

Gunnarstranda frowned sceptically.

'If Stig's telling the truth,' Frølich said, 'he must also have been present. Stig must've seen what happened as well.'

'You may be partly right,' Gunnarstranda said, rapt in thought. 'The two of them were a couple. Two homeless people searching for somewhere to sleep every night. It was freezing cold that Wednesday. They might've found a bolthole near City Hall Quay. It's early in the morning. The victim and the unknown killer approach, they walk along the pier. One pushes the other into the water. Both Stig and Nina are eyewitnesses, but the killer spots only Nina – who makes a run for it.'

Frølich nodded.

Gunnarstranda was still sceptical. At the same time he felt things happening inside his head. Two glasses of bitters and one and a half beers were playing pinball with his brain cells.

'The most interesting bit,' Frølich grinned, 'is what drove Stig to contact you. Why didn't he want to tell you anything at first, but then revealed all half an hour later?'

Gunnarstranda tried to focus.

'Stig contacted you because he was afraid,' Frølich went on. 'He was shit scared and wanted your help. Why was he scared?'

'You tell me.'

'Probably because he contacted the perp after you left him,' Frølich said.

'That's exactly what I can't make tally,' Gunnarstranda said. 'If you're right that both Nina and Stig saw the man push Adeler into the sea, and if you're right that Stig contacted the same man after I spoke to him, why would he wait? Why didn't he contact the killer the day before, why did it only happen after I'd spoken to him?'

'He might've done. Have you got Stig's phone?'

Gunnarstranda shook his head. 'Thorough killer. He took it with him. I tried to find it, but no luck. Telenor say it's probably been destroyed.'

Frølich licked the last bitter drops of his Gammel Dansk. 'You seem dejected,' he said. 'I think you need another one.'

Gunnarstranda peered up. There was another half a litre of beer and another glass of bitters on the table. He smiled wanly. 'This round,' he said, 'but then that's it.'

'My guess is that Stig tried to work out how he could blackmail the killer without any risk to himself. Put yourself in his shoes: he sees a murder committed. He can earn money with his silence. But how? He knows the killer is highly dangerous. If he makes a mistake all he can expect is that his friends will club together for an obituary. Stig must've really put his thinking cap on. When you came along, he saw his opportunity. He must've used you as his insurance policy. First he rings the killer, demands money and agrees to meet. Then he rings you and tells you to come. If the killer plays tough, Stig had you – the police – as back-up.'

Gunnarstranda nodded. This idea was not a million miles off. He remembered the footsteps. The shadow on the stairs. The margins had been tiny. If he hadn't waited for Stig in the stairwell perhaps … No, he couldn't think like that. Stig had been killed by an unknown person. He had nothing to reproach himself with. Gunnarstranda raised his glass. The beer didn't taste good.

'You know you've got an even bigger riddle on your hands, don't you?' Frølich said.

'Really?'

'There are two MOs,' Frølich said. 'One man is pushed into the harbour; Nina is pushed under a train. Whereas Stig is shot. Stig's murder is different. The fact that Stig was shot suggests it *wasn't* the same person who killed all three of them.'

Gunnarstranda nodded. 'Don't you think I've thought about that?' he mumbled. 'I've asked to have Nina Stenshagen's body autopsied. But even if it turns out Nina was also shot, I'm no further on. Adeler drowned, that's irrefutable. There's something here I can't grasp. There's a piece missing.'

'Nina ran off,' Frølich said. 'The killer ran after her. But Stig stayed put. Why didn't Stig go into action and save the man splashing in the water?'

'Stig was handicapped. One leg was amputated. He may well have tried to help. We'll never know, anyway.'

Gunnarstranda cleared his throat and thought aloud again. 'Stig and Nina were both wasted junkies. They'd tried everything. Stig would gladly have extracted the gold teeth from his grandmother's mouth to get money for drugs. If Stig had known the identity of the killer, he was sitting on valuable information. I think he was trying to blackmail the killer.'

'Oslo has half a million inhabitants. How did he get hold of his name and phone number?'

'Hm…' Gunnarstranda said, then had an idea: 'The killer could've been someone well known.'

Frølich grinned. 'A VIP?'

'We do, in fact, have one VIP mixed up in this,' Gunnarstranda said darkly. 'An MP – a woman.'

Frølich shook his head. 'Now you're way off target, old chap. There's something not right about the whole of the Stig angle. Stig was shot. That constitutes a difference, as some of our politicians say. Stig may've been with Nina on the quay and seen who pushed this Adeler into the water. *But* Stig was shot by an armed man. The people who shoot junkies in this country are dealers who don't get their money – or heavies they get to do the job for them.'

Gunnarstranda continued to sit in silence. Everything was going round in his head, but he didn't object.

'There's a much more likely scenario,' Frølich said.

Gunnarstranda didn't much like the idea of a heavy. He knew there was a connection between the three murder victims. He could feel it in his bones.

He tapped his forefinger on his temple. 'The little grey cells say you're right,' he said, and patted his stomach. 'But this tells me you're wrong.'

'"Follow the money",' Frølich said in English, with a grin. 'Shame there's no money to follow.'

'Follow the White Rabbit,' Gunnarstranda retorted, getting to his feet. 'I need something to eat.'

Tuesday, 15th December

1

There was a jug of water with some plastic glasses and a bowl of Twist sweets on the table. Lena resisted the temptation to take a chocolate, although her favourite was on top, in green paper with a coconut filling.

'What's difficult, exactly?' she asked, raising her eyes from the sweets to the woman sitting opposite her.

Soheyla Moestue was Lena's age, of Indian or Pakistani origin. Her black hair cascaded in elegant waves to her shoulders. She looked good in the narrow-striped trouser suit and short, tight-fitting coat over a bright-red blouse. Her clothes made her appear extremely feminine while also radiating authority. Lena wished she had more of the gene some women had that allowed them to emanate womanliness as well as competence.

'Nothing, except that it's the Ethics Council who pass on any information there is. The contents of our – that is, the secretariat's – investigations are secret. I don't know where you've heard that Sveinung had this MacFarrell company on his radar. I knew nothing about them. But it might well be true. We work on companies' portfolios all the time and spend a lot of time on borderline cases. But…' The dark-skinned woman shook her head in doubt and didn't finish her sentence.

Lena was unable to resist the temptation any longer. She took the chocolate on top and peeled off the green paper.

'Sorry,' she said, popping the sweet in her mouth. 'It's the only one I like. I can buy a whole bag of Twist just so that I can eat the coconut choc. The worst is that there seem to be fewer and fewer of them. The last time I bought a bag there were only two.'

Soheyla Moestue poked around in the bowl. 'I like the liquorice ones best,' she said. 'But they've always gone by the time I get there.' She pushed the bowl away.

'I interrupted you,' Lena said. 'You were talking about borderline cases you spend a lot of time on.'

'Exactly. I was about to say it seems so ridiculously far-fetched. Sveinung was a low-ranking employee like me. It's unbelieveable that his job should have anything to do with the drowning incident. When you talk about companies connected with Western Sahara the subtext is that Sveinung's death has something to do with sleaze and political conspiracies. It's…' Soheyla shook her head. 'It's just crazy! Anyone who wants to lobby the SPU – the Oil Fund – whether in investments or whatever, has to go higher up the pyramid, to work directly against people in the Fund or to influence decisions that have already been taken, such as getting the Fund to withdraw its investments from a company. The logical path would be to try and influence the Ethics Council directly or politicians in parliament or, best, in the Ministry.'

Lena nodded. That sounded reasonable. Decisions were taken at a political level, not in a secretariat.

'What I'm trying to say is that there's a very long obstacle course between what Sveinung did at work and the decision the Oil Fund might take in a particular case.' The woman revealed a line of flawless white teeth in a condescending smile.

'Still off the record, and still completely between us, it's simply nonsense to believe that Sveinung's job here in the secretariat might have jeopardised his safety. And I'm saying that as someone who does exactly the same job as Sveinung. I've *never* felt threatened or vulnerable working here and I don't think anyone else has, either.'

Lena pondered this. The woman was right of course. Sveinung Adeler was just a low-ranking official who liked skiing. But, she thought, Aud Helen Vestgård was not at the bottom of the pyramid. She was high up, on the Finance Committee.

Steffen Gjerstad's speculation might well have been right. The journalist in him might have dug up something or other that couldn't stand the light of day. Why else would Vestgård have lied to her face?

Lies are serious when someone has lost their life.

Lena got to her feet. Soheyla Moestue did the same.

'Sorry,' Lena said. 'It looks as if I'm wasting your time.'

The woman smiled disarmingly.

They left the conference room and walked down the corridor side by side.

'One final tiny question,' Lena said as they stopped outside the lift.

'Yes?'

'Do you document the work you do?'

'We produce quite a bit of material, yes, which is sent to the Ethics Council.' Soheyla Moestue pressed the lift button.

'But what is it precisely that you investigate?'

'Ethics. We try to establish whether a company is involved with child labour, whether it conforms to norms and rules regarding emissions, whether they abide by international law.'

'You dig, and that means you probably travel a bit?'

'Naturally. Child labour, for example, has to be documented, on film, photos, in interviews, and that isn't easy. Rumours run ahead of us, things are changed at the drop of a hat. When we arrive at a factory where children are working, suddenly there isn't a child to be seen for miles. A *lot* of what is characterised as "unethical" nowadays is hard to prove.'

'What about Western Sahara?'

Soheyla hesitated. 'Western Sahara is a *big* discussion.'

'Why?'

The lift arrived. The door opened with a little jolt. Lena stretched out a hand and blocked the sensor.

'Morocco has occupied Western Sahara,' Soheyla said. 'And parliament has ruled that the Oil Fund mustn't get involved with businesses that trade with occupying forces. But you have to draw a line somewhere. Even if a company deals with an occupying force, thereby breaking international law, this company has customers and sub-vendors who are not necessarily breaking international law and are independent of the spider in the centre of the web. Do you understand? Sometimes politics is like the surface of water. It's coloured by its surroundings and the eye of the beholder. Whoever has to clarify internal legal issues often has to be better at language than morality.'

Lena looked Soheyla in the eye and could tell that the woman knew which question was coming: 'Was Adeler in Western Sahara?'

'Yes, he was. But, as I said, I don't know specifically what businesses he was investigating.'

'But he went there, talked to people who would undoubtedly dislike the job he was carrying out?'

'Yes, but once again, inflicting any harm on Sveinung would be more stupid than shooting the pianist if you didn't like the music he was playing. Utterly pointless.'

'Would it be possible to read the report Adeler wrote about Mac-Farrell Limited?'

Soheyla shook her head. 'First of all, neither you nor I know whether such a report exists. *If* there is one, it will be not for public consumption anyway. *If* it has to be submitted, the Ministry of Finance is responsible for the case.'

'But to which person in the Ministry?'

'The Finance Minister.'

Lena stepped into the lift and pressed the button. 'Thank you for your time,' she said. 'I may be back.'

The lift doors closed, Lena descended and emerged in Rådhusgata.

2

She had barely stepped out of the lift on the third floor of Police HQ when she was met by Rindal in the corridor. Lena backed away and turned to take the lift down. She wasn't quick enough.

Rindal reacted with surprise and said: 'Just the person I was looking for, at last!' His face had a pink hue. She could almost see steam coming from the scalp under his thin head of hair.

'My office,' Rindal said curtly, spun on his heel and marched ahead.

He sat down behind his desk without a word.

She stood in front of him and stared.

'Door,' Rindal said.

She turned and closed it. Went back.

He tore the paper off a strip of chewing gum and bit into it angrily. 'Tell me something,' he chewed. 'Are you completely off your head?'

Lena didn't answer.

'You've already received one reprimand, but you don't seem to understand. You can't have comprehended a thing. Or why would you go straight from here and cause public consternation by taking a statement from an MP? Didn't they teach you at school that all power resides in Parliament?'

Rindal took a deep breath.

Lena took advantage of the brief pause: 'You weren't here when new information came in.'

'You had all weekend to contact me!'

Lena didn't answer.

'Why didn't you get in touch?'

'I was off at the weekend. I conferred with Gunnarstranda on Monday morning. We concluded that it was urgent to take a fresh statement from Vestgård.'

Rindal swivelled round on his chair and lifted the telephone receiver.

'Gunnarstranda! Here, this minute.'

Rindal smacked down the phone. He sat scowling at her without saying a word. Then he jumped up with such violence that the chair rolled backwards and hit the wall with a bang. He strode to the window. He stood there with his back to Lena.

Lena contemplated his broad back. Wondering if now was the right moment to tell him about the admission that Vestgård made in the end. Lena wasn't willing to take the risk. Best to wait until Gunnarstranda came, she reckoned. Three people, three voices. That would make it easier to manipulate the conversation.

At last the door opened.

Gunnarstranda came in.

Rindal turned away from the window: 'Tell me this minute – is Sveinung Adeler's death murder or an accident? There are people in government offices questioning how we use our resources. There'll soon be a review of the state budget and the police need more money. Do you hear me? We need the cash. We must have new equipment, we must have our overtime covered. We must have more officers. And do you know what that means?'

'Excuse me,' Gunnarstranda interrupted.

'Shut up,' Rindal barked. 'It's in the Bible. It's what you learn as a child: *Don't bite the hand that feeds you!*'

'Is that in the Bible?' Gunnarstranda queried.

'I told you to shut up.'

Lena seized the opportunity. The atmosphere couldn't get worse than this. She said: 'Adeler was killed by an unknown perp. He had wounds to the neck and his shirt was torn after he fell in the water. The fibres from the shirt tally with the fibres found on a piece of wood on the quay. Someone pushed him into the harbour and pressed the wood down on his head and shoulders when he was fighting for his life, and Aud Helen Vestgård can't be ruled out as a suspect.'

Rindal's face went from rosé to lobster.

However, Gunnarstranda managed to get a word in before Rindal recovered: 'The drug addict, Nina Stenshagen, was killed by the same person who killed Adeler. Stenshagen was an eyewitness. She saw the man deliberately kill Adeler. She saw Adeler splashing, heard him shouting, saw him freeze and drown. We know Nina Stenshagen fled the scene chased by the perpetrator. Half an hour later her body was thrown under a train in the tunnel.'

Rindal had a more normal complexion now. 'This theory's based, as far as I know, on the now deceased Stig Eriksen's statement, isn't it?'

'The theory's based on evidence and the statement Stig Eriksen made on the phone before he was shot and killed.'

Rindal contemplated Gunnarstranda in silence. At length he took a deep breath and said: 'Shot and killed. Why aren't you out scouring the countryside to find the killer?'

'Because you asked me to come here. The Eriksen case is closely connected with the Adeler case. They are one and the same.'

'I'm terribly old-fashioned, Gunnarstranda,' Rindal said in an ominously gentle voice. 'Perhaps you could bring me up to date. When did a junkie from Plata have greater credibility than an elected MP?'

Gunnarstranda was about to reply, but Rindal dismissed him with a wave of his hand. 'Firstly,' Rindal said, 'when a junkie's shot it's because the guy's up to his ears in debt and he can't pay. Secondly, the Stig story doesn't hold water. If Stig was shot because he knew something about Adeler's death why do several days pass from the moment he saw Adeler die to when he's shot?'

Lena and Gunnarstranda exchanged glances. Lena quietly hoped that Gunnarstranda had a reply to this question. She left him to answer.

'The perpertrator *can't have known* Stig saw Adeler killed,' Gunnarstranda said. 'The perpetrator didn't know about Stig until Stig contacted him. And he did that after I'd spoken to him. When I asked Stig for information he realised he could blackmail the man with less risk to himself – by using me as back-up. He arranged to meet me and the perpetrator at the same time and place.'

'If that was Stig Eriksen's plan, then it played out pretty badly, don't you think?'

Gunnarstranda shrugged and riposted: 'Now and then things do go wrong, don't they? For you, too.'

Lena watched Gunnarstranda. Thinking about the torch that had malfunctioned – Gunnarstranda's sense that he was just a little too late. But Gunnarstranda didn't mention a word of this now. She decided she wouldn't either.

'You're fantasising again,' Rindal said. 'You're speculating. You're imagining Stig's presence on the quay so that you can make it fit with the rest. I know you!'

Gunnarstranda shook his head.

'Fine. Let's suppose Stig actually did see a man push Adeler off the quay. There's just one little thing that bothers me,' Rindal smiled. 'A minor detail. Alright, Stig sees someone. How could Stig contact this person afterwards? Was this Mr X wearing a T-shirt with his name and address on? Or perhaps he shouted out his name?' Rindal roared with laughter and flung his arms into the air. 'Perhaps this guy shouted: '*Hey everyone who saw me push this poor sucker splashing around in the water, my name's such and such and you can ring me on the following number.*'

Before Gunnarstranda could answer, Rindal lifted his hand like a priest and said: 'Evidence. I want concrete, tangible evidence. A tingle down your spine or your famous gut instinct are not admissable evidence.'

'No problem. We can document the communication between Nina and Stig Eriksen.'

'I said I wanted concrete evidence!'

'We have Nina Stenshagen's mobile phone. *That* is evidence. Nina's phone wasn't used. Nina didn't speak on the phone in the time between Adeler drowning and her dying under the train. Nor can Nina have had time to speak to Stig face to face in the time between Adeler's and her own death. Yet Stig claimed to me that Nina was killed because she witnessed Adeler's death. There's only one answer to why he could maintain this. He was a witness himself. It's obvious. We know Nina and Stig were in a relationship. They were together during the night and in the morning. They both saw what happened to Adeler, but the perpetrator only saw Nina and followed her. Stig was killed when he made his presence known to the perpetrator later.'

Rindal shook his head. 'You didn't answer my question. Seeing someone perform an act is quite a different thing from recognising this person's identity. Your theory stands and falls on the question: *How could Stig contact a person he knew nothing about?* He had no name, no address, nothing.'

Gunnarstranda shrugged. 'I don't know how. I only know he must've contacted him. I'm sure that further investigation will provide a satisfactory answer to that question.'

Rindal sat down behind his desk and swung from side to side in his chair. He was thinking.

Lena and Gunnarstranda exchanged a fleeting glance. They had *almost* succeeded in making Rindal turn.

'There are several weaknesses in the theory,' Rindal said. 'Three bodies and various modus operandi. If the perpetrator killed Svein-ung Adeler in an apparent accident, then eliminated Nina Stenshagen in another apparent accident, why the heck would he shoot Stig with an automatic weapon?'

Gunnarstranda didn't reply with an immediate answer. Lena real-ised he didn't have one. In fact, it was possible his theory was wrong.

Gunnarstranda cleared his throat. 'I've asked Schwenke to do an autopsy on Nina.'

'You did *what*? Do you know what that costs? The woman was sliced into bits by the train!'

'You know we found Nina's blood in very different places from the track in the tunnel. So she'd had *major* injuries inflicted *before* the train hit her. It was time to request an autopsy.'

Rindal scowled, but he didn't object.

Gunnarstranda carried on speaking. 'Nina Stenshagen was shot. Schwenke rang me an hour ago. The blood matches the finds in the bomb shelter. Nina used to work for the Metro many years ago. She was familiar with the network inside the tunnels. She might have sneaked down there for warmth and shelter on cold winter nights. The security service ejected her several times, from the loop under the Storting building, they said. On Thursday morning she ran into the tunnel to evade her pursuer. She was heading for the emergency exit when he shot her in the back. He hid the body, and himself, until the trains resumed. Then he arranged the accident. The fact that Nina Stenshagen was shot explains everything. Nina was already dead when she was thrown under the train. I'm going to deliver the bullet to the ballistics lab at Kripos in person.'

After Gunnarstranda stopped talking, silence reigned, like after a thunderstorm. Broken only by the sound of Rindal pensively swivelling from side to side on his chair.

Rindal cleared his throat. 'Two drug addicts shot dead in Oslo's worst junkie milieu tells me this is where we should look for the killer. But have you done anything? No. None of Nina Stenshagen's relatives has been interviewed; no one in Stig Eriksen's circles has been questioned. Not a single one of our informants has been asked if they've noticed a gunman in their midst. Instead of which, you've been walking roughshod all over our MPs.'

Rindal was getting angrier as he spoke. 'The link between the two shootings and Sveinung Adeler is weak – much too weak. I want you to clarify whether there is a link within the next twenty-four hours. And I want concrete, tangible evidence. The statements of dead witnesses don't count. If, after twenty-four hours, you don't have concrete, tangible evidence that would hold up in court, the Adeler case will be downgraded so that we can concentrate on what should be our focus.'

'Forty-eight,' Gunnarstranda said.

'I beg your pardon.'

'You're experienced, you know as well as I do that twenty-four hours is barely time enough to write the report. You can give us forty-eight…'

'Out!' Rindal shouted.

The two of them were already backing towards the door when Rindal yelled: 'Wait! I haven't finished with you yet!' Rindal pointed to Lena with a quivering finger. 'Fine. Forty-eight hours, on one condition. From now on I don't want any more harassment of MPs or any other respectable people, *capisce?*'

✳

Gunnarstranda had left a carrier bag on the corridor floor outside Rindal's door. He grabbed it as they ambled back to their office.

'Been shopping?' Lena asked, relieved to be able to talk about something else.

'It's my turn to cook this evening,' Gunnarstranda said. 'And what do you make on such a cold day? Fish soup, of course. I make it the way my mother used to.'

He lifted the bag and lowered his voice as if he were going to reveal a great secret. 'I've bought a halibut, the head. Everyone knows fish heads give you the most energy. But halibut is best. It's the most expensive fish, of course, but most people don't know the head is the most valuable bit. So I get the head cheap.' He chuckled, with a secretive, triumphant smile on his face. 'A kilo of halibut costs three hundred kroner while the head costs ten. The guy on the fish counter's just happy to get rid of it. A head like this generally weighs a kilo and a half. This one weighs 1.9 kilos. Two kilos of the world's most exclusive fish for ten kroner, Lena. What people don't consider is that the neck comes with the head, and the neck is the best meat on the fish, over half a kilo of fine, white fish, perfect for soup. First of all, I cut the head lengthwise, using a sharp knife. Afterwards I rinse the brain. Then I let the two halves soak in warm, lightly salted water with a dash of vinegar and a good slosh of white wine for an hour. Just soak – not boil. Afterwards it's bursting with energy. You won't find more powerful soup on this earth. Then I thicken it with butter and flour – good butter, mind you, butter from the dairy – and thin it with stock and cream. And I add sliced carrots and leek. Finally, I use the meat from the neck. Sometimes I add bits of other fish, particularly salmon or trout – the meat has a lovely reddish colour which goes well with the carrots and leeks; some mussels and shrimps are not bad, either, but you mustn't boil or soak shellfish for too long – adding shellfish to a soup is an art form in itself. Season with pepper right at the end. This soup's magnificent. It warms you on cold days and is so nutritious that every spoonful tastes like you're eating liquid sunshine and the new spring. A single plate is an evening meal in itself because the halibut and the cream are fat. With this, we drink a little glass of Chablis, Tove and I, or a Riesling. At any rate it has to be a very dry white wine, with a mineral tang. Personally, I prefer a Moselle. I won't tell you the name. There are some secrets I can share, but not all of them. The taste of the wine is so rich in minerals that every swallow is like drinking the essence of slate and steel.'

The door to the stairs opened. Axel Rise came up. He stopped when he saw Gunnarstranda and Lena. He glowered. 'He who whispers, lies,' he said grumpily.

Gunnarstranda walked past him. 'I've just been sharing a precious secret with Lena,' he said, raising the bag in her direction. 'And it'll stay between us, Lena, *capisce?*'

3

The communal fridge in the corridor was packed with milk cartons past their sell-by date and half-full yoghurt beakers. Gunnarstranda cleared a spot on a shelf and put the fish head there. He was excited about making the soup. But there were things he had to do first. Rindal had asked for evidence. So, evidence he would get.

He caught a tram to the quays by the City Hall. The police cordon was still fluttering on the pier close to Akerhus Fortress. It was fraying at the edges here and there.

Where could Nina and Stig have been?

The icy wind picked up over the open sea, cut into his face and tore at the ends of his scarf. He hurried to shelter behind the low office building in the middle of the quay.

This is where it happened.

Gunnarstranda stepped over the police tape and walked to the edge. Adeler could not possibly have slipped on the wet surface. Gunnarstranda could confirm that. Only if Adeler had been smashed out of his brain would he have fallen in. But he hadn't been. Adeler had been sober.

How long had Adeler survived in the water before he was so frozen that he gave up and drowned? A minute, a minute and a half?

Gunnarstranda continued to the end of the pier. Icy fog hung black over the surface of the sea, steam coiled in thick spirals, rising slowly upwards and dissolving into finer mist, pierced with razor-sharp rays of sunshine, which partially coloured the cloud yellow, red and a smouldering hue, as if this wasn't frost mist but waves of soot after the eruption of a volcano.

Gunnarstranda leaned back and established it wasn't ash falling from the sky but snow.

He walked back to the crime scene. Examining his surroundings on the way. Where could the witnesses to the crime have been?

They were both homeless and crept somewhere every night to sleep.

They must have chosen a place that was sheltered from the wind, where they wouldn't be seen and wouldn't be harassed by the police…

Suddenly he saw where – something that wasn't where it should be. A detail on the opposite quay. At the end of City Hall Quay 2 there was an overturned refuse container.

Gunnarstranda walked back and onto the next pier to check.

Yes, indeed, it was a clever little hiding place. The container was made of plastic, had four wheels and was a metre and a half in width and depth. The lid was open and rested against the wall; that was how they had slept in it, sheltered from the snow and wind.

He peered inside. Yes, someone had slept in there. It was lined with cardboard. Human bodies had clearly been here. And he found a ragged sleeping bag. Just one. The other one, it struck him, wasn't here. Stig had taken it with him. It had been in the building in Grønland, in Stig's little den there.

The two of them had spent the nights here in an empty refuse container insulated with cardboard and air. No one was at the end of the quay in winter, no tourists and no police officers.

But then one morning they had been lying there and had watched as Adeler was thrown into the water from the adjacent quay. They had seen him being murdered.

But the perpetrator had only seen Nina. Why?

Perhaps because she was already up?

At any rate she had fled while Stig was still lying in the container.

Afterwards, when Stig found out Nina had been hit by the train, he had understood. Then he was visited by the police and Stig decided to do something with regards to the killer. This decision would have fatal consequences.

The sleeping bag in the container was evidence. If they were lucky the lab would be able to trace DNA from it and compare it with Nina's body. Some evidence then – but there would be more. Gunnarstranda needed forensics officers to secure the finds. He took a roll of tape from his pocket and started cordoning off the site.

4

'Steffen here. Where are you?'

'At home,' Lena said.

'What are you doing?'

Lena opened the glass cabinet over the bench with the phone to her ear. The crystal glasses she had bought on her summer trip to Prague stood in a neat line. She took one down. 'What am I doing?' She went to the fridge and fetched one of the quarter-bottles from the lowest shelf. Read the label. This was decent stuff. Henri de Verlaine champagne. 'What do you think I'm doing? Shaving my intimate parts, aren't I. Isn't that what all your women are doing when you ring?' With the phone to her ear she twisted off the top.

She filled her glass and sipped the precious drops. Brut. Nice.

Steffen chuckled. 'You win, Lena. You're the princess and I'm bewitched.'

Thank you, and the same to you, she thought to herself in the following silence. She had no idea what to say. It was she who was bewitched.

'This is the point at which you ask what I'm doing,' he said.

Lena hunched up one shoulder and held the phone between her head and shoulder while she drank more bubbly. 'I see,' she said. 'What are you doing?'

'I'm standing outside your door.'

The bell rang at that moment.

Lena stood with the phone to her ear. 'I have nothing to offer you,' she said. 'Nothing.'

'That's good. I brought some champagne with me.'

Lena took the empty quarter-bottle, opened the cupboard with the waste bin and threw the bottle in. 'What brand?' she asked.

'Bollinger,' Steffen said. 'The one James Bond drinks. If you feel like a glass I think you'll almost have to open the door.'

✳

Lena nodded off and in the distance heard that *Retrospect* by Bel Canto was still playing. She opened her eyes.

Steffen came out of the bathroom and asked what the time was.

She reached for her watch on the bedside table. 'Two minutes to eleven.'

After he had gone she lay wondering what she felt. Finally she realised that what she felt resembled sadness. It would have been nice if he had stayed a bit longer. Actually he could have stayed overnight.

The CD stopped playing.

She was hungry.

I could have made some supper for us, she thought. *It's boring to cook good food for one person.*

She went into the kitchen. Without switching on the light. Opened the fridge door. A beaker of natural yoghurt beside a carton of semi-skimmed milk she knew had passed its sell-by date. The remains of yesterday's dinner – half a grilled chicken – lay on a plate beside a jar of Dijon mustard. She took out the plate, twisted off a chicken bone and gnawed at it. She was thirsty now. The bottle of champagne on the sitting-room table was still half full. She had put out flutes because the bottle was Steffen's. But she didn't like drinking from such narrow glasses. The edge of the glass touched the tip of your nose and you had to lean right back to get the last drops. She grasped the half-empty bottle and drank straight from it. She sat at the worktop, not wearing a stitch, picked at the chicken with her fingers, licked her fingertips, grabbed the solid neck of the bottle, lifted and drank more.

Steffen should have stayed the night, she thought. We *could have eaten this chicken, not to mention what we could have used the kitchen table for.* She smiled at the thought. Got up and looked outside.

A car was in the car park with its engine running. A black Fiat 500. Was it really such a popular model?

Hesitantly, she turned her back on the window. Grabbed the bottle and went back to bed. She made herself comfortable with the pillow behind her back and put the laptop on the duvet. Found the Christmas music website. Dean Martin singing 'Baby, It's Cold Outside'. He wasn't wrong.

She tried to think about Steffen, but instead her mind was on the car outside. She had seen a black Fiat 500 cabriolet when she visited Aud Helen Vestgård at her house. The same type of car had passed the drive to her garage half an hour later. And now there was a black Fiat 500 idling outside.

Could it be the same car?

Her stomach screamed yes. Her brain said no. They were three or, at most, two different cars.

In the end she couldn't stop herself. She got out of bed. Went into the hall to the cupboard where she kept her binoculars. The laptop on her bed was playing 'Rudolf The Red-Nosed Reindeer' as she went back to the kitchen. She peered out from behind the curtain. The car was still there. It was odd. It was past midnight, and it was at least twenty minutes since she had last looked out.

She adjusted the binoculars. It had a roof, but the car was a cabriolet, yes, the one she had seen twice before.

It was impossible to see into the car. But she could see the registration number. She put the binoculars down. Grabbed a pen from next to the plate of chicken. *Steffen is having a bad influence on me*, she thought, and jotted the number on the back of her hand.

She cast her mind back. Actually she had made a note of the number the first time she saw the car. She had opened her handbag, rummaged around for a pen and an old receipt. But where was it now? Lena went back to the bedroom and searched. It took time. Her bag was full of old receipts. There. She checked it with the number on her hand. A chill ran down her spine. It was the same car.

She stood for a few seconds trying to gather her thoughts, then slowly crept back to the kitchen and pulled the curtain aside. She looked out. It was no longer there.

Wednesday, 16th December

1

Emil Yttergjerde asked if she'd been to a tattooist. They were standing by the drinks machine in the corridor and Lena was slotting in coins.

She showed him her hand. 'Not exactly Chinese calligraphy,' she said distantly and put the bottle of mineral water under her arm. She had been going to ring him, but now he was here she asked if he had managed to get hold of Adeler's home help.

'Pamina? She keeps ringing and asking about the funeral. And she'd like to work for me, too. I try to tell her to stop pushing. She only does undeclared work and I don't want to cause her any problems.'

'Did she have keys to the flat?'

'She's handed them in,' Emil said. 'She cleaned his pad on Wednesday afternoon and left a note to say he was short of washing powder. So she hadn't been able to wash the clothes in the linen basket. She hadn't seen Adeler for over two weeks.'

Lena went back to her office. She called the Vehicle Licensing Authority.

The car that had been idling outside her block of flats the previous night was owned by the rental company Hertz. Five minutes later she found out the car had been rented to a man named Stian Rømer at Oslo Airport on Wednesday, 9th December.

Her gut instinct that insisted it was the same car in all three instances was strengthened. *Rental car.*

The date – 9th December.

But the name, Stian Rømer, meant nothing to her.

Lena put on her coat and left. She headed for Oslo Station and caught the airport express to Gardermoen.

In the arrivals hall she made for the Hertz desk. The guy sitting in front of a computer was an overweight, unshaven young man with a snus lip. His head poked out of a huge puffa jacket. He stank of sweat and was drinking tea from a paper cup.

Lena showed her ID.

The young man had no idea who had taken the Fiat. The agreement had been made online a long time ago, it was always like that. That was the system. The customer came, was given the keys and signed a piece of paper. He didn't know who had given him the keys. Customers delivered the car with a full tank when they had finished. The keys were in the ignition – and customers got on their plane. No hassle.

'Can you get hold of the guy?'

'Why should we want to?' The man extended his snus lip into a grin. His mouth was like a rabbit's. His front teeth were stained with snus tobacco.

Lena sighed. 'Listen to me. I want to get hold of the man who's rented the car, and I know you have the information I need. OK?'

The man blinked nervously. 'All we have is his credit card.'

'Precisely,' Lena said. 'That's exactly what we want. Can you give me the information on the card?'

✳

When she was back at Police HQ, she found a corner for herself and checked the online telephone directory. The name Stian Rømer didn't exist. There was only one Rømer to be found. Her name was Bodil and she lived in Drammen. Lena tapped in the number and asked to speak to Stian.

'Who's speaking?' The hoarse, slightly tremulous voice probably belonged to someone older.

If they were related, Lena thought quickly, this was the mother, aunt or grandmother.

'My name's Lena. Sorry to ring you like this, but I met Stian in Ibiza last summer and I've been searching everywhere for his phone number or address, and now I just had to try this number. Are you related to Stian?'

'What was that? You met Stian where, did you say?'

'Ibiza. My name's Lena. He might've told you. Did he?'

'No.'

'Can I talk to Stian?'

'Stian isn't here.'

'Do you know where he is?'

'Stian's abroad.'

'Oh, no,' Lena exclaimed, genuinely disappointed. 'You don't say. Where?'

'I don't know.'

'I'd really like to talk to him.'

'I'd like to be able to help you, but Stian's abroad and he can't tell me where he is, either. He might've told you when you met that he works for the Intelligence Service, did he?'

'Yes, he did, but … Are you Stian's mother?'

'Yes, I am. Stian has to sign an oath of secrecy and I'm afraid I can't help you. But if you leave your phone number I can say you rang the next time he's here.'

'My battery's running out,' Lena said, thinking on her feet. 'Where does Stian live when he's in Norway?'

'At home, of course, in Schweigaards gate in Oslo. Can I have your number?'

'Get a pencil and paper quickly,' Lena said. 'My battery's going.'

She could hear the woman putting the receiver on the table to get something to write with. Then Lena pressed 'off'.

Immediately afterwards she used the police phone and rang the Intelligence Service's personnel department. She asked for Stian Rømer. They couldn't help her. She was transferred. She had to spell the name, but still didn't get a response. Then she was transferred to another number and someone put her through to someone else.

It took ten minutes to discover that no Stian Rømer worked in the Intelligence Service.

She put down the receiver.

She had seen a car three times. *Yes*, she told herself, *the same car three times is two times too many*. But not being able to locate the man who drove the car didn't have to mean anything. The bluff about a job in the Intelligence Service could be a fib Stian Rømer had told his mother to avoid her badgering him or to impress her.

A man by the name of Stian Rømer had ordered a car at Oslo Airport the day before Adeler was killed. So what?

Lena sat staring into middle distance. She couldn't get the black Fiat out of her head. She had an uneasy feeling in her stomach. There was something about that car. There was something about Stian Rømer.

That was as far as she got. Lena decided to drop the Fiat mystery and concentrate on reading the Pathology Institute reports.

✳

When Lena straightened her back a quarter of an hour later she heard a familiar voice in the corridor.

She stood up and went out. Ingrid Kobro was in conversation with Rindal. She waved to Lena, who leaned against the wall and waited for Ingrid to finish talking.

Ingrid was close on fifty. But she still looked thirty-nine. Dark hair, not a single streak of grey, clear blue eyes and always a wry, knowing smile on her lips. Her glossy hair might seem dyed, but Lena knew the colour was genuine. When Lena started out in the police Ingrid held a protective wing over her. Unfortunately Ingrid had stopped working for the department six months before and had taken up a higher post in PST, the police security service.

Rindal moved on and Ingrid turned to her.

'Long time, no see,' Lena said, and gave Ingrid a hug.

'I'm here with the sole purpose of talking to you,' Ingrid said.

'That's nice,' Lena smiled. Then she noticed Ingrid's serious expression and felt her smile fade. 'Is it business or pleasure?'

'Business,' said Ingrid Kobro, guiding Lena into an office and closing the door behind them. 'Always great to see you as well, Lena,' Ingrid continued in her soft Sørland dialect. She breathed in: 'Down to business.'

Lena was bewildered.

Ingrid sat down and folded her hands in her lap. 'Lena,' Ingrid said in a serious tone. 'Why are you interested in Stian Rømer?'

In Lena's head a bowling ball started rolling. It knocked down the pins with a bang: being transferred from pillar to post at the Intelligence Service and spelling Rømer's name took on meaning. The questions about her name, address and telephone number…

Ingrid's face had puckered in concentration. 'We at Central Office don't want Oslo PD undermining a case we've spent time and resources on.'

Lena noted the choice of words. '*Central Office*'. Ingrid was flagging up her authority.

'Excuse me,' Lena said with a cough. 'I called the personnel department of the Intelligence Service. I can't understand how I could've come anywhere near you or your people.'

Ingrid deliberated before speaking. 'I didn't know that,' she said at length.

Lena had to laugh.

'What is it?' Ingrid asked with the same crooked smile.

'How can you know that I'm interested in Stian Rømer?'

'We've got the guy under surveillance. He arrived in Norway a week ago and rented a car from Gardermoen. You were interested in it too, weren't you?'

This took Lena by surprise. 'What?'

'We've got you on film and we have a recording of you using your official authority to demand information from Rømer's credit card.'

'Have you been spying on me?'

Ingrid shook her head. 'We're interested in Stian Rømer, and we don't want Oslo PD destroying what we've built up.'

Lena told Ingrid about the car she had seen three times, how it was outside her block of flats after midnight, told her about Hertz and Stian's mother, Bodil Rømer. She told Ingrid almost everything. She held back about Sveinung Adeler and Aud Helen Vestgård.

'If Rømer gets wind of the police investigating him, we may lose him,' Ingrid Kobro said with great earnestness and a suspicious furrow in her brow.

'You would've done the same. You're in the kitchen and see a fishy car outside your block, with the engine running. It's there for a long time, till past midnight, and you know you've seen one like it twice before. Then it turns out it's the same one. I got the heebie-jeebies. For some reason the guy must be watching me.'

Ingrid eyed her, still thoughtful.

'Let's take this from the beginning. Where and when did you see it?'

'The first time? Several days ago. Thursday night. I was about to get into my car in Bærum and saw a Fiat 500 with a man inside. The engine wasn't running and there was frost on the windscreen. It was freezing outside. I drove home and as I was turning down into the garage I looked into my rear-view mirror and saw the same car drive past, fifty metres behind me. I mean, why would a strange car be following me? I reckoned it had to be two different cars – but two cabriolets? Same brand, model and colour? It left me with a tingle in my stomach. But then, last night, there was the identical car outside the block where I live. I jotted down the registration number and it turns out to be the car I saw the first time. You can imagine how paranoid I became.'

'What cases are you working on?'

Lena listed the cases. Without quite knowing why, she left the Adeler affair till last: 'And now I'm busy investigating an official who drowned in the harbour by the City Hall. A so-called suspicious death, which looks like murder. I'm trying to find out what happened.'

'It must be one of the cases you're working on,' Ingrid said, regarding her pensively. But then she suddenly changed her opinion, shook her head and said, almost to herself: 'It just doesn't sound like it.'

Lena asked: 'Have you got a photo of Stian Rømer?'

Ingrid hesitated. 'I need to know you'll co-operate.'

'Why wouldn't I?' Lena pointed to the folder under Ingrid's arm. 'If this man's following me I'd like to know what he looks like. Let me see a photo!'

Ingrid Kobro opened the folder and took out a sheet. A black-and-white photo. The man staring out from the picture could have been an extra in a TV crime series. A round head with cropped hair and a sullen, brutal mouth. Lena passed the photo back, and Ingrid tucked it into her folder.

'Let's take this one more time,' she said. 'You've seen a rental car three times. So there are no other reasons for you wanting to find out about Rømer?'

What was this? Lena angled her head in surprise. 'Ingrid?'

They looked each other in the eye. Ingrid lowered her shoulders. 'You know, we're considering legal proceedings against him, on a prevention basis. That's why I wanted to talk to you now. We're at an early, sensitive phase in the process. We can't risk anything getting out. So we're asking PD to lie low. Don't blow his cover.'

'What is it about this guy?'

'I'm afraid I can't comment on that, even if I'd like to.' She went to the door. 'If you see this car again or the man in the photo, get in touch and leave the car and the man to us, OK?'

Lena nodded. 'Fine,' she said without any enthusiasm.

Ingrid left.

✳

Lena sat in the same place, looking at the closed door for quite a while. Ingrid's message had been unambiguous.

But if Ingrid was going to be able to do anything at all she had better locate the car damned quickly.

Lena began to mull over the conversation. PST was interested in Rømer, but could Rømer be interested in her?

What Ingrid had said meant Rømer wasn't necessarily after her. But why had she seen him three times in her vicinity? If this man was spying on her, the question was why.

Might Ingrid be wrong? Perhaps not. But she was definitely holding back.

Lena weighed up the pros and cons. She remembered the sudden chill she had felt the previous night. Her reaction when she realised that the car outside was the same one that she had seen the first time. One of the most unpleasant feelings you can have is to feel unsafe in your own home. Lena would not accept that. She ached to do something about it.

There was one question she hadn't asked Ingrid: *Is my safety in jeopardy?* Why hadn't she asked? Because she knew what Ingrid's answer would be: WEABS – Wandering Eyes And Bullshit. The answer that meant nothing at all. Ingrid had as good as admitted PST didn't know what Rømer's agenda was. So *no one* knew what his agenda was. *No one* knew who he might or might not be a threat to. Accordingly, Ingrid couldn't know if the guy was spying on her or not.

What about steering a middle course? Checking out his flat, just to be on the safe side?

2

An hour later Lena was on her way down Schweigaards gate on foot. If Ingrid was right that Rømer had *no* interest in her, no harm done, she reasoned. But if Ingrid was wrong, finding Rømer's flat was the best thing she could do.

A large part of Schweigaards gate was taken up by the Central

Station and the bus terminal. So Lena concentrated her search on the apartment buildings in Gamlebyen. She went into every single house entrance and studied the lists of names by the doorbells.

After working her way through all the apartment blocks she still hadn't found the name Stian Rømer. That didn't necessarily mean his mother was lying. Lists of occupants weren't always complete. Rømer could be living in one of the apartments without a name tag below.

She trawled through the side streets looking for the car.

It took her another ten minutes to find the black Fiat. It was parked in Østfoldgata. This was as easy as building Kinder Egg toys. The closest apartment building in Schweigaards gate was short of one name on the occupants list.

Lena crossed the street and scanned the façade. Some windows were lit and inviting. Others were dark. The apartment on the third floor had curtains and hooks on the windows. On the floor below, the occupants liked green plants and flowers.

The apartment on the first floor appeared to be empty. The windows were black and inhospitable. Where the Fiat was parked suggested that Stian Rømer would be living close by. She was becoming more confident now. Rømer lived behind the black windows.

She walked back across the street, stepped over the bank of snow and continued towards the apartment building. The front entrance was locked. She looked around. It was now gone eleven in the morning. If there were any PST undercover officers nearby, they were good at hiding.

Lena went for a recce around the block. When she was approaching the building again she found herself walking behind an elderly woman with a stoop. Two thin legs protruded from under her long woollen coat. The ice cleats under her boots scraped and creaked. She struggled to manoeuvre her shopping trolley on the snow and turned into the right entrance – at least for Lena's purposes.

Lena was kindness in person. 'I'll help you,' she said, and grabbed the trolley.

'Oh, thank you,' said the woman, who appeared to be suffering from some kind of rheumatic illness. She removed the cleats with some difficulty, but she was still stooped. Her big blue eyes peeked up at Lena from under the rim of a brown beret. A dewdrop hung from the tip of her long red nose. She rummaged in her pocket and found a tissue. After drying her nose, she took out a bunch of keys.

'Which floor?' Lena asked.

'Second,' the woman said. 'And there's no lift. It's terrible to get old, I can tell you. Enjoy life while you're young.'

Lena took the trolley in her right hand and supported the woman with the other. She was so thin and fragile that Lena was frightened her thin upper arm would break. The woman struggled with the stairs. She concentrated on raising one foot at a time and almost fell against Lena every time she straightened her leg. A sweet smell of alcohol hovered around her.

The trolley was incredibly heavy. How could the woman have imagined she would be able to get up the stairs under her own steam?

They reached the first floor. The glass in the door to the flat there was as dark and uninviting as the windows looking onto the street. It was as though the door in the gloomy stairwell was pulsating. Lena tried not to look.

She could no longer carry the heavy trolley bag and put it down on a step. The woman wasn't happy with that. 'Bottles,' she mumbled and wanted to go back down.

'I'll fetch them later,' Lena said quickly. 'First of all, let's get you up the stairs.'

'Thank you. That's very nice of you,' the woman said. 'Let's rest a little.'

Lena felt uneasy by the black door and didn't want to attract more attention than was necessary. 'Just seven more steps,' she whispered.

'What did you say?'

'Seven steps. Let's go.'

'I've been to the Vinmonopol,' the woman explained, almost tumbling backwards.

Lena half carried her up the last steps, took the bunch of keys from her hand and unlocked the door. The woman was on her way down.

'Come here,' Lena snapped. 'I'll get the bottles.'

'Thank you very much,' the woman said as Lena trundled the trolley through the door. There was a smell of dust and urine in the entrance hall.

The woman stood, as far as she was able, looking up at her. 'Would you like a drop before you go?'

Lena hesitated. Perhaps the woman knew something about the occupant below. On the other hand…

She shook her head and said a polite 'no'. After waiting for the woman to close the door she turned and tiptoed down the stairs.

3

She stopped by the black door on the first floor and thought: *The car that was spying on you is outside. Two plus two are four. Stian Rømer is inside. You know where he lives, the choice is yours now, either file this information and leave or go a step further and try and clarify the facts. What facts?*

Is he really behind this door? And if so, has he got his eye on me?

Anyway, she thought, if he wasn't living here, if the flat was unoccupied, no harm was done.

She raised her hand and pressed the bell.

No going back now.

Slowly she counted in her head. Thirty … fifty.

No reaction.

No footsteps audible inside the door. Not a sound to be heard.

She raised her hand to ring again.

A chain rattled inside and the door was pulled open.

A man wearing green military combat pants stood looking at her. His chest was bare. It was the most muscular chest Lena had ever seen. Delicate muscles flitted across a rugged six-pack. He had the biceps of a weightlifter. This man could have posed for men's underwear had it not been for an ugly white scar running diagonally from his right nipple, over his stomach, to down below the waistband.

But the man had his right arm hidden behind the door.

'Can I help you?' he asked in English.

His face was sun-tanned, his teeth were white and the suggestion of a smile was mocking. The likeness with Ingrid's photo was striking. They kept eye contact and Lena realised at once that Rømer knew who she was.

At first she was unable to say anything. She focused exclusively on the man's right forearm and hand hidden behind the door.

Lena's mouth was dry, but she managed to clear her throat nonetheless. 'Stian Rømer?'

'English please,' he said, flexing his muscles.

Lena frowned, a little confused.

His neck and left shoulder were adorned with a massive tattoo. She stepped back a pace.

'Please,' the man continued, advancing and stretching out the visible arm after her. 'Come in.'

In there? Not likely. Lena was already on her way down the stairs.

The door slammed shut behind her.

How much time did she have? A minute? Two? He would have to put some clothes on.

The front door was locked. She pushed with both hands, but it remained just as closed when she pushed again. My God, what a fool, it was locked. She flicked the lock and when she banged open the door, fooststeps were thundering down the staircase behind her.

Out. Lena ran, through the gate, not looking left or right, chose right, stumbled and slipped on the loose snow, gasped for air and crossed the street, raced into Klostergata and leaned against the wall.

Here, behind the corner of the house, she waited, panting. Her ears were rushing; she could hear her own heartbeat.

Carefully she leaned forwards to see around the corner.

He was standing on the pavement, scouring the area. A soldier dressed in a short, black hooded jacket and green fatigues.

He was holding something in his right hand. It was a gun. Black, heavy, and the man handled it with a natural nonchalance, as though he were a carpenter with a hammer.

Lena held her breath.

The man scanned the street in both directions, then put the gun in his waistband at the back with practised ease.

Lena was paralysed for a couple of seconds. Her legs almost buckled.

Finally she was ready to move. She backed away a few metres, then she turned and carried on, trying to walk calmly, trying to control her breathing, but instinctively increased her tempo. She ran the last metres to the wall by Minnepark and dived into the narrow opening. Peered out.

The man was charging towards the wall.

Lena threw herself around and ran between the rocks in the little park, which was so small, but now seemed enormous with the deep snow that made it so hard to raise her legs. Her back was in agony and she approached the exit on the opposite side much too slowly, not daring to look behind her.

Out.

She ran. Sprinted. Cast a glance over her shoulder. He was behind her. A machine. High knee pumps and black eyes. He was getting closer. She lost her balance, stumbled and regained it again.

Her coat, her long coat, was preventing her legs from stretching out. Lena tore it off as she ran. Jumped over the bank of snow at the side of the road and into the carriageway.

Now, now, now, she thought, and ran ino the middle of the road. Her feet found traction and she picked up speed. *Breathe!* In, out, in, out. Another glance over her shoulder, the distance was the same. At that moment her pursuer slipped on the ice, half fell, then re-found his footing.

The sight gave her renewed strength. *Breathe in, out, in, out.* She swung her arms in time with her knees. She had the right shoes on and was fit. Glanced back again. Got a strand of hair in her eyes. The distance was the same.

A tram came down Oslo gate. Lena ran inside the rails. The tram stopped fifty metres ahead. People poured out onto the platform.

Lena came level. Dived for the nearest door. Gasping for air, the taste of blood in her mouth. She was ready to drop, close to vomiting. She paused to look back.

The man had stopped on the pavement thirty metres away. They had eye contact. He was also gasping for air. Steam was coming from his mouth.

'Are you coming in or not?'

She was startled. It was the tram driver, a man of around fifty with dark hair in a ponytail and a handlebar moustache.

Lena clambered in, her thighs stiff with lactic acid. The tram set off. Stian Rømer didn't move. They held each other's gaze as the tram glided past.

The House in the Forest, Lena thought – the fairy tale about the girl who was told not to enter the house, but did anyway. *Too late for any regrets now,* she told herself. *You got an answer to your questions, even if you escaped only by the skin of your teeth. Nevertheless, you will have to face the music.* She dug in her pocket for her phone and was fumbling to find Ingrid's number when it rang. She read the number on the display. It was Ingrid Kobro's.

Lena pressed her forehead against the window. Of course PST had their undercover officers out and about. Ingrid probably already knew what had happened.

At that moment a man tapped her on the shoulder. Lena sat up straight and looked at him. Hat, scarf, grey beard.

'Lena,' the man said. 'Answer the phone. Ingrid wants to talk to you.' Then he gave her a sly wink and went back to his seat.

4

Lena straightened up and braced herself when the door opened.

Ingrid Kobro was standing in the doorway.

No hug this time. No slanted smile under twinkling eyes. They stared at each other for a few seconds.

'Do you know how much we invest internationally to build up our reliable sources?'

'Ingrid—'

'Hang on! Do you know what risks such people run when they work for us?'

Ingrid's eyes flashed. 'You don't give a damn, do you. You ignored my order and went straight to the flat after we'd agreed you would keep away from anything to do with Rømer. There's a risk now that we've lost Rømer. Most likely all the work we've done on the guy has been for nothing. You see, he drove straight to Gardermoen, handed over the car and checked in on a flight to London.'

London? Lena wondered vacantly. Why would a man first try to kill her and then take the next flight to London?

'Have you considered the consequences?' Straightaway Ingrid Kobro answered her own question: 'No, you haven't.' She continued: 'Should you care whether other people's lives and well-being have been put in jeopardy? No, sir. You've seen a car and what I or others might think about this case doesn't concern you in the slightest.'

Lena glanced up. 'Why…?'

'Lena,' Ingrid Kobro said in the same harsh tone. 'Listen to what I'm saying now and take good note. Rømer and his business come under PST. Rømer's our case and has nothing to do with you or Oslo Police District. The rental car has been returned. He did it an hour after you got on the tram in Gamlebyen. The man who handed in the car and checked in on a flight to London is on the plane at this minute. In other words, the bird has flown. The man who chased after you has left the country. You don't have a problem now. But we do, precisely because he's gone. So I *have* to know what it is you haven't told me.'

Lena was at a loss to know what to say.

Ingrid Kobro grabbed Lena's arm. 'Lena, is there anything else?'

'What else could there be?'

'For example, the real reason you visited the apartment in Gamlebyen.'

Lena straightened up. 'I wanted to know what he was after, and now I know: he wanted me dead.'

Ingrid inhaled deeply. 'Do you think for one tiny second you could try to consider something else apart from yourself?'

'What?'

'I know you're working on a case with Aud Helen Vestgård. Vestgård's an MP. I want to know why you started ringing round after Stian Rømer. Has that rental car any connection with Vestgård? I'm bloody sick of you working against us. If Rømer's spying on an elected member of the Norwegian Parliament you have a duty to inform me.'

Lena's brain raced.

'Tell me right now!' Ingrid said with force. 'Do the car and Rømer have any connection with the case you're working on?'

'The first time,' Lena said, resigned. 'I saw the car the first time I drove from Vestgård's house in Bærum. The car was parked down the street. I noticed because someone was sitting in the car. But he didn't have the engine running. The weather was absolutely arctic. I thought it odd – that the guy should be in the car, freezing. I wrote down the registration number before leaving for home. When I turned down into our garage I saw the car for the second time. In the rear-view mirror as I was turning. It kept going. That was only two sightings though. I reacted the third time, which was at night. I'd gone to bed, then got up to eat some cold chicken and saw the Fiat in the car park. The engine was idling and it had been there for half an hour at least. It was the same registration number that I'd seen the first time. What else could I believe, other than that he was spying on me?'

'Spying on you?' Ingrid sighed loudly.

Lena reacted. 'What possible other explanation was there?'

'Well, let me tell you a bit about Stian Rømer. He's an ex-soldier and runs a company providing so-called international security. This company earns money on everything from protecting oil pipes in the Middle East to protecting ship-owners against pirates in the Gulf of Aden and protecting African leaders from attempts on their lives. Rømer has recruited people here in Norway – Afghanistan war veterans, for example – but the group also consists of misguided mercenaries, former child soldiers from the Congo, even former foreign legionnaires. This group is extreme, let me tell you. PST, that is, those of us in the section for anti-extremism and organised crime, have spent a lot of time and energy on Rømer because he and his henchmen, among many other activities, sell their services to pirates off the coast of Somalia. There's some evidence to suggest that money from this is going to the Al-Shabaab organisation, which in turn finances and runs terrorist activities. And this is just a tiny fraction of Rømer's story. And in comes Lena Stigersand from Oslo Police District, who happens to see the guy in a parked car outside the house belonging to a Norwegian MP. The same MP who has received a threatening letter. Can you now, Lena, tell me what the reason is for your short-circuit? Why would Rømer be after you, of all people; you, an officer in Oslo PD?'

Lena tilted her head. If Rømer was primarily out to damage Vest-gård, and not her, she really had dropped a terrible clanger. But could that be the case? She tried to concentrate. She went through what had happened step by step. She couldn't make Ingrid's version tally with her own experiences. There was more to it. Rømer had known who she was. When she was standing outside his door he had been the wolf opening to Little Red Riding Hood. But the most frustrating part was that talking to Ingrid about this was like banging her head against the wall. Ingrid was caught up in her own hush-hush arrogance: *Keep out. I know best. This is secret.*

'Whatever conspiracies you and PST are cooking up,' Lena said, 'I'm still convinced the man was focused on me as a person. I wasn't some random plain-clothes civil servant ringing at his door. I could read that in his eyes. He knew who I was. Me, Ingrid, he knew *me*. He wanted to get me in his flat. Why? When I retreated he tried to drag me in by force. Why? Hm? When I ran off he followed me. Why did he do that?'

'If you took the number of his rental car when you first saw him, he might've taken yours too,' Ingrid said. 'Perhaps he wanted to find out who you were. That was perhaps why you saw him in the car last night.'

Lena considered that possibility. Could the explanation be so simple? Her brain had doubts, but her gut didn't.

'I don't buy that,' she answered. 'The only reason he didn't shoot me then and there is chance. I'm sure of it. When he first came onto the street he didn't see me. He tucked a gun under his belt *before* he saw me. If he hadn't he would've fired it. I'm sure.'

Silence hung in the air for a few seconds, as though Ingrid was examining what Lena had said to re-assess the content. In the end she shook her head in resignation. 'Lena, what's wrong with you actually? If the target was Vestgård, of course he would've known who you are.'

They eyed each other for a few seconds. Lena wasn't convinced by Ingrid's argument and knew that Ingrid wasn't sure herself.

Nevertheless Ingrid continued in the same angry tone: 'The fact is that Stian Rømer received a visit from you – a police officer – at his flat and has now taken the first plane out of the country. Our initiative against Rømer has probably been for nothing. But you aren't even aware of the mistake you've made!'

The door slammed after her.

Lena stared at the door. What was Ingrid so pissed off about? Ingrid hadn't had a crazy mercenary on her heels. Nor had she lost a winter coat costing four thousand kroner.

Lena slumped onto a chair.

Her reactions slowly percolated through and continued unabated. The sight of the elite, militarily trained gunman tucking his weapon behind his back. The panic that paralysed her brain when she was making her escape with a terminator on her heels. The taste of blood in her mouth and the feeling when the lactic acid kicked in.

Lena knew one thing: she didn't trust Ingrid.

Saying Rømer had returned his rental car was the kind of soothing statement she herself had made to members of the public numerous times. Empty words to calm their nerves, an empty reassurance.

5

On her way home she first popped by Sultan to buy some fruit and vegetables. The cherries looked inviting and she bought a big bag. She reflected at the same time on the strange fact that while the frost was penetrating the ground in the country where she lived, people elsewhere on the globe were harvesting such treasures in the sunshine.

✳

On the radio Alicia Keys sang about New York while Lena cut up the cos lettuce and sliced tomatoes. She got to her feet and turned up the volume. The song made her think about New York.

Immediately she knew what she was going to do in the summer: fly to New York, check in at one of the smaller hotels on Lower East Side, go to hip boutiques, buy a cool hat, sit on a bench in Washington Square, stroll over Brooklyn Bridge in the crowd of people on the boardwalk, stop and take photos of the Manhattan skyline.

She sprinkled pine kernels into the frying pan.

If I'm well.

She stared vacantly into the air. And gave a start when the kernels crackled. Ugh! It didn't matter whether they were done or not. She scattered them over the lettuce leaves, chopped up a cucumber and made a vinaigrette sauce from olive oil, white wine vinegar, pepper and salt. Treated herself to a bit of Dijon mustard and honey as a finish and mixed it all while adding tiny bits of feta cheese.

After eating she found the Alicia Keys song online and downloaded it. Then searched for other tunes and was lost in this world until Steffen rang the doorbell.

*

Now we are starting a relationship, she thought, when she saw how at home he felt in her flat. However, they weren't completely at ease with each other yet.

They were enacting a kind of rehearsed play. They opened the conversation with empty, tentative phrases and sat down beside each other shyly on the sofa. She continued to talk about nothing, asked if he liked Alicia Keys and made sure not to mention Rihanna because she didn't want to enter into any discussion of Sveinung Adeler. He asked her questions in turn – about music, books, films she had seen. They smiled at common references that were made, sat side by side and sought each other without daring to reveal to the other person what they actually wanted, not until his hand felt for hers. From that moment on they didn't say another word. It was only seconds before he drew her into him.

*

Later, when she jumped out of bed, it was to fetch the bag of cherries. She put one in her mouth and crawled back. He took her head between his hands and kissed her. She passed the cherry into his mouth. He chewed and was soon holding a stone between his fingers. 'Where shall I put this?'

'On the bedside table.'

He put the stone down. There was a clatter as a few Kinder Egg models fell to the floor. 'Sorry,' he whispered.

'Doesn't matter,' she said, bit into another cherry and held it between her teeth. Steffen's mouth came closer to hers. He nibbled at the cherry. The juice began to run down her lip and chin. Steffen licked the juice. She ate the rest of the cherry, took the stone and placed it on the bedside table, knocking another model to the floor, and kissed him on the lips.

It became a game. She bit into another cherry and held it. He bit off a side of the cherry. It tickled when he licked the juice.

'Do you like mangoes?' he asked

'Yes.'

'You have no idea what two people can do with a mango.'

Lena giggled and bit into another cherry.

His lips slowly approached hers. Now they both giggled as he bit into the cherry. She chewed the rest, the juice ran. She choked as she breathed in.

The stone followed. And got stuck.

She couldn't breathe! Her lungs wanted air, but her airways were blocked!

Lena rolled out of bed, crawled onto all fours, gasping for air, but none came, just gurgling sounds, and she held her throat.

Steffen crawled alongside her, a concerned expression on his face. 'What's the matter?'

She *had* to have some air *now*! And she needed his help. She got up and banged herself on the back.

'What's the matter?' Steffen repeated, panicky now, and slapped her on the back. 'Does this help?'

It didn't, couldn't he see? *Air. I need air.*

She staggered into the kitchen, smacked both her hands against her diaphragm, but to no effect. Now she could feel a blackout looming in the far recesses of her brain and had to concentrate to retain a focus on what she had to do. She pushed the table against the wall, wobbled back two paces and threw herself against the edge of the table. Nothing happened except that the table banged against the wall and she saw a naked, panic-stricken Steffen standing in the doorway waving his mobile, but she couldn't hear what he was saying. She had to have air and she threw herself against the table again, her diaphragm hit the edge of the table, even harder than the first time.

The stone pinged against the glass of the kitchen clock.

Lena's lungs sucked in oxygen like bellows. She supported herself on the table with her arms and breathed in, out, in and looked up.

Steffen was still in the doorway, looking at her with the same worried eyes. 'What happened?'

'The cherry stone got stuck in my throat,' Lena panted, trying to breathe normally. 'Before we start on the cherries again, I think we should do a little course on life-saving skills.'

She told him to stand behind her and hold her around the waist. She showed him how to fold his hands and press in situations like this. They were close.

It was so quiet in the flat that they could hear the radiator hissing.

'Lena,' Steffen whispered.

'Yes?' she whispered back.

'I want you to drop the Adeler case.'

She opened her eyes. What was that?

'What you told me,' Steffen went on. 'About the guy going after you with the gun.'

'Stian Rømer? Don't worry. He's left the country.'

'Stian? Do you know his name?'

'I'm a detective.'

Steffen stepped back. 'The guy chased after you with a gun!'

'Steffen, walking on the pavements in town is dangerous. An icicle can fall on your head.'

'I mean it,' he said, perfectly serious. 'He could've fired the gun. You could've been shot and killed.'

'I almost snuffed it just now,' Lena said dismissively. 'Killed by a cherry stone.'

He looked at her. 'Are you annoyed?'

She looked back. That was a question she didn't want to be asked by men. It was a question she had taught herself never to answer.

'Sorry,' she said. 'I know you meant well.'

He looked down. He seemed distant. The atmosphere was very different now, charged. 'Are you going to stay over?' she asked and could feel she wanted him to, genuinely.

He shook his head and smiled weakly when he read the disappointment on her face. 'Next time maybe. I have to work this evening.'

Thursday, 17th December

1

She woke up before the alarm clock went off. It was ten minutes to six and she felt as fresh as water from a spring. Enough time to fit in an early-morning ski run on the illuminated piste.

The lights on the track hadn't been switched on yet, but the moon was high and white and the cover of snow shone a bluish grey. Together they gave a few metres' visibility. When she had almost finished the round she sensed a movement between the trees by the car park. She didn't have time to feel fear before she saw a figure leap out.

Lena screamed and threw herself down in the snow.

She lay still listening. Nothing happened.

Slowly she raised her head.

It was a deer. It was standing a metre from the tips of her skis, watching her.

The deer carried on, strutted past with light, creaking steps and was gone, in the darkness.

Then came the next reaction.

The silence that, hitherto, had felt wonderfully liberating suddenly felt threatening. The shimmer of the snow was no longer beautiful but grey and opaque. The snowdrifts and the dark tree trunks were possible hiding places for enemies.

After struggling up onto her skis, she covered the final metres without sensing anything but a fear of the dark and her own heartbeat. She removed her skis and hurried to the car while glancing fearfully in all directions.

When the car had started she forced herself to wait for a minute before moving off. She was back in Minnepark, running helter-skelter for the exit, her long coat preventing her from lengthening her stride. She told herself: *The man has left the country. It was one incident. You mustn't let one incident at work destroy the pleasure of skiing.*

✳

Once in her flat, she headed straight for the shower. Stood for ten minutes under the stream of hot water, reflecting, thinking that the water was not only cleaning her body, it was also purging her mind of unpleasant thoughts. All her imaginings and suspicions swirled down the drain with the soapy water.

In the kitchen she felt like she had just woken up again. She prepared her favourite breakfast: yoghurt with walnuts, slices of mango, banana and apple. The mango was ripe to perfection and the juice went all over her fingers as she cut it up.

Lena was eating her breakfast and reading the yoghurt pot when the telephone rang.

It was Gunnarstranda: 'Have you read today's *Dagens Næringsliv*?'

Lena, the phone held to her ear, was about to open her mouth over a spoonful of food. The spoon quivered in the air. 'No,' she said, prepared for the worst.

'Listen,' Gunnarstranda said. 'I'll read you the front page: "TERRORIST GROUP INFILTRATES OIL FUND". The intro is as follows: "There are many who would like to influence the decisions of the administrators of Norway's biggest war chest. Some are open about it while others sneak through back doors. Today *DN* can reveal that an African terrorist group nurses close ties with members of the parliamentary Finance Committee and employees in the Government Pension Fund Global."'

Lena put down her spoon. Her head buzzed as she formulated the question that had destroyed her appetite.

'What's the journalist's name?'

'Someone called Gjerstad,' Gunnarstranda said. 'Steffen Gjerstad. But I haven't got to the point yet.'

For Lena every word had a resonance and an echo. She pushed the plate away.

'This is photo reportage,' Gunnarstranda said. 'I'm looking at pictures of Sveinung Adeler and Aud Helen Vestgård on a street in Oslo. They're standing and talking to an unknown third person who, the article maintains, lives in Stockholm and is affiliated to the political movement Polisario. They fight for Western Sahara's independence and, according to the newspaper, are regarded as terrorists in some circles. There are pictures of the same three going into a restaurant in Grefsen. The article poses the question, why is a Storting MP – who, conveniently, is also on the Finance Committee – going into a restaurant with a civil servant from the Finance Department and a man with connections to the guerrillas in Western Sahara? And there's an answer as well. Let me read aloud from page five. It's subtitled: "Occupation":

'"The resistance movement Polisario has been agitating for international investors to withdraw their proprietary rights in companies working under the auspices of or in co-operation with Morocco, the occupying power. It is well known that the Government Pension Fund Global has acquired companies that work in this area. *DN* sources confirm that the Oil Fund's Ethics Council is examining certain companies in this portfolio. These investigations were being carried out by Sveinung Adeler – on the right in the photo. Adeler participated on Wednesday, 9th December in a secret meeting with representatives from Polisario and the parliamentary Finance Committee. A few hours after the meeting this same Adeler was found floating in Oslo Harbour. The leader of the police investigation, Lena Stigersand, has made it clear to this newspaper that the police regard the death as suspicious."'

'What?' Lena screamed. She jumped up in alarm.

'I'm looking forward to seeing Rindal's face when he reads this,' Gunnarstranda said.

'Has Vestgård made a comment?'

'Vestgård's declined to comment on the article. Ditto the Finance Committee and the Ethics Council. By the way, there's a nice photo of you here, taken on City Hall Quay.'

Lena looked out of the window. Daylight was slowly making inroads into the December day and she already felt tired, like after a long overtime shift.

The case she was working on had been dragged out of her dusty desk drawers into an arena of camera flashes and shouting and yelling. Actually, though, that didn't bother her.

Steffen had lied.

He had known about the third person at the restaurant that Wednesday night. He had not only known about the guy, he had photos and they had been printed in the newspaper.

'Are you there?'

'Yes,' Lena said. 'I'm just thinking.'

'Then think about this,' Gunnarstranda said. 'The photos in the paper prove there was a third man at the table with Adeler and Vestgård. Now we have photos of the guy. Once again there is proof that Vestgård lied to you. But there's also someone who knows more than we do: the photographer who took the pictures.'

※

After he had hung up, Gunnarstranda lifted the receiver and dialled Rindal's number.

'Gunnarstranda here,' he said when Rindal answered. 'Usually I ask you stupid questions, Rindal, so I'm asking if you've read today's *DN*.' He winked to Emil Yttergjerde and held the receiver away from his ear so that his eardrum wouldn't be damaged by the noise level of Rindal's explosion.

When Rindal paused for breath, Gunnarstranda asked: 'The deadline you set for the Adeler case, does that still apply?'

There was a bang as the receiver was slammed down.

'What was the answer?' Yttergjerde asked. 'Has the deadline been dropped?'

'It has been dropped,' Gunnarstranda said.

2

Lena drove down to the city centre and gazed at the traffic as if she had a plastic filter in front of her eyes. Why did Steffen write the article? Why hadn't he said anything last night? All she could remember now was the puzzled figure waving a phone as she fought to gain her breath. Why had he just stood there?

Her spiral of thoughts grew wider and more paranoid with every turn.

She pulled into a parking space in front of a Spar supermarket. Switched off the engine and remained staring into the distance.

Should she, shouldn't she?

There was no question. She had to.

Her hand on the phone trembled as she tapped in his number.

She dreaded every dialling tone.

'Hi, Lena.'

'You know why I'm ringing, don't you.'

'I have a hunch.'

She said nothing. He was the one who should be talking. He was the one who kept quiet about this last night.

The silence on the line grew, became heavy and awkward. But she wasn't going to break it. Not now.

'I'd been thinking of calling you late last night,' he said at length. 'But the atmosphere was so strange when we parted...'

'You quoted me, Steffen, without permission. What's more the quote was inaccurate. I've never said anything of the kind and you know that.'

He went quiet again.

She waited for him to speak. But he didn't say any more. 'Are you there?' she asked.

'I apologise unreservedly,' he said. 'It was a mistake.'

'You knew all the time about the meeting between the three of them and you said nothing to me?'

'Lena, listen. This is important. I only saw the photos last night. I found out about the third person in the restaurant last night. My source was there on Wednesday, that ninth of December and took photos. Before I saw them I had no reason to believe anything other than that Adeler met Vestgård on his own. I didn't know about a third person, not until late last night. I left you for a meeting with my source. When I was given the photos you were asleep in bed.'

'I'm investigating this case,' she said firmly. 'It's best for everyone if you're more open with me than you're being now.'

There was a silence at the other end.

She closed her eyes. Hating what she was going to say, but she had to: 'You and I cannot continue like this, sorry. Last night was the last time, Steffen.'

Total silence. He said nothing. Was he going to hang up? It was bad enough to break up with a man, but to do it in this way was worse. Why didn't he say anything?

'If it should become necessary to take an official statement from you, I cannot be present,' Lena said, feeling a mixture of sadness and anger growing in her chest.

'Taking a statement? Lena, calm down.'

What a tone! Lena wasn't sad any more, she was furious. 'I don't want to be taken off a case just because you and I slept together, you know.'

In the ensuing silence, she was able to count slowly to five.

'Lena, I don't want things to be like this between us.'

Didn't he understand anything? She had told him it was over!

'We each work in our own worlds,' Steffen persisted doggedly. 'Right now these two worlds are clashing, so we have to be careful what we say. We have to discuss, tidy things up. I don't want my banal job to ruin what we have or indeed any part of my private life. I'm sure you don't either.'

'You and I cannot carry on,' she said. 'And I think you'll realise that if you give it some thought.'

'Don't break up with me over the phone,' he said. 'Give me a chance. Let's meet and have this out.'

'The problem is that you're not open with me,' she said. 'We're not communicating. You write things about me you're not entitled to write. That's no good.'

The phone crackled in the silence.

'Please, Lena. Let's meet and sort this out.'

'Answer me one thing,' she said. 'How could you not inform me?'

'It was late,' Steffen said softly. 'I was under pressure and had a deadline. The paper wanted us to go public. You were in bed asleep. I made a decision. Maybe it was a mistake. All I can do is offer you my apologies. But it's precisely because of situations like this that we have to talk and clear away any obstacles that our work puts in our way.'

'Who took the photos?'

'Don't ask, Lena. He's my deep throat. I can't tell you. If we meet this evening, face to face, we can work out what information we can share.'

She couldn't be bothered with this any more. 'The photographer was there and might be sitting on important information about where Adeler went afterwards. I work for the police. You have to understand that I cannot accept you withholding such information. Bye.'

Immediately after she hung up, the phone rang again. She switched it off.

3

'Things are on the boil here,' Gunnarstranda said as Lena came into the R&R room. 'And all the press are asking to talk to you. They want to know more about Adeler's death.'

Lena hung up her coat. Thinking distractedly that she ought to go and look for the one she lost yesterday.

The phone rang.

Axel Rise, who came through the door at that moment, took the call. He listened, silent and patient. Then handed the receiver to Lena with an inquisitive expression.

She shook her head.

Rise put the receiver back to his ear and said: 'I can put you through to the Press Office.' With which he hung up. '*Verdens Gang*,' he said to the other two, turned round and went out again.

Gunnarstranda watched, then shook his head.

'What's the matter?' Lena asked.

Gunnarstranda opened his palms. 'Can't make that guy out. He seems to clock in and then he's off.'

He turned. 'I suppose it's none of my business though.' He took the newspaper. 'There's something about the timing of these photos,' he said. 'If they were taken on Wednesday night, why have they only come out now?'

Lena didn't want to go into this speculation. Her focus was elsewhere. May as well get it over with, she thought, and braced herself: 'I've spoken to the journalist.'

Gunnarstranda looked up.

'Apparently *Dagens Næringsliv* got the photos last night, but they refuse to release the name of the photographer.'

'It can't be a coincidence that this is coming out now,' Gunnarstranda said. 'Someone's burst the dam and the person who did it must be profiting in some way.'

Lena had no more to add. She went to her own office.

4

She logged on. And googled MacFarrell Ltd. The hits she found told her more or less the same as what Steffen had told her, plus a little more. Mac-Farrell was a huge multi-national concern with many irons in the fire. Phosphate was just one of the concern's investments. One article showed pictures of planned fertiliser production plants. No articles about the shortage of phosphate in the world, no doomsday prophets. Just dry facts, and photos of workers in red overalls and red safety helmets. A smiling man clambering into a big vehicle with immense wheels.

So that's what it looked like, Lena thought, when you depleted the world of its most important resource.

Could the issue be as simple as Steffen had portrayed it? Why would the world go under if it ran out of fertiliser? Hadn't the world lived for several thousand years with natural agriculture, with the use of natural muck from animals or compost from plant fibre? This was basic life-cycle knowledge that children learned at school. Farmers produced food from animals that returned nutrition in the form of manure and where there was insufficient manure they supplemented it with other forms of natural compost.

On the other hand, the fertiliser industry was enormous. One of the biggest producers was the multi-national Yara, previously known as Norsk Hydro. This producer was in turn dependent on a supplier like MacFarrell.

This was also basic school learning: the intensive use of fertiliser made agriculture more efficient, increased capacity and facilitated food production in areas that otherwise wouldn't be able to produce food.

She gave herself time to read Steffen's article thoroughly.

Then she noticed something she hadn't picked up on when Gunnarstranda read her the excerpts on the phone: Steffen didn't write the name of the relevant company. She read the text through again. She was right. MacFarrell Ltd wasn't mentioned in the article.

Steffen's piece suggested a political conspiracy. The paper was saying that a politically suspect foreigner and a democratically elected Norwegian were cooking up some jiggery-pokery with a Norwegian official who might subsequently have been murdered.

She fell into a reverie. Rose to her feet. Took a few steps, walked back. Sat down. Fumbled with the keyboard. Why hadn't Steffen written the name of the company? He was an investigative journalist after all!

She googled the organisation Polisario and skimmed through articles and reference material. The organisation was founded when the Spanish colonists withdrew from Western Sahara in 1973. There was warfare in the 1970s. Morocco held power in the towns while the independence movement controlled the desert and attacked the Moroccan army from bases in Algeria. Since then Morocco – to control the rebels – had built a long wall that divided the country lengthwise.

Most internet sites told the same story: Morocco and Moroccan immigrants plundered Western Sahara's natural resources while the local population was forced to live on barren terrain in poverty.

Lena went onto the CIA's websites and searched for organisations labelled terrorists. She couldn't find the name Polisario and concluded it wasn't on their lists.

She repeated the search in various forms, putting 'Polisario' with 'terrorism', but there were no hits.

Why did Steffen Gjerstad write that *in some circles* the organisation were regarded as terrorists?

No one regarded Polisario as terrorists, it appeared.

If Gunnarstranda was right, she thought, if someone had a particular interest in having these photos published, was Steffen allowing himself to be used?

Lena doubted it. The photos were of general public interest. The journalist who wrote the article knew the MP was lying to the police about her presence at the meeting. Lena had told him that.

So the question was: Was she being used by Steffen?

She ruminated. Regretting the phone conversation. If she and Steffen had met face to face she would have confronted him with this.

Lena turned to scanning the online newspapers. Most had run Adeler's death as the main story. But the articles referred mostly to Steffen's column; the journalists made them their own by adding comments from some opposition Storting MP.

A couple of the newspapers had tried to get comments from Polisario, without success, however.

Lena closed her laptop and got up. She glanced at her watch. Today she would get the results of her test. What would be worse:

talking to the doctors or to Rindal? She dismissed the thought. *That's not how you should be thinking*, she told herself. *This is just a variant of the Birkebeiner. It is a long race with a variety of challenges. But you have to finish.* She went into the corridor and knocked on Rindal's door.

5

She opened the door and went in.

Rindal was sitting behind his desk. He looked up, his eyes dark. 'There's a photo of you in the papers,' he said grumpily.

Lena closed the door behind her. She cleared her throat. 'Apparently the photos at the restaurant were taken by a secret source – an informer.'

Rindal continued to eye her darkly, without speaking.

Lena coughed and continued. 'As the informer was outside the restaurant and took the photos *before* they ate, he might know what happened *after* they ate as well. It may be worth the effort of finding him.'

Rindal's eyes were still cold. 'How do *you* know this?'

She nodded towards the newspaper. 'I know the journalist a bit.'

Rindal lifted his head, like a dog when it scents blood. 'A bit? You know the journalist … a bit?'

'Yes, a bit.' Lena refrained from elaborating.

'How well do you know the guy?'

Lena didn't answer.

'Is he a childhood pal?'

She shook her head.

'Is he a sweethea—?'

She cut him off. 'Don't take this any further than necessary. I've told you I know the guy. Let's move on.'

Rindal watched Lena with a sarcastic smile, as though he could read her mind.

She looked down.

He sighed and shook his head in resignation. 'Have you discussed the whole or parts of the investigation with the journalist?'

'No. The photo of me was taken when we lifted Adeler from the harbour on Thursday morning. Steffen Gjerstad was one of the journalists by the cordon trying to get a comment.'

'Beyond that you haven't discussed this case with Gjerstad?'

'No.'

'He's quoted you. You say the police consider Adeler's death suspicious.'

'I don't remember having expressed anything of the kind. I rang him early today and discussed this point with him. I also asked him who took the photos at Flamingo Bar & Restaurant – to get the name. But Steffen wouldn't tell me. And justified himself by saying he protected his sources.' She coughed again. 'I had the impression this was a special source. He referred to him as a type of deep throat.'

'Steffen, eh?' Rindal said, eyeing her more closely. 'So you're on first-name terms, are you?'

She nodded.

Rindal subjected her to an equally cold stare.

She glared back defiantly. She blinked, but she held his eye.

'I think we should do this by the book,' he said at length and lifted the phone. He rang *Dagens Næringsliv* and asked to speak to the editor concerned.

Rindal introduced himself in authoritative fashion and asked for the name of the person who had taken the photos of Adeler and Vestgård.

Why did he want it?

Rindal sighed condescendingly. Because the police were in the middle of an investigation and apparently the photographer was one of the last people to see Adeler alive.

Rindal listened to the editor's response with his brows knitted in irritation.

He put down the receiver, furious.

'He didn't want to say?'

'Talked about press ethics and protecting their sources. We're investigating murder for Christ's sake!'

'I have a suggestion,' Lena said.

Rindal arched his eyebrows.

'A press conference,' Lena said. 'That'll take some pressure out of the situation.'

Rindal was silent, but he didn't make an objection.

'This case is Steffen Gjerstad's scoop,' Lena said. 'He refers to his source as a kind of deep throat – so he's working in a team with one or several other persons who will necessarily have an agenda. This newspaper doesn't generally cover crime. I don't think they're particularly interested in Adeler's death or our investigation. This is a newspaper that focuses on general politics and specifically the international role of the Oil Fund.'

'If you know the journalist, couldn't you get him to whisper the name of his source in your ear?'

She chose not to answer. Looking him in the eye without saying a word.

Rindal averted his gaze. 'You've suggested a press conference. Why?'

'In this way we reduce the case to what it actually is: a death in the harbour. We need witnesses. Today's coverage has blown up the media's interest in the case. I think we should exploit the media interest instead of fighting it. We now have a unique opportunity to speak to all of Oslo live.'

Rindal angled his head pensively. 'It *could* work ... it might indeed. But are you prepared for it? A press conference is like walking into a minefield. Walk far enough and sooner or later you'll step on a mine and be blown up.'

Lena didn't answer. There was nothing to say.

Rindal got up, tucked the paper under his arm and went to the door.

✳

They found Gunnarstranda, Emil Yttergjerde and Axel Rise in the conference room.

Rindal put the paper in front of Gunnarstranda and without wasting time on pleasantries said: 'I want you to check out this Polisario guy.'

'They've got an office in Stockholm,' Gunnarstranda said.

'Go there. Get the man's statement. Find out when he came to Oslo, how long he was here, ideally why, and what he discussed with the other two. Make sure you find out where he was when Adeler took a dive into the sea.'

He nodded to Lena.

She returned his look, bewildered.

'Your suggestion,' he said with a smile. 'Don't be so modest.'

Everyone looked at her.

Lena cleared her throat once and then again. 'I'm summoning a press conference here at Police HQ this afternoon. The aim is to exploit the current media interest and get in touch with anyone who might've seen Adeler during the night or early morning.'

When she turned to go she looked straight at Rindal.

'After the press conference you and I are going on a trip to the island of Ulvøya,' he said.

'Ulvøya?'

He nodded and left.

Lena glanced at her watch. Suddenly she had a full programme for the day. And therefore very little time. She had an appointment with the doctor in forty minutes.

6

The low sun dazzled her as she drove along the narrow roads between the buildings at Ullevål Hospital, looking for a parking space.

But there wasn't a single gap in the lines of parked vehicles. In the end she couldn't afford to search any longer. She chose the emergency option. Drove half onto the pavement. At least her car wasn't blocking the traffic there.

When she sat down in the waiting room and flicked through the old magazines she tried to focus on the pictures instead of looking at everyone else waiting.

Before long she had gone through the whole pile and sat staring at a recipe revealing the secret behind juicy chicken filets. She read the article through for a second time without managing to take in the content. She put the magazine down. And met the look of a pale, grey-haired man sitting on a chair who had just looked up from a newspaper. Beside him sat an even paler woman wearing sunglasses and a blue turban-like hat.

Lena thought to herself: *I'm strong. I haven't given the lump a thought for a long time. It's a minor issue. I don't belong here. Why isn't anything happening?*

At last a door opened and a plump, uniformed nurse appeared. Several pairs of eyes were directed at her. The secretary nodded at the pale man, who got up and went in.

Lena looked at her watch, annoyed. She should have been in twenty minutes ago. Were there still people waiting for their turn before her?

Ten more minutes dragged by. She considered getting up and asking what was going on when the plump nurse reappeared in the doorway and called Lena's name.

✳

The doctor was an unshaven man with round glasses and a crew cut. His voice was soft and his mouth radiated a warm sensitivity when he spoke.

Lena observed the situation from deep inside herself.

'Are you OK?' the doctor asked. 'Would you like anything to drink or…?'

Lena blinked and fought her way back to reality. 'No, thank you.'

The plump nurse knelt down beside Lena, who closed both eyes and heard her voice from far away:

'It's a shock of course. But you have to view being given radio-therapy so quickly as positive. It means there's a low risk of anything spreading. In your current situation it's important you focus on the positives and prioritise these more than the negatives. I know that's easy to say. But, as the doctor said, the prognosis is very promising.'

A door closed and Lena opened her eyes.

The doctor had gone out. The bastard had gone out! What kind of doctor was that? *Who tells people they have breast cancer and then just goes out?*

Lena stood up. She was giddy, but regained her balance.

The nurse held her hand. They looked at each other.

'I haven't got the time,' Lena said.

'You haven't got the time for what?'

'This. I have a demanding job.'

'Illness never comes at the right time,' the woman said with com-plete understanding. 'But from now on it'll pay to rank your job and everything else lower than the illness. What's most important for you now is to get well.'

'To survive?'

'To get well,' the nurse said in a gentle tone and handed her a pile of papers. 'Everything's new, Lena. There are so many things you'll wonder and want to ask questions about. They'll come when you've recovered from the shock. You'll find many of the answers in this material. But of course you can phone or email us too. Anyway, I'd advise you to come to the information meeting. Then you'll get to know other patients in the same situation, and you can ask as many questions as you want.'

✳

That's my Christmas present this year, Lena thought, as she walked to her car like a somnambulist.

She was a somnambulist. The air was robust and offered resistance. It felt as if she were moving in jelly.

She unlocked the car door and fell rather than sat down.

She cursed aloud when she saw a parking fine tucked under the windscreen wiper.

She opened the door and pulled out the yellow ticket. Tried to tear it into pieces. But it was made of some kind of plastic that you couldn't tear. She threw the fine into the dirty snow and stamped on it.

Finally she spat on the ticket in her fury.

An elderly lady in a dark cape stopped on the pavement and stared at her.

Lena composed herself and got back into the car.

The lady in the cape passed.

Her phone rang. It was on the car seat next to her.

She took it and put it to her ear. 'Yes?' she said hoarsely.

The voice in Lena's ear belonged to her mother. 'Hi, Lena. I'm out buying Christmas presents. You'd better tell me now what you'd like,' her mother said.

Lena didn't have the energy to talk to her. Or with anyone. Not now. 'I'll ring you later, Mum. I've got a lot on my plate just now.'

She hung up and switched off her phone.

She drove slowly out of the hospital complex and turned up to Vestre Aker Church. Her car climbed the hill and Lena registered that there were no other vehicles by the entrance. She stopped and looked at the treetops stretching bare branches up to the sky. Actually, though, she saw nothing. She thought nothing. When the cold began to creep into the car, she opened the door and got out.

The snow between the graves was an unsullied white. The dirt from the traffic and the exhaust fumes didn't reach as far as here.

A narrow path had been ploughed down the hill to the gate at the bottom by Blindernveien. She ambled down. Stepped over a pile of cleared snow and waded up to the middle of her calves in the snow between the gravestones, which protruded from the white blanket like crooked hats. You could almost imagine they had been garnished with cream.

She knelt down in front of the red-granite gravestone. Closed her eyes and evoked the image of her father – the way she wanted to remember him.

She knelt down on the snow with her back to the street.

She waited. What was she waiting for? A miracle?

She closed her eyes again and listened to the sounds around her: the laughter of children playing in the nursery outside the fence, the dull drone of traffic, the bang of a window as it was shut. The vague rumble of a plane that passed overhead, high, high in the sky. She heard some people talking in low voices on the snow-free path nearer the church.

The moisture from the snow was soaking through the knees of her jeans. She was wet, but she didn't feel it.

She didn't have a handkerchief with her, or any tissues. She used her hands, ran her fingers over both cheeks in a vain attempt to wipe away her tears. Took a deep breath and got up.

At that moment there was a loud bang right behind her. She sank to her knees

Glass shattered.

She rotated one hundred and eighty degrees.

A black Mercedes had wrapped itself around a lamppost in Blindernveien. Smoke was coming from the bonnet of the car.

Lena reacted as if on autopilot. She was already on her way to the fence. Jumped over it and landed in the snow. She was racing towards the car when the door on the driver's side of the wreck creaked open.

Lena came to an abrupt halt, fearing the worst.

The edge of the door hit the road. The hinges must have gone.

A shoe and a trouser leg appeared in the doorway.

Another shoe and another trouser leg.

A young man manoeuvred his way out of the car – apparently completely unhurt. The man was wearing a blue blazer and light-blue jeans.

He stood brushing down his jacket and jeans. Then he cast a resigned look at Lena and said: 'An E-Class Mercedes and the air-cushion fails in a crash. You can't believe it, can you. I'm going to take this up with the dealer.'

Lena just looked at him, speechless.

The man really was unhurt. He smiled sheepishly. 'Slippery today,' he mumbled and looked up. 'The weather's milder. That's why.' He lifted both palms as though he was weighing the air. 'Think it's going to snow.'

This must be a sign, Lena thought, breathing in deeply. It felt like she was inhaling new strength.

She fumbled in her pocket for her phone. Tapped in the number. 'It's me, Lena.'

'Your job,' her mother said. 'Sometimes I don't understand how you can stand it.'

'You were wondering about a Christmas present,' Lena said, turning in through the gate to the cemetery and starting to walk up the hill to where her car was. 'I haven't managed to give it much thought yet. But I was thinking of popping by one evening. We have to plan a little.'

'I quite fancy baking a *kransekake*,' Lena's mother said. 'I finished the *sandkaker* yesterday.'

'*Krumkaker*?'

'Two boxes full.'

'*Gorokaker*?'

'Done them, too.'

'*Serinakaker*?'

'I've baked them, and *Mor Monsen kaker*. But I thought I'd hold back on the doughnuts until the twenty-third.'

'Hm,' said Lena, unlocking the car door. 'So all that's missing is in fact a *kransekake*.'

7

Before he left for Stockholm, Gunnarstranda wanted to revisit the Metro crime scene. To avoid the din in the tunnel he rang Torleif Mork to requisition a man to unlock the emergency exit from the outside and switch on the light.

A youngish guy in padded overalls was waiting at the traffic lights in Grønlandsleiret. Gunnarstranda promised he would close the door after him and went into the bomb shelter alone. Now the electricity was working. The SOC officers had chalked a circle around the blood stain where Nina Stenshagen had been shot.

He stopped and examined the blood stain.

The neon tube above his head buzzed. He looked up. The cable shone white where it had been repaired. Someone had definitely torn down the cable and shorted the circuit. The 'someone' was very probably the gunman.

They both had and didn't have pictures of him. The CCTV footage showed a dark, erect figure walking with his head down and his hands deep inside his jacket pockets. Strolling along, his face hidden under the edge of a hood. What Gunnarstranda knew was that Nina had entered a train at Jernbanetorget Station at 06:20. On the film you could see a figure in red slip in through the door while the man with the hood went through the door behind a second later.

Gunnarstranda had been to the ops room and fetched the pictures from Karl Johans gate. They had some of Nina, but none of her pursuer.

What kind of person was this guy who had managed to follow someone while evading all the CCTV cameras?

The guy must have had some past familiarity with these cameras. He knew where they were and how to avoid them. This person had drowned Sveinung Adeler. This man had killed Adeler with intent and, despite the fact that he was armed, disguised the murder as an accident. He had disguised the murder of Nina as an accident too. But he hadn't managed to do the same with Stig Eriksen.

The sharpest pictures were of the platform in Tøyen. An athletic man wearing a short jacket with a hood covering his head. Hands in his pockets. Presumably he was holding a weapon as he walked. He was planning to kill the poor, terrified woman in front of him. When Nina jumps down onto the track he follows without a break in his stride. Single-minded to the nth degree. Then the chase through the tunnel, running on the track, jumping away and squeezing back against the wall as a train whistles through. It is dark in the tunnel. The only sources of light are a few luminous green exit signs. When she flees up the stairs to the emergency exit he is right behind her. They are both out of breath. Nina gropes her way through the darkness. He listens for her breath, sees her floundering shadow along the wall. He shoots. The sound must have been like an explosion in the bomb shelter, a long, resounding echo. He doesn't hear her fall.

The man shot Nina before she pushed open the door. He shot Nina with the same weapon that had killed Stig Eriksen. So he was the type who *didn't* get rid of the weapon after a murder. Why not? What did that say about him as a person?

There was something military about a man who kept his own weapon. Killers on the street acted differently. They shot their victim with a stolen weapon and immediately disposed of it.

Gunnarstranda walked towards the stairs leading down to the tunnel, where a train roared through. He tried to imagine the scene. Nina groping in the darkness, up the stairs and on towards the emergency exit. The man rushing up behind her, raising the gun and firing.

After Nina falls the man finds himself in a dilemma: should he leave her and head for the door, or…?

If the body is found here, shot, the police will raise the alarm and study the Metro's surveillance cameras. So he isn't sure if the cameras have caught his face or not. For that reason he chooses to hide the body.

That must have been his intention. Hide the dead body first and then leave the scene. But then the lights are switched on.

Gunnarstranda visualises it: the man towering over the body and suddenly finding himself and the victim bathed in light.

This is a new situation. He must realise what is happening. An alarm has gone off and the search team are on the way. Another argument for getting out. But no. The man has a cool head, he sticks to the plan, hides the body under the ventilation pipe, pulls out the light cable and shorts the lights in the bomb shelter. In the darkness he wriggles under the large ventilation pipe and pulls up the ladder to hide.

He lies still and hears the search team come, sees the beams from their head torches sweep along the walls. He listens to what they say and waits until he is alone again. By now he knows how to solve this dilemma once and for all: by throwing the body in front of the first passing train.

The perfect murder – almost.

He didn't know or perhaps he didn't think that the emergency exit door would trigger an alarm that would reveal his presence. Nonetheless, the perpetrator was a confident, coldly calculating person with no sympathy for his victim, a person who was not held back by doubt or conscience. A psychopath.

Gunnarstranda crouched down and studied the rust-red stain. He wouldn't get any further in here.

8

Lena changed into her uniform with ten minutes to go. By then she had already written three cheat sheets. It was important to know what to say, not to stammer and stutter. Afterwards she found Rindal, who seemed to be in a good mood. His shirt front bulged like a swallow's chest, he cast an eye down himself with a smile on his lips and threw a few air punches to ensure his cuff links would shoot out from under his jacket sleeves and reveal their presence.

'Where's your jacket?' he asked.

'My mother says blue suits me better than black,' Lena said, brushing a strand of hair off her uniform shirt. 'It matches my eye-shadow.'

Rindal smiled again. 'You do the talking,' he said. 'And don't say anything you can't back up.'

They walked side by side down the corridor. Heels click-clacking on the floor.

Like on a TV programme, it occurred to Lena, casting a glance at herself in the glass pane beside an office door. She ruffled her hair and double-checked until she was happy with what she looked like.

They took the stairs down. As soon as they turned into the corridor, the flashes started going off.

Ram full.

Lena worked her way to the table with the microphones. She scanned the assembled crowd. Steffen was nowhere to be seen.

She scoured the faces, craned her neck to see the faces of the people standing partially hidden behind others.

The conclusion was simple: no Steffen.

Rindal cleared his throat and signalled.

Lena took the microphone and welcomed everyone.

An overweight journalist with a mane of wavy blond hair put up his hand. Lena ignored him. She read from her notes:

'On the morning of Thursday, the tenth of December, at 08:11, the police received a message that a person had been seen floating in the harbour between City Hall Quay 1 and City Hall Quay 2. The caller was the captain of a Nesodden ferry. The ambulance service arrived on the scene at 08:16. The man was pronounced dead. The Pathology Institute has since confirmed the cause of death was drowning and death occurred at some point between 05:00 and 06:00 on Thursday morning. The victim was identified by the police as Sveinung Adeler, thirty-one years of age and a resident of Oslo. It was a very cold night, the minimum temperature was twenty-five degrees below zero, and the deceased man was found wearing thin clothes. The temperature of the water was around freezing point. In such conditions the critical body-cooling time will be very short – one to two minutes. As no witnesses to the incident have come forward, we will continue to investigate the case to clarify the circumstances surrounding the death. In this regard the police would be interested to talk to anyone who might have seen anything around the time Adeler fell from the quay, which was at some point between five and six o'clock on the morning of the tenth of December. We would like to talk to anyone who was in the vicinity of City Hall Quay, Aker Brygge or the square outside the City Hall during this time. We would also like to talk to anyone who was with the deceased or observed him earlier in the evening or night.'

She glanced at her watch. 'We have allowed a few minutes for questions. I believe *Dagbladet* is first.'

'You just described Adeler's death as an incident. In *Dagens Næringsliv* you're quoted as saying Adeler's death is regarded as suspicious.'

'Whatever appears in *Dagens Næringsliv* is *Dagens Næringsliv's* responsibility,' Lena said. 'Is anyone from *Dagens Næringsliv* present?' She scanned the audience.

All heads turned, but no one came forward.

Several hands went up. The *Dagbladet* journalist stood up. 'You didn't answer the question. Adeler's death – is it regarded as suspicious or not?'

'The job of the police is to determine what actually happened,' Lena said. 'I think TV2 is next.' She nodded to a blonde woman in her early twenties, who then stood up with a microphone by her mouth.

'*Dagens Næringsliv* suggested Adeler's death might be connected to the Norwegian Oil Fund's investments in Western Sahara? What is the police reaction to this?'

'The police are investigating the circumstances surrounding a death. Our work consists in clarifying what actually happened on Thursday morning. We don't concern ourselves with Adeler's employment or any speculation linked to his area of expertise.'

A disgruntled chunter ran through the assembled media ranks.

Lena raised her voice. 'The police mandate is to determine Adeler's movements on the night of the ninth and tenth of December in such a way that we can explain how he could end up in the sea and drown. Once that is done, the police will draw their conclusions. Therefore the police need information from the general public. Anyone who knows anything about Adeler's movements on Thursday night, please come forward.'

She nodded to the *Aftenposten* delegate. 'Yes?'

'What comment can the police make on the news that Sveinung Adeler was in the company of Aud Helen Vestgård and a political extremist before he died?'

'Adeler was in contact with many people before he died. That's our comment.'

The journalists were beginning to shout over one another.

Lena straightened the microphone and asked for silence. 'Adeler had dinner at the Flamingo Bar & Restaurant in Grefsen on Wednesday evening. Witnesses have said he left the restaurant at 23:00. The police are interested in Adeler's movements from this moment on until he drowned and we need all the assistance the general public can give. Our information line is open around the clock. *Dagsavisen*, please.'

'Adeler worked for the Government Pension Fund Global. What is the police comment?'

'We have no comment to make.'

'Does this mean the police consider the *Dagens Næringsliv* revelations untrue?'

'We know it's true that Adeler was at a dinner until eleven pm. Adeler drowned between five and six am. As I have said, the police require assistance from the general public on this matter.'

Several of the audience shouted out.

Lena nodded to a journalist with the *VG* logo on his chest.

'Have the police interviewed Aud Helen Vestgård in this case?'

Lena said: 'The police have interviewed all the relevant witnesses in this case.'

Lena looked across the audience.

Steffen was still nowhere to be seen.

Rindal looked at her with raised eyebrows. She shook her head. They started packing their papers.

'Thank you for attending,' she said into the microphone.

'Excuse me,' said the journalist from *Verdens Gang*. 'We have more questions.'

She followed Rindal. They had to plough a way out.

✳

Twenty minutes later she and Rindal were driving out of the centre in Rindal's silver-grey Mercedes.

Lena had sat in the passenger seat still wearing her uniform. It was rush hour and cars were advancing at a snail's pace.

Should she, shouldn't she? If she contacted him he might misunderstand. On the other hand, she needed to know. Lena decided to grasp the nettle.

She wrote a text and made it impersonal. And sent it to Steffen:

No sign of DN at police press conf???

She put the phone on her lap. Seven whole minutes passed before the phone vibrated. Message from Steffen:

We don't cover criminal cases. But I miss you! Give me a chance. Let's meet face to face – at my place tonight at 9. Tidy up, clarify, you set the agenda, promise, what do you say?

Lena looked out of the car window, to the west. High, high up, delicate clouds tinged magenta red by the setting sun were drawing a veil over the sky.

She ought to have gone straight home after work. She needed to find literature about cancer, radiotherapy and chemotherapy. She should be informing herself about what she would have to go through. She should have told her mother she had the same illness her dad died from. But she didn't have the energy.

She closed her eyes and knew things couldn't go on like this. She *had* to tell her mother about the cancer. She *had* to tell Gunnarstranda and the others at work. If she was going to give Steffen the chance he asked for, she would *have* to tell him, too.

What she was actually longing for was a state of mind where she didn't have to think about anything. And these days Steffen was the only person who had managed to transport her there.

You fool! Don't forget what he did to you!

Yes, you, you stupid woman!

Have I actually been using the man as a kind of euphoria-producing drug? she asked herself.

No. She opened her eyes to think about something else. The sun was low and dazzling. Soon it would turn and start making the days lighter, but there wouldn't be any normal daylight until well into February. Where would she be then? Behind a folding screen in a hospital corridor? Or hiding in a flat behind blinds, trying on wigs?

They were approaching the Ulvøya turn-off.

If I meet him this evening I can push him for the source, find out who took the photos, she mused, and weighed the phone in her hand. Finally, she tapped in the following text, which she sent.

OK.

9

There were two big cars in the drive of the immense detached house with a view over Oslo Fjord. A black Audi A6 beside a silver Lexus. Two free spaces beside these. Not a bad drive, Lena thought, as Rindal parked.

'Now I know where to park when I go swimming in the summer,' she said.

Rindal remained as reticent as he had been during the whole journey.

The sign on the door was made of brushed brass: IRGENS.

They were expected, the door opened before Rindal could ring the bell. The man who opened it was in his seventies. He was wearing a checked, dark-brown tweed suit with a waistcoat and a watch chain over his stomach. This gave him a slightly aristocratic, British appearance, which was emphasised by the cool gaze that came from under bushy eyebrows and a haystack of thick, grey hair.

Irgens shook hands with Rindal and nodded briefly to Lena. A deep, half-moon bag under each of his grey, watery eyes reinforced the arrogance of the man's gaze.

He surveyed them in silence as they hung up their coats.

Afterwards he held open the door to a hexagonal office where every wall was clad with shelving.

In a dark leather armchair sat Aud Helen Vestgård, dressed for the occasion in a tightly fitting sombre dress and black high-heeled boots.

She leaned forwards and gave Rindal her hand, with an accompanying smile, then leaned back and nodded in a measured way to Lena.

'Please take a seat,' Irgens said, stretching an arm towards the suite where Vestgård was already ensconced.

They sat down. The chairs were upholstered in leather and creaked with every movement they made.

Rindal finally took the trouble to explain to Lena who the man with the owl eyes was: 'Herr Irgens is fru Vestgård's and herr Råholt's lawyer and business manager.'

'Aud Helen would like to make a statement,' Irgens said.

The MP was reduced to a schoolgirl – she was nodding like a teenage swot towards the teacher's desk. 'Shall I do it now?' she asked, batting her big blue eyes at the lawyer.

Irgens explained that for the sake of form he had asked Aud Helen to write down her statement and that Rindal would be given a copy after she had read it out.

Lena was impressed, both by the lawyer's authority and ability to ignore her completely.

Aud Helen Vestgård stretched an arm to the shelving and took down two sheets of paper that had been resting on some books. She cleared her throat, then began to read in a limpid voice:

"'I, the undersigned, Aud Helen Vestgård, met Sveinung Adeler and Asim Shamoun at an unofficial engagement on Wednesday, the ninth of December at 20:30.

Asim Shamoun is the father of my eldest daughter, Sara.'"

Vestgård looked up from her papers and went from one face to the next as if to check their reactions before clearing her throat and continuing:

"'Asim Shamoun is the local representative in Scandinavia of the Polisario organisation. He lives in Stockholm. He and I met for the first time in Paris in 1988, when we were both studying at the Sorbonne. Our child, Sara, was born in 1989. Asim Sharmoum is passionate about his country and the rights of his people. The reason for our meeting on the ninth of December of this year was that Asim had been approached earlier this autumn by the Government Pension Fund Global's Ethics Council via Sveinung Adeler with regard to a company operating in the occupied areas of his homeland, Western Sahara.

Asim and Sveinung Adeler had exchanged letters regarding the matter. Since then there had been some developments and Asim thought it would be useful to pass on information about these and changing conditions in his home country. Sveinung Adeler, however, hadn't answered his many letters. Asim rang me at the end of November and asked me to talk to Sveinung to persuade him to meet Polisario. I tried to explain to Asim that Adeler probably wasn't answering his letters because he had all the information he required. I explained the procedures to Asim and that there would be no point meeting Adeler, who was only a case officer on the Ethics Council and had absolutely no political influence.

But Asim thought it was his right on behalf of Polisario to inform the Oil Fund's Ethics Council about all the relevant information regarding the relevant company's activities in Western Sahara as well as Morocco's occupation of the country. He insisted on my arranging a meeting with Adeler and he rang me several times about this. In the end, I succumbed. I contacted Sveinung Adeler at the beginning of December.

Sveinung concluded that a meeting with Asim could be construed as standard research and agreed to the dinner.

Asim landed at Oslo Airport on Monday, the seventh of December. He was picked up by Sara and stayed at my house with my family from the Monday to Thursday, the tenth of December. He spent Tuesday and most of Wednesday with Sara.

Asim and I met Sveinung Adeler at the Flamingo Bar & Reataurant on Wednesday, the ninth of December at 20:30. In this way Sveinung had a lutefisk dinner before Christmas while helping me out with a problem. Asim had an opportunity to inform him about his country. It was a win/win situation for everyone. Adeler came well prepared. It became apparent in the conversation over the meal that Sveinung was already familiar with the information that Asim had. He was also able to tell Asim that he would make a comprehensive presentation to his employer, the Ethics Council, who would make their recommendations on a completely independent basis.

Asim and I left Adeler at 23:00. We took a taxi home. Sveinung was going somewhere else and turned down our offer of a lift.

When we left him he was standing outside the entrance of the restaurant. He had assured us he would take the first taxi that came along.'"

Aud Helen Vestgård's voice gave way. Her eyes were shiny and she had to clear her throat several times for her voice to carry:

"'Unfortunately Sveinung had an accident during the course of the night and drowned. I thought it was terribly sad to receive the news of his death. At the same time it is a fact that this accident occurred many hours after our meeting. Asim travelled home to Sweden on Thursday morning, before we knew anything about the accident.

I found out about it on Thursday afternoon. My husband, Frikk Råholt, called me and told me the news. By then the name of the drowned man had been made public in some online newspapers. My husband and I discussed the situation. We arrived at the conclusion that we wouldn't subject either Asim, my daughter Sara or myself to unnecessary media attention because of this case. We considered there was no point in dragging my or Asim's name into the police investigation. It was our opinion that this exposure would only result in gossip and unfortunate political speculation, so there was no point. Since then it has transpired this was *a misjudgement, which I am the first to deplore. The consequence of my low profile with regard to the police and press was speculation and that led the police, to an unnecessary degree, to waste resources on fruitless work. I am the first to regret this as well.*

That said, it is an incontrovertible fact that neither Asim nor I had any contact with Sveinung Adeler after 23:00 on Wednesday, the ninth of December. Asim and I took the taxi home. He stayed overnight with my family, and my husband, Frikk, drove him to Oslo Airport the following morning.'"

Vestgård lowered her papers.

Lena and Rindal exchanged glances.

Rindal folded his hands and laid them on his knees. 'Think how much easier this would've been if you'd told all of this to the police the first time we visited you,' he said.

Irgens coughed.

Rindal took the sheet of paper Vestgård passed him. 'Thank you anyway,' he mumbled.

Vestgård, pensive, took a deep breath. 'There was so much going on. Asim's a very committed patriot. If you ask me, the most important thing for him was to meet Sveinung and ensure the information got through.' She opened the face of her palms. 'It's a cultural thing. Oral and written communication have different weights in our culture and his.'

Lena glanced at the others. She supposed that Vestgård demeaning herself to include her in the discussion had to be interpreted in a positive light.

'You were photographed by an as yet unidentified person' Lena said. 'Did you see anyone with a camera inside or outside the restaurant?'

'No. But I would assume many of the guests had a phone with a camera. Lots of photos were probably taken, but don't ask me to give a description of anyone. I didn't notice any cameras.'

'What unfortunate political speculation did you fear?'

'What do you mean?'

'You say Adeler considered this meeting as standard research. Then you say you lied in your statement because you and your husband feared political speculation – what speculation?'

Vestgård hesitated. She gave a heavy sigh and turned to face Irgens.

'Today's newspaper coverage is probably a good enough answer,' said the man with the owl eyes.

'Today's newspaper coverage is today's newspaper coverage,' Lena said. 'Aud Helen Vestgård is sitting here, but do I take it she won't answer the question?'

A silence hung in the air. Irgens stared at Lena with stern eyes. Vestgård's lips quivered with fury.

Lena decided to tighten the vice: 'Adeler's death was no accident,' she said.

No one said anything. If a strand of hair had loosened itself from Lena's curls, she was sure they would have heard it. She looked up at Rindal, who stared back coldly. But he didn't stop her.

'The police have forensic evidence that the drowning was murder. For investigation reasons this information was not released to the general public. But I'm sure you understand that it's of the utmost importance that you tell us all you know about his movements…'

'I've told you everything,' Vestgård interrupted angrily. 'For God's sake that ought to be enough.'

For some strange reason it's me against the rest of the world in this room, Lena thought. 'Does the name Stian Rømer mean anything to you?' she asked.

Vestgård frowned as though she were thinking and then shook her head.

Irgens interrupted at that point and turned to Rindal: 'You have the statement. Any more questions?'

Lena watched Vestgård, who evaded her gaze.

How was Lena to interpret this body language? Did the name Stian Rømer mean anything to this woman or didn't it?

It was impossible to say.

Lena said: 'You've lied to the police twice. Why should we believe you this time?'

Vestgård didn't answer. She sat looking Lena in the eye for a long time, then slowly turned her head to Irgens.

The lawyer took Rindal's hand and squeezed it. 'Are you happy now?'

Lena was annoyed. 'I just asked a question.'

Irgens ignored her. 'Aud Helen's statement is of course entirely confidential,' he said to Rindal. 'It has been made exclusively to the senior officers leading the investigation to clarify any unfortunate details. There has been some non-disclosure, yes. But you're intelligent people. The tabloids have already labelled the child's father a terrorist. You appreciate what a strain this is already for the child. You also appreciate what unfortunate speculation will ensue if this information about paternity or the relationship between Shamoun and Aud Helen reaches the public. We are relying on your discretion.'

Irgens stood up and went to the door. He opened it and stood aside. The audience was over.

10

Rindal was silent behind the wheel on their way back. As he turned into Mosseveien to head towards the city centre Lena could wait no longer and broke the silence. 'Who is that guy actually?'

'Irgens goes way back,' Rindal said. 'He's an institution.'

Once again they fell into silence.

Lena decided she would drop the lawyer. There were other topics she would rather pursue.

'I just can't get it to tally,' she said at length. 'Why would Vestgård lie to me twice just because she was young and wild in the eighties and had a child with an African? What was she risking by telling me that? It's much worse to lie to the police than it is to confess she's had a child out of wedlock!'

Rindal said nothing. He just stared in front of him.

'Why was it so bloody important for Shamoun to meet Adeler?'

'You heard why. He wanted to have some influence. It was Adeler's job to listen to people like Shamoun. Incidentally, I couldn't care less why the woman lied,' Rindal said. 'And nor should you. This meeting was initiated by the top boss. The fact that Irgens had Vestgård come to his house and condescended to open his door to you and me means Vestgård isn't lying any more. You can bet your ass on that.'

Lena looked out. It was dark already.

This time Rindal broke the silence. 'Stian Rømer – what was that about?'

'His name came up.'

Rindal pulled in and stopped. He turned in his seat and looked at her. 'Wrong answer, Lena. The name didn't come up. You dug it up. Do you think I'm a complete idiot? Lena, listen to me. Aud Helen Vestgård is involved in Polisario through this Asim Shamoun, whom she can't escape because the guy's the father of her child. What's more, the police interest in Stian Rømer is hush-hush. Our job is to find a gunman. We'll do that; you and I and Gunnarstranda will do that because it's our job. And our job has nothing to do with the Secret Services, do you understand? Have you got that straight?'

'When Ingrid Kobro briefed you about Stian Rømer, did she tell you the guy ran after me with a gun?'

'Of course. But he isn't after you any more.'

'Nina Stenshagen and Stig Eriksen were shot and killed,' Lena said. 'Stian Rømer's the nearest I've been to a gun – after we fished Adeler out of the harbour.'

Rindal breathed in before continuing in a low voice. 'This job's like being a bullfighter. Think *corrida*, Lena. It's a fight. But to win the fight you have to pass, to feint and sense the right moment. Charging over and killing everything in your path is a tactic you should leave to the bull. Let the bull try to gore you, let the bull charge forwards, you perform a pass and wait for the moment with your sword because you'll win. Actually I have this imagery from Gunnarstranda,' Rindal grinned. 'You can play many a good tune

on an old fiddle, isn't that what they say? Anyway. We'll crack this
case. We'll win. We'll feint, Lena. So let's leave Stian Rømer to the
Secret Services – at least as long as he's out of the country. You and
I can rely on Ingrid Kobro, for the time being. Anything else isn't
worthy of a matador.'

Rindal handed her the statement he had been given by Vestgård.

'What shall I do with this?' Lena asked.

'This is evidence. File it away. You're leading the investigation.'

Lena took the two sheets.

'What about the guys in the team? Shouldn't they be informed?'

'Gunnarstranda, Rise and Yttergjerde,' said Rindal, detailing the
team. 'I'll ring each and every one of them.'

11

The first thing Lena did when she was back at Police HQ was to file
Vestgård's statement. First of all she categorised the statement with
a stamp: CONFIDENTIAL in big blue letters on each side. Now it
was official.

Afterwards she looked at her watch. She had several hours to kill.
She drove to the apartment in Vogts gate.

❋

It was the second time Lena had unlocked Adeler's letter box. Bills,
unsolicited advertising leaflets and a parcel from amazon.com, which
appeared to contain a DVD. No personal letters. Not so much as a
Christmas card.

The seal she had put across the door was untouched.

She broke the seal and went in.

She switched on the hall light, closed the door behind her and
surveyed the flat. It was as quiet as a mausoleum.

Now Lena went to work, systematically opening drawers and

examining their contents, object by object. She took out clothes from cabinets and went through trouser and jacket pockets, took out all the trainers and returned them. The laundry bin was a woven basket. She removed the lid and emptied it. Two pairs of jeans. Three track suits, a number of pairs of boxer shorts, two pairs of long johns and a little pile of socks. She went through everything, item by item, checking pockets.

She found nothing.

But what was she looking for? Mostly she was looking for Sveinung Adeler. She visualised the tall, fair-haired man he must have been, sitting on the sofa watching TV, getting up and going to the kitchenette to get some ... sweets?

She opened the kitchen drawers, no sweets. So Adeler was not the kind of person to have a stock of chili nuts or goodies to munch while watching a film. He had been a fitness junkie with an iron will.

The Sveinung Adeler Lena visualised was also a tidiness junkie – a person of punctilious habits; someone who didn't leave notes everywhere and didn't save old newspapers; someone who put everything in its place, who spent time and energy on keeping the place neat.

Such characteristics are often carefully thought through, Lena reflected. Many such pedants have an annoying effect on others and their fastidiousness is commented on. Tidiness freaks will tend to justify their sense of order by pointing to their efficiency and the results they achieve. But this absence of a personal touch in such a private space as a flat could go one of two ways, she reasoned, it might either appear frightening or it was a symptom of vulnerability.

Lena concluded that Sveinung Adeler lived and operated on at least two fundamentally different levels. He had a job during the day and he had a home without the tiniest trace of his job. In his flat there were no notes, circulars, documents or books that revealed what this guy did for a living. Not even a payslip.

Sveinung Adeler trained, he did the Birkebeiner. Where were his skis?

He had a storage room, thought Lena, a cellar room for skis, poles and boxes full of old diplomas, Asterix magazines and discarded computer games. *But*, she reminded herself, *before I look there I have to go through everything here with a fine-tooth comb*.

In the bedroom she opened the drawer in the bedside table next to the double bed. Three glossy magazines. One copy of *Sports Illustrated* and two copies of *Playboy*.

Lena flicked through the pages with glossy photos of women in corsets, stockings and stiletto heels reclining on sheepskins in front of fires.

She put the magazines back and looked under the bed. No shoebox of old love letters or pictures of barrack life during military service, nothing.

She went into the sitting room. Surveyed the wall of films. Carefully pulled out the odd DVD box, all of which were Hollywood's version of reality: muscular men running through streets or throwing themselves from rooftops with guns in their hands.

She went to the window and looked out onto a shopping mall. That's where reality was, she thought, watching customers trudging along the pavements behind lines of parked cars. An elderly man in a long winter coat and an unfashionable hat schlepping two bulging carrier bags had to rest and put down the bags. He carried on, met a bank of cleared snow and managed with some difficulty to get over it, first with one bag, then he went back for the other.

Lena turned her back on the window. She sat down on the leather sofa and stared at the widescreen TV. Lifted the remote and switched it on.

A head appeared, a CNN news anchor.

Lena switched it off. Would she really have to leave this flat without discovering one single tiny secret?

The most revealing side of sticklers for tidiness is what they tidy away. She looked at the kitchenette. The somewhat rotten smell of rubbish told her there was a bin bag under the worktop.

Lena got up and found a half-full bag in the cupboard under the sink.

She emptied the contents onto the worktop.

Disgusting coffee grounds and the stinking leftovers of food, packaging and two ballpoint pen tops.

Lena poked through the rubbish with a fork from the kitchen drawer and found some scrunched-up paper. Most of it was advertising. But between the colourful leaflets there shone a corner of something white: a folded envelope. It was addressed to Sveinung Adeler, but there was no stamp.

To find a private letter in this clinically impersonal abode made her hands tremble.

She fumbled as she opened the envelope. Inside was a small, folded note. A short message written in blue ink:

Got your message, but couldn't reach you on the phone. Wednesday after 11 pm is fine. Look forward to seeing you.

L

Lena clenched her fist in triumph. This was a lead – a concrete lead.

The person who had written this note might be a girlfriend, someone his parents knew nothing about.

Or was she a date? Or maybe just a good friend?

Where was the line between a friend and a girlfriend?

Would a good friend have written '*Look forward to seeing you*'? Would a good friend have *looked forward* to meeting Sveinung Adeler at eleven at night?

First Adeler goes to a work dinner. Then he says goodbye to work and duty.

The mysterious L had to be Adeler's date, but what kind of date?

Lena re-read the note: '*Got your message*'. The choice of words suggested they had met several times before.

The three people had parted outside the restaurant in Grefsen. The taxi pulled up beside them. Adeler turned down the offer of a lift. He was going on a date with the mysterious L.

Vestgård had no idea about Adeler's arrangement, so Adeler couldn't have said anything – but might that mean his relationship with the unknown L was secret? For all Lena knew, L might be an acquaintance from his home patch of Jølster. If so, the Chief of Police in Jølster would be able to find out.

Lena remembered the reports sent from Jølster. Sveinung Adeler's family had made no mention of any girlfriend. Nor had they listed anyone whose name started with an L.

Lena tried to imagine Adeler after a good dinner, late at night, wanting to take a taxi alone because he was going to see L, who was *looking forward* to seeing him.

If the mysterious L was a kind of girlfriend, it was, to put it mildly, strange that she hadn't contacted the police. Adeler was supposed to meet her after eleven and ended up drowning before day had dawned.

This mysterious L must have something to hide.

What if L had some dangerous friends?

Who has dangerous friends?

Could L be a prostitute?

No, hardly likely. Adeler had two thousand two hundred kroner in his pockets when he was found. He had withdrawn three thousand from a cashpoint the same day. So Adeler's expenses in the course of the evening had been eight hundred, give or take, depending on how much cash he'd had before the withdrawal. The dinner had been reasonably priced; they hadn't drunk much. According to the woman who served them Adeler had paid his share of the bill and he had done so in cash.

Presumably Adeler hadn't bought any sex during the night. In all probability the mysterious L was not a prostitute.

Lena read the message again: *Got your message, but couldn't reach you on the phone…*

Lena had contacted Telenor and asked for a print-out of the activity on Adeler's mobile phone. She still didn't have it. High time she reminded them. She looked at her watch. She had an engagement and needed to get home.

12

Lena reckoned it would take her about twenty minutes to drive from home and through the town. She planned to leave so that she would arrive around ten minutes late.

The car was freezing cold as she got in. She let the engine idle, wriggled out and scraped the ice from the windscreen. She had to lean over the bonnet and got snow and road salt on her trousers. With a handful of clean snow she rubbed off the salt stain. The cold soon penetrated through her clothes. Shivering, she got back in behind the wheel, turned the heater on full and set off.

Was it wrong to give in to Steffen, to meet him so that they could 'discuss'? She had no idea. All she knew was that if they found any common ground she would have to tell him, loud and clear, that she had cancer. What would happen then? Would he be afraid? Would he beat a retreat? Would he think – *I don't want to be involved with a sick woman!*?

Fine. Then it was clear. Nothing more to discuss. They would go their separate ways. It had been nice for as long as it had lasted. So long. Farewell.

Or would he react in the opposite way?

What if he did? Would that be alright or not? What did she actually want?

Wrong, she thought at once. *You mustn't expect anything. You have no right to expect specific reactions. He has his own life to lead and must be allowed to react in his own way. You and he…*

She braked for the red lights and turned the heater down. Unzipped her jacket.

What have I got myself into with this man?

How many times had they met? First, a nice evening. Then, next morning, she is misquoted in the newspaper. When she says adios he immediately offers an apology and says they have to talk, disentangle their private lives from work.

He was dead right about that. They each had their own jobs, but they had become entangled because of Sveinung Adeler.

She gave a start when the car behind her hooted. The lights had changed to green. The car leapt forwards when she let out the clutch and moved off.

He was the one who had asked to meet to sort out their differences, to tidy up the grey zone between the relationship and work. *That* had to be the top priority now. Define the circles they moved in: this much is job, this much is shared…

In which case, she thought, slightly dejected, this was *not* the right moment to tell Steffen about the tumour.

But if it wasn't, when was?

If, if, if!

Admit it! You've finished with a guy over the phone and now you're running back into his arms.

We've known each other … how long? I've had my life turned upside down in that time, but have I the right to involve him in it?

Would it be right to include illness in the upcoming conversation? To be kind of asking for sympathy? To lay it on the line: *Listen up, I'm ill, I might die in a year or two, what do you say? Are you going to stick it out with me or are you going to do a runner?*

Wouldn't it be equally inhuman not to tell him about the illness? *So what shall I do?*

She was reminded of what the nurse had said: 'Illness never comes at the right time'.

She spotted a gap in the line of cars on the opposite side of Hegdehaugsveien, parked, her mind elsewhere, and sat for a few minutes thinking before she got out. They had never met at Steffen's. She had never seen how he lived, his private world.

*

When she rang the bell on the door it was opened at once. She went inside, feeling a little embarrassed. They stood for a few silent seconds checking each other out. *He's embarrassed too*, she thought.

On the wall by the entrance there was a 1950s film poster. Cary

Grant and Ingrid Bergman. And the film title: *Notorious*. The poster was framed, but there were creases and marks to suggest it had been folded. In fact, it looked like the genuine article.

'Is that an original?' she asked, hanging up her jacket and looking around. Warm colours, two big hooks for outdoor clothes, a shelf for shoes on the floor.

He nodded. 'You're late,' he said.

'I had to work,' she said. 'Top-secret stuff. Mustn't tell outsiders what I'm working on. Professional ethics, you know.'

He took the jibes with downcast eyes. It couldn't be helped. It felt wonderful to say what she felt.

She kicked off her boots.

'What are you staring at?' she said.

'You. You look great. You are a—'

She pressed her forefinger against his lips. 'Don't say any more. If you exaggerate I'll stop believing you.'

He removed her hand. Pulled her close to him.

She gently pushed him away. 'Now you're going a bit too fast.'

He smiled.

It was contagious. She smiled back. 'I thought I was setting the agenda.'

He splayed his hands.

'I have to ask you something,' she said, going into the sitting room. It was spacious with a broad white sofa down one wall. There were posters with pictures of old film stars above the sofa. Bogart, Lauren Bacall, Rita Hayworth, more attractive men and glamorous women whose names she didn't know.

'Do you collect them?'

'*Collect* may be going a bit too far. I think some old film posters have style.'

He had set a table in the kitchenette. Pink prawns in a large bowl on the table. White bread, lemon and a green bottle of Riesling. White serviettes, even lit candles.

She stepped closer to the glass-framed posters. There were titles like *The Strawberry Blonde*, *The Devil Thumbs a Ride*, *Kiss Tomorrow Goodbye*.

She turned to him. 'I've got a question for you and I want an honest answer. Do you truly believe, upon mature reflection, that members of the parliamentary Finance Committee are conspiring with a foreign resistance movement to use a low-ranking official to manipulate the Oil Fund?'

She gave him a broad smile. It was her gesture to him, an invitation to laugh together, to smile away the seriousness of the situation and extinguish the strange antagonism that lay smouldering in some intangible place between them. The question was intended to clear the area they had to chisel out for each other – the relationship between work and private life.

But Steffen didn't smile back.

She wanted him in a light, humorous mood. 'I suppose you realise this conclusion would make for a juicy debate?'

'That's not how it works,' he answered sombrely. 'You're police and I'm a journalist. We do different things. We have different angles on the same topic. We printed the photos because they were in the public interest. Why? Well, because Vestgård was present at the dinner. The Ethics Council talking to Polisario is not in the slightest bit dramatic. Nor when it happens over a meal. But when the meeting is set up and organised by Aud Helen Vestgård you have to question to what extent a low-ranking official is working in a neutral, unprejudiced capacity, simply because Vestgård is not just anyone. She has status. She has authority. It's *obvious* that this meeting between the three of them is in the public interest.'

'I don't want a quarrel with you,' she said, 'But there is one thing to say. I went onto the CIA's homepages and Polisario is not on any lists of terrorist organisations.'

Steffen pulled an irritated grimace. 'That's not the point,' he said.

'But *you* claim they're terrorists.'

He dismissed her argument with an angry flick of his hand. 'The photos carry the article. And they prove that any work Adeler did with regard to Western Sahara is worthless!' Steffen raised his index finger and wagged it to emphasise every word. 'If the Ethics Council or the Oil Fund have made decisions based on Adeler's work with Western Sahara the decisions *have* to be reversed. We live in a country with a free press. Officials working for the Ethics Council are supposed to be neutral. They're not supposed to be pandering to one side of a disputed territory and taking up a position according to what Norwegian politicians say they should!'

Lena interrupted his flow. 'How can you know this? You have no idea what they talked about!'

'And what do you know?'

'Do you know what they talked about at the meeting?'

'I told you. I have a source. My deep throat knows what was said at the meeting. We don't publish the photos for fun, you know!'

'Is Vestgård your source?'

'Are you crazy? Of course she isn't.'

'What was said at the meeting?'

'I can't tell you that now.'

So that was how he sorted out a relationship. She shook her head and sighed.

'Vestgård lied to the police,' Steffen persisted. 'The one person who knows about that is *you*. The photos we published prove that a Norwegian MP is lying. Why is she lying? There's only one explanation. She has a private agenda with regard to the Government Pension Fund Global and Polisario. It's the duty of the press to bring such matters to public attention. Or do you think I should keep my mouth shut? Should the press lie down, crawl and meow just because Vestgård's an MP?'

'The press shouldn't lie down,' she said, 'but it does have a duty to quote its sources correctly.'

He smiled disarmingly. 'I apologise for that. I have done already.'

Lena was once again amazed at how quickly Steffen's mood could change.

However, she simply didn't believe in Steffen's alleged scoop. She had greater faith in Vestgård's version. Lena would have liked to tell Steffen he was on a wild-goose chase. She could have told him there was no secret alliance between Vestgård and Polisario, that the connection between them was about two students who fell in love and a pregnancy in Paris slightly more than twenty years ago. But Lena was unable to do that. She had sworn an oath of confidentiality.

Here we are, she thought, *together and apart. He keeps his secrets and I keep mine.*

There was a lengthy silence. When she raised her head she looked into his open face. 'You're still here,' he said warily.

She gave a smile of resignation.

'Shall we eat?'

She glanced across at the table, the bowl of prawns and the wine. Deep down, she knew it would be a mistake to sit down at the table. It would be a mistake to stay here any longer. A mistake to go to bed afterwards. A big mistake, she thought, watching him move towards the table and open the bottle. She sat still and watched him pour, watched him take both glasses and pass her one.

'*Skål*,' he said softly. 'To us.'

Lena closed both eyes and took a sip from the glass.

✳

It was night. The light from the streetlamps outside cast a yellowish-grey gleam over the room.

Lena lay in Steffen's broad bed looking at the floorboards. They ran parallel along the floor and tapered slightly near the wall. She imagined they continued behind the wall and tapered again until they met at a fixed point far away.

Lena let her eyes wander across the wall. Focused on the door. There was a light on in the room behind.

The door handle moved.

The door opened, slowly.

A little girl stood in the doorway. She had plaits and was wearing a tattered dress. Her tights were twisted round her thin legs. The girl beckoned furiously for Lena to get out of bed. Lena glanced at Steffen. He was fast asleep. She got up carefully and swung her feet to the floor. Pulled on her jumper, which hung over the chair, and followed the girl, who was already out of the door. Lena moved quickly down the stairs. It was cold under her bare feet. The cold went up her bare legs. The girl was always half a staircase ahead. The door slammed shut as they ran out. It was freezing cold outside. Lena told the girl to wait, but she just kept running, waving her arms and shouting that Lena had to hurry. A bit further down the dark street an open gateway shone. There was an orange, glowing light inside, as though it were on fire. The girl disappeared. Lena stopped. She didn't want to go on, didn't want to go into the reddish glow. She called that she wasn't going in. But her cries were drowned by church bells peeling. Then a shadow leaned over her. She screamed.

And woke up.

She was looking straight into Steffen's face. 'What's the matter?' she asked, befuddled.

He just looked at her in confusion. 'I can hear something ringing,' he said sleepily.

Then she heard the sound. An alarm! A shrill, piercing sound rent the air.

'I can smell burning,' Steffen said.

Immediately Lena was awake. She jumped out of bed. Pulled on her underwear, tights and jumper.

He was still in bed, calmly staring up at her.

'That's a smoke detector,' she said. 'An alarm.' She put on the rest of her clothes and opened the door a fraction.

The sound was coming from the staircase outside the flat. There was a stronger smell of fire in the sitting room. She ran through the room, into the hallway, and unlocked the door.

People were thundering down the stairs. The smoke detectors were getting louder and grey smoke poured in through the door opening. At that moment another smoke detector went off. It was above her head. The noise was ear-splitting.

She slammed the door shut. Turned to Steffen. He was wearing trousers and a vest and holding his ears. 'Fire,' she shouted.

Steffen hobbled around putting on his shoes and socks.

'We've got to get out,' Lena said.

'How? There's no balcony.' He pulled a jumper over his head. Went to the window and looked out onto the street.

She pulled on her boots and jacket. It was cold outside, but outside was where she was going. Lena opened the front door. Running feet crashed down the staircase, which was pitch black. Smoke immediately billowed into the flat. 'Come on,' said Lena, grabbing his hand.

Friday, 18th December

1

Gunnarstranda always woke up early when he stayed in a hotel.

It was five o'clock in the morning and the noisy air-conditioning was on. He knew he wouldn't be able to go back to sleep.

He looked at his alarm clock on the bedside table. Switched off the alarm. He thought about Tove.

At that moment the phone rang.

'I was thinking about you,' Tove said. 'So I thought you would be thinking about me and it wasn't too early to ring.'

'You're right. I was,' he said.

'How's the weather in Stockholm?'

'Haven't managed to see yet, but I would guess it's like yesterday. Cold.'

'How was the visit to Polisario?'

'In fact, the trip's been a waste of time. Asim Shamoun hadn't seen anyone with a camera outside the restaurant. This paparazzi guy must've concealed himself well.'

Tove roared with laughter at his resigned tone. She could never understand how people could regard a flight abroad as failed if you had access to a duty-free shop at the airport. 'Have you had a nice time then?'

Gunnarstranda sat up and swung his feet to the floor.

'Asim Shamoun's a passionate man, an enthusiastic reader of newspapers. He gets so caught up by an article or an item that he stands up and paces around the room, takes a pair of scissors, cuts out the extract and puts it somewhere for safekeeping. Then he turns the page, reads a book review and becomes as enthusiastic as before, cuts out what he's read and puts notes in his pocket. While he and I were talking he went through what he'd read and cut out while waiting for me. Five pieces of paper. So I sit watching the guy thinking, what does he do with all this paper? I ask him. And he says: "I keep them". Do you understand? No archive or filing system. Presumably he puts everything in a cardboard box or in the rubbish bin. The last note's forgotten as soon as the next one's been cut out. The guy's a dreamer. Today will bring a new enthusiasm. Perhaps he's up now, walking around his room. He picks up the scissors and cuts, finds some old paper in his pocket, which he throws away, then reads on and exclaims: "Would you listen to that! What eloquence! Listen to what the man has written!"' Gunnarstranda grinned.

'Reminds me of Torstein, my ex-husband,' Tove said.

'Similar,' Gunnarstranda said. 'Asim Shamoun's a well-meaning, nice, innocuous man.'

'When are you coming home?'

'This afternoon. He's insisted on driving me to the airport.'

'Did you find out what you wanted?'

'Yes indeed. But what a waste of time coming to Sweden. I could've just rung the guy.'

2

A big fire engine with a ladder blocked the pavement. The compressor in the vehicle droned. Three powerful searchlights cut through the darkness and cast a yellow light over the scene, making it seem unreal.

A firefighter wearing a mask trudged through the door and into the artificial yellow light.

A smoke diver, Lena thought, shivering in the cold air and stifling a yawn. She had no idea how long it had been since she stumbled out of the very same door.

The smoke diver tore off his mask and collected the residents around him.

Lena moved away from the wall and joined the circle. The man had a scar on his top lip, Lena noticed. A harelip. His face reminded her of something. She scanned her memory to no avail.

He announced that they could return to their flats now.

It was a sleepy group of people who slowly ambled back into the block. An aged woman with a fur coat over her nightie stood apathetically staring into the distance. One of the firefighters took her arm and led her back in. A young couple had their arms wrapped around each other. An elderly man wearing a coat over his striped pyjamas hadn't heard the announcement and asked what was happening.

Steffen and the smoke diver with the harelip came over. 'He says the build-up of smoke was caused by someone having lit some old rags in a zinc bucket at the bottom of the cellar stairs,' Steffen said.

Lena was unspeakably tired and pulled her jacket tighter around her.

'That would never have caused an actual fire,' the smoke diver assured them and continued on his way to the immense fire engine. The man clambered into the driver's cab. The compressor stopped at once.

She turned to Steffen. The previous night she had been in agonies about what to tell him. She hadn't mentioned or hinted at the tumour once. They had barely spoken. She had slept maybe two or three hours. It seemed unreal watching firemen joking and laughing as they handled heavy machinery, gas masks and protective equipment.

'I'm going to work,' Steffen said. 'For me this is a story.'

Lena yawned. She felt most like going back to bed. But she took his point. Journalists can't report on world events from their bedrooms.

'Shall I drive you?' she asked, motioning to her car parked by the pavement.

'Don't even think about it,' he said. 'I'm off now. I'll think up a few well-formulated sentences on the tram.'

She nodded.

He cleared his throat. 'What's the time?'

She automatically pulled up the sleeve of her jacket. No watch. 'It's on your bedside table,' she said.

He put his hand in his pocket and brought out a key. 'Here. While you're up there take a shower, have some breakfast and put the key in the letter box when you leave.'

She took the key. And watched the figure hurry away beneath the streetlamps without so much as a backward glance.

✳

The engine roared as the fire vehicle drove off. She turned to the block of flats. The searchlights were gone. The darkness of the night was back. People had returned to their flats. The front door was wide open. A small child with plaits ran in and up the stairs. Lena smiled and followed. The child was like the girl in her dream.

It felt odd to be on her own, going to unlock the door to Steffen's flat. She walked up the stairs slowly. The windows in the stairwell were open to ensure proper ventilation. Nonetheless, a smell of smoke still lingered inside the walls. There was total silence. You wouldn't believe the residents of this block had just been dragged from their beds.

It was quiet, like when you duck your head under water and hold your breath, that kind of quiet.

She swung around the landing and looked straight at the door to Steffen's flat.

She stopped.

The door was ajar.

She had one foot on the landing and one on the first step. Craned her neck. The door really was unlocked, with a gap of a few centimetres.

But hadn't she slammed the door shut after them as they raced out … how long ago? An hour?

She couldn't remember, only the panic and the haste.

She walked slowly up the last steps. Concentrated and tried to recap what had happened:

The murky staircase. She remembered that. The darkness and the thick smoke; the fear she shared with the other residents dashing out of the building.

Why had the stairs been in total darkness? The person who set fire to the rags must have switched off the light. Now a dim ceiling lamp lit the landing.

She had run out of the flat first. Of course. Steffen had followed her. He must have forgotten to shut the door.

But how could he have done?

They were on their way out of what they supposed was a fire. Draughts allow fires to spread. How could they have forgotten to close the door?

Ah, the crew of firefighters. They had a master key. They must have been in to check everything was alright.

Lena relaxed. At that moment the silence was broken by running feet on the floor above. It must have been the girl with the plaits.

The sound broke the oppressive atmosphere. Lena lifted her right hand and pushed the door open to its full extent.

She walked into the hall. She was dressed. It was six o'clock in the morning. The car was outside. It would be best to get her watch and then drive home, have a shower and a bite to eat before going to work.

She placed her foot on the threshold, but stiffened when she heard a sound.

Someone was inside, in the sitting room.

Lena stood still and breathed through her open mouth.

Someone had simulated a fire. The residents ran out. And now there was *someone* in Steffen's flat, someone who didn't belong here.

The glass over the film poster reflected parts of the sitting room. Above the face of Ingrid Bergman, who was looking at Cary Grant with bedroom eyes, she could see the sitting-room window, the sofa…

The glass frame that held the film poster reflected the blind spot behind the door. She could clearly make out a shadow in the reflection.

But the shadow wasn't human. It was a lampshade. Lena breathed out and went in.

She continued into Steffen's bedroom. No smoke had seeped in here. The room smelt of sleep.

She took her watch and walked to the door, fastening the strap. The situation was reminiscent of something, but what? She went on into the sitting room. And looked up.

She read the title of the nearest poster: *Kiss Tomorrow Goodbye*.

A second later she was lying on the floor with an icy pain in her head. She saw the man's shadow in the glass frame. She rolled over onto her stomach. The very next moment she was being pressed into the floor. She screamed as he pulled her up by the hair and forced a knee into her back. At that moment she registered a nauseating taste in her nose and mouth. She saw Humphrey Bogart laughing. His smiling mouth stayed the same size as his head shrank. It became smaller and smaller and finally merged into the black darkness.

3

Out of the speakers came Arab music. Flute laments accompanied a man's voice that sang with a pronounced vibrato. Asim Shamoun's shoulders swung in time with the music. With one hand on the wheel and his eyes firmly on the traffic he turned the music up a little higher. The drums came in. He flicked the fingers of his left hand. Sang along with the refrain.

Gunnarstranda looked out at the bare trees whizzing past. A couple of kilometres away the tower at Arlanda Airport stood out. A plane was on its way in to land, its tail low. The wheels were out as if to break its fall.

In a way it was sad to say goodbye. Gunnarstranda liked the man at the wheel. Asim Shamoun was open and generous. The day before he had been almost angry when Gunnarstranda insisted on paying for dinner himself, and now he had personally driven the Norwegian policeman from Södermalm to Arlanda to make sure he left OK.

'Just one thing,' Gunnarstranda said as Shamoun came to a halt outside the departure terminal.

Shamoun raised both eyebrows and switched off the CD player.

'Did Adeler – the official – know you're the father of Aud Helen's daughter?'

Shamoun laughed good-naturedly.

Gunnarstranda, who had spent the whole of the previous day in this man's company, knew the laughter was a front and he probably wouldn't answer. 'Come on,' Gunnarstranda said. 'Aud Helen arranged this meeting for you. The official must've been given an explanation as to why she was bothering to mediate, to organise the meeting?'

'Aud Helen asked me not to mention Sara,' Shamoun answered at length.

'She asked you to keep the relationship between you and your daughter quiet? Why?'

Asim Shamoun shrugged. 'It wasn't relevant. We weren't going to discuss private relationships at the meeting. It was to be exclusively about MacFarrell, my homeland and the occupation.'

'But she must've flagged up a reason to the official? From what I gather, you'd been trying to get a meeting with Adeler for ages and had been told "no" time and time again. Then Aud Helen comes onto the scene. She must've said something to him to make him change his mind?'

Shamoun shrugged again. This, clearly, was not something he was comfortable with.

'What was Aud Helen's explanation for how she'd been able to arrange this meeting?'

'Why do you ask?'

'I don't know,' Gunnarstranda admitted openly. He didn't want to talk about the gut instinct he was feeling right now.

'She told me to say she and I had met at the Norwegian Embassy in Stockholm when she was on the Standing Committee for Foreign Affairs – and that was how we had got to know each other.'

Gunnarstranda pondered. He couldn't understand why Vestgård would be so furtive, and he could read in Shamoun's eyes that the man was uneasy about this as well.

'Is she ashamed that you're the father of Sara?'

'No.' Shamoun shook his head and held both hands up in defence. 'I don't think so. Sara's over twenty now, and that thought has never struck me – never.'

'But it's not common knowledge in Norway that you're Sara's father, is it?'

'No; why would it be? Aud Helen is a free western woman. She has two daughters from different men. I'm one of them, but I belong to Aud Helen's distant past…'

Gunnarstranda continued to ponder. He couldn't make this fit. 'Sorry,' he said again, 'but can you imagine *any* reason at all why she didn't want Adeler to know the two of you had a past?'

Shamoun shrugged. 'None. You'd better ask Aud Helen. But she arranged this meeting only with extreme reluctance.' He smiled apologetically. 'My apologies, but I don't like talking behind Aud Helen's back. That is to say, my impression was that her resistance was tied up with our relationship. She didn't want Adeler or anyone else to know I was Sara's father.'

'But have you experienced this reluctance to admit the relationship between you before?'

Shamoun reacted. 'Why are you so curious?'

Gunnarstranda was slow to respond. He felt he was onto something important, he felt his trip to Stockholm had finally paid off. 'Because we've pushed Aud Helen from one entrenched position to the other,' he said. 'Yesterday she presented a personal statement to the investigators leading the case in which she told them Sara was your child. The fact that you're Sara's father has raised her above all suspicion. That's why it seems entirely illogical that she would insist on keeping the relationship with you hidden.'

Asim laughed. 'You're forgetting one thing. I represent Polisario. I'm politically controversial. Aud Helen has a political career to protect.'

Gunnarstranda nodded. He could understand that. Nonetheless, Aud Helen Vestgård was a politician, he thought. She knew Sveinung Adeler well. Sooner or later Adeler would have discovered the past she shared with Shamoun. Sooner or later. Why would she conjure up a different relationship with Shamoun from the truth? This he didn't understand. There had to be a motive of course. For some reason it suited Vestgård's purposes that her relationship with the man who represented Polisario remained a secret for as long as possible.

But Asim had assisted him as much as he could.

Gunnarstranda shook his hand and thanked him for the lift and all his help. He got out of the car.

As soon as the door was closed the Arab rhythms began to throb from inside. The car moved off. The music died away. Gunnarstranda turned and went to check in for the flight to Oslo.

4

She was on her way to a lighter, though blurred, surface. Water, she guessed. When the light came closer she was able to distinguish additional features. She wasn't under water. She could breathe. She felt hands groping her body. In her pockets. These sensations grew weaker. She looked down, beneath her, into the darkness. But she didn't want to go down and fought to ascend. There. The light and the surface were coming closer and closer.

Something wet hit her in the face and hair. Alcohol! It was strong and it made her cough. He was splashing alcohol over her!

Upright. She was standing upright. Lena just managed to open her eyes. She was leaning against a man. She was in Steffen's flat. The man was pulling her towards the front door. Her legs gave way. But he held her up. He was strong; the arm holding her upright was like a steel cable.

She was on the stairs, going down. It was easier now. She wanted to fall but couldn't. The arm holding her was vice-like.

The icy air on her face told her she was outside. Her legs gave way again. When she opened her eyes she saw her own car in the light beneath the street lamps.

She half fell into the car and curled up on the passenger seat. She tried to get out, but the door was slammed shut. Then she had no more energy and leaned her head against the window.

The plan was to find the handle and open the door. But there was no chance.

Her hands hurt and she looked down at her wrists. They were bound with cable ties. Everything was beginning to spin round. She was nauseous. Almost as though she was drunk out of her skull. She swallowed, but the nausea was still there.

When she could finally see without images spinning round, she saw lines of headlights. Cars coming towards them. So he was driving in the opposite direction to the rush-hour traffic, out of town. But it was hard to see, hard to think. Her head and upper body fell against the door every time the car turned. The lights from the oncoming traffic swept over the face of the man behind the wheel. She had seen him before. He had run after her with a gun in his hand.

What did he want?

The nausea was intense. She felt better if she didn't move.

The windscreen wipers thrashed to and fro.

She raised her hands and aimed at the wheel.

The pain travelled from one temple to the other as his fist hit home.

The glove compartment.

He said something and pulled her into a sitting position by her hair. The brutal fist struck again.

Through the pain she heard the glove-compartment door fall open. The glove compartment was open in the darkness.

She closed her eyes. They stayed closed for a long time. She had no idea how long. Once again she fought to ascend to the surface. It was faster now. The poison was on its way out of her body.

When she opened her eyes wide there was no oncoming traffic lighting up the driver's face. The windscreen wipers were no longer working.

The glove compartment.

She leaned forwards, thrust her hands in and screamed with pain as he struck. She closed her eyes and mouth and waited for the next blow. It didn't come.

But she had her fingers around the pepper spray.

The car wasn't moving.

A cold gust of air blew into the car as he got out. He was going to come around the car and drag her out. But she had the spray. She braced herself.

The door opened.

She pointed the spray at the man, who knocked it out of her hands.

The next second she was lying on the ground. The snow was soft and cold. She waited for the punches and kicks. But they didn't come. Slowly she got to her knees.

Car headlamps lit up a narrow path that had been cleared in the snow.

Where was he?

She scoured the darkness.

'Here,' the voice said.

She twisted her head in his direction and screamed when she got the pepper spray in her face.

Burning hot spikes pierced her eyes and nose. She screamed so loudly her voice went falsetto.

A single clear voice in her mind: *Get out of here!* She buried her head in the snow, ate the snow, bored her eyes into the snow.

*

When she resurfaces, it is not a slow ascent towards light above the water. She simply opens her eyes. They are not ablaze as before; the pain is more like a glow, a throbbing pulse in a smouldering burn.

She sees he has cut the cable ties around her wrists. What does he want?

Why has he cut the ties?

She stands up. She has two legs, two arms and ten claws and she uses them. Kicks at him, scratches him. She falls and he grabs her foot. He drags her across the snow, her jacket rucks up, her bare back scrapes over snow and ice.

She smells salt and seaweed. She hears the beating of waves and she knows what is about to happen.

He pulls her to the edge where the sea awaits.

She kicks out. She knocks him off-balance and he lets go of her, and she rolls downwards. Her head hits the rock face and she has hair in her mouth as she rolls towards the sea that is waiting to swallow her up. Her hands scrabble in panic for a hold and her fingers fasten onto a thin branch to break her fall.

She gasps for breath.

The waves below are licking their lips.

Suddenly the air is knocked out of her lungs and she groans again. Sees the shadow of a boot launching a kick. *I'm going to die*, she thinks. *I'm going to die, but not on my own.* She lets go of the branch and makes a grab for the boot with both hands. And gains a hold. She clings to his calf. He shakes his leg, but his calf is all that is holding her to life. He is strong. His foot lifts her off the ground. She clings on. Won't let go. The next time he can't raise his foot as high. She uses her body weight to grip tighter.

Her strength is ebbing away.

Then something happens.

She can feel that he has lost control of his body. He keels over. She starts with surprise and hears the heavy body hit rock.

She is slipping towards the sea.

That is when she realises she is no longer slipping. She is lying still and stretching her toes. They met an overhang on the way down, something anyway. She can't see what.

Where is he?

She can't see anything. Only hears waves beating against the cliff.

He is down there, below her somewhere. She casts around for a crack, finds one and sinks her fingertips in it. Grips tight and tries to look down the slippery rock face.

Day is slowly dawning. She can make out the shelf her feet are resting on. A small ledge in the cliff, a rugged shelf, the kind children can dive from on hot summer days. She has to go down further and her frozen, numb fingers find another crack in the rock. She isn't thinking, only acting.

But then gravity wins. Her body starts slipping. Her jacket catches. This time it is her stomach that takes the brunt of it as she slides towards the sea and death. But then her body comes to a halt. Her feet have found another ledge in the wet rock. The spray from the waves soaks her hair and face.

She rests and looks around her.

He is nowhere to be seen.

What happened?

Why did he lose his balance?

Where is he?

She can hear nothing. Stays where she is.

It is getting lighter. But she can't hear anyone, can't see anyone.

She is hungry. She is wet, cold and stiff. But she doesn't want to be swallowed up by the waves.

I don't want to drown, Lena thinks. *I'm going to survive and afterwards I'll get healthy. I'll squeeze that bloody tumour in my breast to nothing. I'll beat it even if I have to suffer shooting pains that are worse than this.*

She raises her right leg and searches for a foothold. Now her left leg. Push, slip, stretch upwards.

A clean bill of health, she thinks. *First this; afterwards a clean bill of health.*

She clings to the rock face, possessed by one sole thought: to heave herself up another half a metre. Her left leg finds a foothold, she puts her weight on her foot, raises herself another half a metre from the waves. Her stiff fingers fumble for the branch that saved her before. But she is exhausted, she has cramp in her forearm, she is losing any feeling in her fingers and she can't rely on her own strength.

At last she finds the branch and pushes off with both legs. She can feel the centre of gravity in her body shifting. Now the angle is with her. She can let go without sliding back down, but she daren't let go. She is soaked with sweat in the freezing cold and scrabbles her way back through the snow to her car.

5

She rested her head against the wall as the hot water cascaded over her shoulders. The water formed her hair into a wet, heavy plait and ran down her back as she breathed through her open mouth and tried to place her body where the jets from the showerhead were strongest. She couldn't get enough hot water. It was steaming, but she turned the temperature up higher and it was almost painful as the water worked on her grazes, cuts and stiff muscles. She had no idea how long she had been in the shower. The only thing that had any meaning was letting the water soothe the pain and run and wash away the grime that had accumulated in her mind. She opened her eyes and glimpsed her red skin through the steam and thought: *Is it possible to burn yourself without feeling the pain?* She answered the question herself. No. She was repeating this answer when the telephone rang. She let it ring, fleetingly wondering who might be ringing her now, today. *Who is missing me?* She turned up the temperature and clenched her teeth so as not to scream, until she could no longer stand it and rotated the dial the opposite way. Freezing cold water streamed down over her body, but she felt no shock, she could only confirm that the water was cold. She lifted her face and let the cold water run, determined that it would make all the sensation in her skin disappear entirely. It didn't happen though. Instead she began to tremble. *This is no good*, she thought, and turned off the water. She gasped for breath as though she had given everything in a final sprint. She stood like this, leaning against the glass partition, until her breathing was normal. Then she got out of the cubicle and examined her body in the mirror. A cut over one eye. That could be explained. Worse was the cut over her ear. She had grazes over her stomach and hips, and red bruising over her shoulder blades. Slowly and carefully she rubbed in some cream.

What had actually happened early today? He had waited for her in the flat, hit her over the head and splashed alcohol over her. Why?

Presumably to make her seem drunk, get her down the stairs and...?

He had been waiting for her, it struck her. He had been waiting in Steffen's flat.

She sat on the edge of the bath and was rubbing in cream when the phone rang again.

She got up. Put down the jar of cream. Went out of the bathroom and over to the unrelenting telephone. She lifted the receiver.

'Gunnarstranda.'

'Just a mo,' Lena said quickly.

'Yes?'

Lena collected her thoughts. 'You're back from Stockholm?'

'Just this minute. Thought I'd have a chat with you, sift through the important details of the trip instead of writing an essay.'

'We can do a bit of sifting now.'

'Rindal rang and told me about the child Vestgård had with Shamoun. So I broached the subject. And I got quite a surprising answer. According to Shamoun, Vestgård had told him not to mention to Adeler that they'd had a child together.'

Lena could feel how sick she was getting of this woman's intrigues.

'I reckon she's up to jiggery-pokery again,' Gunnarstranda said.

Lena didn't answer.

'Why are you at home?'

'Overslept,' Lena said quickly. 'Fell on the piste last night.' She regretted her words at once. This was the excuse she had been going to use later.

Gunnarstranda was silent for too long. Of course the old fox scented something or other.

'What was that again?' Gunnarstranda asked at last.

'Hm?' Lena said artlessly.

'The stuff about the piste.'

'We can talk about it later,' Lena said hurriedly. 'I'm on my way now. Bye.' She rang off.

✳

She didn't go to work at once. She went into the bathroom and then to bed.

When she threw back the duvet it was because she had given up on her resolution to get a bit of shuteye. But her watch said something else. She thought she had been in bed for ten minutes. Actually she had slept for two hours. She looked at herself in the mirror. That's the first time you've slept with your eyes open, she said.

Steffen asked me what time it was. He gave me the key and told me to go in and get it. Someone had been waiting for me in the flat. Why?

6

She found a parking spot on the corner of Hausmanns gate and waited. Stared intently at the front entrance of *Dagens Næringsliv*. Half an hour passed before a Highways Authority vehicle drove slowly past and stopped. The man behind the wheel waved a hand as if to chase her away. In the end he made the effort to get out of his van. The man had a little soul patch and carried a ticket machine in his belt as if it were a revolver. She opened the door and showed him her ID card. 'Police.'

The man's eyes flickered with uncertainty. 'You can't stay here. You're blocking the way for pedestrians.'

'Beat it,' Lena said in a monotone. 'Buzz off. Now.'

The man met her eyes and backed away without a protest. He got into his van and drove off.

Lena adjusted the mirror. *Do I look demented?*

The door of the newspaper building opened. Monica, Emil Yttergjerde's girlfriend, had come outside for a cigarette. Lena slid down her seat. She remembered Emil saying Monica worked in reception there. She didn't remember when he had said it though. *This is ridiculous*, she thought. *Here I am, hiding in a car from friends.*

No, a voice protested in her head. *This isn't ridiculous.*

Steffen begged me to go last night. He invited me over. He said to go to his place. He said to go in and pick up my watch…

Monica had draped a long, elegant woollen jacket over her shoulders. She was in constant motion in the cold weather, tripping with her feet while smoking feverishly. The jacket was multi-coloured and multi-patterned. Monica was a girl with a passion for handicraft.

A Volvo estate pulled in by Monica, who presumably knew the driver. She bent down and spoke to him through the window. She threw down the cigarette, turned and went back in. The Volvo idled. The front door opened again. A familiar figure appeared. It was Steffen. He walked around the car and got in. The car drove off. Lena started up and followed. She switched on the radio to hear something other than her own thoughts. Rod Stewart was singing that tonight was the night. Not her style of music. She pressed to find a station with music she liked as she followed the car to the right, into Storgata, then left in front of the old Schous Brewery and up Thorvald Meyers gate. The Volvo took a left and stopped in front of the library in Schous plass.

Lena found a gap in the line of cars and parked. She switched off the radio.

The driver of the Volvo turned out to be a female photographer – a woman in her twenties, wearing a duffle coat, a fashionable fur hat and a pink scarf, which she had wound round her neck like a collar. Steffen waited with his hands deep in his pockets while the woman took photos of the library. He said something to her. She looked up from behind the camera and said something in return. Steffen grinned and stepped in front of her as she once again knelt down with the camera raised. He posed. She lowered the camera and shooed him away, a baby-doll smile on her face.

A journalist and photographer at work. And Lena spying on them. This was ridiculous. What would she say to him?

A man was waiting for me in your flat. A man who wanted to kill me. Did you let him in?

How could Steffen have done that? Steffen had given her his key. They had both been woken in the night by the alarm. Steffen had been as sleepy as she had been. He couldn't have had anything to do with the fire. It was her who should take responsibility for everything that had happened. It was Lena who had tracked down Stian Rømer. She was the one who had defied Ingrid Kobro's orders. Rømer had chased her through Gamlebyen. Rømer had gone underground afterwards.

That was how it must have been! Rømer had found Steffen via her. The man must have been spying on her. Rømer was in the rental car the night Steffen had been at her place. Rømer had found out where Steffen lived. When she fell straight into the trap last night he had been waiting outside Steffen's flat until she and Steffen turned out the bedroom light. Then he had given them another hour or two until he was sure everyone was asleep. Then he had gone into action.

But why?

Why did Steffen want me to go to his flat? Why did the man run after me? Why did he want to kill me?

She didn't have a clue.

Lena took a deep breath and raised her head.

She looked straight at Steffen, who was standing by the library and looking back at her.

He raised a hand and waved. 'Lena!'

She didn't want to talk to Steffen. Not now. She turned the ignition key. The engine started.

He walked briskly towards the car. Lena didn't want this. She rammed into first gear. A horn blared. She didn't give a damn and moved into the carriageway. She accelerated. Looked in the mirror. A van driver was flashing his lights and behind it Steffen was standing with his arms raised and a bewildered expression on his face.

'Ugh!' Lena banged her hand on the wheel. She was flushed, embarrassed. She wanted to get away.

7

The first person she met on her way into Police HQ was Emil Yttergjerde. He held her arm.

'What happened to you?'

Lena stroked the cut above her eye with her forefinger. 'Herpes. Terrible.'

Yttergjerde frowned. 'Herpes is a lip sore.'

She nodded. 'Oh, you mean the cut over my eye?'

'What did you think I meant?'

Lena shrugged. 'Hard to know. I fell on the piste. They turned the lights off before I'd finished.'

'You coming out for a beer tonight?'

Lena didn't need long to think about that. 'Yes,' she said.

The nurse had said she should make the most of good moments. A beer after work was a good moment.

✳

She had to control her paranoia, and resumed her work on the mysterious L. She tried to organise the numbers on the list Telenor had finally provided for Sveinung Adeler's mobile phone.

Finally she looked at the results without being any the wiser. But at least she had managed to work out that one of the numbers was an unregistered mobile. She rang the number and was told that the phone was switched off or was in an area where there was no coverage. She drummed her fingers on the desk. Something told her this was worth examining more closely.

She rang Telenor, asked them to trace the phone, thanked them and rang off. Then went through the list of numbers again. This time she concentrated on the calls Adeler had received on the Monday, Tuesday and Wednesday – the days before the famous dinner in the restaurant.

Adeler had spoken to a lot of people, but he hadn't used his phone much during working hours. As the date with L was on Wednesday evening he must have made the arrangement one day, or several days, before. At 10.27 on Monday, 7th December he had rung a landline number outside Oslo from his mobile.

Why had Adeler used his private phone in working hours this time?

Maybe he had gone out somewhere to be alone when he rang? In which case, why had he wanted to be on his own? Perhaps because he wanted a more personal conversation?

Lena dialled the number. It was the switchboard for the duty-free shops at Oslo Airport.

✳

So many strange things I do in this job, Lena thought twenty minutes later. By then she'd had four further telephone conversations. She had been promised a list of the employees at Gardermoen Airport whose first names started with L. Once that was done she sat staring at the wall.

Behind her someone coughed. She swivelled round in her chair. Emil Yttergjerde was standing in the doorway. He had his coat on and was pointing to his watch.

8

Monica was waiting for them in the hall below. Lena avoided eye contact, slightly ill at ease with having spied on her earlier in the day.

Monica suggested the Asylet. Neither Lena nor Emil had any other suggestions.

They sat down at a long table where there were already a lot of police officers from Sentrum Police Station.

Lena drank white wine, not beer. It was good – a light, chilled Chardonnay that made the glass sparkle. Lena was well through her second glass before Emil had finished his first half-litre. That didn't go unobserved.

'Wow,' Emil said. 'Keep going like that and we'll have to carry you home tonight.'

Lena ignored the comment and went to the loo.

It happened on her way from the toilet.

She came face to face with Steffen.

And pulled up sharp.

'Hi,' she said automatically.

He looked into her eyes for several long seconds. Then he said a curt 'Hi' and pressed past her.

She watched the door to the gents' toilet close behind his back.

People streamed past her, back and forth. Lena was motionless while others were in motion, as if she were a big rock in the middle of a fast-flowing river. Her head buzzed. She heard waves beating against the rock face. She was back there. Clinging to the rock face while the sea stretched up its arms for her.

The door to the gents was constantly opening and closing. But Steffen didn't appear.

How long had she been waiting there?

She had no idea.

The door to the gents opened again.

Steffen stopped when he saw her, stood aside for someone and was alone again. An attractive man in scruffy clothes. Almost a rocker. Unshaven, long hair and gentle movements.

'Christ, you still here?' he said.

She tilted her head, puzzled.

'You didn't seem so interested earlier today.'

'Something happened,' she said in a low voice, 'after you went to work.'

She straightened her head and met his gaze.

'Whatever it was, it must've been pretty special,' he commented in a cool tone.

This is all wrong, she thought. *You can't talk about Stian Rømer now*. But she wanted to.

She cleared her throat. 'After you left…'

She didn't get a chance to continue. 'After last night,' Steffen said with a glower. 'After what happened last night, you spy on me at work? And when I try to talk to you, you drive off. What is it with you? What are you up to?'

Lena's whole body was ice-cold. She didn't want this. 'Did you find your key?' she asked with no emotion in her voice. 'When you got home?'

'It was where it should be, in the letter box. But don't you change the subject, Lena. Not now.'

'I didn't put it there.'

'Oh?'

The expression on his face was at once enquiring and unsure. 'If you didn't, who did?'

She searched for the liar in his eyes, but didn't find one. Steffen just looked lost and uneasy.

The silence that persisted between them became oppressive. People squeezed past them on their way to and from the toilets.

'I'm a bit curious as to what you wrote about the fire that wasn't a fire,' she said.

'What?'

'Earlier today you said you had to go to work because the fire in the block had become a news story.'

'Oh, that…' He summoned a distant smile.

'Didn't you write anything?'

'It was a way of speaking.'

'A way of speaking? You left without having any breakfast, without changing clothes, without checking to see if anything was damaged in your flat. I heard you clearly. You said the fire was a news story.'

She tried to hold his gaze, but couldn't.

'Lena, what's the matter with you actually? I went to work because I had to go to work, and what concern is that of yours?'

At last she had eye contact.

'I was actually on my way out,' he said.

She nodded.

Suddenly he opened his arms and hugged her.

She was unable to react. Her body was stiff all over.

He released his grip and looked her in the eye. 'Lena, what's the matter?'

'I've got cancer,' she said.

She might just as well have slapped him; the effect would have been the same. His face was open and vulnerable as he blinked. And blinked again. His eyes began to flicker.

'Is there anything I can do?'

'I don't think so. You go now. Do what you must.'

She turned to leave him.

He grabbed her hand. Clearly he regarded the situation as absurd and weird as she did.

'Yes?' she said.

'Tell me about it,' he said.

'About what?'

'About what you said.'

'Have you got the time?'

He waved his arms helplessly. 'Tomorrow?'

The boat had slipped its moorings. The distance between them grew with every word they said. She pretended she was mulling over his suggestion. 'Call me tomorrow,' she said.

He nodded and gave her another quick hug before turning and

leaving. On his way out of the door he sent her a final glance over his shoulder. Raised his hand in a wave. 'You were kidding, weren't you? About something happening today?'

She raised a hand and waved without answering.

The door slammed behind Steffen.

Lena hadn't moved. *I've got cancer.* That was the first time she had said the word aloud. The way she said it, the sound the word took on, was eerie.

Steffen had asked if there was anything he could do, as though she was telling him she had missed the last bus home. He hadn't even asked what type of cancer it was. He hadn't been interested. He had turned and asked her to tell him about it when he realised he hadn't reacted well.

No, she said to herself at once. She had no right to judge his reactions. She was the one who had brought up the subject. It was the wrong place and the wrong time. She was the one who had created the difficult situation. Or had she?

Illness never comes at the right time.

Lena tore herself away and went back to her table.

Monica stood up to make room for her. 'I saw you talking to Steffen,' Monica said.

Lena looked at blonde Monica with somnambulist eyes.

'Monica knows him,' Emil said. '"The Hanger-On". Monica works at *DN*.'

Lena was still looking at Monica, who smiled shyly. 'Some of the journos are naughty and call Steffen the Hanger-On, apparently because he usually hangs onto others' coat tails instead of doing the digging himself. The atmosphere between some journalists is a bit competitive,' she added, by way of apology.

Lena blinked. It was strange to hear Steffen being slandered like this. 'The Hanger-on'! How humiliating that must be for him. Nonetheless, it didn't please her. All thoughts of Steffen were painful. She didn't want to think about him any more. She wanted to drink.

But she was torn out her trance when Emil Yttergjerde waved a hand in front of her face. 'Lena, anyone at home? Feel like a beer and a brandy?'

'Yes,' Lena said. 'Very much.'

Saturday, 19th December

1

Her eyelids felt like two stamps with the gluey side down. She could barely open them. But she would have to. The light flickered. Horrible, bright light penetrated between her eyelashes.

There.

The room was light. So it had to be later than nine o'clock in the morning. Her stomach felt like a lump of clay. Impossible to budge.

Why? She didn't know, but knew she should keep perfectly still.

I'm looking up at a ceiling, so I'm alive, I exist. But where?

She was looking straight at a lamp. The shade was a plate decorated with pictures of Donald Duck.

She moved her head to the left while trying not to irritate her stomach too much. The cupboard was awful. An IKEA model from the previous century. Broad brown doors and white side panels.

There was a wooden chair by the bed. Over the chair hung a pair of long gentleman's underpants, blue.

Where on earth was she?

Sweat broke out over the whole of her body. Another attack of nausea was on its way.

I've got a hangover, she thought, *but where am I? What day is it?*

She sniffed and found the reason for her upset stomach. The smell of fried eggs and bacon. *My God, what a terrible stench!*

She groaned aloud.

Then she heard someone move in another room.

At that moment the seriousness of the situation came home to her. She was in bed with a stranger! It was a double bed with only one duvet. She lifted the duvet.

Oh, my God, I'm stark naked in a stranger's bed.

What happened? What have I done?

She looked around feverishly for her clothes. They were nowhere to be seen.

Who was in the adjacent room?

Lena tried to sit up, but another bout of nausea forced her back down.

The person or persons in the other room were approaching the door.

She had to defend herself! What should she…?

Lena watched the door handle, her eyes rigid. It went down. The door opened slowly.

A bearded face with a thatch of hair revealed itself in the doorway.

'Awake?'

It was Frank Frølich.

'You!' Lena exclaimed. 'What are you doing here?'

'I live here.'

'Oh,' Lena said, pulling the duvet up to her chin.

Frølich entered the room. He threw her a garment. Her light-blue panties – which landed on the floor.

'What are you doing with my underwear?'

'Nothing. I just thought you might like to dress before breakfast.'

Lena stared at him in shock.

'Hang about,' he said and left the room. A few seconds later he returned with a pile of clothes, which he laid on her bed. 'If you want a shower there are towels in the bathroom cabinet.'

He made to leave.

'Frank!'

'Yes?'

'I don't feel well.'

'You've got a hangover.'

'I don't remember anything.'

He smiled and his eyes had that mischievous look.

'Be honest,' she said.

'About what?'

'Now. I need you to be totally honest with me … now.'

'Aren't I always?'

He turned round with a big grin on his face. 'You're wondering if we were drinking last night. You can bet your bottom dollar we were!'

'You know what I mean!'

'Mean?'

Lena was sweating feverishly.

'You're wondering if we…' His grin spread wider and he winked at her. 'If you and I … Wish I could say yes,' he said, 'but you were in no state.' He looked at her with the same mischievous eyes.

She didn't want to hear any more. She held her ears as her cheeks burned.

'I had to carry you in here, and I slept on the sitting-room sofa.'

She was sweating, still blushing, but she ventured a smile. 'Now you're joking,' she said tentatively, searching for something in his eyes that could confirm what he had said.

He shook his head and coughed. 'If you're feeling better and the offer's still on the table…'

'No,' she said quickly. 'Go away. I have to get dressed.'

He turned to go.

'Frankie,' she said.

'Yes?'

'Did I say anything about myself of a private nature?'

He wrinkled his brow. 'You were off on your usual number – your father dying etc etc etc. Sorry, but I always close my ears when you start on that one.'

'Did we talk about illness?'

'No. Why?'

'Nothing.'

He went and closed the door behind him.

She sat up in bed. Her hands were shaking. What had actually happened that morning? Why had it happened to her?

She closed her eyes. Remembered the car trip, which was as

fragmented as the previous evening and night. The fist that hit her. She had seen him before. He had ripped open the door and flexed his muscles. Stuffed a gun in his trousers and charged after her. Stian Rømer.

He had recognised her when she opened the door. He had wanted to drag her into the flat. And yesterday morning he had been waiting for her in Steffen's flat.

Frankie knocked on the door. 'Are you coming? Shall we eat?'

'Coming,' Lena said, starting to get dressed.

2

The sight of Frankie Frølich with egg yolk in his beard was too much for her. Lena couldn't think about food and left without eating. She had listened patiently to Frankie's directions – which Metro station and where to change. His words were forgotten as soon as she stepped out of the lift. But there were three taxis in a line outside. She walked straight over and got in the back seat of the front one. The car was driven by a lean man smelling strongly of perfume and talking Arabic on his phone the whole time.

✳

She was at her desk by twelve, but still couldn't bear the thought of food.

It's like being in a plane, she thought. *You sit by the window as the plane goes in to land in thick cloud. Now and again you see green fields and houses on the ground, then you see nothing but white cloud, and when it clears you see other houses, roads and streets.*

The swish of windscreen wipers. The beating of waves before he keeled over and was gone.

And yesterday: on the razzle and talking nonsense. She was embarrassed by her behaviour. The mere thought of drowning your sorrows in alcohol was wrong. She had to focus.

What shall I focus on?

The mysterious L. The tangible clue in the Adeler case.

Telenor had emailed her to say that the unregistered mobile Adeler had rung was located in Frogner, Oslo. We-ell, Lena thought, Frogner was a big area. If the mysterious L was the owner of the phone she was a woman in one of Oslo's most populated districts, stretching from Majorstua to Bygdøy. If the phone was on the peninsula, Telenor's base stations would pick it up. Lena decided to try the second name, a Lisbet Enderud. Address: Bygdøy allé.

What had she found out? Adeler had rung the duty-free shops at the airport. A woman who worked there went by the name of Lisbet and lived in West Oslo. But Lena knew nothing about this Lisbet. It could be a dead end.

Lena looked up the name anyway. Lisbet Enderud, who lived in Bygdøy allé, was also registered as having a landline.

Lena rang the number and got an answerphone: '*Hi, this is Lisbet. As you can see, I'm not at home right now. Leave a message and I'll call back.*'

Lena waited for the tone, then left her name and telephone number.

As soon as she put down the phone the fax began to chunter. She turned her head and watched it. A sheet of paper rose slowly from the machine. Dutifully, Lena got up. Walked over and took the first sheet. Immediately she broke into a sweat. She looked into the corridor. No one around. Nevertheless, she closed the door.

She had hung onto the man's leg. She had caused him to fall into the sea. She didn't want to talk to anyone about it, not yet.

Several more sheets followed. Lena collected them as they came out and rolled them up.

The machine continued: it spewed out a series of photos.

They were photos of a body, a man who had drowned. Unidentified. There was a message with them:

Could anyone offer any information to help identify the deceased?

The dead man's face was beaten and bloodstained. His clothes were in tatters. His skin was cut and grazed. Both eyes were splodges of red. Pecked at by seabirds, Lena guessed. The body lay distorted between rocks at low tide. Ice on the ground.

Stian Rømer's dead body had been found.

That could have been me, Lena thought. She swayed and had to hold onto the wall. The moment was back. Numb fingertips on the cold, icy rock face. Waves beating below. Her hanging onto his leg and feeling him lose his balance.

She took a deep breath. Breathed out. Breathed in again.

This is not my fault! This is what he was trying to do to me!

But then he lost his footing and fell.

Lena relived the moment. She was clinging to the man's leg.

She heard footsteps in the corridor. Straightened up, took a deep breath. Held the fax machine with both hands.

Someone knocked on the door.

Lena, sweating, didn't move. *Go away*, she thought, panic-stricken. *Don't try the door, just leave! Go away! Now!*

The machine spewed out sheet after sheet.

Lena stared blindly at the accompanying text to the photos: the body had been found by two small boys playing in the rocks in Kadettangen. The photos were sent by Asker and Bærum Police District.

Should she take a peek, see if the person outside had left.

At last! The final sheet. The machine fell quiet.

There. The fading sound of footsteps. For safety's sake, she waited a few seconds, in case another fax came.

When she was sure there were no more sheets to come, she put on her outdoor clothes.

She had to talk about this man and there was one person in particular she wanted to confront.

Lena set off for the headquarters of the Police Security Services in Nydalen.

3

At the reception desk of PST she asked to speak to Ingrid Kobro. The man behind the glass partition lifted the phone and swung round on his chair. Then he stuck out his head and told her to deposit her phone in one of the wall lockers.

Lena said she didn't need to go inside or hand in anything. She waited.

Ingrid came down in the lift to meet her.

Now there were a lot of people in the reception area. A group of visitors had arrived for a tour. A lot of commotion regarding lockers and mobile phones.

Lena asked Ingrid to wait until they were alone. As soon as the barrier closed behind the visitors, Lena passed the wad of photos to Ingrid, who flicked through them quickly.

'This is the man you claimed was out of the country. His body's been washed ashore at Kadettangen in Sandvika.'

Ingrid Kobro flicked through with renewed energy. Studying the face of the dead man.

'Two small boys were playing there earlier today. They noticed a lot of seabirds pecking at a bundle by the water's edge. Asker and Bærum have just faxed over the photos in the hope that other police districts can identify the body. I think you might be able to help them.'

Ingrid glanced wordlessly from the photos to Lena and back again.

The doors opened. A chubby woman in her fifties came in, nodded to Ingrid and stopped by the electronic barrier.

Ingrid and Lena stood silently watching as she produced a smart card and bustled through.

Ingrid met Lena's gaze and said with great earnestness in her voice: 'He can't hurt you any longer, Lena.'

Lena took a deep breath. For a second she was tempted to tell her about the mock fire, the attack in Steffen's flat, the journey in the car to Asker, the nightmare at the edge of the cliff and the man who fell into the sea. But she restrained herself.

However, Lena was unable to restrain her fury. 'Are you married to your bloody job or what?' she snarled. Then continued in a whisper: 'You lied to me, Ingrid. Fine, I lie sometimes too; everyone does. But you let the job take priority and you lied to my face. That wouldn't've mattered much either, had it not affected my personal safety. The guy continued to walk around with a gun in his back pocket after he'd tried to use it on me once already. What is it about your job that makes all the cloak-and-dagger-stuff you do more important than my safety? Have you thought about that? Eh?'

Lena turned on her heel and left.

Ingrid followed her. 'Lena, wait!'

'I *know* he checked onto the flight!'

'But did you check the passenger list afterwards?' Lena asked, and read the answer in Ingrid's pensive expression.

'The easiest trick in the world,' Lena carried on angrily. 'Check onto a flight with no luggage and take the train back instead of boarding. And you lot boast you have competent undercover agents!'

Ingrid grabbed Lena's arm, but she shook her off.

They stood face to face. 'He's dead,' Ingrid Kobro said. 'He can't hurt you. And now I want you to hear what I have to say. And you'd better obey: I'm ordering you not to say a word about this person. I'm ordering you not to say a word to Asker and Bærum.'

'Are you going to hush it up? Asker and Bærum have already faxed the photos all over the country.'

'Be quiet for two seconds and listen,' Ingrid snapped. 'I'm ordering you not to say a word about Stian Rømer, to forget him. Have you got that?'

Lena was speechless. She turned and started to walk away.

Ingrid followed.

Lena stopped.

'Have you understood what I'm ordering you to do,' Ingrid asked with a stony expression.

The seconds ticked by.

Ingrid waited. Her eyes still flashed as she lightly smacked Lena's shoulder with the roll of documents.

'Yes,' Lena said, and breathed in, out, then in again and sensed she was finding her balance.

She left Ingrid Kobro without a backward glance. She walked down the road slowly, thinking at every step:

Ingrid knows.

Ingrid knows I know what happened to Stian Rømer. But I don't care. I can't do anything about Ingrid Kobro's thoughts or conclusions.

In her heart she knew Ingrid had already turned round and taken the lift back up to the offices behind closed blinds.

She marched down to the city centre. Warm from the exercise, she caught a bus to Bygdøy allé.

4

She got off at Frogner Church. The bus stop was like a young forest with all the Christmas trees for sale. Imported blue spruces, silver firs, Norwegian spruces – even the odd pine – stacked against one another.

Lena searched for the address of the woman Adeler had rung on his mobile phone during working hours. She lived in one of the art nouveau blocks with curved balcony fronts about fifty metres down from the bus stop.

Lena went to the front entrance.

She checked the nameplates by the bells. Lisbet Enderud's name was by the bell at the top right.

She pressed the button.

Nothing happened.

She pressed again.

The door stayed locked.

Lena crossed the street, leaned against the wall and peered up at the windows of the top floor.

As she had nothing else to do, she decided to wait.

She waited for two uneventful hours. On the other hand, she did learn quite a bit about Norwegian rituals when buying a Christmas tree. Some busy men grabbed a tree at full speed and hurried away with stooped backs and their eyes on the ground as though they were ashamed of the purchase and wanted to go into hiding as soon as they could. Others, generally older women, were good friends with the Christmas-tree seller, asked him how he was, and his family, listened to his recommendations and what he thought about so many trees being imported from Denmark … and there's us in Norway, surrounded on all sides by forest. Sometimes couples came pulling their children on toboggans. These customers took their time, examining tree after tree while the young ones played between the spruces. An older woman in a mink coat complained about the price and reminisced about the old days when she and her husband went into the fields to pick up loose spruce branches, which they pressed into holes they had drilled into the trunk of a pathetic specimen this seller's predecessor had tricked them into buying one Christmas Eve when he was almost sold out and couldn't be bothered to drive back to the farm for more trees.

Lena told herself she would have to remember to buy a Christmas tree one of these days, drive by her mother's afterwards and put it on the veranda. Do it tomorrow, she thought, well in time for Christmas Eve, anyway.

Well in time? Christmas Eve was around the corner and she hadn't finished getting presents yet.

While she was thinking this, it struck her she didn't have the energy to rack her brains for presents. She had too much else on her mind.

After two hours the windows on the top floor were still dark.

On her way home she popped by the bookshop at the bottom of Bygdøy allé. She went to the back of the shop, to the shelves to which books that didn't make it onto the front display tables were consigned. This was where Lena found the books she liked. She found several this time, too. But she wanted them for herself. So she gave them a miss and drove home to change into warmer clothes.

✳

It was past five in the afternoon when she got into her car and drove back, found a free parking space by Gimle terrasse and strolled towards Bygdøy allé. A little later she nodded to the Christmas-tree seller, who was busy pulling the trees through the funnel that enclosed the trees in netting. Lena had dressed like the seller, in blue nylon overalls, moonboots and a leather hat with earflaps.

It was an ordeal doing surveillance in sub-zero temperatures. Lena kept warm by moving. For variation she leaned against the wall, went for brisk walks up and down the pavement or jumped up and down, hidden by the Christmas trees.

'Anything in particular you're after?'

Lena gave a start. It was the tree seller. His light-blue eyes flashed under the fur cap. His cheeks were as red as apples and his wry smile revealed that one front tooth was a crown that was much whiter than the rest. In his hand he was holding a tall, slim tree with shiny needles.

'This one would suit you,' he said with a wink. 'It matches your personality.'

'It's a bit too big,' Lena said, embarrassed, and uncertain as to how she should tackle this advance. 'I'm celebrating Christmas with my mother, and she has a low ceiling.'

The tree-seller nodded and turned to find alternatives.

'The tree's nice,' Lena said quickly, 'but actually I'm not after a tree now. I'm working.'

'Working?' the tree-seller said, mystified.

'Counting cars,' Lena answered. 'I'm checking the traffic here in Bygdøy.'

A young couple came along the pavement and started moving between the trees. 'Customers,' the tree-seller said with an apologetic expression and walked away.

He's going to come back, Lena thought, and crossed the street in case he did.

✳

Just before seven a shadow waved from the driver's seat of a black BMW. It drove past and pulled in to the bus stop. It was Iqbal from the undercover section. He buzzed down the window.

'You've got an hour,' he shouted.

'Two,' Lena shouted back. 'I haven't eaten and I'm dying for the loo.'

'One and a half,' Iqbal said.

She took two hours. Balkan Kebab had the best food, but at Bislett Kebabhouse the service was faster. Lena was handed the food at once. She was starving and wolfed it down with a Coke. But it wasn't enough. She fancied something sweet.

I'm ill, she told herself. *I can allow myself to push the boat out.* So she set a course for Pascal's in Drammensveien and bought two cream sponges covered with marzipan and decorated with, among other things, red and green flowers that doubtless contained artificial sugar and unhealthy preservatives. She made short work of them, licked her fingers and concluded that cake-making was a profoundly unacknowledged art form. The taste of rum cream, vanilla, chocolate, almonds, marzipan and strawberry exploded in her mouth, causing the freezing temperatures to recede and morph into a sensual tingle on her skin. Afterwards she felt like more and wondered what was happening to the body she inhabited. It never used to behave like this. The sweet things she normally indulged in were fruit and yoghurt.

✳

It wasn't only her body that was behaving differently. Her beloved Micra was starting to be affected by the cold too. At first she noticed danger signs from the interior light, which was dimmer than normal when she opened the door. On turning the ignition key a grating moan came from the starter motor. She tried again. Same result.

Nervous, Lena let it rest for a few seconds, then turned the key for a third time. The engine started and she patted the Micra's dashboard as though it were an old friend. 'Good ol' boy!'

She drove back to Bygdøy allé, waved to Iqbal and searched for a parking space. Finally she found one in Gabels gate.

When she was back on her plot she saw the Christmas-tree seller was packing up. Nevertheless, he offered her a coffee from a steel Thermos. Lena accepted and took a paper cup half full of what resembled liquid asphalt. She couldn't even swallow it. Anyway, she was ill and was supposed to stay off coffee and alcohol and drink vegetable juices bursting with antioxidants.

As soon as the seller turned away she poured the caustic brew down the grille by the kerb.

She perked up when the door to the block of flats opened. But the residents who came and went were elderly women in long coats or old gents with skinny legs in slacks and scarves loosely knotted around their necks.

Whenever the door closed behind the person entering, she gave them sufficient time, then leaned back and looked up. The windows of the flat on the top floor remained dark. Her icy breath took on a rainbow aura when she exhaled under the street lights.

The last shops were closing. The tree seller slammed the sliding door of his VW Transporter shut. He waved to her and asked if he would be seeing her again, tomorrow for example.

Lena shrugged.

'I've kept back this one,' the seller said, showing her a tree that was a shorter version of the previous example – nice and compact with shiny needles. 'Same tree, with a metre lopped off.'

'Beautiful,' Lena said. 'Perfect, but I can't take it with me. Sorry.'

'See you,' the seller said optimistically. He waved through the window as he drove off.

*

By the time midnight came, Lena was frozen stiff. She had been fantasising for hours about the cakes at Pascal's and gave herself another ten minutes before admitting defeat.

She hated giving up.

The ten minutes passed and Lena counted her buttons. Shall I, shan't I?

A bus drove past slowly and pulled in to the stop. It drove on. Leaving a young woman. Lena watched her. Fashionable fur hat over a mass of blonde hair that fell down her back. The woman ran across the street, light on her feet. She wore a short white jacket cut in at the waist. Her tight trousers emphasised curvy hips and a lithe backside that men would certainly give a second look. The woman opened the correct door. It closed behind her.

Lena stared up at the windows on the top floor. She imagined what was happening in the block and could almost hear the lift ascending through the floors. She visualised the woman searching for the keys in her bag and switching on the light...

The windows on the top floor remained dark.

The last hope. Enough was enough.

Lena strolled back to Gabels gate and the car. When she opened the car door there was just enough electricity in the battery for a dim glow in the ceiling light. Which went out as she was watching.

Lena got in anyway, pressed the accelerator once and optimistically turned the key.

But her good ol' boy had had it. A dry click was all that could be heard.

This was not her day.

'Home,' she said aloud, got out of the car and locked it. Strolled slowly back, up the hill to Bygdøy allé to find a taxi rank. When she was level with the block of flats she sent a final glance up at the flat she'd had under surveillance.

The window on the top floor was lit.

5

The package he had ordered online was in the letter box. On the rare occasions Gunnarstranda received a parcel he behaved like a child. His hands were shaking and he didn't have the patience to untie the knots or look for a pair of scissors to cut the tape in a civilised fashion. He ripped the package open. The more obstinate the packaging, the more vicious his assault.

While he was struggling with it, Tove sat watching him with arched eyebrows. She said nothing.

At the top of the pile of CDs was the soundtrack to the film *Ascenseur Pour L'échafaud* by Louis Malle.

This CD was also wrapped in plastic. His fingers skidded across the plastic. He tried with a fingernail, but that was no use, either.

Tove arched her eyebrows once again. She leaned forwards and took a knitting needle from a bag on the floor. It pierced the plastic. 'Thank you.'

Gunnarstranda could finally sit comfortably and pull the headphones over his ears. He wore them because Tove was a TV fan. She liked to have the TV on twenty-four hours a day, and there was a constant stream of noise from the room – junk TV, news programmes, church services, whatever. Sound or no sound. The TV was on whether Tove was on the phone or reading a newspaper or a book.

He knew she wouldn't object if he turned off the TV. But if he did, and put on Miles Davis, for example, Tove would probably start talking.

That in turn would lead to him either switching off the music or asking her to be quiet.

He didn't want Tove to be quiet. But that was the way he was wired. He could not talk to people while Miles Davis was playing.

The solution was therefore to insulate the sound of music in headphones while Tove had the TV on.

Miles Davis was dead by the time the CD came out. Miles had always recorded on vinyl and had consequently taken into account that listeners would have to get up and turn the record manually.

Recordings generally had two concepts, one on side one and one on side two. The first side of *In a Silent Way* was an eighteen-minute-long melody borne by a hectic drumbeat. The other side was a lyrical composition in three parts. Gunnarstranda had always thought it an absurdity to listen to Miles Davis without being able to turn the record. However, this CD was the soundtrack of a film, so the music wasn't tied to an A and a B side.

Gunnarstranda was impressed that a French film director in the late 1950s had managed to persuade Miles to record a soundtrack for a whole film. What was more, it was beautiful. The harmonic progression was spare and melancholy, not unlike the soundscape on the classic *Kind of Blue*. But the only musician Gunnarstranda knew on the CD was the drummer, Kenny Clarke.

Sipping from a glass of Upper Ten on the rocks, he relished the trumpet solos as he absent-mindedly stared at the TV screen showing the news. He tapped his left foot to the beat – and stopped.

The screen was filled with the face of Frikk Råholt.

Gunnarstranda pulled off the headphones and asked Tove what the item had been about.

Uninterested, she glanced up from the paper where she was trying to do a Sudoku. 'He's giving up.'

'Giving up? Politics?'

The face of Frikk Råholt had gone now. It was the weather forecast.

Gunnarstranda located the remote control and zapped through the channels.

On TV2 News the story was still hot:

'*According to TV2's information, Frikk Råholt will take over as a consultant for the PR agency First in Line. Råholt, who has built up a large network over many years as a politician, will be a lobbyist with great authority and force. Råholt's move from being an MP at Storting to serving employers for a lucrative salary will stoke the debate about the realities behind government, says—*'

Gunnarstranda lowered the volume.

'Why are you so interested?' Tove asked.

'Actually I don't know,' he said. 'I only know I'm intrigued.'

'What are you listening to?' she asked.

'Miles.'

Tove took the CD with pictures of the film on the cover. 'I've seen that one,' she said. 'The woman is that French…' Tove snapped her fingers as she remembered the name. 'Jeanne Moreau. The trumpet playing is when she wanders alone through the Paris night.'

Tove grinned when she saw his surprise. 'You like music, I like Jeanne Moreau. Sometimes you get both at once. Nice, isn't it?'

On the TV there was archive footage of Råholt's political career.

Gunnarstranda turned up the volume again. Råholt's voice was mellifluous. He said politics was about achieving goals.

'What many people forget is that we politicians are actually salesmen,' the mellifluous voice said.

Gunnarstranda sighed.

'What is it?' Tove asked.

'My brother was on the picket lines at Linjegods in seventy-six and was attacked by the police.'

Tove smiled. 'Good job you weren't working for the police then.'

Gunnarstranda shook his head. 'The point is that my brother said he was drawn to politics for ideological reasons. That cuckoo there,' Gunnarstranda pointed to a smiling Råholt waiting for another question from a fawning journalist, 'he belongs to a generation that has turned politics into buying and selling.'

Tove didn't answer.

'Why do we have to *see* all the people they interview on TV?' Gunnarstranda said. 'In the old days they filled the gaps between programmes with a picture of an aquarium and we could rest our eyes watching the fish. They should've kept that.'

Tove lifted the remote control to switch off the television.

Gunnarstranda raised both eyebrows in surprise. 'Are *you* turning off the TV? Voluntarily? I'm impressed.'

'I can take a hint,' Tove said, walking over to the stereo. 'Let's have a bit of culture.'

6

Lena rang the bell on the top right. After a few seconds the lock buzzed. She pulled the door open and entered.

There was no lift.

She almost became hot walking up all the stairs to the top floor.

Lena was about to ring the bell when the door opened.

The woman standing in the doorway was at that indefinable age between twenty-seven and thirty-five. She was wearing tight black trousers and a short jumper revealing her navel. Her hair was honey blonde but with dark roots showing. She smiled in anticipation, showing her upper teeth, pointed, bent slightly inwards.

A bit like a shark, Lena thought, and said: 'Lisbet?'

The woman nodded.

Lena was wondering how to phrase the reason for her visit. This led to them looking at each other without speaking. The blonde spoke first.

'You're a policewoman,' she said. 'I've seen you on TV.'

Lena nodded. 'This is about Sveinung Adeler.'

The woman pulled a kind of apologetic grimace. 'I heard your message on voicemail and I was going to answer you tomorrow.'

She kept looking at her watch as if to signal how late it was.

'Can I come in?' Lena was already undoing the zip of her overall.

The flat was stylish. Sparsely furnished, but both the sofa and the broad armchair could have been displayed in one of the fancy boutiques in this area – clean lines, muted colours. Some glass shelving. A few magazines and a lot of textbooks stacked in piles on a dining table of solid wood. Lit tea-lights on a work table. Stereo with mini speakers.

Some CDs scattered across the floor in front of the stereo. Lena tried, unsuccessfully, to read the titles. What came out of the speakers was some indie rock Lena recognised: Arcade Fire.

Lena sat down on the sofa.

The woman in the middle of the floor stood watching her – clearly ill at ease.

'Would you mind turning the volume down a bit?'

The woman took a remote from one of the shelves. The sound vanished.

'You didn't need to turn it off completely.'

The woman didn't answer.

'I've come here to ask you whether you signed yourself L when making a date with Sveinung Adeler on Wednesday, the ninth of December at eleven o'clock in the evening.'

The woman hesitated for a few moments before nodding and sitting down on the sofa as well.

'It was our second meeting.'

Lena said nothing, waiting for her to continue.

'The first time was a month ago. In town. Very stupid actually. I was out with some girls. Just having a last shot at a bar. I met a guy and, well, he came back with me.'

'And you met another time?'

'After a few days he texted me, wanting us to meet again. Actually I wasn't sure it was a good idea.'

'A good idea?'

'I'm in a relationship with someone else. Engaged.'

Lena said nothing.

'But then he rang and we talked … and then he rang again. In the end I said yes. Of course I realise now I behaved stupidly. I even told Sveinung I was in a relationship, and a lot besides. But I wanted it too, to meet Sveinung.'

'You know he's dead, I suppose.'

'Yes.'

'When did you find out?'

'A couple of days ago.'

Lena was quiet, waiting for an explanation.

'I've cut myself off for the moment.' She nodded towards the pile of books. 'I read round the clock when I'm not working at Gardermoen. So I'm not always up-to-date with events. I saw you on *Newsnight* and my jaw dropped. Sveinung dead – what the…?'

'We asked people to come forward if they knew anything.'

Lisbeth didn't answer.

'But you didn't contact us?'

'No.'

'Why not?'

'I was in total shock. So there was that. And I'm supposed to be engaged. So should I ring the police and tell them I've been unfaithful? If everything finishes with Olaf, I don't want it to happen like this. If it does, I'll do it on my own initiative. He doesn't need to know about all of this.'

Lisbet looked at her watch. 'He's coming here, by the way. She got up. 'I thought it was him ringing now, but it was you.' She took a phone from the windowsill. 'And I have a feeling this conversation won't finish that quickly.' She sent Lena an enquiring look.

Lena nodded.

The woman tapped in a number and put the phone to her ear. When there was an answer she went into another room and closed the door behind her.

Lena sat listening to her talking in a low voice behind the door. She was so annoyed. This girl was banging another guy on the side and failed to inform the police when they were asking for information!

Lena's eyes wandered around the walls. She was envious of the two designer candlesticks on the table.

Lisbet had finished talking and was standing in the doorway watching her.

'Well?' Lena said.

'Can I offer you anything? Something to drink perhaps?'

Lena shook her head.

Lisbet came over and sat down. They remained in these positions, each sitting in their corner of the sofa looking straight ahead.

'Tell me what happened on Tuesday night.'

'Sveinung came here at about half past eleven.'

'How long did he stay?'

'Till early in the morning.'

'Time?'

'Around five maybe.'

'Did he say where he was going when he left?'

'Home, I would suppose. He didn't say, but I asked if I should ring for a taxi. Out of the question. He wanted to walk. He was like that, I think – a fitness freak … Of course, it was sad that he slipped into the water, but…'

Lena waited in the ensuing silence.

'After seeing you on TV and hearing what you said I thought about Sveinung. It was really tough. I didn't feel anything. It struck me I didn't know anything about Sveinung – nothing private, not even whether he liked fried eggs for breakfast. I mean, we had fun together, but he never said anything about himself. And so I thought: did *I* reveal anything of myself at all? What if *I* was suddenly gone like that? Would he, for example, have been able to say anything about me, something nice? I had no idea. It was frightening. I don't know if you can understand that.'

Lisbet looked at Lena, who decided to ask another question:

'What did you do when he left that morning?'

Lisbet didn't answer. She looked into middle distance. Her eyes were moist. She blinked.

'For example, could you get someone to confirm that you *didn't* follow Sveinung Adeler?'

'Who would confirm that? Olaf, my bloke? After all, he was in Berlin.'

'What was he doing in Berlin?'

'His job. He works for the Norwegian Export Council.'

'Could I have his name and address?'

'Why?'

'Because you were cheating on a guy who was possibly pushed into the harbour half an hour after he got out of your bed.'

Lisbet's eyes were no longer moist.

'We want to eliminate Olaf from our enquiries. Do you understand?'

'But I know he was in Berlin. He has a phone with a German SIM card. I rang him that night, in Berlin, only an hour before Sveinung arrived.'

'I still need his name and address.'

Lisbet continued to hesitate. 'Does he have to know the reason for your questions?'

Lena jumped up from the sofa.

'What's the matter?' the blonde woman asked nervously.

'You've withheld information from us for long enough!'

Lisbet got to her feet without another word. She went to the work table with all the books and took a pen from beside some loose papers.

✳

A little later, as Lena was strolling down to the crossroads of Bygdøy allé and Gabels gate, she glanced at the car that had been frozen to death. It really did look like a corpse with a thick, solid, grey layer of rime on all the windows, even over the paintwork.

Lena carried on towards the centre. It was past midnight now, and no one was around. She sluiced all thoughts of Sveinung Adeler and Lisbet out of her head. She had a whole free day ahead of her. Now she focused on finding a taxi, getting home and drinking a quarter of bubbly in bed. She felt she could sleep for several days.

Monday, 21st December

1

Lena didn't think about Sveinung Adeler or the woman he was with the night before he drowned until she got on the bus on Monday morning. As soon as she plumped down on the bus seat her phone rang.

It was Gunnarstranda.

'Did you see the note I found in Adeler's flat?' Lena asked. 'The mysterious L at the bottom is Lisbet Enderud and she lives in Bygdøy allé. She and Adeler—'

'I knew I'd seen the handwriting before!' Gunnarstranda interrupted.

Lena was quiet and fell back on the seat as the bus set off.

'In her notes. Lisbet Enderud's the name of the girl who signed the threatening letter to Vestgård. I compared the notes with the letter to see if it was her handwriting.'

Lena felt faint.

Gunnarstranda chuckled. 'The girl lives in Bygdøy allé, eh? Sweet blonde with lots of textbooks lying around?'

'That's right.'

'That's her,' Gunnarstranda said.

Lena gulped. The trail she followed on Saturday night was growing warmer.

The silence on the line told Lena that Gunnarstranda was thinking the same.

'I'll ring you back,' Lena said, looking at her watch. 'No, I'll see you in ten minutes.'

Lena hung up and tapped in the number of Lisbet Enderud. The phone rang twice before she picked up.

'It's me again, Stigersand,' Lena said.

'Hi,' Lisbet said. 'What is it?'

'I'm ringing because I have to ask you something. Last Friday you were contacted by a short bald cop wearing rubber overshoes who asked you about a threatening letter. Is that correct?'

Lisbet was able to confirm this.

'Has anyone else asked you about the letter?'

'No. My jaw dropped when I heard. Mostly because of the letter, but also because the strange guy said he was a police officer.'

Lena thanked her.

'Can I ask you something?' Lisbet said.

'Yes.'

'Have you spoken to Olaf?'

'When we do, we'll inform you.'

Lena rang off and concentrated on establishing a chain of events:

Gunnarstranda had visited Lisbet on Friday, 11th December. Axel Rise should have done it the Thursday before, but he hadn't. So Rindal must have been given the threatening letter job by PST a *few hours after* Adeler was found drowned.

When could the letter have been received at parliament? As the letter contained a threat against an MP it was quickly handed onto PST, who presumably did a speedy assessment and sent the letter on to Rindal who…

The letter must have been delivered to parliament on Thursday morning – the same day that Adeler was found dead. This wasn't just probable. It *had* to be like this. If the letter had been received the day before, on Wednesday, someone in the department would have gone to see Lisbet that same evening or night.

Lena concentrated on recapitulating the order of events:

Sveinung Adeler is out with Aud Helen Vestgård and Asim Shamoun on Wednesday evening. They part company at eleven. Half an hour later Adeler arrives at Lisbet's flat. They're together all night, and he leaves her at around five in the morning. Half an hour later, at the latest, he is pushed into the harbour and held down with a plank and drowns. The killer pursues the eyewitness, Nina Stens-hagen, to the Metro, onto the train, off the train and into a tunnel. He shoots Nina, camouflages the murder as an accident and disappears without trace.

Shortly afterwards, presumably at about nine, the morning post is opened at parliament and Vestgård receives a death threat signed by Lisbet Enderud.

Gunnarstranda didn't think the letter could have been written by Lisbet. His theory was that the death threat was a pointer – a letter sent to Vestgård from an unknown person, to discredit Lisbet.

In other words, *someone* – the letter-writer – wanted to lead the police to Lisbet Enderud. Why? And why her? And why threaten Aud Helen Vestgård?

Three questions. Lena didn't know the answers. However, she knew what the questions and the answers had to mean: the death threat *must* have had something to do with Adeler's death.

Of course, they had to check out Lisbet's boyfriend. That was a job for Emil Yttergjerde, she thought, and rang him at once.

With the phone to her ear, she let her gaze wander over the advertisements in the bus. The driver stopped. Several more passengers got on.

On the seat in front of her a man was reading a newspaper with pink pages.

Lena craned her neck and looked over his shoulder. She saw a photo of Aud Helen Vestgård and Asim Shamoun.

He turned over the page.

Immediately Lena broke into a sweat. What was in today's paper?

2

Lena jumped off at Jerbanetorg and walked against the flow, into the concourse of the old Oslo East Station, looking for a newspaper kiosk.

The story was hinted at with a little teaser in the margin on the front page: '*Vestgård Dismisses Controversial Meeting*'.

Lena was taken aback by Steffen's toned-down vocabulary. What had previously been put forward as a political conspiracy was now reduced to a controversial meeting. Lena bought the newspaper and flipped through to the article. The teaser turned out to be inaccurate. Vestgård didn't dismiss anything. She hadn't been interviewed or asked about anything. It was the journalist, Steffen Gjerstad, who was doing the dismissing with – in Lena's eyes – an unusually unpleasant revelation: *Dagens Næringsliv* had *discovered* that MP Aud Helen Vestgård had had a child with the man responsible in Scandinavia for fronting the civilian façade of a military and *very controversial* resistance movement. Here Steffen had moderated his language as well. The word 'terrorist' was eliminated.

What irked Lena was the fact that Steffen had been told about Vestgård's highly confidential statement. That was anything but good news. There was a leak in their group. No doubt about it. *Someone* was telling Steffen what was going on. Lena had a fairly clear idea who. She *knew* the people Steffen knew and who would willingly give him information. But it was one thing knowing and quite another having tangible proof.

Lena rang Steffen as she was striding up the hill to Police HQ.

'Hi Lena. Thought you would ring.'

Lena got straight to the point: 'Who told you about Vestgård and the child she had with Asim Shamoun?'

'You know I'm a journalist, Lena. I don't reveal my sources.'

Fuck you, Lena thought.

'I wanted to ask you quite a different question,' Steffen said.

Lena hung up before he had finished talking.

She went in and ran up the stairs.

On the fifth step Steffen called her back.

She switched off her phone.

She continued to the third floor and went straight into Rindal's office.

The newspaper lay on his desk.

Rindal was standing by the window. He glanced at her. 'I suppose it's obvious, but I have to ask you anyway,' he said. 'Are you the source?'

She shook her head.

'I want to hear an answer,' Rindal said coldly.

'No,' she said. 'I haven't said a word.'

'Someone has,' he said. 'Someone has passed on information given to you and me in the strictest confidence to this journalist. You know him personally. You admitted that earlier.'

Lena was startled by his choice of words: *admitted*? Was this an interrogation?

She steeled herself and answered calmly: '*Admitted* is the wrong word. I told you in confidence that I know the journalist. But you can be sure of one thing: I am *not* his source.'

Rindal fixed her with a stare. Eventually he cleared his throat. 'You and I had a private conversation with Irgens and Vestgård. We guaranteed them discretion as we left.'

'Everyone in the investigation team was informed afterwards,' Lena countered. 'There are many of us who know, many of us who might've spoken to Steffen Gjerstad and—'

He raised a hand to stop her.

She fell silent. She was talking nonsense. There weren't many people who had contact with Steffen. There were two. Her and Axel Rise. As Lena *wasn't* the source, Axel had to be Steffen's source. But she couldn't bring herself to say that aloud. She was no squealer. She would have to take this up with Axel personally.

Rindal took a piece of paper from the desk.

'We've been accused of a dereliction of duty. *You* have been accused.'

'Me?'

'Irgens.'

'Irgens?'

'He says Vestgård made her statement on condition there was

total discretion. He's demanding an investigation into the leak and has informed our internal committee, SEFO, that you have an intimate relationship with the journalist who penned this article. They've decided you need to be investigated.'

'And what do you say?' Lena exclaimed in disbelief.

'Lena, you're right. There are many people who could be the journalist's source. But you're leading the investigation. You were present in Irgens's office when the information was given and you know the journalist. You're in a relationship with him, isn't that right?'

'A relationship?'

'Wake up, girl. Tongues wag. It's well known here that you're in a relationship with the journalist. Even Irgens knows!'

Lena was silent. She was thinking: *How can Irgens know?*

'I'm going to have to suspend you while you're being investigated,' Rindal said.

She closed her eyes and braced herself to ensure her voice carried. 'Listen to me,' she said, concentrating. 'We're making progress. I was doing surveillance work until midnight on Saturday. I now know where Adeler was after the dinner with Vestgård and all Thursday night. I just need a little more time.'

'You can put this in a report. You can inform Gunnarstranda.'

'Listen to me,' she repeated.

'I can't, Lena. There's a complaint. At this moment you're being investigated for possible dereliction of duty. There's nothing else I can do but suspend you while the investigation's ongoing. It has to be like this. If you give it some thought, you'll understand!'

Lena didn't want to hear any more. She went to the door. Stopped. Turned on her heel and said: 'You were present too.'

Rindal eyed her without speaking. She looked down.

The silence lasted. She inhaled and met his eyes again. He said nothing. It was impossible to read his expression. But he wasn't going to answer, that much was clear.

'What will you do,' she asked, 'if the leaks persist after I'm suspended?'

He shook his head, as though coming round after intense reflection. 'What do you mean?'

'Who are you going to give the boot if the leaks persist?' she asked in a firm voice.

Wrong formulation, she thought instantly. Now he could talk his way out of it.

Rindal breathed in. 'You aren't being given the boot, you're being suspended because you're under investigation. No one's passing sentence on you!'

Without another word, she left the office.

She marched down the corridor, looking neither left nor right. She had cancer. She had to focus on things she could do something about. What the 'Gene Hackman' Rindal did or didn't do was beyond her control.

Lena pulled up sharply as she came face to face with Axel Rise. He stopped, too.

They stared at each other. Rise's eyes wandered.

'Steffen says hi,' she said.

'Right. Say hi back.'

'Actually I think you see more of Steffen than I do,' she said.

He didn't answer.

'Yesterday, for example. Do you know I've been given the blame?'

'What are you talking about?' Axel Rise asked in a measured tone.

Lena went up close to him. 'You're his source here. I know that,' she said in a low voice. 'If you were a man, you'd admit it to me,' she went on. 'I'll have to take the blame anyway. Was it you?'

He shook his head condescendingly. 'Me? Was it me? Have you gone crazy? Take a look at yourself before you try to drag others into your own personal mayhem. Keep me well out of this.'

She couldn't be bothered to argue and squeezed past him without dignifying him with a further look.

'You've got problems,' he shouted after her. She didn't hear the rest. His words drowned in the chaos of her mind.

A few weeks before, being suspended would have been synonymous with a catastrophe. She wouldn't have been able to cope for a second. Now she couldn't care less.

*

Her thoughts churned around the conversation with Rindal. *It's well known here that you're in a relationship with the journalist.* Steffen had *not* contacted her after their meeting at the Asylet. Instead he had written an article that had led to her losing her job, which would make her a leper in the eyes of many of her colleagues. The so-called Hanger-On wrote in such a way that others lost their jobs.

But Steffen couldn't know that. After all, she wasn't his source.

But now? I'm suspended. I'll never get the killer behind bars.

Yes, I will, she decided. *This goes beyond a job. I'll get to the bottom of it!*

What she had to go on was that Sveinung Adeler spent his last night with a woman. *Someone* had issued a threat to an MP and pointed a finger at this woman. What was the logic behind these events?

Lena had done this before. Looked at events separately – as though they were scattered across a board – it was like studying a teeming mass of stars in the sky. It was like looking at dots that weren't actually dots. It was simply a question of looking long enough, focusing on one individual element at a time. In this way the correct picture, the links and the system to the chaos would appear. She knew that deep inside her. She had all the information. It was just a matter of sifting through it.

The suspension – what happened in Rindal's office – was part of the unknown logic that drove the events in this case. A *feigned* threat on Aud Helen Vestgård's life.

Press coverage that placed her – a detective – in a poor light, to put it mildly.

That was it. The answer lay there. The big what-was-it-all-about. All she had to do was tease it out.

3

She jumped off the bus by Frogner Church. An unending stream of noisy vehicles went past as she waited for the green man at the lights. He was taking his time. When she turned she looked straight into the face of the Christmas-tree seller.

'How's the traffic?' he shouted.

She didn't understand what he meant and tilted her head.

'Weren't you counting cars?'

'Ah, yes, of course.' Lena pointed to the cars racing past. 'It's not going too badly,' she shouted back. 'Traffic's on the increase.'

The tree-seller grinned and lifted his Thermos with an enquiring look.

She smiled back and shook her head.

The green man. Lena crossed the street and stood outside the block of flats where Adeler must have emerged on Thursday morning, half an hour before he was killed.

If Adeler walked from here, how long would it have taken him to City Hall Quay?

She decided to walk the same stretch and time herself.

After checking her watch, she set off at a cracking pace down Bygdøy allé. It had been freezing cold that night and Adeler had been wearing no more than a white shirt and a suit. No coat, no long johns, no woollen underwear, not even winter boots. He must have walked very fast in the hope of building up some heat.

Why had he gone on foot? Presumably he had been hoping to catch an early tram or bus in Solli plass.

Lena glanced to the right as she crossed Gabels gate. Her car was still there. Another yellow fine under the windscreen wiper. She couldn't care less about the fine, but she would have to call for help to get the car started.

Seven minutes at a fast pace and she was in Lapsetorvet. She went left along the tramlines, but stopped after a few metres.

This wasn't the shortest way to the harbour. The quickest way from here would have been to walk straight on.

Why had she decided to turn left?

The answer was obvious: she had turned left because that would be the logical route if Adeler was walking home. If a tram rattled by he would only have had to jump on. But most importantly: going via the harbour would be a detour.

Lena stopped and thought.

It wasn't logical for Adeler to choose the route via the harbour. It had been so cold that morning that anyone with their wits about them would have tried to flag down a taxi or get on a tram or bus – even if he was fit and sporty.

Why had Adeler chosen a route that was absolutely illogical?

The answer was equally obvious: Adeler *wasn't* on his way home.

Lena stood motionless, picturing the scene:

It is somewhere between five and six o'clock in the morning. The crack of dawn. Adeler has eaten, drunk and made love. It is the middle of the week. He will be going to work in two or three hours. The logical option would be to go home and change his clothes.

Then the certainty hit home: Sveinung Adeler was on his way to work!

She was on the right track now. She knew it in her bones. The secretariat was in Rådhusgata. It wasn't far from from Lisbet's flat in Bygdøy allé. He just needed to go to Solli plass, carry on a few hundred metres and then cross past the City Hall Quays. There was no point taking a taxi. Adeler was fit and focused after a night out on the town.

He went straight to work – of course! He would be early for work, but so what? The state operated on flexi-time. If Adeler turned up a couple of hours early he could then go home early.

But Adeler never arrived. He met someone on the way, ended up in the sea and drowned.

Lena concentrated. Adeler had been walking alone in Bygdøy allé. On the way he either met his killer or the killer caught up with him.

A meeting? That was unlikely. A casual encounter that resulted in murder? Probably after a robbery. But they had found a wallet, bank cards, more than two thousand kroner and a valuable wrist watch on the body.

The killer had caught up with Adeler. *Someone* had been waiting outside the block of flats in Bygdøy allé, *someone* had followed him and carried out an attack on the quay, the same way *someone* had been waiting for her, she thought darkly.

Her pocket vibrated. The phone. She took it out. The display showed it was Gunnarstranda.

'First of all, my condolences,' Gunnarstranda said. 'I know Rindal has made a big mistake, so you don't need to tell me he's a sack of shite. But I'm going to be taking over your work while you're sucking your thumb, so I need a briefing.'

4

She found Gunnarstranda at Kafé Justisen with a cup of black coffee in front of him.

Lena sat down.

They looked at each other.

He didn't say a single word. He laboriously peeled the paper from a sugar cube.

Now and then the man's reticence could get on your nerves. 'You wanted a briefing?' she said as he studied the sugar cube in great detail.

Annoyed, Lena beckoned to the waitress. She disappeared behind the counter. Lena became even more annoyed. Didn't she have eyes in her head?

'I think it's time for you to get out of Otta,' Gunnarstranda said absent-mindedly.

'Hm?'

The waitress was suddenly at the side of the table. She was holding a cup of steaming tea in her hands. She placed the cup on the table in front of Lena.

'Tea,' Gunnarstranda said. 'I ordered it for you. Green tea, apple flavour. That's the one you usually drink, isn't it? I know you don't eat between meals. So I haven't ordered any food. Have a look around you.'

Lena looked around. A few weary old boozers with glasses of beer in front of them alongside the windows. At the neighbouring table three youths discussing something or other. Behind them an immaculately dressed gentleman was eating what was known as *porsjon*, bacon and egg on rye bread.

Gunnarstranda floated the sugar cube on his coffee. When it had absorbed enough he popped it into his mouth and sipped the coffee. He lowered the cup. 'We used to rent a cabin in Gudbrandsdalen,' Gunnarstranda said, 'me and my wife, Edel, who died some years ago. Whenever we needed anything we had to drive to Otta to do our shopping. Well, Otta's a small place, and Gudbrandsdalen is a popular tourist trap. At weekends and Easter there were probably as many cars in the narrow streets as in half of Oslo. People were pissed off. If they drove, there was a traffic jam; if they walked, there was a queue; if they went shopping, there was a queue; if they went out to eat, there was a queue. A shopping trip could produce so much adrenalin and stress that people would get into fights if anyone jumped the queue to pay at the cash desk or the post office. Edel, she was much more clear-sighted than me. She said she couldn't stand it any more. "Well," I said. "Where do you want to rent a cabin then? Or perhaps you want us to buy one?" "No," she said. "But we can go shopping somewhere else." She was right, of course,' Gunnarstranda smiled, stirring his cup. 'We got out of Otta and never went back.'

Gunnarstranda lifted his cup and looked Lena in the eye.

'And the point you're making is?' Lena said, meeting his gaze unflinchingly.

Gunnarstranda put down his cup without taking a sip. He searched for words. 'She couldn't have children, Edel. That was her great sorrow in life. It was a sorrow she took with her when she became ill. It was my sorrow too, for a very long time. But now it's not so important. Edel died ages ago and I've got over not having children.'

Lena had worked with this man for many years, but she had never heard him open up. She didn't even know he had been married. But Lena wasn't sure she wanted to know these kinds of details.

'I'm not sure you should be so personal,' Lena said gently. 'Those of us who know you aren't used to it.'

'If you stop what you're doing and look around,' Gunnarstranda said, 'if you look at yourself, what's actually important?'

'In my life? Being successful. If you mean my job, the answer's the same: being successful.'

Finally Gunnarstranda sipped his coffee. 'But if you think a bit further than your job and today, what *is* actually important?'

Lena looked down at the table cloth. Being healthy, she thought, but she didn't want to talk about that, not now. However personal Gunnarstranda wanted to be. She decided to change the subject. 'I don't wish to talk about that.'

'I don't mean a particular worry or a fear of death or any terrors you might have.'

She raised her head and looked him in the eye. Did he know? No. Gunnarstranda couldn't know. No one else but her could know.

Gunnarstranda locked eyes with her, smiled faintly and shook his head a little patronisingly. 'Don't be afraid,' he said, 'I don't know anything you don't want me to know, but the reason I asked you to come here is that I can see there is *something*. I like you, Lena. But I've been a cop all my adult life and now I can see a colleague of mine is about to lose her grip, or perhaps I should say "jump on the wrong train". So I want you to stop and look around you. *Something* or *someone* is giving you grief. In such situations it's important to stop, look up and imagine you're a bird hovering aloft and looking down. The bird sees a wide swathe of countryside with a wealth of possibilities. But right below there's a little place with a lot of people jostling and pushing and shoving and cursing and screaming to buy a loaf of bread or a newspaper. And in the midst of this sweaty herd of angry people is you, stamping and fighting, wasting loads of energy on utterly crazy things. But getting out is so easy. Just take a step to the side, find a new angle. *You* have to make yourself the main person in your life. Don't reduce yourself to being an extra in the lives of others. To achieve this you have to see yourself in a wider context than one police case, or a particular worry, or a fear of death that has you in its grip and is making you blind.'

He fell silent.

She fell silent.

They gazed into each other's eyes for a long time. She had no idea what to say, but she liked what he had said, she liked it that he understood.

It was Gunnarstranda who broke the silence. He bared his teeth in a broad grin. 'This was our first and I hope last Get-Outa-Otta conversation,' he said. 'Now I'm ready for the briefing.'

5

She went through the online newspapers. Forced herself to look for deaths, drownings, accidents. She found nothing. News of the body that had been washed ashore in Kadettangen, outside Sandvika, hadn't reached the papers.

So PST must have put a lid on the case.

Could that be possible? Lena got up from the worktop. The pan was sizzling. The kitchen began to smell of crispy bacon. Lena filled the pan with onions and garlic. The prevailing smell now was reminiscent of holidays in Italy. When the pasta came to the boil she still had a few minutes to wait, so she took the opportunity to manoeuvre the Christmas tree through the balcony door. She leaned the tree against the corner. It wouldn't stand on its own. She crouched down and held it straight. The tree really was small, but with her mother's old tree-stand it would be higher and fit perfectly into her flat. Lena used a clay pot as a support and got it to stand upright, more or less.

She went back in, forked up a strand of spaghetti and tried it. *Al dente*. Perfect. She rinsed the pasta.

Lena was treating herself to her favourite meal: *spaghetti alla carbonara*: pasta, bacon, fried onions and garlic, topped off with raw egg yolks. Sideplate: a wholemeal roll from Åpent Bakeri. And to drink: pure Norwegian water.

Lena ate with intense concentration, as if she had never seen food before. At the end she mopped up the remaining sauce with the roll. She might be ill, but there was nothing wrong with her appetite.

When the plate was empty she was still hungry for more, but she controlled herself. Instead she brewed up some green tea and sat down with the laptop again.

This time she clicked on the bookmark she had made when she was searching for Steffen Gjerstad's articles. Single-mindedly, she combed through all of them. There was some truth in his nickname, the 'Hanger-on'. His name was often in the byline next to other names. She narrowed the search to articles written by him alone. Started to scroll. She yawned with boredom, but straightened up when she found an article about the homeless in Oslo.

The picture had been taken one summer's day, by Spikersuppa in Karl Johans gate. Two people were sitting on a bench: Nina Stenshagen and Stig Eriksen.

Lena studied the picture. After reading the article through once she read it again – word by word.

The myriad of stars in the sky was no longer a myriad. She had distanced herself now and she saw in the chaos the contours of a system. She lifted her head and closed her eyes, feeling what it did to her to see the connections forming.

The man I've been to bed with, she thought, and was close to throwing up. She swallowed and stood up. With her forehead against the wall she swallowed until her nausea had gone. She tried to breathe normally. Which was easier said than done. But do it she would. She felt empty, like after an exhausting ski run. Lifted her hands and inspected them. Waited until her fingers stopped trembling. Then she picked up her phone. She dialled Steffen's number.

It rang and rang. Finally he answered. 'Gjerstad.' The formal tone was so artificial it was almost embarrassing.

She cleared her throat, unsure whether her voice would carry. 'I was made the scapegoat,' she said. Her voice was carrying. She cleared her throat anyway and asked: 'Was that the idea?'

'Oh, it's you. What are you talking about now?'

'I'm talking about your recent article. I've been singled out as your source and I'm now under investigation. Have you been contacted regarding this case?'

'Suspended?'

'Yes, suspended. Shall I spell it for you?'

The silence lasted a little longer. 'Can I buy you lunch?'

Lena looked down at the article with the photo of Nina Stenshagen and Stig Eriksen. She smiled to herself.

'On one condition,' she said.

6

Gunnarstranda opened Rindal's door a fraction and Rindal beckoned him in.

There was a special news bulletin on the flatscreen TV on the wall.

'I've had a long and detailed discussion with Lena,' Gunnarstranda said. 'She's a good officer. I was thinking of asking you to review her suspension.'

'Shhh,' Rindal said, pointing to the screen.

Frikk Råholt was holding a press conference. He confirmed his acceptance of his new job as consultant at the PR agency First in Line.

Råholt's delicate face filled the screen. He said how pleased he was that the truth about Aud Helen's relations with Polisario's Stockholm office had come out in today's papers. Truth was beautiful and precious.

The truth was that his wife had neither been involved in politically subversive activities nor acted in any other fantasy scenario. The matter boiled down to something as simple and humdrum as caring for a child and to two people working together as responsible parents after a love affair in Paris more than twenty years before. But the press had presented wild claims that some funny business was going on between the Oil Fund and a completely legitimate political organisation! The press coverage was the scandal. The poor case officer, who unfortunately drowned, was only doing his job! Anyone who had seen how segregation was practised in Western Sahara could not understand how it was possible to use this poor country's political situation to turn a Norwegian politician having dinner with her ex into a media circus!'

Frikk Råholt raised his head and stared into the camera. This was a scandal the Norwegian press should learn from. 'Many editors and journalists should examine their consciences,' Råholt said. 'The Norwegian press lacks self-regulation. The bar for what the press allows itself is getting lower and lower. The only authority that can do anything about it is the press itself. We need freedom of speech, but even more than that we need a debate about media culture,' Frikk Råholt said, locking his eyes onto the camera. 'My wife is a living example of what an unpleasant burden it is to front politics publically,' he added, then had to cede attention to the news anchor, who presented the next item: the enormous amounts of money Norwegians spent on Christmas presents.

Gunnarstranda glanced over at Rindal, who lifted the remote and turned down the volume.

'What do you reckon?' Rindal asked.

'I don't think the leak about the MP's past with Shamoun came from us at all.'

Rindal clocked Gunnarstranda from across the table, a sceptical expression on his face: 'Why not?'

'Because Råholt can sit there puffing himself up without any fear of comeback. Now he'll become the most obese lobbyist this country has ever produced.'

Rindal smiled for a few seconds then shook his head. 'I don't follow your train of thought.'

'This happening now is no coincidence,' Gunnarstranda said. 'I can feel it in my gut, in the marrow of my bones. Soon there'll be more. We haven't heard the whole story yet. What I'm sure of is that this man wants to steer the ship. There'll be more, believe you me.'

'Such as what?'

'The official who drowned was examining a mining company operating in some ethical grey areas.'

Rindal smiled condescendingly. 'So the Adeler case is tied up with this? Have you gone mad?'

Gunnarstranda shook his head. He pointed his forefinger at his stomach.

Rindal shook *his* head. 'Your stomach's lying. Keep your feet on the ground and use your brain.'

'Do you imagine the lobbyist is holding a press conference for no reason?' Gunnarstranda asked.

Rindal sighed. 'Listen: Frikk Råholt's a politician. That's all there is to it. He's stoking the fire. Naturally. He's exploiting the situation. He's a matador in the ring, playing to the crowd. He's a winner. That's all. The leak came from here.' Rindal tapped his finger on the desk. 'You and I are both grown-ups. We don't imagine things.'

'Who's profited from this situation so far?' Gunnarstranda asked sombrely. 'Both Råholt and Vestgård. There's only one loser: Lena.'

Rindal fixed Gunnarstranda with a heavy stare. 'We both know Lena's been to bed with the journalist.'

'Lena's loyal. She's not the source.'

'I can see you're fighting for a colleague you like,' Rindal said. 'I like Lena too. But that doesn't mean she hasn't leaked information. The journalist could've got into her laptop or overheard a phone conversation for all we know. The point is that at some level Lena has shown poor judgement. In this situation we should leave any conclusions to SEFO. The world isn't about conspiracy theories and, if you give it a little thought, you know that. Listen and take note:

we've been accused of leaking confidential information. I have the head of the investigation sleeping with the journalist who publishes said information. So I have to act. I can't afford to slip up. *Capisce?*'

Gunnarstranda looked at him. '*Sayonara*,' he said.

'I beg your pardon?'

'You don't need to suspend Lena. You can take her off the case and give her admin tasks for a fortnight until this is over.'

Rindal contemplated Gunnarstranda, his brows knitted in annoyance.

'We police are much too square-headed in our thinking,' Gunnarstranda said. 'We focus too much on punishment and rewards instead of leadership.'

'That's enough,' Rindal snapped. 'Do your job and I'll do mine.'

'Actually there's another protagonist who's profited from this case,' Gunnarstranda said, getting up. He walked to the door. Opened it and left.

'Who?' he heard behind him.

Gunnarstranda stopped, turned and leaned against the door frame. 'One of the companies Adeler was investigating; goes by the name of MacFarrell. But you won't find the name in the papers or anywhere else.'

'Where did you hear the name?'

'From the loser – Lena. The only person who didn't have enough sense to keep the name quiet.'

7

Lena left her flat and met the new day, which was as dark as winter can be. She crossed the salt slush in Stortingsgata and continued quickly down towards Hotel Continental.

Lena's birthday was on 1st April – April Fools' Day all over the world. Most people had made a point of this over the years – friends, teachers, fitness coaches, boyfriends. Only one person had never made a joke about her birthday.

The day of her fourteenth birthday her father was waiting for some X-ray results. He was coughing a lot, but that was all. She celebrated the day with her mother and father in the Theatercafé. Lena had asked for a Sony Walkman as a present and had received it. They had ordered walnut cake for dessert. When the waiter came, the lights went out in the restaurant. The orchestra played 'Happy Birthday'. The waiter served the cake with sparklers crackling around him.

Every single 1st April in the years since then there had only been two of them to celebrate.

Lena had adroitly avoided the Theatercafé since. She had always come up with veiled excuses for not going there. The Theatercafé was an expensive place. People from the provinces went there in the hope that they would meet celebs from the city. It was a place for financiers, the media, stars and groupies of all shades.

Now she was going in through the classic portals for the first time in almost twenty years. She dreaded seeing the same things: the tall windows, the mezzanine with the orchestra, the rotunda, the buffet counter.

At the same time, however, Lena was happy. She was happy because her thoughts of a reunion with the café were on her mind, not the man she was going to meet.

She strode over to the cloakroom, took off her red woollen coat and passed it to the man behind the counter.

All the fashion bloggers swore by a short black dress. Lena had followed their tip. Her dress stopped in the middle of her thighs where equally black tights carried smoothly down to her ankle-high boots with low heels. Even the small handbag matched the dress, a treasure she had bought in Paris on her thirtieth birthday: Chanel 2.55 – black and elegant.

She turned and went into the restaurant, exactly ten minutes late.

She stood for a few seconds looking around. It felt like walking up a steep hill in her childhood. Slopes in reality are smaller and gentler than you remember.

This was only a café, a room crammed with people.

Conversation between all the guests created a loud booming sound beneath the ceiling. The din was wrapped in a concentrated Christmas fragrance: it was a bouquet that collected the scent of individual perfumes and mixed them with a pungent atmosphere of aquavit, *lutefisk*, creamed peas, roast pork and pork ribs, mutton ribs steamed for hours over beech twigs, sauerkraut with caraway, and puréed swede and pork sausages spiced with ginger, rounded off with floury potatoes, crowned with fresh coffee combined with the delicate odour of exclusive cognac. The place was packed. Steffen's press card must have enabled him to get a table. The head waiter met her with a broad smile. She ignored him and craned her neck to find Steffen. She spotted him at a table for four facing Stortingsgata. He was sitting with his back to her, but jumped up from his chair when she appeared at the table. His eyes told her she had hit the bullseye with her clothes. She backed away when he went to hug her.

He didn't allow the rejection to upset him; he gallantly proffered a hand and pulled out a chair, as though he had done nothing else but dance attendance on women all his life.

They sat down.

A waiter came over to the table. 'Something to drink first?' he asked politely.

'I have some Chablis.' Steffen held up a glass by the stem.

She hesitated. Both the waiter and Steffen looked at Lena patiently. She pointed to the menu. 'Sancerre.'

After the waiter had poured her wine, they raised their glasses.

'Chablis, soft and sweet,' Lena said.

He arched his brows. 'Sancerre, sulky and sour.'

He twirled the glass between his fingers.

He stared at her.

'We had an agreement,' she continued. 'I came here on the condition that you'd tell me who your source was.'

'It was Axel Rise,' he admitted at once.

'Prove it,' she said.

'Prove what?'

'Give me some proof that it was Rise who tipped you off about Shamoun, Vestgård and their child! I've been suspended because of that case. Your say-so isn't enough. I need proof.'

Steffen put a hand into his inside pocket, pulled out a document and passed it to her.

Lena straightened out the sheets of paper. It was Vestgård's statement. The same text she'd read out to Lena and Rindal, with Vestgård's lawyer, Irgens, present.

'You're lying again,' she said.

He stared at her.

'The document I filed was stamped, by me personally. These two sheets are blank. No stamp. This isn't a copy of my document. Axel Rise can't have given you this.'

He looked down at the two pieces of paper without uttering a word.

Lena folded them and put them in her bag.

'I don't know how he did it,' Steffen said. 'But I do know where I got them. From Axel Rise.'

She looked him in the eye. 'I don't believe you,' she said coldly.

He spread his open palms in resignation. 'Then don't.'

As if I were the dishonest one, she thought, and said: 'Tell me what Axel Rise's agenda is. Why is he feeding you information? What have you got on him?'

'Rise has a sick child.'

At last he had said something that was the truth.

'There's a clinic in Germany,' Steffen said, rubbing his thumb against his forefinger. 'Outside Frankfurt. Naturopathy. Cleaning blood, the full programme. So-called alternative medicine. No support from the state. Rise has to pay the whole whack himself. That clinic costs money.'

'You pay Rise for information?'

He didn't answer.

'Does your editor know this?'

Steffen looked back at her, still silent. His hand sought hers. For a fraction of a second she eyed the hand. Blue and green numbers and letters in biro. It jolted a memory, something that happened a long time ago. She smiled weakly. Was about to look away, but his hand drew her eyes back:

A hand covered in writing. Numbers. Numbers and writing in blue and green ink. Numbers. Numbers she had seen before. Where had she seen the numbers before? It was a phone number. It was a number she had dialled herself.

It was a number belonging to Bodil Rømer – the mother of the man who tried to kill her.

For a moment time stood still. Sound vanished. The waiter, who was on his way to the neighbouring table, didn't move.

It was a brief moment. But he must have noticed. 'What's the matter?' he asked.

Lena got up. 'Won't be a minute,' she said, put her handbag under her arm and walked out through the glass door. She took a deep breath. Then rushed to the cloakroom. Handed the man behind the counter a coin, grabbed her coat with both hands and staggered out.

Tuesday, 22nd December

1

She set off after him. Her eyes were fixed on his back. She picked up the pace to catch him. The man just walked faster; the distance stayed the same. Lena began to run. She closed the gap and stretched out a hand to grab his shoulder. Her hand fell short. He climbed into the cab of a lorry. The man was wearing some kind of uniform. He looked like the smoke diver who had got into the fire engine outside the block where Steffen lived. The man turned. At last she would see who he was. The man twisted his head round. At that moment she looked away. *No, don't look away!* She fixed her eyes on the man again. Once again she saw a profile turning towards her.

A loud noise woke her with a start.

She was sweaty, clammy, but didn't move a muscle, terrified of what lay behind the bang that had woken her.

She listened to the darkness. The flat was totally silent. She could hear nothing, not even the traffic outside.

The bang must have been in her dream. Was that possible? Could you hear such a realistic sound in your dream?

At last she plucked up the courage to move. Stretched out an arm and took her watch from the bedside table. The small, luminous hands showed ten past two in the morning.

She lay awake. Trying to focus on ordinary things, normal things, domestic things. For example, she had a frozen car to see to. That had to be sorted. She got out of bed, went to find her phone in the sitting room and texted Frank Frølich. Then went back to bed.

She was woken by the phone ringing. It was light outside. Lunch time for people who were working. She picked up the phone.

It was Gunnarstranda: 'I've got some good news and some bad news,' he said. 'Which do you want first?'

'The bad news.'

'You've got to get out of bed.'

'And the good news?'

'Your suspension's been countermanded.'

She wondered how she felt about that.

'You'll be a desk rat for a few days, that's all,' Gunnarstranda said.

'There's something I have to talk to you about,' Lena said, and launched into it: 'Steffen Gjerstad, the journalist.'

'What about him?'

'Six months ago he interviewed Nina Stenshagen and Stig Eriksen.'

There was silence for a few seconds, then Gunnarstranda coughed. 'Did he tell you that?'

'No. I found his article on the internet. One report in a series about people living in extreme situations. A guy living all year round in a hunting lodge in Svalbard, one digging for gold on Finnmarksvidda and these two homeless drug addicts living in a city.'

'So you're thinking Gjerstad is someone these two knew?'

'Yes,' Lena said, holding her breast for the first time for a while. She could feel the tumour. It ached. The whole of her breast was sore.

This silence lasted a little longer than the previous one.

'What are you actually trying to tell me?' he said.

'I think Gjerstad's the killer.'

Gunnarstranda said nothing.

'Why aren't you saying anything?'

'I'm thinking,' Gunnarstranda said.

Was he sceptical? Lena had never been so sure of herself. 'I'm waiting to receive the final confirmation today,' she said.

'How?'

'I'm going to Drammen to confront a witness.'

*

Frankie had answered the message.

He picked Lena up at just after two in the afternoon.

She asked him to stop at the Shell petrol station in Østre Aker vei. He drove in and stopped by the front door. She got out and went to buy some jump leads.

'I've got plenty of them,' he sighed when she got back in. 'You could've saved your money.'

'I need them anyway,' Lena said, not wishing to discuss the matter.

The Micra was where she had left it, covered in more ice than ever. She put the yellow fine in her pocket before Frølich had a chance to comment.

While he manoeuvred his Toyota into position she unlocked the door of the Micra and opened the bonnet. Lena hated everything to do with electricity. The mere thought of getting an electric shock could make her hysterical. And she tended to be oversensitive to static electricity. It wasn't unusual for her to get a shock just touching a car. Now she had to connect two car batteries and was already sick and tired of men's patronising attitudes towards her ignorance.

'Now you'll see,' Frankie said, swaggering over to the engine.

Lena opened the packet of jump leads. 'I have to be able to do this myself,' she said, pushing him away and taking one cable and attaching one clamp to the plus terminal. She took the other clamp and looked down into the engine of Frølich's car.

'There,' he pointed.

'I can see it,' she said, looking for the plus sign.

Frankie was impatient. 'There,' he said.

'I told you I could see it,' Lena said, about to attach the clamp.

'Not there,' he said, annoyed. 'There!' He went to take the clamp out of her hand.

'I'm doing it!'

She attached the clamp to the terminal without any further protests. This was child's play, she thought, examining the second cable.

Frølich watched her with a mildly condescending look.

'Yes?' Lena said.

'It's earth.'

'I know it is!' She attached the clamp to the opposite terminal on his battery. The cable was still too short to reach, so she attached the other end to the edge of the bonnet. 'That's earthed now.'

'Clever,' he said. 'Let's try.'

Lena didn't know what was clever, but she got into the car and turned the ignition key. The starter motor turned over as if the battery was new. The engine started. She put her foot on the accelerator. The car ran like a dream. Frankie removed the jump leads and closed the bonnet lid.

'Everything OK?' he shouted over the din of the engine.

She nodded. 'Thanks, Frankie!'

'Drive around for half an hour before you switch off the engine,' Frølich said, 'so that the battery can charge up.'

She nodded, waved as she let go of the clutch and turned the heater on full.

2

It was as hot as a sauna in the flat. Lena had taken off not only her jumper but also her short-sleeved top, which was sticking to her back.

'You don't need to offer me anything,' she called.

'What was that?' came a voice from the kitchen.

The lady really was hard of hearing. Lena gave up. She leaned back against the sofa. Then she spotted an ant parading along the windowsill. An ant! Lena's eyes widened. This was late December, winter, icy outside, frozen ground. How could an ant be wandering around in here? She followed it. It continued on its indefatigable journey. She leaned over and placed a finger in front of the ant. It climbed over her finger and down to the other side. Whoops! The ant fell from the windowsill and vanished in a crack above the radiator.

Lena jumped up, pulled the sofa back half a metre and knelt down to find it again. No ants on the floor. She presumed it was dead. Burnt to death on the radiator. It had survived half a winter here against all the odds, but then was killed because of her curiosity. It was a catastrophe. She tried to peer into the crack between the radiator and the wall to see it again.

'What are you doing?'

Bodil Rømer stood in the kitchen doorway. In her hands she was holding a porcelain tray with two porcelain cups, a jug of cream and a sugar bowl.

Lena blushed and sat up.

'I thought there was a bit of a draught,' she said, 'and I was feeling to see where it came from.'

'My husband was always repairing that corner,' Bodil Rømer said, and came in. She put the tray down on the small round table. Placed a cup for each of them.

'You don't need to serve anything,' Lena said. 'I don't want to be any bother.'

'You will have a cup of coffee, won't you? And a few cinnamon snaps. These cinnamon snaps are from Kiwi supermarket and are much better than the ones from Rema. You're right, there is a draught. There's a radiator behind the sofa. But I struggle to bend down. Would you turn the radiator up a bit?'

Lena, who was still withering in the heat, got to her feet and knelt down beside the sofa. No ants. Yes, there it was, and it wasn't alone. There was a little colony flourishing in the dust behind the radiator. An ant-hill in the sitting room! What might this woman have under her bed?

'There we are,' Lena said, straightening up. 'Now you'll be lovely and warm in here.'

She turned and looked straight into the face of Bodil Rømer, straining to hear her.

'Have a cinnamon snap,' said Bodil.

Lena took a heart-shaped biscuit and put it on her plate. She wondered what to say in order to point the conversation in the direction she wanted. She thought she would make some small talk first, then search for an opening. But the heat was still suffocating. This flat with its heavy curtains, even heavier door curtain, heavy furniture and ants on the floor was making her slightly claustrophobic. Suddenly Lena thought she had ants crawling up her legs and felt an acute urge to scratch; she longed to get out.

She stood up, squeezed between the sofa and the table and walked into the free area in the centre of the room.

'What's the matter?' Bodil asked.

'Draught,' Lena said. 'I'm a bit sensitive to draughts.'

'Dearie me,' Bodil said. 'It's true, it is cold. I'll turn up the heating!'

Lena was barely listening. She was back to when this woman's son pounced on her and she was hanging from the side of the cliff for grim life.

No, she told herself. *What happened was not my fault. He was the one who dragged me towards the edge. He was the one who wanted to throw me off.*

Lena closed her eyes. She was counting days. Bodil Rømer apparently thought her son was still living abroad. Why? Why hadn't Ingrid Kobro informed her of her son's death? And why did this woman have such a sad face?

'Imagine you meeting Stian on holiday and coming here to visit me. You're a nice girl.'

'So stupid of us not to exchange phone numbers,' Lena said, 'but that's how holidays are. Before you know what's happening you're on your way home, and it's only then you remember what you forgot to do.'

'I'll tell Stian you've been here next time he drops by. I'll tell him to hold onto you!'

I'd better get to the point, Lena thought. 'Lovely coffee,' she said with a smile.

'Oh, I'm forgetting myself,' Bodil said, got up and filled Lena's cup. She held the jug with both hands. Now Lena noticed that her hands were crippled. Three of her fingers curled into her palm in an unnatural way. Arthritis, Lena thought. At that moment their eyes met. Bodil put down the jug and hid her hands in embarrassment under the table.

Lena's feelings of guilt grew. She turned to the wall.

And she found herself looking straight at a school-leavers' photo. The writing underneath told her this was the last year at Drammen Gymnas. She took the picture down and studied it.

Bodil smiled. 'Yes, that's Stian's school photo.'

Lena scanned the heads wearing the famous red *russ* caps; the photo was nineteen years old. She had no idea what Stian looked like nineteen years ago.

But then her legs gave way beneath her and she had to support herself on the wall.

'What is it? Aren't you feeling well?'

Lena shook her head. If she had been hot before, she was cold now. 'I think I've found Stian,' she said, putting the photo on the table and pointing.

''No,' Bodil said, pointing to the photo with a deformed hand. 'This is Stian,' she said, with a crooked little finger. 'You were point-ing at Steffen, his friend, but they're very similar, I'll give you that!'

Lena kept a poker face and managed to simulate a smile. 'How stupid I am. I can see it now. I met both of them there on Ibiza. Stian and Steffen were on holiday together.'

'No change there then,' Bodil said. 'Steffen and Stian, they were like the *Katzenjammer Kids* – utterly inseparable.'

'Has Steffen tried to contact Stian recently?'

'He's rung, but I can only tell him what I've told you. Stian's abroad.'

3

As Lena was driving through Lierskogen Forest, down the hill towards Asker, with Oslo spreading in front of her like an inverted starry sky, she had an idea. She reviewed it once and then a second time. It got better the more she thought about it. Approaching Sandvika, she picked up her phone and rang Gunnarstranda. He was in Tanum Bookshop on Karl Johans gate, buying Christmas presents. They agreed to meet at the skating rink nearby, in Spikersuppa.

She found a place to park at the bottom of Roald Amundsens gate and found Gunnarstranda talking to Frank Frølich by the statue of Henrik Wergeland. Metallic music was blaring out of the loudspeakers. Crowds of children were floundering round and round the little rink, which was bathed in light.

Lena joined them.

'I've just heard you've been rehabilitated,' Frølich said. 'Congratulations.'

Lena shrugged. If Frankie was bitter she could understand. 'I'm sure it's a gender thing,' she said, 'like everything else.'

Both of them looked at Gunnarstranda, who was sorting the books in his carrier bag.

'It was Rindal's doing,' Gunnarstranda said. 'He succumbed to persuasion. Actually I think he's got a soft spot for you, Lena.'

Frølich was off to catch a bus from Universitetsplassen. The two of them said goodbye to him and walked slowly towards the Storting building.

'This idea of yours, is it to do with Gjerstad?' Gunnarstranda asked.

She nodded.

Gunnarstranda pulled a sceptical grimace. 'You still think Gjerstad drowned Adeler?'

She nodded.

'And shot Nina Stenshagen and threw her in front of the train, and shot Stig Eriksen?'

Lena didn't answer.

'In which case, where did he get the weapon? I don't like to know too much about my colleagues' private lives. But when you were together did you see a pistol? ... I don't mean that euphemistically.'

Lena still said nothing. She knew about one person who had run after her with a weapon – and who knew Steffen Gjerstad. A man who had waited for her in Steffen's flat.

Should she tell Gunnarstranda? She didn't have time to think that through.

'If you think that Gjerstad's the killer, then it's not enough that he interviewed the two who were shot. You need proof. You need to be able to prove that Gjerstad was present at the harbour with Adeler. And you need a motive. Why did he kill Adeler? Also you need the weapon Nina and Stig were shot with. Also you need to be able to explain why Aud Helen Vestgård received a death threat. Have you got the answers?' But Gunnarstranda clearly couldn't be bothered to wait for an answer. 'Let's go,' he said. 'I'm getting cold.'

Lena realised the moment had come. 'Hang on,' she said. 'As I said, I've got an idea.'

Gunnarstranda stopped.

'I think I know how we can lure whoever pushed Adeler off the harbour into the light,' she said.

'How?'

'Stig Eriksen and Nina Stenshagen are not necessarily the only ones to have seen what happened that morning,' she said. 'We can leak another name. We use informants to spread this information. So far the killer's eliminated all the witnesses. If we leak a name, he's bound to try and eliminate the third as well.'

Gunnarstranda made no secret of his opposition to the suggestion: 'Provocations like that are illegal. Furthermore,' he continued thoughtfully, 'if we invented such a witness we'd need a decoy; and we won't get one because we would've informed Rindal and he would've refused to let us go ahead.'

Lena turned to the old university building. Beneath the Christmas decorations she could see Frøhlich waiting for a bus with his hands in his pockets. Lena stretched out a gloved hand and pointed.

'A civil servant who's been suspended from duty can't be suspended twice,' she said.

Gunnarstranda shook his head. 'Provocation is a no-no,' he said. 'It's a shot in the dark. You never know if you've hit, and if you do, you won't know what until long afterwards.'

'So you're not in favour?'

Gunnarstranda didn't answer.

'You *are* in favour?'

Gunnarstranda took a breath and was about to answer, but she got in first:

'If Frankie says yes, are you still against the idea?'

Lena walked off without waiting for an answer. She marched towards the university building.

✳

Gunnarstranda watched her progress. Lena crossed Universitetsgata on red and shouted to Frølich, who came to meet her. Frølich listened without batting an eyelid. Then he nodded.

Gunnarstranda breathed heavily. Frølich had agreed, just as he had feared he would. Gunnarstranda rested his hands on his hips. He turned and strolled in the opposite direction, towards the Storting.

Lena caught up with him.

'We have a plan,' she said with a broad smile.

'As I feared,' Gunnarstranda said.

She sensed his disapproval at once, and asked: 'But what can really go wrong?'

'In 1949 three aeronautic engineers ran a rocket-sled test in California,' Gunnarstranda said. 'One of them was called Edward J. Murphy. Afterwards he formulated something that has become known as Murphy's Law.'

Lena sighed.

They walked along side by side without speaking until they reached Egertorget.

'Have you got a better suggestion?' Lena asked finally.

Gunnarstranda shook his head. 'Let's talk more about this tomorrow.'

✳

They went their separate ways. Lena continued a few metres down Karl Johans gate. But she was unable to let go of the idea.

She stopped. People were rushing back and forth, shoulder to shoulder.

They had to coax Steffen out of hiding. But how could they get Gunnarstranda on their side? The answer was as clear as day. She had to be honest. All her cards on the table. She couldn't hush up the Stian Rømer business any more. Lena closed her eyes. Something inside her bristled. *Why? What are you afraid of? You have to say what happened, to get it out of your system.*

It was obvious. She had a choice: either go home now and forget the whole thing or take this to the bitter end. What should she do?

Lena turned and walked back. Slowly at first, then faster. She had to go back home. Where was he? Where could he have gone? She guessed to the bus stops in Akersgata and turned right.

But Gunnarstranda was nowhere to be seen. She quickened her pace.

She saw his characteristic figure in front of the windows on the ground floor of the *Verdens Gang* building. Gunnarstranda was dialling a number on his phone.

4

Gunnarstranda was using the light from the windows to find the right number. He rang security at the parliament building. They were able to inform him that Frikk Råholt was still in his office.

Gunnarstranda walked towards Møllergata and down the drive to the underground car park for parliamentary staff. There, he stood outside the gate. Regardless of whether Råholt used his private car or not, Gunnarstranda assumed he would have to come out this way. He waited for just under a quarter of an hour as a steady stream of officials passed him, some in cars, some on foot.

Råholt left on foot. The opening of the car park shone yellow behind the silhouette wearing a dark winter coat and walking into the street at a brisk, efficient tempo. When the gate closed again Råholt's delicate facial features could soon be distinguished in the half light.

Their eyes locked and Råholt stopped.

'Yes?' he said.

'Gunnarstranda, Oslo PD.' Gunnarstranda went to the trouble of showing the ID card he had hanging around his neck.

Råholt went to the trouble of studying it.

'What's this about?'

'A number of relationships. It would be to your benefit to allow me a few minutes.'

Råholt tilted his head and gave Gunnarstranda an enquiring look.

'This is primarily about a job you took on for First in Line.'

'I haven't started working for them yet.'

'So how come I know your client list?'

Råholt didn't bat an eyelid.

'Let me fill you in on the context first,' Gunnarstranda said. 'My colleague was suspended because she was supposed to have leaked a document to the press. I know she didn't. However, I now have the document that *you* personally faxed to the journalist from your home address. The journalist gave it to me.'

Råholt still said nothing. He just watched the police officer attentively.

'And you don't deny it,' Gunnarstranda prompted. 'One of your clients is MacFarrell Ltd. You don't need to deny that either. I'm like the detective in old comics. I know everything.'

Råholt tilted his head again. 'Not bad,' he conceded with a slight smile.

Gunnarstranda folded his hands behind his back. 'This mining company has hired First in Line – you, in other words – to influence government decisions so that the Oil Fund will maintain its commitment, as it's so nicely put.'

'How on earth can you make such a claim?'

'Look me in the eye and tell me I'm wrong,' Gunnarstranda said.

Råholt said nothing.

'MacFarrell hired you and you've kept your part of the bargain by systematically feeding confidential information to a journalist by the name of Steffen Gjerstad.'

'That's your contention,' said Råholt. 'Mine is that I've solely given advice to a multinational concern about how to position themselves with regard to the Norwegian public.'

'Given advice? First of all you smear an official on the Ethics Council. Then you leak a document to a journalist – a document your wife asked to be treated in total confidence. That's pretty state-of-the-art advice.'

'That's your contention,' Råholt said.

Gunnarstranda turned to go. 'At any rate you've confirmed what I wanted to know.'

Råholt held him back.

Gunnarstranda stopped.

'What are you going to do?' Råholt asked.

'What do you think I'm going to do? What do you think I draw my pay for?'

Råholt smiled at him. 'Then you might do your job better than your red-haired colleague? You might collect evidence before you begin to harass people with accusations?'

They eyed each other. 'Let me put it this way, Frikk Råholt. If you'd been on my social level I would've asked if your wife bakes bread.'

'And why would you have asked that?'

'Because I'd tell her to start baking tools in it – a file for example.'

'Oh, my goodness me,' Råholt smiled. 'What have we here? A comedian?'

'But you're not on my social level. You belong to that circle of people who get away with crime. I've been a cop too long to care what happens.'

A car pulled up in front of the drive.

Råholt waved to the driver, who waved back.

'My wife,' Råholt said.

Gunnarstranda looked at the car. 'Does she know?' he asked.

'Does she know what?'

'Does your wife know that you used her to smear Adeler? That you rang the journalist Steffen Gjerstad and told him your wife and Asim Shamoun were having dinner with Adeler on Wednesday, the ninth of December?'

'You don't give in, do you. Are you wired?'

Gunnarstranda shook his head. 'We police are banal enough to obey the law.'

'Let me answer you in this way,' Råholt said. 'I keep no secrets from my wife.'

'But Shamoun didn't know?'

Råholt cast a quick glance at the car.

'He didn't know,' Gunnarstranda said. 'Unlike you and your wife, he's decent. You've played your cards well, I'll give you that. When Gjerstad uncovered the so-called meeting between the Oil Fund, the Finance Committee and Polisario, your employer MacFarrell had the "scandal" that would achieve the right result. Polisario, as it were, conspiring with an MP to influence the Ethics Council rendered the case officer, Adeler, tainted and his eventual report valueless in the eyes of the public. Leaving MacFarrell squeaky clean in the eyes of your average Norwegian. Taking the company off the Oil Fund portfolio after the "revelation" would create an unparalleled political storm. And once that goal was achieved, you could exonerate your wife and kick the ball into the long grass. You could leak the truth. The link between Polisario and your wife wasn't political, it was a family relationship.'

Råholt nodded towards the car, his face taut. 'Can you see someone's waiting for me?'

'But it must've been a shock hearing Adeler had drowned that morning, eh?' Gunnarstranda said. 'The scenario you had set up took a turn you hadn't planned. How did that feel? The moment you realised you weren't the Almighty?'

Råholt took a deep breath and said in a patronising tone: 'Sveinung Adeler's death never had anything to do with the matter. This has always been about his report.'

Gunnarstranda nodded.

'Of course. I'll go along with that. The official was not your concern. His death didn't change anything. Cheating the public was not important. You and the journalist made up all that shit and smeared it over Adeler. He was dishonest and tainted, even if the man was dead and unable to defend himself. Nothing meant anything. You steamed ahead.'

'Moralising is for hypocrites,' Råholt intoned. 'And you don't look like a hypocrite, Gunnarstranda.'

The police officer nodded. 'Explain one thing for me anyway,' he said.

'Ask, and I'll see.'

'Why?'

'Why what?'

'Why use your wife and her child in such a cynical way? Why is it so bloody important to cling onto the new job? What is it about it that legitimises lies, manipulation, slandering the name of the deceased and leaking confidential information that has dramatic consequences for others?'

Råholt stepped forward two paces. They were so close Gunnarstranda could smell the man's after-shave.

'Well I never. What a hypocritical and ridiculous man you are,'
Råholt said in hushed tones. 'You said yourself you were on a different level from me. Well, that's true. And now you're wondering
why I'm giving up one job and starting another? Surely that can't be
so difficult to understand? I want to feel good about myself; I want
to fulfil myself and I want power! Do you know what that means? I
want to make decisions. I want to see results. Someone with power
and influence has to be where decisions are engendered. There's no
more to understand than that.'

'But you can't have had Gjerstad working for you gratis,' Gunnarstranda said. 'You bought the journalist. Anything else would've
been too risky. How much did you pay him?'

Råholt didn't answer.

'Let me guess,' Gunnarstranda grinned. 'He has a public position
and he joins you in the agency, First in Line?' Gunnarstranda nodded
to himself. 'Makes sense, and it explains why he did what he did; but
do you really think it was a smart move?'

Råholt still didn't say anything.

'I may not know as much as you about advanced forms of communication. But I'm a cop and I know something about crooks. You
and your wife will evade the legal system this time. I'm fairly sure of
that. But remember he's got something on you, this journalist. He
knows who you are at heart and knows your methods. Are you sure
you haven't made a move you'll live to regret?'

Råholt cast down his eyes, pensive.

The car door opened. Aud Helen Vestgård got out and leaned
against the open car door with an anxious expression on her face.
'Are you coming, Frikk?'

'I'm coming,' Råholt said, with a friendly smile for Gunnarstranda. 'Anything else, Mr Detective?'

. Gunnarstranda shook his head.

Frikk Råholt walked to the car and slid onto the back seat. The car reversed from the car park and turned. There were three women in the car. Aud Helen with her two daughters.

Råholt waved as the car passed Gunnarstranda.

'*Sayonara*,' Gunnarstranda said, watching the vehicle disappear.

After it was gone, he turned. 'You can come out now,' he said in a louder voice.

✳

Lena came out of the shadows and into the light.

'Eavesdropping on other people's conversations isn't polite,' Gunnarstranda said.

'Råholt will get away with it,' she said. 'I was made a scapegoat, but he can do as he likes.'

'The rule of power,' Gunnarstranda said.

'Are you still against faking a press conference about a third witness?' she asked.

'Why do you want to do this?' Gunnarstranda asked, looking straight at her. 'Honestly.'

'I'm a hundred per cent sure Steffen Gjerstad is the killer,' she said.

'So it's revenge?'

Lena shook her head. 'This is what our job's about! He's a murderer and has to be punished.'

'Provocation of this kind would be illegal. What about your role as a police officer and your relationship with law and order?'

'Of course, but…'

'But?'

'I'm sure Steffen Gjerstad's killed someone and I don't want him to get away with it!'

'Three people have been murdered,' Gunnarstranda objected. 'Which one did Gjerstad murder?'

'It must've been Steffen who pushed Adeler into the harbour and held him down with the plank.'

'That's what you *think*. It's not something you know.'

'But Nina Stenshagen saw what happened. She knew Steffen…'

'And who shot Nina? Who shot Stig?'

Lena and Gunnarstranda looked each other in the eye.

Lena took a deep breath and cast off. 'Someone by the name of Stian Rømer,' she said.

Lena closed her eyes. She had done it; she had let the cat out of the bag. She opened her eyes. But she could read nothing in Gunnarstranda's face.

'So you think there were two assailants on the quay that morning?' he asked.

'There must've been,' Lena said. 'Nina was a witness to Steffen killing Adeler. She knew who Steffen was and for that reason was dangerous to him. I think Stian Rømer shot Nina Stenshagen on Steffen's orders.'

'Let's talk a bit about Stian Rømer,' Gunnarstranda said.

'I know they knew each other. They were childhood friends.'

'The Stian Rømer who chased you in Schweigaards gate and was armed?'

'Don't you think that happened?' Lena retorted.

'Of course I believe you, but at the moment Rømer isn't in the country,' Gunnarstranda said.

Lena didn't answer.

Gunnarstranda stared into her face: 'That's what PST's trying to have us believe anyway.'

Lena averted her eyes. 'Don't you believe them?'

'What I've been told is that Rømer took a plane to London after his failed attack on you in Gamlebyen.' Gunnarstranda allowed the silence to hang in the air for a few seconds. 'If that's true, it won't be so easy to nick him for murder now.'

They gazed hard at each other. Measuring each other's strengths. 'I know PST are wrong,' Lena said after a while. 'He didn't take any plane.'

They continued to measure each other up. Lena waited for the question she dreaded. Her mind was racing. How should she present what happened?

But the question never came.

'Let's assume you're right,' Gunnarstranda said. 'Let's assume it was Gjerstad who drowned Adeler and that the mercenary, Stian Rømer, shot the witnesses. What would Gjerstad's motive be for killing Adeler?'

'I don't know,' Lena said, unsure whether she was happy about this side-track or not.

'Then I'm sure you'll understand why I'm asking you if you're just out to avenge a love that went wrong.'

Lena shook her head. 'This isn't revenge. I've finished with Steffen. And I do mean finished,' she said. 'Råholt's just admitted that he and Steffen had collaborated to bring a scandal down on the Ethics Council and Polisario. Well, Steffen took the photos at the restaurant. Steffen appeared at the harbour when we were recovering the dead body. He spoke to me then, but he omitted to say he knew the deceased. He only told me that a few hours later, when he was outside Adeler's flat waiting for me to come out. And it was only then he told me he had recognised Adeler when we lifted Adeler out of the water. And it was only then he told me where Adeler grew up – in Jølster. And he told me Adeler was a conceited namedropper and a fitness freak. All of a sudden Steffen knew *a helluva lot* about Adeler. Why didn't he say any of that at the harbour? All the journalists outside the cordon were interested to hear if we could identify the dead man. Steffen knew who had drowned, but chose not to say anything. Why was he waiting for me outside Adeler's flat?'

Gunnarstranda nodded thoughtfully. 'That's a lot of questions you're asking,' he said. 'But they don't necessarily have the same answer. Let's suppose you go ahead with this charade to lure the journalist out of hiding. Don't forget the journalist has an ally in Rise. How could you carry off this ruse without it being revealed?'

Lena ruminated. 'Rise's friendship with Gjerstad can be used,' she said. 'When we feed him the name of the fake witness, we have to keep the plan to ourselves. He should be told the name, that's all.'

'And how will we do that?'

'You just used the word "we",' Lena said with a smile. 'You're almost convinced.'

Gunnarstranda shook his head and replied: 'It's no good you *feeling* Gjerstad is the man. You have to be able to prove he was at the crime scene, that he had the opportunity and a motive to kill. You don't *know* if Gjerstad was there at the harbour when the murder took place.'

'If he was there he had the opportunity,' she said.

'But have you got a motive?' Gunnarstranda riposted.

'I'm sure there's a motive,' she answered.

'But you don't know what it is.'

'No. But the person who killed Adeler also eliminated the eyewit-nesses. If we let it leak out that there was a third witness near the quay, the man will attack that third witness.'

'You still don't have the motive behind Adeler's murder. Remem-ber Murphy's Law. If it runs true to form, all you'll achieve is a charge that has to be dropped because the attack on the decoy is an illegal, provoked act. Then the killer goes free and you've gambled away any chance to nab him.'

'But there'll still be reasonable grounds for suspicion. We can question him.'

'The man will refuse to make a statement on the recommendation of his solicitor. Then it's only a question of time before he goes free. No, Lena, the risk's too great,' Gunnarstranda concluded. 'There'll be no operation with a third witness.'

Gunnarstranda turned without another word, and went.

Disappointed, Lena was left watching the low-gravity, slightly skew-whiff figure.

Suddenly he turned and fixed her with a stare. 'How can you be so sure Rømer wasn't on the plane?'

She gulped, and shouted to make her voice heard: 'I've been instructed by Ingrid Kobro not to say.'

A cowardly answer, she thought, leaning back. The snow that was drifting down was invisible in the night sky, but thick and

impenetrable in the yellow glow around the streetlamps that succeeded one another in a straight line.

She lowered her head, ready for a confrontation. But Gunnarstranda had set off again without a word.

The snow lay like a fine layer of powder on the road, muffling
sound. A tractor with a snowplough at the front and a snowblower
at the rear came into Youngstorget. The orange flashing lights were
reflected on the walls around. Even the roar of the diesel engine
became a muffled growl. Christmas, Lena thought, trying to remember back. She hadn't noticed a silence like this in snowy weather since
she was a little girl.

Lena leaned against the wall, watching the small figure of Gunnarstranda, who hesitated for a few seconds by the steps to Møllergata
19, the old Nazi HQ, then turned and crossed the street. Soon the
silhouette of the police officer had merged with the shadow from
the towering building. The snow was falling heavily now. Soon his
footprints would be small depressions in the thickening carpet.

Lena filled her lungs with air, turned and strode off in the opposite direction.

5

A Christmas song was audible from down the corridor: John Lennon
and Yoko Ono's 'Happy Xmas. War is Over'.

No doubt about that, Lena thought, walking over to her pigeon
hole. Quite a pile of post had accumulated. It was full to overflowing. She grabbed the pile and flicked through it as she walked to the
office.

In the middle there was a thick, brown C4 envelope.

She was about to put it back in the pile when she saw it had
been sent by the Finance Department – the secretariat of the Ethics
Council. Lena raised her eyebrows.

She went into her office and opened the envelope.

In it was a stapled wad of typewritten sheets of paper. On top was a yellow Post-it:

Hi Lena,

Nice to meet you. Thought the following would interest you. The report is finished, as you can see, but we haven't sent it on. As Sveinung's dead, the case has been handed over to another officer, who will present his own conclusions. As this report no longer forms part of the official case, we can make an exception and allow you to peruse it. Naturally, the condition is that you treat this document as confidential information. Happy Christmas!

Soheyla M

This had to be a sign, thought Lena. Soheyla Moestue had been so correct and formal when Lena made enquiries in the secretariat. Soheyla hadn't even wanted to investigate whether her colleague Sveinung Adeler had written a report on his journey to Western Sahara. Now she was sending her the whole file that Adeler had put together on MacFarrell Ltd.

'*The report is finished, as you can see, but we haven't sent it on.*'

Lena re-read the sentence.

She checked the date on the front: Wednesday, 9th December.

'*…finished … but we haven't sent it on*'.

The secretariat hadn't sent it on. Why not?

Because Sveinung Adeler died during the following night.

Lena had to talk to Soheyla Moestue. She looked at her watch. It was evening. No one was at work now, but it would soon be Christmas and people were out and about early and late. Lena pulled out her desk drawer and found the little cardholder where she kept all her business cards. Yes!

On Soheyla Moestue's card there was a mobile number.

'Thank you for the report,' she said when Soheyla picked up. Then she got to the point: 'Just one thing though. Why wasn't the report sent to the Ethics Council? Was it really stopped?'

'Can I ring you back? I'm in a shop,' Soheyla said.

'Yes, of course,' Lena said. 'I think I know why, but I need to hear you say it.'

'The case has been given to another officer,' said Soheyla in a stressed voice. Lena could hear children shouting and the ringing of a till in the background. 'As Sveinung's dead he can't justify his conclusions. So we asked for his report back when we found out he was dead.'

'Back?'

'Yes, it went by post on Wednesday, the ninth of December. The following day, on the Thursday, when it was clear Sveinung was dead, we asked to have all his documents returned as, of course, he was unable to clarify them. The report you're holding was never discussed. But I knew none of this when we two talked a week ago.'

'Thank you very much,' Lena said, and left her to do her shopping in peace.

Lena leaned back in her chair and could feel everything slotting nicely into place. The date on the report explained what had happened.

Sveinung Adeler, who was reporting on a company operating in occupied Western Sahara, on behalf of the Ethics Council, had received another request from Aud Helen Vestgård to meet Polisario. Meeting Polisario should have been a trivial matter – unproblematic. But it was quite a different business doing it at a restaurant in Oslo on the initiative of – and in the company of – an MP who had arranged the meeting. This context lent it a certain significance and impact. What at the outset would have been the normal investigations of a case officer could, in this new light, be interpreted as ceding to political pressure and lobbying. Naturally Adeler would have taken this into account. He was a young man with a career in front of him; a climber and a name-dropper; a party member who didn't say no to an MP who condescended to call him and ask him out. However, he was in a dilemma. Adeler had no idea what Vestgård's intentions were with such a meeting, but he was bound to have looked for a way of evading the taint of impropriety that attached itself to her invitation.

How could he avoid potential political pressure in this situation? How could he avoid future speculation concerning his neutrality and reliability because of this meeting?

Lena smiled to herself. Adeler had taken the only correct course of action. He had stopped work on the MacFarrell case *before* the dinner. In so doing he was able to counter possible criticism later: the meeting that evening didn't affect his work – the report was finished and had been sent for approval beforehand! That was obvious. *That* was how it must have been. Nothing at all mysterious about it. Adeler had washed his hands of the case in advance!

Lena flicked through the report and decided to go straight to the conclusions and read the last page first. Then she skimmed through page by page and took a deep breath.

Lena wasn't tired and fed up any more. She was wide awake when she picked up the receiver.

6

Elvis was singing 'Blue Christmas' on the stereo and Tove was sitting with a large Christmas card in her hand when Gunnarstranda came in through the door.

Tove got up, lowered the volume and showed him the motif on the card. 'From Torstein,' she said. The card was A4 size with a portrait of Elvis Presley. She opened the card. 'Eh *voilà*,' Tove said with a grin.

A sombre, slightly grating Elvis-voice rose from the card: 'Merry Christmas, Baby!'

Gunnarstranda gave a nod of acknowledgement and removed his winter coat, which he had almost managed to brush free of snow. 'Christmas,' he said, kneeling down and unzipping his boots.

'By the way, regards from Torstein,' Tove said. 'He's better.'

'Anything new?'

Gunnarstranda stood up and put his boots on the shoe shelf.

He went into the kitchen and put on the hot-water tap to warm his hands, which were red from the cold.

'New?' Tove mulled over the question. 'Torstein's latest theory is that all geniuses die when they're thirty-seven years old. He put forward Rimbaud, Mozart, Henrik Wergeland and Jesus Christ as proof, and claimed the reason for the phenomenon is that the digit sum of thirty-seven is ten and of ten it is one and the number one is a symbol of a genius.'

Gunnarstranda turned off the tap, took a towel and dried his hands. 'The digit sum of twenty-eight is also ten,' he said.

Tove nodded. 'I used that argument, too. But Torstein had an answer to that. His theory is that geniuses die when they're nineteen, twenty-eight, thirty-seven, forty-six, fifty-five, sixty-four, seventy-three, eighty-two or ninety-one.'

'What about one hundred?'

'No geniuses become a hundred,' Tove said, and added: 'According to Torstein. And thirty-seven is a kind of peak, age-wise.'

Gunnarstranda considered this claim. 'Miles Davis. He died when he was sixty-five. Which makes eleven and the digit sum of eleven is two. The theory doesn't hold water.'

'Torstein has never understood jazz,' Tove said.

The telephone rang. Tove got up again and moved towards it. Gunnarstranda admired the swing of her hips as she did so. She took the receiver and held a thoughtful finger to her chin. They exchanged looks.

'For you,' she said, passing him the receiver.

'I'm in the bath,' Gunnarstranda said.

Tove shook her head. 'Lena Stigersand,' she said.

Gunnarstranda took a deep breath. 'I just went outside and you can't see me in the foul weather.'

She shook her head again.

Gunnarstranda took the receiver.

'Please be brief,' he said.

'I've found the motive,' Lena said, laughter bubbling in her throat. 'It's here on the table in front of me.'

7

It was a few minutes after midnight when Gunnarstranda turned off Østre Aker vei and continued towards the satellite town of Haugenstua.

He found Ole Brumms vei and drove up the little hill to the car park before the railway crossing. He parked. Got out and strolled towards the blocks of flats and the paths between them where the snow had been cleared. Yellow stains on the piled-up snow revealed that this housing co-op allowed dogs.

He was going to see Axel Rise – if this man was in Oslo and not in Bergen. All Gunnarstranda knew was the house number, not which floor Rise lived on.

The front entrance turned out to be in the middle of the block, closest to the railway line and the forest.

Gunnarstranda rang below and there was no response. When he went to press the bell for a second time the front door was opened by two young boys in jackets slightly too big for them and who, judging by their appearance, came from the Middle East. Both were grinning and exchanged glances when they saw him.

Gunnarstranda went in. There was a smell of frying oil. The lift was waiting. He entered and took it to the top floor. Then he went out and started walking down the stairs. He read the nameplates on all the doors, floor by floor. The problem was that many residents didn't have a nameplate.

Neither did Axel Rise. Gunnarstranda recognised his motorbike boots though. They were parked tidily on a plastic mat outside a door on the fourth floor.

Gunnarstranda rang the bell.

Nothing happened.

Gunnarstranda looked at his watch. It was twenty-five to one. He was tired and impatient. He took his bunch of keys and used the ring to hammer repeatedly on the door and yelled: 'Police! Open up in the name of the law!'

Soon afterwards he heard Bergensian swear words through the door.

The security chain rattled.

'You? What do you think you're doing?' Rise groaned. He blinked sleepily into the bright light. All he was wearing was light-blue boxer shorts and a hairnet.

'My gran had one like that,' Gunnarstranda said, pointing to the hairnet. 'But she only wore it when she had curlers in. Have curlers gone out of fashion?'

Rise automatically put a hand to his head and smiled sheepishly. At the same time there was a rattle of locks. Two neighbouring doors opened a fraction. Frightened faces peered out.

Rise sighed. 'You'd better come in.'

Gunnarstranda went into a dark, poorly ventilated bedsit dominated by a wide bed. In front of it was an almost equally wide TV on a stand.

No chairs, no table.

Axel Rise pulled on a pair of jeans lying on the floor. He went towards the kitchenette where he opened the door of a low fridge. 'Can I offer you anything?'

Gunnarstranda shook his head.

Rise fetched a red can of Christmas brew and sat down on the bed. He was a sight with his long hair in a net and his bare chest – truly bare, except for a large hairy mole between his nipples. It resembled a lucky charm – the scalp of a gonk troll.

Gunnarstranda remained on his feet.

'And what brings such worthies to these parts?' Rise asked.

'We have a leakage problem,' Gunnarstranda said.

'The bladder, eh?' Rise grinned. 'Is that why you didn't want a beer?'

'I think you know what I mean, and I also think you can help me to solve it,' Gunnarstranda said.

Rise took the remote control from the floor. He switched on the TV and zapped through the channels until he found one with car-racing on. Then he made himself comfortable, and said: 'Shut the door after you as you leave.'

Gunnarstranda stood in front of the screen. 'Eighty per cent of the earth's population are idiots,' he said. 'It's what's called the 80:20 rule. You can have a conversation with the twenty per cent. The other eighty per cent are all knuckleheads. Isn't that depressing?'

'You're in the way,' Rise said grumpily.

'I asked a witness once where she lived,' Gunnarstranda said. 'She said she couldn't remember whether it was Nesodden or Notodden. She mixed them up. I told her Nesodden was a few hundred metres from here – I even pointed across Oslo Fjord to where it was. Nesodden's the bit of land you can see out there in Oslo Fjord. However, Notodden's a town a hundred and fifty kilometres from Oslo, so the question is fairly simple, I told her. "Do you live five hundred metres from here or a hundred and fifty kilometres?" And you know what she answered? "How the hell do I know?"'

'What are you talking about?' Rise said.

'This is my offer to you. We're close to a breakthrough in the Adeler Case. We'll be there tomorrow. If you tell me right now, without any trickery, why you didn't do your job when you were instructed to check out Aud Helen Vestgård, you'll still be in the team and involved in clearing up the case. Otherwise you're out. But you won't only be out. I'll tell everyone why. Oslo PD will become a living hell for you, and every single police district where I have contacts. You've got thirty seconds.'

Gunnarstranda pulled up his jacket sleeve and counted the time.

Rise eyed him from the bed. 'You're a strange bugger, you are,' Rise said.

'Time's up,' Gunnarstranda said, and headed for the door.

'Alright then,' Rise yelled.

Gunnarstranda turned.

Rise switched off the television. He sat collecting himself for a few seconds. 'I went there, to where she lived – by Frogner Church. While I was ringing her bell an old pal of mine – Steffen Gjerstad – came along. He patted me on the shoulder. He'd been waiting for someone from the police to show up. He asked if I was going to take the statement of a woman who'd sent an MP a threatening letter. I asked him how he knew. Steffen told me he knew the woman. They go out a bit and have fun. He wrote the letter and signed it using her name. The threat was just messing around. He'd done it for a joke.'

'Steffen Gjerstad? The journalist? And he was waiting outside her flat, waiting for the police?'

'Yes,' Rise said. 'He was waiting there to clear up a misunderstanding! He regretted writing the letter. It had been a stupid idea. He assumed the police would react and was waiting outside to sort it out with them.'

Gunnarstranda had to grin. 'Imagine how happy he must've been to see you turn up. A policeman he knew. Do you live in Nesodden or Notodden, Rise?'

Rise got up from the bed. His eyes flashed. 'It was a minor matter. Steffen had written the threatening letter and signed her name as a prank. But after putting it in the Storting postbox he regretted his actions. He realised she could get into a lot of trouble. So he stood outside the door so that he could clear up the misunderstanding when the police came. When I showed up he asked me for a favour: if I'd drop all the fuss with statements and testimonies and so on, which wouldn't do any good. The case was solved. He admitted to writing it. The letter was a jape. They were always playing jokes on each other. I dropped the case there and then.'

'But he lied to you. The woman has no idea who Gjerstad is. You could've found that out for yourself, if you'd bothered to do your job and talk to her.'

Rise didn't answer. He blinked with heavy eyelids.

Gunnarstranda shook his head. 'Where's the policeman in you? After all, you're holding a letter that threatens an MP's life. And you don't even bother to talk to the woman?'

'Steffen's my friend.'

Gunnarstranda turned his back on him and walked to the front door.

Rise followed him into the stairwell. Gunnarstranda pressed the lift button.

'Why do you want information from me when you've got nothing to give me in return?' asked Rise.

'What do you want to know?'

'You said you were close to a breakthrough. What breakthrough? When? Where?'

'Shouldn't you be more interested in finding out why Steffen Gjerstad lied to your face?'

Rise blinked.

Gunnarstranda said nothing.

'Tell me what the breakthrough is,' Rise repeated, his eyes burning.

The stooped figure in the doorway at that moment seemed so tragic that Gunnarstranda took pity on him. He cleared his throat and spoke in a low voice so as not to disturb the neighbours. 'Lena received a telephone call. A guy told her he had information about the Adeler case. The guy said he was near City Hall Quay 2 and saw what happened on the night of Wednesday, the ninth of December. Lena kept her cool, thinking we'd got some media-hungry bastard who'd spotted a chance of getting into the papers. She told him to come to Grønland HQ and tell her all he knows. Then he rang off. Lena thought "what the hell". But then I was talking to another junkie. And he told me a pal of Stig Eriksen's used to hang around with the two of them – Stig and Nina – and that this guy had rabbited on about knowing something about the man who was lifted out of the water by the quay and the cops weren't doing their job properly. That changed things a bit. We may well have a living witness to the murder of Sveinung Adeler. As soon as we can haul the man in, we've got the case solved. We just have to find him. Apparently he lives in a hostel when he isn't sleeping rough. I might be counting our chickens, but we intend to nab him tomorrow, and as soon as we do, we've got an eyewitness. With the info we have already, plus an eyewitness, I'm a hundred per cent certain we can make an arrest tomorrow.'

The lift pinged.

Gunnarstranda grabbed the handle, but didn't open the door.

'Who is it? What's his name?'

'His name's Dag Enoksen.'

As Gunnarstranda told him, Rise was already heading back into his bedsit.

Gunnarstranda raised his voice: 'Take it easy. Plata's a small area. Lena'll find Dag Enoksen, maybe even tonight.'

Axel Rise turned in the doorway.

Gunnarstranda opened the lift door. 'If you really want to do yourself a favour,' he said, trying to catch Rise's eye, 'ask your journalist pal why he lied to your face. Ask him why he wrote the threatening letter. Ask him why he threatened Aud Helen Vestgård in particular, and ask him why he signed the letter with the name of a woman he didn't know and had never met!'

Rise didn't answer. He closed the door.

Yep, Gunnnarstranda thought to himself. *Sick child or no sick child. It really is a shame about that man.*

1

Lena lifted her plastic cup and sipped the mulled wine. It tasted of end-of-term celebrations: a lukewarm mixture of spices with some chopped almonds and raisins floating on the surface. Everyone had to drink mulled wine before Christmas. In kindergartens, at schools, in the workplace, in shops. You couldn't move in one of Oslo's festive streets for people trying to force this tepid, sweet plonk on you.

I suppose I'm being very negative, she thought. But there was something about the almonds that made her throat go dry. Or perhaps she was just allergic?

The guy with the Sinatra hat and baggy pirate pants obviously found the silence a torment. He sat with his head down and was taking deep breaths, as if searching for something to say. He seemed a little delicate to be running a hostel for drug addicts. But Lena didn't know him. He was probably very competent at his job.

Lena slurped down some more of the sickly sweet drink and politely said no when the guy straightened up and told her to help herself to a cinnamon biscuit.

The taste of bought cinnamon biscuits also reminded her of school. Rehearsing a play, feeling stupid acting, being dressed up in a home-made costume that didn't fit, reeling off daft lines, knowing someone you really like is loyally watching from the darkness of the auditorium. The demands of family conventions: turn up at the end-of-term party, drink lukewarm mulled wine and take a photo of your promising child playing the part of Joseph or Mary or the Angel Gabriel.

Lena was never given the role of Mary or the angel. Red hair and freckles were a bad start for the audition. On her CV she didn't even have the role of wise man visiting the baby Jesus in the stable. Usually she was Shepherd 1 or Shepherd 2. She had been the innkeeper who turned away Joseph and Mary. More often than not she was in a flock of non-speaking angels, wearing a halo made of pipe-cleaners on her head and singing 'A Child is Born in Bethlehem'.

When she asked her mother about this, she couldn't remember anything; generally it was her father who had attended and taken a photo of her.

Was *that* the mystery behind her unease? The loss of her father? Not being able to share memories with him? She dismissed these thoughts.

The fact was simple enough. It was now 23rd December. She had bought presents for most people, but not yet for her mother.

If she managed it this afternoon, she would pop up with the Christmas tree so that Mum could decorate it in time – before the big day.

Tomorrow the two of them would be together from early afternoon. They would go to the cemetery together and light candles on Dad's grave. Afterwards they would go back to her mother's and finish the mutton ribs. She had remembered to buy them, fortunately – smoked and salted, from a lamb that had definitely grazed in the mountains. Now she had only to soak the meat in water this evening. She *mustn't* forget.

Lena looked at her watch. She also had to buy swede for the mash. She could do that tomorrow as well. But there was some peeling and slicing to do before *Sølvguttene*, the choirboys, rang in Christmas tomorrow – otherwise Mum would get the screaming abdabs.

There was a radio on the windowsill. Modern. It had a digital clock. Lena could see it still wasn't five o'clock. So she still had enough time. The shops would be open till late this evening, on the 23rd.

The guy with the Frank Sinatra hat couldn't stand the silence any longer. He switched on the radio.

Bells chimed. Violins, then Jussi Björling's velvet voice filled the room. He was singing 'Silent Night'.

She couldn't stop herself.

The young man with the Sinatra hat gave such a start he almost fell off the chair. 'What's the matter?'

Lena didn't answer. She was unable to say a word.

'Are you in pain?'

Lena shook her head. It poured out. Tears, snot. She stood up and went over to the radio. Switched it off. She was sobbing with her forehead pressed against the wall.

She heard the young man pacing back and forth. She turned. He looked pale and upset.

She straightened up. 'Have you got a serviette or something?' she managed to stammer out.

'Yes, of course.' The young man whirled around and and left the office. Came back. With a kitchen roll in his hand.

Lena took it. Wiped her eyes and blew her nose. She could never listen to Jussi Björling singing her father's song. That was how it was. But she didn't have to explain that to anyone.

She sat down.

The man sat down too and looked at her warily. 'I've heard about people who burst into tears. For no reason, like. Must be terrible.'

Lena said nothing. She sniffled. And cast a glance at her watch.

This inspired the man in the Frank Sinatra hat and pirate trousers to change the subject.

'Time flies,' he said.

Silence invaded the room once again.

'Yes, it does,' said the man with the Sinatra hat. There was a nervy side to him now and he kept shooting glances across at her. Not knowing what to do with his hands. He took his hat and fidgeted with it.

Lena was beginning to recover. 'Cool hat,' she said, wiping under her eyes again. 'Where did you buy it?'

'Kiel, in the mall there. Karstadt.'

Lena nodded. The choirboys, she thought. She could manage them. 'Silent Night', 'In the Bleak Midwinter', even the song about the Christmas star that shines above the midwife's house. But not 'O Holy Night'.

He had sung it, in church, with the full choir behind him. The thought and memory drew forth a sob. Tears sprang into her eyes.

A nervous twitch went through the man's body.

She was unable to stop the next sob. Then she filled her lungs with air.

Think of something else! Think of a less emotional subject. Think about the incident in Steffen's flat. The feeling you had when you were fastening your watch strap and you saw the floor coming towards you.

She leaned back and stared at the chair the man was sitting on. Over the back hung a shoulder bag.

Lena's mother liked bags with a lot of pockets. *That's what I'll buy her*, she thought, closed her eyes and breathed out, relieved to have found an idea for a present at last.

A bell above their heads rang, loud and shrill.

Lena and the man with the Sinatra hat exchanged glances.

'Client?' Lena said.

The man looked up at the bell high on the wall. 'Bit early,' he said. It rang again.

'Don't think this is a client. It seems too energetic.'

The man stood up and went into the corridor. Lena finished her plastic cup of tepid mulled wine and grimaced.

Soon afterwards the man came back. His face wreathed in smiles.

'What is it?' Lena asked.

'The guy asked after Dag Enoksen.'

Lena got up, went to the window and pushed the curtain aside a fraction. She peered out. 'And you said what we'd agreed?'

'Yes.'

'Thank you,' Lena said, and took out her phone. She stopped in the doorway and turned.

'Right, have a good Christmas,' she said.

'And you, too,' he said.

Lena hurried out of the hostel.

No one to be seen in Waldemars gate, only the red lights of a car on its way up the hill towards St. Hanshaugen.

She stood watching it for a few seconds, then turned and hurried down the pavement. Things were happening. They had set the line and now the fish was biting. She rang Gunnarstranda.

2

Gunnnarstranda roared out of town, northwards, along the E6. He thanked Lena and wished her good luck.

'Where are you?' Lena asked, clearly surprised.

'In my car,' Gunnarstranda said. 'I'll give you a call later.'

He passed Skedsmovollen and took a right at the next turning, to Sørum. After a couple of kilometres he left the main road and went down a narrow but snow-cleared road leading to a tiny village of low prefabricated houses. As the road became narrower, the distance between the houses increased. Soon he passed an old timber house where a small red tractor with a mounted snowplough was parked in front of a dilapidated garage. Gunnarstranda had come here many times and knew the way. He made for the next house on the left. It was lit up, as it was every Christmas, like an American Coke advert. Loads of red, green and yellow chains of lights adorned the ridge of the roof and the house entrance.

Gunnarstranda turned into the farmyard.

He reversed the car and pulled into the side. Switched off the engine. The lights went out. Through the large windows he could see inside the house. Preparations were being made for a party. A teenage girl was setting a dining table. A teenage boy was walking around with a box of matches, lighting candles. The match was burning dangerously close to his fingertips. The next candle was one too many. The boy burned himself, dropped the match and feverishly blew at his fingers, then lit a new match.

Gunnarstranda took the phone lying on the passenger seat.

He found a number he had saved. It was Ingrid Kobro's private number.

Before tapping in the number he glanced again at the house. Through the windows, now, he could see Ingrid Kobro coming out of the kitchen and saying something to her daughter. Ingrid was wearing a purple dress.

She turned away from the window.

Immediately afterwards he heard her voice in his ear.

'I'm outside,' Gunnarstranda said. 'I can see you aren't alone. So it would be much easier if you came out, rather than me going in.'

'You can probably see I'm busy,' Ingrid Kobro said, hesitantly.

'We're very close to an arrest,' Gunnarstranda said.

'Just give me a few minutes,' Ingrid Kobro said.

3

All the Christmas illuminations cast a yellow, almost orange, glare over the street. A Father Christmas with a sack on his back came walking towards her. Lena passed the Father Christmas. She stopped and stared.

He had disappeared. Which way could he have gone?

Well, there was no doubt where he was going.

She walked briskly towards Kiellands plass. Knowing she needed back-up. She had a bad feeling.

A handful of pedestrians were waiting at the traffic lights. A family. The mother in a black niqab. The father was struggling with a pram on the snow-covered pavement. A little girl was holding her mother's hand and looking up at Lena, who was still on the lookout for a man in a reefer jacket. The traffic was getting heavier, buses and taxis were passing.

She rang Emil Yttergjerde.

'Nothing doing here,' Emil said. 'Just freezing my arse off.'

'He's wearing a navy-blue reefer jacket,' Lena said. 'He's on his way, dead certain, but I've lost sight of him.'

Green. Lena crossed the street.

'Where are you?'

Lena shouted over the din of the traffic. 'Kiellands plass. I've just passed the Ila block.'

'Should show up soon then,' Emil said.

'Pass the message on to Frankie,' Lena shouted, and hesitated.

'Already have done.'

'Say…'

'Say what?'

'Say it's fine if he wants to pull out.'

Yttergjerde's laughter was almost drowned in the roar of a diesel bus. 'Do you mean that?'

'Yes, I do. I don't like this guy going missing. It's not a good sign.'

She didn't want a discussion with Emil. She hung up and shot off down Maridalsveien.

The thought that Frølich was sitting alone at this moment made her increase her speed. It had looked like a piece of cake. Nothing could go wrong. But before you could say Jack Frost, there was a sudden glitch.

She jogged on down. The fresh snow was heavy underfoot. Of course, the snowploughs didn't bother with the pavements. Lena looked over her shoulder. The cars behind were stopped on red. She jumped over the pile of snow along the kerb and into the road. While she was running, her mind went over what had happened a few minutes before.

She had seen the back of a man through a window in the block of bedsits.

Less than a minute later she was in the street, but she couldn't see anyone.

Why hadn't she seen him outside the block?

What had she seen?

A car! Of course. She ran faster. A car hooted. She jumped over the snow back onto the pavement. It was a taxi. She waved. It stopped. She threw herself onto the rear seat. 'Oslo Station,' she gasped. 'The multi-storey car park.'

4

'Yeees,' Frølich intoned. 'I'll be on my guard if I see a car.' He rang off and looked around. Cars everywhere.

He sat playing on his phone. Out of sheer boredom he played one of the older games. He had been sitting on a wooden chair in this multi-storey car park for several hours. The air was bad and the only sound to break the noise of the ventilation pipe was the crunch of tyres on concrete when a car rolled down the ramp at the other end of the building. A false alarm every time.

Playing a game was meant to pass the minutes. A strange figure ran to and fro across the screen while bombs dropped. Frank Frølich held the phone with both hands, using his thumbs on the arrow keys. He was obviously out of practice. He could barely get going before a sneaky bomb wiped out the poor guy, so he had to start again. It wasn't particularly cold, but his fingers were still freezing and his bottom had begun to feel like wood. If you sat motionless for a long time the cold sneaked up on you anyway. Frølich adjusted his position on the kitchen chair as he surveyed the spacious, empty car park. There were hardly any cars parked.

He started the game and managed to keep going for a whole minute. He was getting the knack now. Amazing how quickly you were hooked, he thought, then lifted his head and listened. Was that a sound?

No. It was a bomb killing the poor guy on the display.

He was shivering and about to restart the game when a car accelerating on the floor above broke the silence. A customer leaving. Probably the fiftieth in the last half-hour.

Frølich put his phone in his pocket. Soon yellow headlights came down the ramp and the crunch of studded tyres drowned the sound of the engine. He waited for the driver to switch off. Frølich looked up. He was dazzled.

And wary.

The car passed him and parked right at the back.

Frølich listened to the engine idling. He was waiting for the driver to switch off his engine.

Why didn't he? Didn't he realise the exhaust fumes polluted the air?

As soon as the thought arose, he reacted on autopilot. *Now* he was on his guard. Instinctively he jumped up. Took two steps backwards and sensed rather than saw the shadow that launched itself at him. He twisted away ninety degrees and in so doing saved his own life. The knife that was pointed at his back cut through his jacket and tore into his side.

Frølich grabbed the man's arm, swung him round and forced him down. Received another stab in the process. In the thigh this time. He screamed as the blade cut into his flesh. The man rolled away as Frølich fell.

Frølich stayed down, holding his thigh. Blood pumped out between his fingers.

He saw Lena running over. Raised his head. Behind her was Emil Yttergjerde.

'I need someone who can patch up stab wounds,' Frølich groaned. 'Tell them it's urgent.'

Yttergjerde knelt down, took off his scarf and wrapped it tight round Frølich's thigh, near his groin. The whole of his trouser leg was wet and red, and it was impossible to see if the bleeding was stopping.

At that moment there was the clang of a metal gate slamming shut. The man was getting away!

Frølich and Emil exchanged glances. 'We'll sort this,' Emil said, without much conviction.

Frølich turned his head and saw Lena sprinting for the gate.

5

The concourse was packed with people slowly surging back and forth. There were parents holding hands, or their children's, young women side by side pushing prams, boys in a group with their phones and cameras out, girlfriends walking in fours, giggling. It was a dense mass of jackets of all colours and the gaps there were between people were filled with bulging carrier bags of Christmas presents. Lena pushed her way forwards, trying to focus on Steffen's navy-blue jacket further ahead. One minute it was visible, the next lost in the crowd. He wasn't wearing a hat and with every step his hair bounced off his neck. Trying to reduce the distance between them was like swimming against a strong current. People walked at a leisurely pace, pushing shopping trolleys, stopping suddenly or standing still and chatting. Bodies were everywhere and had to be nudged to force a way through. In return she was shoved and sworn at. Her thought-processes were blocked. She thought of Frølich and blamed herself.

Why hadn't she run into the car park straightaway?

Why hadn't she taken the car number when she first saw it? And where was Steffen now?

There. He was making for the escalator and looked over his shoulder. For an instant she caught his eye.

Now he was headed for the Metro. Lena broke into a run. Reached the long escalator going down. Took two steps at a time. Ahead of her she saw Steffen push people aside. Lena ran after him and received a shove in the back from an irritable man trying to manoeuvre a suitcase. She caught a glimpse of Steffen ahead, rounding two small children and colliding with a woman, who dropped two bags. He ran down to the platforms. Lena jumped over the bags and followed after him. She could already hear a train pulling in. She heard the doors open and reached the platform in three strides. The train stopped and waited. Had he got onto the train or not? She walked slowly alongside the carriages. Staring in through the windows and every open door she passed, scanning the platform. She couldn't see him. She couldn't bloody see him!

The signal sounded for the doors to close. She sensed a movement at the end of the platform. At that moment she hurled herself on board. The doors closed.

The train picked up speed. It was too late to jump off now. Was he on board or not? She looked out of the window at the platform. No reefer jacket. But the train was travelling faster and faster. Soon the people on the platform were one long blur. Then the train was in the tunnel.

She made her way forwards. Ploughed a passage between the passengers. Some looked at her, some looked at the ceiling, some clung to their bags of shopping. She pushed on.

It was impossible to see into the carriage ahead. She began to have her doubts. Had she lost him?

The train accelerated now. The carrriages lurched on the bends. Lena had to hold on tight.

The train roared into Stortinget Station.

The train came to a halt.

The doors opened. Lena got out and walked along the platform.

He was nowhere to be seen among the disgorged passengers. She stood by a door in the front carriage. One foot on the platform and one in the carriage.

Someone moved by the door ahead.

Again they had eye contact. Ten metres separated them. He was standing in one doorway. She stood in the other.

They held each other's eyes. He raised a hand, a wave.

She stood still, staring back.

The expression in his eyes was vacant and cool. Not a single feeling, she noticed. Presumably there had never been any.

Last-minute passengers raced down the steps and threw themselves in.

Would he step out or hop back in?

She didn't move.

The passengers had found seats.

Lena and Steffen were still watching each other.

The shrill signal indicated that the doors were closing.

She waited, waited and waited.

When he jumped out, she took a step to the right.

The doors slammed shut. He tried to prise them open and force his way back in. Without success. The train set off. He let go of the door.

The train disappeared into the tunnel.

The two of them were left on the platform, eyeing each other. Now she could read an unfamiliar expression on his face, a kind of half-embarrassed grimace. She understood. She had just observed a shred of dejection. The failed fugitive.

As he moved towards her she stood her ground.

Soon no more than a single metre separated them.

'Bodil sends her regards,' Lena said.

'Who?'

'Bodil Rømer, the mother of your best friend.'

He didn't answer this time. But his eyes flitted around.

'That was a digression,' she said. 'What I meant to say was you're under arrest.'

Her phone rang. She took it from her pocket and glanced at the display.

'Just answer it,' said Steffen, who seemed to have regained his composure.

It was Rindal. He wanted to know where she was. 'Stortinget Station,' she said. 'Metro.'

Rindal wanted to know if she had everything under control.

'Yes,' she said, and hung up.

'And what now?' asked Steffen after she had put the phone back in her pocket.

Lena didn't answer. He had heard what she said. If he wanted to pretend he hadn't, that was his business. She motioned to the stairs with a nod of the head. 'Shall we go?'

He didn't move for a few seconds and looked at her in surprise, as though wondering if she was serious. In the end he shrugged his shoulders and made a move.

They walked slowly, side by side, up the staircase to the large con-course. There weren't many people around. Steffen headed for the escalator.

Lena stood beside him, on the same step.

'Jesus,' he sighed. 'Now you're taking this a bit far, aren't you?'

Lena didn't answer.

A dark-haired teenage girl slowly glided down on the adjacent escalator. The girl looked at her first, then at Steffen. He thrust out an arm and pointed threateningly. 'You, look away!' he shouted.

The girl was shocked and continued with her eyes downcast.

Lena wondered how she should interpret the outburst. She had never seen him do anything like that. But now he seemed as calm as before, as though the incident had never taken place.

They were approaching the top of the escalator. They both stepped off. Both stopped. People who had been behind them on the escala-tor walked past and away.

They were alone. 'Give me the knife,' Lena said.

It took him time to answer. 'What if I scarper?' he said at length.

She clocked him from the side. His choice of words was childish. The idea was childish. She didn't answer.

'What will you do if I scarper now?'

'As I said, this is an arrest. If you resist arrest, that'll be added to the list of charges.'

'Charges? What charges?'

A man glided up on the escalator. One of the Metro's own employ-ees, wearing a uniform with a rucksack on his back.

Lena waited until they were alone again. 'You attacked and injured a person in the multi-storey car park,' she said. 'You've made it clear you're dangerous. It would be better for everyone if you handed over the knife voluntarily.'

He smiled weakly. 'Odd situation this, don't you agree?'

'Give me the knife,' she repeated calmly.

'My God, just listen to you.'

'Steffen!'

'I haven't got it. I threw it away.'

She fixed him with her stare. His smile was a rigid grimace, but his eyes were cold. This arrest was not developing as it should. And now Lena was unsure what to do. It was difficult to think. The escalator chuntered. On the brick wall behind Steffen was a ladies' lingerie poster. The model was looking at her with her chin raised provocatively.

Impatient, he moved. 'Shall we go?'

'You'll have to give me the knife first.'

He shook his head authoritatively. 'It was your suggestion,' he said. 'You suggested going.'

What he said didn't make sense. But Lena was quiet. If he still had the knife on him it had to be in a sheath. *He's either got it on his belt or in a pocket*, she thought. *As both his hands are free now he will have to give himself away when he makes a move.*

At that moment the escalator stopped working. The chunter came to an end with a click.

The sudden silence was as shrill as an alarm in her ears, and she averted her eyes so as not to give the game away.

But had Steffen heard the change? Impossible to say.

Every second that dragged by made the silence resound more loudly in Lena's ears. No footsteps, no noise from the train, no telltale rush of air.

Her mouth was dry. She ought to say something to distract him. But she didn't have the words. Then she saw that Steffen had noticed. He raised his head, listened and tried to work out what was different. She stepped back a pace to centre her bodyweight. But her movement was a signal. She caught his eye for a fraction of a second, read what he was thinking and saw the lunge before he crouched down.

His knife was in his boot.

But now her balance was just right.

There was a flash of steel as he got up.

She kicked out. Striking him in the kneecap. He screamed in pain and fell like a log. She launched herself. Landed on top of him. Got both his arms in a half-nelson. He twisted like a snake.

'I practise this twice a week,' she hissed. 'Lie still!'

He tried to turn again. She got a knee in the small of his back with her weight behind it and jerked both arms upwards. He screamed again. She let him. Counted slowly to three and loosened her grip by a couple of centimetres. He fell quiet.

Then came the sound of running feet. 'I told you I had everything under control,' Lena shouted, annoyed.

There were three of them. Police dressed as robots: visors, vests and helmets. All three with guns at the ready.

Steffen was now supine and still.

She found the knife. It was on the ground. The blade was long and wide. There was a clattering sound as a foot kicked it away.

The foot was clad in a worn overshoe.

'Now perhaps you know why I don't like police provocation,' Gunnarstranda said, taking a hand from his pocket. He closed hand-cuffs around Steffen's wrists.

✳

Lena went up the stairs first. Her legs ached and she was trembling. Lactic acid, she thought. She had been petrified, but had had no time to notice it.

A large group of curious bystanders had gathered by the police cordon.

Lena and Gunnarstranda squeezed their way through and got into the operation commander's car. From the back seat they watched an armed police officer help a limping Steffen Gjerstad into a van, which drove him off.

Lena felt sick. Her hands were shaking. She put them into her lap so they couldn't be seen.

'And Frankie?' she asked.

'He's fine, considering the circumstances. The duty doctor patched him up. I think he's on his way home.' Gunnarstranda looked at his watch. 'If he's lucky, he'll just catch *Dinner for One* with Freddy Frinton. But he's probably not interested.'

6

Lena went into the observation room and sat down. The screen showed profiles of Gunnarstranda and Steffen Gjerstad. The digital clock flashed in the right-hand corner. It would soon be eleven o'clock at night.

'Axel Rise and Frikk Råholt are using you as a scapegoat,' Gunnarstranda said. 'That's the situation.'

Steffen didn't answer.

'Axel Rise has said in a statement that you confessed to him that on Thursday, the tenth of December you faked a threatening letter and put it into the Storting postbox for Aud Helen Vestgård. Frikk Råholt, for his part, has said in a statement that he bought services from you. He ordered reportage for which you took photos of Vestgård, Adeler and a Polisario at a dinner and you wrote about the meeting in a later article.'

Gunnarstranda pushed some papers across the table. 'You can read their statements yourself.'

Steffen folded his hands behind his neck. 'And what are you accusing me of?' he asked with a grin. 'Illegal student prank and inappropriate paparazzi activity?'

'There's more,' Gunnarstranda said matter-of-factly. 'Axel Rise says you gave him money for the name of a witness who could point out Adeler's killer. You said to Rise you were running a spread in the newspaper and needed the name to do an interview. Axel Rise told you the witness's name was Dag Enoksen. But you didn't do an interview. Instead you attacked Enoksen with a knife. Why?'

'Do you believe I threw Adeler off the quay?' Steffen asked.

'We can talk about Adeler first, that's fine,' Gunnarstranda said. We can come back to Enoksen. You could tell me who threw Adeler off the quay, as you've just stabbed an eye witness.'

'I can give you more than one name,' Steffen said. 'I can tell you what happened. The man who killed Adeler is called Stian Rømer. He's vanished off the face of this earth and the last person to see him alive is a colleague of yours – Lena Stigersand.'

Lena got up. She stood for a few seconds thinking before she opened the door and went into the corridor. She marched over to the interview room, opened the door and went in.

'Lena Stigersand has joined Steffen Gjerstad in the interview room,' Lena said to the tape recorder. 'It is now 23:00 hours,' she added and sat down.

Steffen smiled at her.

'I have a suggestion,' Steffen said.

'Oh, yes?' Gunnarstranda said.

'I confess.'

'Nothing would please me more,' Gunnnarstranda said.

'I confess to buying services from Axel Rise, but I'll do it on one condition.'

'Which is?'

'You listen to what I have to say. I'll tell you what happened to Adeler if Lena tells me what happened to Stian Rømer.'

Steffen stared straight at her.

The silence hung in the air until Gunnarstranda coughed.

'The more clarity we can establish around this Rømer, the better. Don't you agree, Lena?'

Lena looked at him. Then turned away. 'Agreed.'

Steffen focused on Gunnarstranda. 'But I talk to you, and only you,' he said.

Gunnarstranda turned to Lena. 'Will you leave us alone for a bit?'

Lena swallowed the humiliation and got up. She left without a word.

7

After closing the door behind her she almost collided with Ingrid Kobro.

They both came to a halt.

It was a strange situation. Two old friends meeting face to face then looking away, as a result of their own and the other's discomfort. It was Lena who reacted. She wriggled past without saying a word. She took a few steps, stopped and glanced over her shoulder.

Ingrid Kobro was watching her from where she stood.

'Surely things haven't got that bad between us, have they?' Ingrid said. 'We can still say hi, can't we?'

Lena looked down. 'Hi,' she said without any warmth.

Ingrid nodded. 'And hi to you, too.' Ingrid appeared to be searching for words.

'Is anything the matter?' Lena asked.

It was Ingrid's turn to look away. 'I hear you've made an arrest.'

Lena nodded. 'Sorry to be so direct,' she said, 'but it's Christmas Eve tomorrow and almost midnight now…'

Ingrid Kobro nodded.

'What are you actually doing here?' Lena asked.

Ingrid put on a thoughtful expression.

'Is it because we've made an arrest?'

Ingrid just looked at her.

Lena couldn't be bothered to wait for an answer. She turned and went back into the observation room.

On the screen, Gunnarstranda asked: 'Who is Stian Rømer?'

Steffen's face replied: 'A pal. We grew up in the same street.'

Lena sat down.

Shortly afterwards someone fumbled at the observation-room door. It opened.

In the doorway Ingrid Kobro was struggling with a cup of coffee in each hand. 'Can you help me?'

Lena stood up and held the door for her.

Ingrid Kobro sat down, smiled warmly and said: 'Almost like in the cinema, isn't it?' She nodded towards one cup of coffee. 'That's for you.'

Lena was rigidly watching the screen.

Steffen's head said: 'After school I studied political science at Blindern. Stian did his military service and went into the forces.

He signed up, serving first in Bosnia and Kosovo, afterwards in Afghanistan. Then left to start his own business. Since then it's been all action for Stian. He's been in South America and North Africa a lot. That was where we met, quite by chance a few weeks ago. I was doing some research for a series about Norwegian state finance and was travelling through Morocco, Mauritania and Western Sahara. I stayed at the Kenzi Farah Hotel in Marrakech – pretty posh. I was lying there by the pool, on a sunbed, relaxing. I open my eyes and see Stian, my old pal, at the bar. At first I thought it was a chance encounter. But it wasn't. Anyway. Stian and I had a few jars and he explained he was working in security now for several companies there. He was organising big surveillance and intelligence operations. Two evenings later he turned up again, at my hotel room, with his pockets full of dollars this time. He would pay if he could dictate what I wrote.'

Steffen changed his sitting position. 'The whole of Stian's plan was crazy. I said so, too. "I'm a journalist," I said. "I don't write for money," I said. But Stian was a soldier and didn't understand things like that.

'On the sixth of December I arrived back in Oslo. A day or two passed and up he popped again, this time in Oslo. Full paramilitary deal – undercover, the whole business. I told Stian I didn't want his money.'

Gunnarstranda coughed. 'When he offered you money in Marrakech was that on behalf of this company, MacFarrell?'

Steffen shook his head. 'Stian would never have told me who was behind it.'

'But the article he asked you to write was about this company's activities?'

'Yes.'

'Frikk Råholt says he asked you to take photos of Adeler's meeting with Polisario and Aud Helen Vestgård.'

Steffen nodded.

'Say it out loud,' Gunnarstranda said, 'for the tape recorder.'

'Yes,' Steffen said in a clear voice and breathed in deeply with his eyes closed.

'Are we talking about Wednesday, the ninth of December?' Gunnarstranda asked.

'Yes. He needed photos and a spread in the paper to smear Adeler and the projects he was working on in Western Sahara.'

'And you took the photos outside a restaurant in Grefsen?'

'Yes.'

'Who was with you?'

'Stian Rømer.'

'Tell me what happened.'

'Stian had a hire car. We waited in it. At about eleven, the three of them finished their meeting. They came out, shook hands and left. Good atmosphere. They were good photos, too. Two of them – Vestgård and Shamoun – got into a taxi and went. Adeler stood around for a few minutes. He hailed a taxi that was dropping someone off. Stian and I followed the taxi into town. It came to a stop in Bygdøy allé. Adeler walked to a door and rang the bell. Stian got out of the car and pretended he was visiting someone in the same building. He stood beside Adeler. When the automatic lock buzzed for Adeler, they both went in. A little later Stian came back. He said Adeler was visiting a woman. The name on the door was Lisbet Enderud. So what should I do? In any case I had to confront Adeler with the restaurant visit – show him the photos and demand a comment. But I had no idea how long he would be with the woman. I considered ringing the bell there and then, but decided to wait to talk to him alone. Stian found a parking spot with a view of the front door. We both sat waiting in the car. Time passed. Adeler was there for ages. Stian woke me at a bit past five in the morning. Adeler was by the front door. I was groggy, but I got out, intending to talk to him. As I crossed the street, he was a long way off, way down the hill. I followed him, but it was easier said than done. Eventually, though, he slowed down and I caught him up by the quays. We continued side by side and he asked what I wanted. I was polite – I said I had photos of the meeting at the restaurant and only wanted to know what was being discussed. He refused to answer. But he had spoken to me first, so I pushed a little harder. I asked why the man from Polisario was backed up by a top Norwegian politician during the interview. Was he doing research or what? I asked if Vestgård's party affiliations would invalidate his report. Could the public rely on everything being above board? I asked who paid for the meal, if he'd received an offer from Polisario, money for example. His face went paler with each question. He understood the gravity of the matter, that was for sure. The man changed personality. He lost his temper and started to threaten me. Which was quite frightening because he was a powerful man. Then I said – and it was true – that the newspaper was going to run the story whatever. It was his decision not to say anything, but it would be stupid, I said, because then he couldn't influence what I wrote, could he.'

Steffen leaned forwards. He tapped his forefinger on the table to emphasise his point: 'Adeler flew at me. I did nothing. But Stian was there. Stian had followed us. When Adeler came at me, Stian was there instantly. I didn't see what happened. I only know Adeler was splashing in the water when he should have been on land. Do you hear me? The fact that Adeler fell into the sea was his own fault. And I was unable to prevent what happened. I ran up the pier next to the quay to find a lifebuoy. It was a long way down to the water and Adeler wouldn't have had a chance in that temperature. I had to find a lifebuoy. But what happened then? I ran straight into that junkie woman. "Help me", I said, but she just stood there watching, perplexed.'

'Where did you run?' Gunnarstranda asked.

'Up the pier. I bumped into that woman.'

'Which pier?'

The question caused Steffen to lose his composure. 'What do you mean, which pier?'

Steffen ended up not answering the question, but continuing the account.

'I ran straight into her. "Where are the lifebuoys?" I shouted, but the woman just backed away from me. I cast around. Couldn't see any lifebuoys, couldn't see anything. Usually there are lifebuoys hanging on the quay, aren't there? But I couldn't see any. I ran back and still couldn't see any. Stian had gone. The junkie had gone and Adeler wasn't moving. He was floating on his stomach, dead as a dodo. What could I do? Nothing. So I left.'

Gunnarstranda coughed.

Steffen looked at him.

'Was that the pier closest to the fortress?'

Steffen considered the question. 'Yes.'

'Sure?'

'What difference does it make which pier it was?'

'Your credibility makes a difference, especially because you've demanded another account in return.'

Steffen again lost his composure. 'Yes, it was the pier closest to the fortress. I'm sure. Can we move on?'

'And you ran straight into Nina Stenshagen?'

'I don't know what her name was.'

Gunnarstranda rummaged through his papers. He pushed a piece of paper across the table. 'I think you know what her name was. You've interviewed her. But…' Gunnarstranda raised a hand to nip the man's reaction in the bud. 'Let's just clarify these events. You ran down the pier nearest the fortress and collided with this woman. That's what you said, didn't you?'

Steffen looked at the photo Gunnarstranda was indicating.

'Yes.'

Gunnarstranda cut a sceptical grimace.

'What is it now?' Steffen asked impatiently.

'I can't make this add up. You see, we've reconstructed the course of events to some extent, and we can document that the woman was on the pier to Quay 2, the next quay.'

Steffen fell quiet.

Lena used the opportunity to sip her coffee, which had no taste at all. She glanced at Ingrid, who said: 'Decaff, sorry.' Ingrid motioned to the screen. 'This is exciting, isn't it?'

Lena didn't answer. Her whole body was tied in knots, but she wasn't about to announce that.

On the screen, Steffen's face spoke. 'You're wrong,' he said.

Gunnarstranda shook his head. 'As I mentioned, we've reconstructed what happened. The person who pushed Adeler in grabbed a plank from the pier to Quay 1. Which he used to force Adeler under the water. You're claiming Rømer did that.'

'I am not!' Steffen riposted.

'Who did then?' Gunnarstranda asked. 'You've just said there were three of you. Adeler, Rømer and you.'

'What I meant was he didn't use a plank.'

'But now you're contradicting yourself. You just said you didn't see what happened.'

Steffen fell quiet again.

'One of you did it,' Gunnarstranda said.

'Your reconstruction's wrong.'

Gunnarstranda shook his head. 'I believe a lot of what you've told me,' he said. 'For example, I believe you and Rømer were waiting in the car while Adeler was visiting a woman. I believe you fell asleep and you ran after Adeler. I believe you did catch him up,' Gunnarstranda said. 'I believe Rømer followed you and Adeler. I believe he saw you two arguing about something. But I don't believe it was Rømer who pushed Adeler into the harbour. I think he saw *you* do it. Then he reacted and ran up the pier to Quay 2, perhaps to find a lifebuoy. There *he* bumped into Nina Stenshagen. She and Rømer watched you forcing Adeler under the water. Nina Stenshagen ran off and Rømer followed her.'

Steffen shook his head. 'You've got it all wrong.'

'Alright,' Gunnarstranda said. 'You admit at least that you were on the quay between five and half past. A few hours later you're back there when Lena Stigersand and Emil Yttergjerde from Oslo PD arrive at the crime scene. What did you do in the meantime?'

Steffen responded with a vacant stare.

'You've already admitted you spent part of this time writing a threatening letter. Why did you do that?'

Steffen shrugged. 'For fun.'

Gunnarstranda shook his head. 'Remember everything you say affects your credibility. I believe this is why you wrote the letter.' He pushed a pile of papers across the table and turned them so that the front sheet was visible. It was Adeler's report.

'What is it?'

'This is the report Adeler wrote about MacFarrell.'

Steffen blinked. He eyed the report and blinked again.

Lena was brought back to reality by low, crunching noises. Ingrid was eating cinnamon biscuits from a dish on the table.

A sound from the screen drowned the crunching. It was Steffen grabbing the papers and placing them back down on the table.

'You asked why I wrote the letter. Well, Adeler was floating on the surface of the water. He was dead, that much was obvious. So there was no point writing an article about the meeting the evening before. I needed a new angle.'

'Angle for what?'

'For the story. Of how a Norwegian politician was using her power and influence to steamroller the neutrality of the Ethics Council. Well, Adeler had been with this woman that night. The point was that the letter connected Lisbet Enderud's name with Aud Helen Vestgård. If I uncovered that story first I could follow up with the meeting and everything else bit by bit. Investigative journalism, pure and simple. First the link between Lisbet Enderud and Adeler and afterwards the photos of Adeler, Vestgård and Shamoun.'

'Goodness me,' said Ingrid, taking another biscuit from the plate. 'We've got a cool customer here. A murderer who likes to construct his own news.'

Lena reached out for her coffee. But her hand was shaking. So she gave up.

'You waited outside Lisbet Enderud's flat later that morning,'

Gunnarstranda said. 'When Axel Rise came along you asked him not to interview the woman about the letter. Why did you do that?'

Steffen splayed his arms. 'I'd been thinking. The letter was a hasty solution. It was clumsy. I was out of control. First of all I couldn't know for certain if the threat would be made public or leaked to the press. If it was, the story could travel on different routes from those I wanted.'

'So you'd found a better angle?'

'You could put it like that.'

'What sort of angle?'

'I'd got to know Lena Stigersand.'

Ingrid and Lena exchanged glances.

'How did you get to know her so quickly?'

'It was chance. I met her when she went to Adeler's flat. I took the initiative. She seemed OK, we found the vibe, and she seemed keen.'

Gunnarstranda sat up on his chair. 'Gjerstad, you're going to be charged with murder.'

'It wasn't me,' Steffen repeated once more.

'It's my belief you killed Adeler for your own personal benefit. You killed Adeler because that morning, while you were at the harbour, he told you he'd already handed in the MacFarrell report. You hadn't anticipated that. As he'd already written his report, the splash in the papers you'd planned was of no value. On top of losing a scoop you would lose a lucrative number that Råholt was offering you. I believe you killed Adeler to shut him up. With Adeler dead you could still run the story. With him dead he wasn't in a position to deny or disprove the contents of your big splash – that said he'd been bought and paid for by one of the parties in a conflict zone. In that way you'd still be able to do the job for Råholt and earn the cash you'd been promised.

'You've admitted being at the crime scene where Adeler was murdered. The eyewitness Nina Stenshagen was shot and killed by your friend Stian Rømer. This eyewitness had spent the night on City Hall Quay with another eyewitness – Stig Eriksen. Both of them were shot and killed with the same weapon. I believe Stig Eriksen contacted you after I told him Nina had been murdered. And when he did, you decided it was time to get rid of him. Rømer shot him at your behest.'

Gunnarstranda turned and picked up a box from the floor. He put it on the table between them and removed the lid. 'Both Nina Stenshagen and Stig Eriksen were shot and killed with this weapon – which belongs to Stian Rømer.'

He took a semi-automatic gun from the box and put it on the table. 'Have you seen this gun before?'

Steffen scrutinised the gun without a word.

In the observation room Ingrid stood up. 'That must be my signal,' she said cheerfully. 'You'd better watch, Lena, and give me a grade afterwards.'

Ingrid Kobro went out.

Lena studied the screen. Someone knew more than her in this case. That was clear enough.

The door of the interview room opened.

Ingrid entered, carrying a briefcase. She sat down.

Steffen was still so engaged by the weapon that he barely reacted.

Ingrid stretched out her arm and switched off the tape recorder.

Steffen followed her hand with his eyes.

'My name's Ingrid Kobro and I work in PST, the Police Security Service. Don't worry. We'll run the tape recorder again soon. The weapon on the table belongs to your friend Stian Rømer. Of that there is absolutely no doubt. He was in possession of this weapon when it was seized in Kadettangen outside Oslo a few days ago. Here's my offer to you: you just heard what the police consider to be your role in this affair. The Director of Public Prosecutions is willing to waive some points in the charges against you on certain conditions.'

Steffen, silent, watched her.

'You can, of course, reject this deal. You can deny you killed Adeler with malice aforethought and possibly avoid imprisonment. But even if you do deny this charge you'll probably find it hard to wriggle out of being an accessory to murder. It would be the DPP's word against yours. To refute the charge of complicity, there will be more than the charge of murder to face. You've already admitted taking part in a conspiracy against an MP. You've admitted sending a death threat to the same MP. Even if you didn't personally hold the gun that was fired, you conspired in the premeditated murders of Nina Stenshagen and Stig Eriksen. Furthermore, you conspired against a police officer – Lena Stigersand. You and Stian Rømer planned an assault on her in your flat. Rømer carried out the attack after you'd left the premises. I'd like you to take a look at these photos.'

Lena was startled. How could Ingrid know this?

Ingrid opened her briefcase like a woman on a market stall opening her purse. At length she had a wad of photos in her hand. Lena got up from her chair, but it was impossible to see the pictures on the screen.

She spun round and went to the door. She opened it. And came face to face with a man barring her way.

Lena tried to push him aside.

He was like a rock.

'Shift.'

The man shook his head. There was something familiar about his appearance. He had a scar on his top lip.

'I've seen you before,' Lena said.

'PST,' he said. 'I'd appreciate it if you'd go back and sit down.'

'There are some photos in the interview room I'd like to see.'

Ingrid's voice on the screen made Lena turn:

'The photos show your friend Rømer carrying a lifeless Lena Stigersand to her car. As you can see, her hands are tied with plastic strips. She is being taken away against her will. What I'm trying to tell you is that these photos prove Rømer is performing unlawful transportation – kidnapping. And it happened in your flat. After the photos were taken, Rømer drove this woman's car out of town to the sea at Asker. These photos show him dragging Lena towards the water. One of our officers decided to step in. Thereby thwarting the plan both of you had made.'

Lena turned to the door again.

'Me,' said the man with the harelip, tapping his chest. 'I was the fireman that morning.'

Lena remembered. The man in front of her was the smoke diver who had spoken to the residents outside the block where Steffen lived.

'So,' said Kobro's voice on the screen. 'The DPP's willing to drop the charge of premeditated murder in the case of Sveinung Adeler. Also complicity in the premeditated murders of Nina Stenshagen and Stig Eriksen. We're also willing to drop the death threat against Vestgård, which of necessity falls under the terrorism clause; the same applies to complicity in the conspiracy against Lena Stigersand, so long as you sign this declaration.'

She pushed the document across the table.

Steffen looked at her with raised eyebrows.

'You hereby declare that you saw Stian Rømer alive and well at the Kenzi Farah Hotel in Marrakech on the third of December.'

Steffen took his time. Silence hung over the interview room.

'What do you think?' asked the man with the harelip. 'Is he going to sign?'

Lena's mouth was dry. She barely heard the question.

'What will the charge be in the end?' Steffen said in a business-like fashion.

'If you sign, you'll be charged with manslaughter as a result of pushing Sveinung Adeler into the sea during a fight, plus gross negligence for not trying to save him.'

Steffen mulled this over.

'Together this makes wilful manslaughter,' said the smoke diver in a dry voice. 'Twelve years at least. But he doesn't realise.'

'It's the plank that makes it premeditated murder?' Steffen asked.

Ingrid Kobro nodded.

'But the plank won't be mentioned in the charge?' Steffen asked with a look askance.

'Correct,' Ingrid said.

Steffen ruminated further. Eventually he said: 'I don't remember if I was at the Kenzi Farah Hotel that day.'

'We were there,' Ingrid said. 'We saw you and have both of you on film. We weren't interested in you then, but in Stian Rømer.'

Lena switched off the screen.

She headed for the door again.

The man with the harelip held her back. 'Rømer's death mustn't get out,' he said. 'A lot of people's lives and safety depend on him being officially in Mogadishu, Somalia, today. Lots of people who risk their lives on a daily basis and those of their closest families depend on Gjerstad signing the deal right here and now.'

'How can you say that?'

The man deliberated for a few seconds, then said: 'What if there's a man pretending to be Stian Rømer in Mogadishu at this very moment? What do you think will happen to him and the players around him if the real Rømer turns up in Oslo – dead?'

Lena took a deep breath. There was nothing she could say. The man watched her in silence.

'You were there?' Lena said at last. 'In Asker? When I got the pepper spray in my face?'

The man nodded. 'We were keeping an eye on Rømer. We'd been on his heels the day before, when he was searching for a place to dump you. We didn't know what he was up to. It was only when he took the car and drove you out of town that we knew where he was going. We were in position when you arrived. As I said, we didn't want to harm Rømer, but it couldn't be avoided when he tried to kick you into the sea.'

'We?'

'There were two of us.'

'You threw him in?'

The man shook his head.

'You shot him?'

The man with the harelip nodded.

'I didn't hear a bang.'

'You weren't supposed to.'

'It was dark.'

'We used lasers.'

'I could've fallen!'

The man nodded again.

'I could've died.'

'I doubt that. As I said, there were two of us – both ready to step in if you were in difficulty.'

'But you allowed him to carry out the whole plan. Light the fire on the stairs, the attack, the car journey…'

'We had no idea what he was up to. When it became clear he intended to drown you, we stepped in.'

Lena looked down at her hands. They were trembling.

'I thought it was my fault he fell.'

The man didn't answer.

'He could've shot me in the flat.'

'I doubt that,' the man said. 'That would've put his pal, Gjerstad, in a very tricky spot.'

Lena closed her eyes. She grabbed the door handle.

'Where are you going?'

'Out,' Lena said. 'Away from here.'

✳

Lena didn't go away. She stood motionless in the corridor until the door opened and Ingrid Kobro emerged from the interview room.

'Did he sign?'

'Yes.'

Ingrid Kobro folded the piece of paper in her hand and looked at her watch. 'It's past midnight. Now we can say "Happy Christmas".'

Lena nodded wearily. She turned away and went into her own office. The word Christmas had set off alarm bells in her head.

It was Christmas and she had actually committed the cardinal sin. She had forgotten to soak the mutton ribs. Mum would never forgive her.

She had to shake her head at herself. Mum's forgiveness? Mutton ribs? What was she like?

She closed the door behind her and leaned back against it. For a long time. She was still there when she heard footsteps in the corridor. The footsteps faded.

It had to be Gunnarstranda taking Steffen to the custody suite. Should she or shouldn't she? There was no question. She had to!

She ripped open the door and hurried along the corridor. On the steps she saw the lift was already on its way down. She descended the stairs at a gallop and got to the bottom just as Gunnarstranda was about to open the gate to the cells.

'Steffen!'

Both men stopped and turned.

Lena asked: 'Why did you do it?'

Steffen stared at her with empty eyes. 'Do what? The charges have been radically revised. I don't know if you're aware.'

'Why did you take part in planning the fire? Why did you let the guy wait for me in your flat?'

Steffen turned to Gunnarstranda with a questioning look on his face, but Gunnarstanda shrugged and said: 'I'm deaf in that ear.'

'Shared guilt,' Steffen said. 'Stian couldn't accept that you knew his identity and wanted to do something about it. On the practical side, you gave me the idea when you got the cherry stone stuck in your throat.'

Lena had to count to ten. She propped herself against the wall.

She and Gunnarstranda sent each other a look.

Gunnarstranda grabbed Gjerstad's arm to hurry him along.

'Wait,' Lena said.

Both men turned. 'Since you think you're so bloody clever, Steffen,' Lena said, 'there's one little thing you should know.'

He looked at her, curious.

'You needn't have killed Sveinung Adeler.'

Steffen's eyes glazed over.

'Didn't you read it? Let me tell you what he wrote on the last page:

"*In this case it is necessary to draw a distinction.*" I know it off by heart, Steffen. I memorised it so that I could tell you when we met: "*MacFarrell Ltd only has owning interests in the plants; they play no part in the production. Because the concern necessarily receives profit from its activities and through its ownership indirectly maintains the production in occupied territory, there will always be controversy about whether this kind of interest violates recognised principles of international law. However, this level of ownership is not enough to have any direct influence on the decision-making authority of the production company.*"'

Lena paused for dramatic effect, then continued: 'So Adeler came to the sensational recommendation that the Government Pension Fund Global *didn't* need to withdraw from MacFarrell. Even if everyone believed the opposite to be the case. MacFarrell was frightened they would be forced out. Råholt was sure the Oil Fund would force out MacFarrrell and was paid an enormous fee to lobby the decision-makers. He was so sure of the outcome of the official's investigations he paid you money to smear him. When Adeler told you he'd already handed in the report you should've taken the trouble to ask what his conclusions were. Had you done that, you would've known there was no point in bumping him off.'

Gunnarstranda pulled Gjerstad into the custody suite with Lena shouting after him: 'There was no point! Do you hear me, Steffen? You screwed up!'

The door slammed.

She waited.

For ten minutes.

Then Gunnarstranda returned.

'Are you still here?'

She nodded.

Gunnarstranda's voice was low and sympathetic as he spoke: 'Gjerstad told me you were ill, Lena. Is that true?'

She nodded.

'When you're served up that kind of diagnosis it's absolutely understandable you come unstuck at the edges,' Gunnarstranda said. 'I've lost people who were very close to me; in fact everyone I know has had someone who's been affected by that illness. Everyone understands. You have colleagues who'll cover for you. You need to rest, Lena. You have to go through a very tough course of treatment. I know you and I'm sure you'll beat it. But only if you focus! Do the sensible thing. Go home and celebrate Christmas like other people. Think positively. Take sick leave and get well. Life's not a motorway on the Po Plain. Life's a struggle with a few uphill climbs. Sometimes we solve the problems as easy as winking. Sometimes we have to be patient. That's the most important quality you can have as a cop. To know your own limits. We have to maintain law and order. The power lies elsewhere. It's in parliament, in the government and the courts.'

Lena stared, knowing he hadn't finished.

'In the press, too, sometimes,' Gunnarstranda said with a characteristic little smirk. 'That's what they think anyway. Come on,' he said, taking her arm. 'We're going the same way, so we can share a taxi.'

✳

They sat side by side in the back seat of the taxi without speaking. The car passed through quiet Oslo streets. Inside there was a smell of Wunderbaum air freshener. The driver had lowered the music on the radio and the windscreen wipers were on intermittent in the snow.

Gunnarstranda coughed. 'Are you celebrating Christmas with your mother?'

Lena didn't answer.

'What's up?' he asked.

'The man with the hare lip – where does he come from?'

Gunnarstranda shrugged. 'Sounded like Fredrikstad.'

'I mean which police department.'

'No idea. Think he's been with PST for quite a while. Why?'

'I wonder what kind of people PST are … or become.'

Gunnarstranda looked at her sideways.

'It suddenly struck me they've been following Rømer ever since he landed in Gardermoen.'

The taxi stopped for the lights.

The driver turned up the volume on the radio. It was Bing Crosby singing 'White Christmas'.

'What if PST saw everything that happened in the harbour that morning?'

Gunnarstranda didn't answer.

'My guess is they were there and saw the lot,' Lena said. 'But they didn't step in and they said nothing to us. Think about everything that happened, and it's all because they think they're working in the most important service in the world and what is paramount in life is to keep mum.'

'I doubt they were there and saw what went on.'

'But what if they were?'

Gunnarstranda heaved a sigh. 'If the sun didn't exist, neither would we,' he said. 'But the sun rises every morning. Think of the future, Lena. Tomorrow it's Christmas Eve and it'll be better for you and your mother if you remember to soak the mutton ribs.'

Sunday, 7th March

Footsteps creaked on the snow-covered path. The thrum of a car engine was the sole sound to break the winter silence as a figure hoisted a shovel and mattock over her shoulder, stepped over the heaped snow at the side of the road and waded into the blanket of snow, which reached up over her knees. The white expanse glistened. The bright sun hung low in the sky and made the bark on the tree trunks glitter like gold.

The woman dug her way down in the snow, to the ice layer, squinted into the sun and carried on. It was important to keep warm. Beneath the loose snow there was an older, compressed layer which required a great deal of muscle. The woman worked systematically and rhythmically, digging away a rectangle of two metres by four. She dug down deeper. Soon the snow was up to her waist.

Then the job of hacking into the ice started. With every swing of the mattock a shower of tiny fragments of ice shot into the air. The rays of sun didn't find their way down into the hole. Matt pieces of ice lay on the ground until they were shovelled away or crushed to powder underfoot. The mattock had two ends: a pick, and a blade like a small axe. The shaft was a little loose in the welded rim. At the start the debris could easily be removed with the shovel, but the deeper the mattock went into the ice, the more energy it took to lever the chunks loose. She worked up a sweat. Her breath froze on the edge of her fur hat. Now and then she straightened up and measured the depth with the shaft of the mattock. Thirty centimetres of blue ice and still no water. Forty centimetres and no water. Fifty centimetres and no water.

There! The pick was stuck and water was bubbling up. The sight of it made her redouble her efforts. She wriggled the mattock loose and then smashed the hole wider. Now she was pushing loose fragments and debris under the edge of the ice as the water rose. When the hole was clean and square she had to create a step into the water. Splinters flew as the axe blade hacked one out.

She put the mattock down. It stood like a crooked pole in the snow. Now the engine was the only sound to break the silence. The exhaust fumes rose like a grey sculpture into the frozen air. She walked back to the car, using her previous footprints.

On the seat in the car were a towel, a blanket and two ice picks, pointed implements with handles. The walk back to the hole was faster. She stopped by the edge, looked at the black water, pulled the mattock over and sliced off a jagged piece of ice protruding into the water by the step. Removed her woollen mittens. Instantly the cold gnawed at her fingers. She laid her jacket on the snow. Undid the zip at the side of her thermal trousers. Folded her clothes nicely. Loosened the laces of her boots and kicked them off. She stood barefoot on her puffa trousers. Brushed away the snow. Took off her woollen jumper, woollen shirt, thermal tights. Finally, she peeled off her bra and panties. She stood there naked in the sub-zero temperature. Her skin steamed; in seconds the sweat was transformed into invisible frozen mist. She could feel the frost biting and numbing her skin, yet she stood still. She wanted to be cooled down and thoroughly cold before she moved. The water temperature would be two, maybe three degrees. She wanted it to feel warm when she went in. That was why she was bathing her body in the Siberian air, waiting, naked, beneath the blue sky – white skin yellow-ish against the whiteness of the snow. Short, red hair, blue eyes, red lips, pink nipples and a little red scar on her left breast. The sun was already setting. It had cast a barely visible, yet heavy shadow over the countryside. The late-winter sunset was close. The tree trunks no longer shone like gold. The crystals in the white carpet of snow over the ice no longer glistened; the tree trunks no longer cast shadows. Grey mist in the sky became pink as though it were the final convulsions of a dying sun. She still waited. But she was no longer warm. She was shivering. Her hands trembled, and her thigh muscles were tense to the extreme as she set out. She went down the step and lowered herself into the water. Her body was a white log that sank into black matter. Feet, calves, knees, thighs, breasts, arms, neck, head – the whole of her body sank beneath the water to meet the all-decisive moment. Now she could choose to die, finish everything, give up, continue her journey through this purgatory of coruscating pain, to sink further to the great mother of all anguish as she descended with open eyes, the hole a light patch in a dark, all-consuming nothingness.

In that moment she fought with death once again. Her body began to ascend, towards the light patch – it became white, it became the thread to which her life was attached. She gasped for air as her head broke the surface of the water. Her movements were automatic: her hands gripped the ice picks, all her muscles tensed as she pulled herself up in one immense leap; she dragged herself over the hard edge scratching her breasts and stomach. She felt nothing, she concentrated solely on her breathing. She dried her body, wrapped it in the blanket, consciously breathed in and out to transfer oxygen into her blood while her fingers searched for her clothes, put them on. Panties, bra, tights, shirt, jumper, everything was slow, her clothes wouldn't slide on smoothly over her damp skin. Breathe – in, out, in, out. Don't give in to the urge that had crept up on her, to drift into sleep. She forced her feet into her boots, succeeded, without losing her balance and falling over. It was becoming harder to resist the desire to sleep. She couldn't stand the pain any more, grabbed her jacket and trousers and hurried back to the warm car. Her fingers trembled, her lower lip quivered. Her legs moved more slowly, the snow seemed impassable. Her biceps were sore from just carrying her clothes. Her fingers were numb. It was a fight to open the car door, to scramble in. To close the door behind her.

When – at long last – the warmth returned, her skin tingled as her blood burst its way through the thinnest, finest blood vessels in God's creation. She thrilled with the sense of it, sat with closed eyes relishing the Creator in action, life returning, forcing out the paralysing cold and infusing her skin with heat, energy and vibrancy.

*